WRITE FOR YOU

TITLES BY MEGAN BYRD

Take a Chance on Me

One Sweet Love

Merry & Brett

Stuck With You

Write for You

Write for You

MEGAN BYRD

ARDENVILLE PRESS

For Anna,
and all you other amazing librarians

1

Anna

"HURRY UP, ANNA! We're almost out of time."

I glance up at the clock, then to the five anxious faces crowded around me. Ducking my head, I force myself to focus on the task in front of me. Sweat trickles down my neck and my clammy hands fumble with the dial. I haven't used this type of lock since I was in high school. Even then, I wasn't the best at remembering which way to turn the dial and how far to go. Is it left, right, left or right, left, right?

I guide the dial to each number set before me, but when I pull the shackle, it doesn't release. Huffing out a frustrated breath, Josh shoulders me out of the way, wrenching the lock from my slippery fingers. "I'll do it."

He nimbly guides the dial and, a few seconds later, there's an audible click. The group sighs collectively. Josh guides the lock through the clasp, then opens the trunk. He reaches in, then thrusts his hand into the air, a skeleton key on display. He hands it off to a modelesque brunette with a wink. She giggles, then races to the door, jams the key into the lock, turns it, and pulls the door open. Cheers go up around the room.

My eyes flit to the black clock with bright red numbers on the wall above the door. It flashes 05:11. Plenty of time. What was Josh so worried about? I can't believe he gave up on me so quickly. Of course, he didn't seem to have much faith in my abilities from the get go.

While we waited for our escape room to open, he casually mentioned that my book smarts probably wouldn't help me much since the aim of the game was clues and challenges. Has he not read *The DaVinci Code* or an Agatha Christie book? There's a whole genre devoted to solving mysteries and puzzles. It's how I knew what the cryptex lock was earlier in the evening. But whatever.

I should have known things weren't going to work out when he spent dinner mansplaining escape rooms like I'd never heard of them. Hello, this date had been my idea! Which turned out to be a poor one because I learned Josh is uber competitive and doesn't like to let other people figure things out on their own. Actually, maybe it was good for me to see this side of him. It will lessen any guilt I might feel about turning down a second date from him. Not that I think he's going to ask.

Realizing I'm the only person left in the room, I walk through the door, down the hall, and to the lobby where I'm just in time to see the beautiful brunette hand Josh his phone back and whisper something in his ear. His eyes light up and he gives her a wolfish smile, along with a suggestive wink. Witnessing my date shamelessly flirting with another woman might have hurt if I had any interest in him or if this wasn't just another awful evening in a long string of terrible dates.

I've been on MeetCute for almost a year and have yet to go on a date worthy of the app's name. There was the guy who "forgot his wallet" after making reservations at The Aristocrat, one of the swankiest restaurants I've ever set foot in. Another guy was thirty minutes late for our pottery lesson, which meant instead of making coffee mugs, we ended up with ashtrays. Not something I have any use for.

However, neither of those compare to the guy who, after I ordered a bowl of soup, asked for a second spoon instead of ordering his own meal. I managed two bites before he plunged his spoon into the bowl. The clam chowder was delicious, but I couldn't eat another bite. Who does that on a first date? It's just gross. A shudder runs through me at the memory.

On the drive to my apartment, Josh has his alt rock music blasting through the speakers. My smart watch tells me too much time at this decibel level could affect my hearing. At least I don't have to scramble for something to say. There's nothing else to do but call the time of death on this date.

When Josh pulls up to the curb, my hand's already on the door handle, but I still have manners. "Thank you for dinner."

I wonder if he'll thank me for the escape room, especially since he seems to have netted another date out of it. "Welcome. Take care of yourself, Anna."

He reaches toward me, and I freeze. Is he going to try to kiss me? My panic turns to confusion when he pats the top of my head. Is he petting me like a dog? Okay, it's official. Worst. Date. Ever.

I grit my teeth in an approximation of a smile and hustle myself out of the car. I slam the door and give a little wave, but Josh has already pulled away from the curb, so he probably missed it. Oh well.

On the way up to my apartment, I open my phone and cancel my MeetCute account. A year of nothing but duds is more than enough evidence online dating isn't for me. I'm going to have to find some other way to meet Mr. Right because he's obviously not on dating apps.

Inside my apartment, I drop my purse on the kitchen counter and grab the mail, thumbing through it. Mostly bills and junk, but then I spot a familiar light blue envelope. I drop the rest on the counter, kick off my shoes, and plop down in my favorite flower-printed reading chair. It's a wingback recliner I picked up at a yard sale. It had ugly green upholstery, but I recovered in a gorgeous blue-gray fabric with purple, cream, blue, and tan flowers. It's my favorite piece of furniture in the entire apartment. Much nicer than the beige couch and love seat that make up the rest of the combination living room and library.

Sliding my finger under the envelope flap, I carefully pry it open, then slide out the matching blue paper. Unfolding it, I smile at the monogram at the top of the page: MBW. It's a very masculine font, quite suitable for the sender. My eyes race down the page, devouring the words.

January 5

Dear Anna,

Happy New Year! I hope you had a fun celebration with your friends. I'm sorry about your dating struggles, but am glad you can laugh at the absurd. I apologize on behalf of the male species for the rude behavior you've experienced. We're not all ill-mannered buffoons (at least I hope not). I hope you know you're a remarkable woman who deserves someone who cherishes you for the precious person you are.

Work is going…slowly. I'm really struggling to move forward with my current project. I have a looming deadline, but just can't figure out the character's big goal. Do they want to save their country or is there an overarching desire that makes saving the country a necessary part of their trajectory? Have any ideas?

Not that I expect you to miraculously solve my writer's block, but perhaps a new perspective would be of use. I tried my agent, but he's all about war and vengeance and weapons, which is not the story I want to tell. You are a kind, sensitive soul who might have something unique to share. No pressure, though. I'd hate not to receive a letter from you just because you don't have an answer for me. How would I find out if you'd finally met Mr. Right on that dating app of yours?

I'm thinking about getting a pet. Not sure what kind. Something that can keep me company while I write, but also doesn't require tons of maintenance or attention. Is that too selfish of me? Should I just get a pet rock or a plant to tide me over? Please advise.

Sincerely, Winston

M.B. Winston asked me for advice. Twice! I doubt Josh would ever ask me to help with something. Not that I care what Josh thinks. But M.B. Winston is an award-winning author of young adult science fiction novels. And he wants my help! Sure, one is a pet question, not exactly rocket science, but still. Science fiction isn't my favorite genre, but I've read all his books since we became pen pals.

How did I become pen pals with a famous author? Just lucky, I guess. About a year ago, a light blue envelope with my name on it was left at the circulation desk of Pack Memorial Library where I work. It was a very kind note thanking me for helping him with some research. I don't remember the incident, though to be fair, I see hundreds of people every day and help whenever and wherever I can. He included an Asheville PO box, inviting me to respond. I looked up his name, which is how I discovered he's an author. A thorough internet search did not uncover a website, social media, or even a picture, so I have a name but no face. He doesn't even have an author photo in the back of his books (I checked). Which is fine. I don't need to know what my pen pal looks like. He's been kind and funny through our letters. Every time I mail a letter off, I wait in anticipation for the next little blue envelope to arrive in my mailbox. Yes, I am using my actual address. I don't think he's a creeper, but I suppose you never know.

I think we're officially friends because M.B. Winston used to sign with his full name and now just uses his last, which sort of sounds like a first name. Of course, I'm pretty sure M.B. Winston is a pen name. All online references are to his books. It occurred to me once that he might actually be a she, but the more we've sent letters, the more confident I am that Winston is a man.

It's kind of fun having a mysterious pen pal. Since he's local, it makes me wonder if I've seen him around and not known it. Does he remember what I look like? My appearance has changed since the first letter. I had short pink hair I'd started growing out. I recently dyed it a pretty auburn, and it's almost to my shoulders. My co-worker, Penny, says I look like a completely different person now.

Setting the note on the side table next to the chair, I search online for advice about writer's block to see if there's anything useful I might pass on. Because I'm a librarian, I also run a search for relevant books in our system. When I'm finished, I grab my box of mishmash stationery from the bookshelf and rummage through it until I find an orange card that says "You got this!" on the front. I grab a pen from the box, then use the box as a writing surface. I tap the pen against my lips while I think through what I want to say. First, the pet situation. Next, the writer's block. And finally, if I haven't run out of room yet, I can talk about tonight's terrible date. I know it'd make him laugh.

January 9

Dear Winston,

I feel like pets are an essential part of being a writer. Gertrude Stein had a poodle named Basket. Langston Hughes, Truman Capote, and Dorothy Parker also had dogs. Hemingway had his six-toed cats. Lord Byron had a bear, Flannery O'Connor kept a menagerie of birds, George Orwell had a goat, and Virginia Woolf owned a monkey. However, pets are a lot of work, so if you'd prefer to focus on writing without having to take a pet for a walk or clean up after accidents, I'd suggest a plant. Not only are they pretty to look at, but they produce oxygen and help purify the air in your home.

Here's a list of some plants that are fairly low maintenance and hard to kill: Pothos, Bromeliad, Snake Plant, Cacti, Chinese Evergreen. There are others, but I don't want to overwhelm you. Besides, it depends on which store you visit as to what's available. In the meantime, I've included something to keep you company until you make a decision.

I wish I had some sage advice for overcoming writer's block. I searched our online database to see if there might be any books with wisdom to impart. I was unsuccessful, but found something I'm having sent to you. It might not be any good, so donate it if it isn't useful. The tracking app says it should be at your PO Box within the week.

In the meantime, perhaps a tale of woe can help spark something for your story. I had a date with a guy I connected with on MeetCute (terribly inaccurate name for an app by the way). We went to dinner where he spent half the meal mansplaining escape rooms to me even though I had been the one to suggest we tackle one together as part of our date (insert huge eye roll). At least the food was good.

I learned my date is very competitive and essentially took over the challenges in the room. I'm surprised the other guests didn't rise up and mutiny against his overbearing "leadership." If that wasn't bad enough, when he wasn't pushing people out of the way to open locks, he was flirting with the other women in the room. I get we didn't exactly click, but come on. Rude much?

Anyway, here's the icing on the cake. When he dropped me off, he patted my head like I was a dog. Who does that?! After that humiliating experience, I've officially canceled my MeetCute membership. Looks like I won't be finding love online.

Hope my tragic dating life helps you feel a little better about your writing struggle. Perhaps you can use some of it in your new story. Thanks for listening to me vent. I feel a little better now that I've shared my frustration with you.

Sincerely, Anna

2

Brody

THE CURSOR BLINKS on the screen, taunting me from the top left corner of the blank page. I've been staring at my computer for over an hour, but nothing is coming to me. My fingers drum out a random pattern on the wooden top of the cubicle I'm occupying. I lean back in my chair, tilting my head up toward the ceiling. There's a water stain on the drop tile above me shaped like a hippopotamus, its mouth wide open like it's about to chomp. It makes me think of that old game, Hungry Hungry Hippos. I thought the green one was the best.

My stomach growls at the thought of food, but I remind my body it doesn't get food until my brain gets in gear and writes something. My gaze drifts along the ceiling and I spot another stain that looks like a giraffe. And there's a lion's head. It's practically a menagerie here in Pack Memorial Library. I chuckle, then quickly glance around to make sure no one heard me laughing to myself. Thankfully, I'm the only one occupying a cubicle in this part of the library.

On the far side of the room, two librarians are conversing at the circulation desk. The rest of the room appears to be empty. Plenty of quiet to work in. If only I could work. My gaze swings back to the women up front. The woman on the left is petite, with straight black hair that falls halfway down her back. She's wearing tan slacks and a lavender top. The other woman is tall, with pretty reddish hair and brilliant blue eyes. She has on a flowery dress that flows down to her calves. I see the two together often, making me wonder if they're good friends outside of work. The redhead, Anna, waves her arms around and the other woman throws her head back, her mouth open wide in unfettered delight. I can hear her laugh from here. Anna puts a hand on the other woman's shoulder and makes the universal sign for quiet. She then turns to scan the room.

I duck my head back down into the cubicle. My cheeks are warm with warning that I might have been caught staring. Watching the women was a welcome distraction from my writer's block, but what I really need is some inspiration. I place my fingers over the keyboard, trying to imagine what their conversation might have been about. Perhaps on her way to work, she was behind a truck whose back doors flew open and out fell a crate of rubber duckies that spilled out all over the road. And they were the squeaking kind, so the cars driving over them set off a cascade of squeaks and squeals. An entertaining thought, but not sure how that would translate into something for the science fiction novel I'm supposed to be writing.

Ciara Thieros is struggling to keep the country together, battling a nefarious group of lords trying to undermine her leadership so they can stage a coup and use their power for their own gain. I'm drawing a blank on how this is supposed to play out.

Such is the life of a discovery writer. I tried to be one of those people who create an outline and then write each chapter as I'd previously laid it out, but it turns out my characters don't like this method. They prefer to reveal their personality, quirks, and desires as the story progresses. It's an interesting process. When I'm in the groove, my characters will speak to me and tell me what's happening.

Of course, that hasn't happened in a while, which is why I'm struggling with this one. Since it's supposed to be a sequel to *Into the Unknown*, I know who Ciara is, but she's changed from the strong, confident teen I left at the end of the first story. Now she seems fragile and insecure. I'm not sure what has happened in the interim, but I hope she'll tell me soon so I can get on with the story. In the meantime, I'm sort of writing in the dark, hoping my typing will break something loose.

I decide to write about one of the new side characters and figure out how they fit into Ciara's world. He shall be called Rylan unless he tells me otherwise. What was he doing in the first book? He was hustling in the market, trying to support his mother and little sister with his technological skills. He can fix anything mechanical and hack into even the most secure systems.

Rylan begins talking to me and I'm sucked into another world. It feels good to be writing, watching rows of black letters spooling across and down the page on my screen. It barely feels like work as my fingers obey the commands of my mind for words. I ignore the typos as more and more thoughts come to me, knowing I need to capture these ideas now before they fly away. My mind is locked into this other world, a window opening up and allowing me to peer in and record what I'm seeing. I'm right in the middle of what feels like a pivotal moment when a throat clears nearby, startling me out of my writing trance.

I blink, confused about where I am. My laptop comes into focus along with the wooden walls of my cubicle. A hand rests lightly on top of the wall to my right. I swing my gaze up and freeze when I meet a pair of brilliant blue eyes. My heart rate immediately picks up and sweat breaks out across my forehead. My face flames and I look away. What is she doing here at my cubicle? Was I unconsciously making noise while I wrote?

She smiles warmly. "Sorry to disturb you, sir, but the library is closing. I have to ask you to leave."

My blush burns harder as I realize my mistake. My mouth opens and closes as my brain struggles to catch up. I've already forgotten what she said. Did she ask me a question? I have to get out of here. I manage to stutter out one word.

"S-sorry."

My pulse pounds in my temples, and I know it's time to go. I stand quickly, saving the document before closing my laptop. Keeping my head down, I pick up my bag and shove my computer and phone into it, zipping it closed. The chair feet whine against the laminate floor when I slide the chair in too quickly. I give her a nod without meeting her gaze, and hightail it to the exit. I walk down the hall to the parking garage. Safely inside my silver Subaru Crosstrek, I cross my arms over my chest and alternate tapping each shoulder while taking deep breaths. My heart beat slows and I relax against the seat.

I unzip my bag and retrieve my phone. It's a quarter after six. The last time I noted the time it was four thirty. I guess I really found my flow for a bit there.

I chastise myself for not setting an alarm. A few seconds of forethought could have prevented the incident with Anna. Did she smell like lavender? I caught a hint of the scent before my brain went haywire.

To be fair to myself, I didn't know I was going to actually find some rhythm with my writing today. Still, I should have an automatic alarm set for ten minutes before closing, so it doesn't happen again. One, because I don't want to be surprised again and two, I hate the fact that I'm responsible for staff having to stay late. It may have only been a couple of minutes, but she might have had somewhere to be tonight. I don't want to make her late anywhere. From my observation of her in the library, Anna seems like a social butterfly, so I'm sure she has plans of some sort.

I take a moment to remember the feeling of her warm smile directed at me. She didn't look mad that I was still in the library, but she doesn't seem like she's ever upset about anything. Maybe she's one of those people who can go with the flow. I cannot. I like structure and clearly laid out expectations and deadlines.

Well, I don't like deadlines when one is looming and I have nothing to turn in. Like right now. My manuscript is due in a few months, but I don't have anything close to a rough draft, which means I'm way behind where I should be. Today, I got a little work accomplished, but it was mostly just working out the major players and the setup. Sure, it's better than nothing, but it's nowhere near the eighty thousand words my editor is expecting.

The loud clang of the parking garage door slamming shut grabs my attention and my eyes shift to the rear-view mirror. It's Anna and the other librarian. I watch as they hug and then head off in different directions. The dark-haired woman heads up the deck and Anna walks past the trunk of my SUV and unlocks the white vehicle two spots down.

I'm still mulling over the embarrassment of losing track of time when the sound of something shattering makes my head snap up. Sensing trouble, I'm out of my car in a flash and headed toward the noise. I only take a couple of long strides before I see Anna crouched down between cars. Her shoulders are shaking a little, but I can't see what's happening from my position.

"Ouch!"

I take another step and bend down, my heartbeat pulsing in my throat. "What happened? Are you hurt?"

She stiffens, probably unaware of my presence. I try to think of something reassuring to say.

"I'm first-aid certified. Let me help."

She turns, her shoulders relaxing when she recognizes me.

"Oh, it's you. It's no big deal. I just dropped a mug and cut my finger on a sharp piece."

She holds up a finger, a bright spot of red on the tip.

"We should clean it up just to be safe. Be right back."

I straighten up, grab the first-aid kit I keep in my trunk, and return to her side. I pull on a pair of disposable gloves before reaching for her hand. I stop before I touch her, holding my palm up. She places her hand in mine and I swab it clean before applying some ointment and a bandage.

"That's not too bad. No shards in the skin."

"Thanks," she says and sniffs.

I meet her eyes for the first time and realize she's been crying. I grab a travel pack of tissues from my kit and hand them to her before busying myself with carefully cleaning up the broken coffee cup. One of the larger pieces says *THIS IS HOW I ROLL* with a drawing of a book cart beneath. After gathering as many pieces as I can, I take them and my used medical supplies to a trash can near the doors that lead to the library. Then I concentrate on organizing my kit, unsure what to do next, but not wanting to leave her while she's upset.

"You must think it's silly I'm crying over a coffee cup. A friend gave it to me the first day I started working as a librarian. It had a lot of sentimental value."

"I-I'm sorry."

She sighs. "It's not your fault. You didn't have to clean it up, but thank you."

Now that all danger has passed and I'm not in responder mode, my nerves are ratcheting up by the second. I need to get out of here before my vision gets fuzzy at the edges. Convinced she's okay, I nod, my throat too tight to respond, then stand up and retreat to my car. Safely inside, I close my eyes and focus on my breathing to help calm down. When I open my eyes again, Anna's car is gone.

I look down at my khakis and button-down shirt. The knees of my pants are dirty from kneeling on the parking garage floor. I look like a college professor or architect or someone who does intellectual stuff. I like to dress up to get myself into the work mindset required to focus and get stuff done. It hasn't really been working lately, but it's become my weekday uniform. One less thing to think about so I can concentrate on storytelling. However, after two near panic attacks, I'm itching to get into something more comfortable and head outdoors for a bit.

I start the car and head for home, running through possible places I can go this evening. Getting out into natural locations that are secluded appeals to me on multiple levels. I can think clearly when I'm out in an expansive area, surrounded by trees or rocks, with vast swaths of blue sky. I'm fairly introverted by nature and don't mind being alone. After all the unwanted attention I received as a kid, I will never take anonymity and solitude for granted. Which is why I try to look nondescript and unobtrusive at the library. I want to be just another face with no name.

I know it sounds silly to want to be left alone when I chose a profession that practically requires one to self-promote in order to be successful. I didn't mean to become a writer, and certainly not a semi-successful one, but life sometimes takes turns you don't expect. At least I've been able to do things on my terms to have a fairly quiet life, though I'm in danger of becoming unemployed if I can't get my sequel written. However, I'm a man who fulfills his obligation and am on the hook for one more book to my publishers, so I'm going to get this thing written if it kills me.

3

Anna

I REACH INTO the backseat of my car and grab my work bag, purse, and lunch box, ready for another glorious day of work at the library. Shutting the door with my hip, I root around in my purse until I find my key fob and press the lock button, satisfied when the exterior lights flash and my car honks. I rotate through the various charms and keys until I find the one that unlocks the exterior door to the library hallway. The door is a little unwieldy with all my bags, and I have to set down my lunch in order to grasp the handle and pull with all my body weight while simultaneously turning the key in the lock. Luckily, I've done this dance so many times it's ingrained in my muscle memory.

Sticking my hip into the opening, I bend and grab my lunch before sliding inside. The door makes a loud thunk behind me. I walk down the long hallway, smiling at the pretty blue and gray tiles on the floor. I always thought it was a pleasant surprise to have such a lovely floor in a hallway that leads between the parking garage and Haywood Street, a thoroughfare of downtown Asheville.

Three quarters of the way down the hall, I turn right and use a different key to open the door to the library. This door is much easier to open, so my lunch gets wedged under my arm as I turn the key and pull on the handle. It's dark inside, which means I'm the first one here. I flip on the lights, smiling as the overhead fluorescent bulbs light up row after row of bookshelves. I walk behind the circulation desk, opening a drawer for my lunch and purse, and dropping my bag in a chair. I tuck the keys into the pocket of my cardigan for easy access, then turn on the work computers.

I take a lap of the main floor and make sure everything is where it should be. I pass by the security desk, and meander over to Bookends, our used bookstore. I unlock the door and prop it open, then walk along the first row of fiction shelves. All the books are upright, so I turn right and make my way down the first aisle between the shelves, straightening books that have fallen over and pulling out books that were pushed too far in. When I've finished in fiction, I loop around the horseshoe-shaped new release section, making sure all the titles are visible to patrons. I then wend my way through periodicals, audio books, and nonfiction.

Satisfied that the books are ready for the day, I turn on the patron computers and push in chairs that were left out from the day before. I stop by the cubicles scattered around the room, making sure no one has defaced them. We have rags and cleaner behind the counter for just such issues. Thankfully, all the users were respectful of our space.

The library door bangs shut and I hear a hearty, "Hellllllllooooooooooo."

"Hey, Penny!" I call from the other side of the library, making my way quickly to the circulation desk where my best friend and fellow librarian, Penelope Ruiz, is setting down her stuff. Her long black hair is fashioned into a stylish braid crown. "Oooh, you look like a princess with that hair."

Penny smiles and wraps me up in a quick, tight hug. "Thanks. If you grow your hair long enough, I'll show you how to do it."

I run a hand through my almost shoulder-length hair. It's only been ponytail length for a few months. "That would be fantastic, thanks."

"Sure thing. Have you checked the book return out front yet?"

"Nope. Just finished doing my lap. Everything looks good."

"Great. I'll grab the cart and go check it."

While Penny heads out front, I empty my bag onto a section of the desk. I've recently been given the task of applying for grants that could benefit the library. There are grants for continuing education for staff, technology, programs, and materials. My boss, Jen, says to apply for everything I can find because we will use whatever we get.

Penny comes in with an empty cart. We don't have a backlog of returns from last night, so Penny gets online to check interlibrary loan requests we can pull from our stacks while I start on grant paperwork.

When the library opens, a large group of parents and children enter the main floor and head downstairs. They're here for the story time that starts in thirty minutes. Soon, other regulars arrive.

There's Trudy, who likes to bring her knitting and sit in a chair while listening to an audio book. I'm sure she could do that at home, but I know her husband passed away a few years ago. If I lived alone after years of being part of a family, I might find a public space to feel more connected as well. Lately, I've noticed

Sergei, another regular who retired after years of being an orchestra conductor, sit next to Trudy and chat for a bit when they're both in the library. I wonder if there's something brewing there.

While I'm pondering this, the introverted professor sneaks in the door and walks swiftly to his cubicle at the other end of the room. I don't actually know if he's a professor because we haven't had a real conversation, but he always wears khaki pants and a checkered button-down shirt with brown dress shoes. Of course, wouldn't he be teaching during the day instead of holing up in the library? Maybe he teaches classes at night. Of course, he could have some other job, but I'm drawing a blank on what that occupation might be.

Though after yesterday when he barely met my eyes and stuttered a little before dashing off, I have second thoughts about him being a professor. He didn't seem very comfortable, though maybe he was just embarrassed about being asked to leave. He was much more self-assured when caring for my wound in the parking garage, but, once again, left a little suddenly. Maybe the crying made him uncomfortable? I do feel a little silly about that part. I'm sure I can get a replacement mug if I really want. It shouldn't matter that he wasn't a sparkling conversationalist. He was considerate and competent, even if he was quiet. We all act weird at times. I'm certainly not one to judge.

I glance over at the cubicle and see the top of his head disappear below the wall. Was he just looking this way? Probably just adjusting his chair. When I kindly kicked him out of the library last night, I had a good chance to see him up close. He has dazzling green eyes that look really good with his thick black hair. His nose is a little crooked, like he might have broken it once. He's always clean-shaven, which shows off his strong jawline. How did I not notice how handsome he is before now?

Penny comes up and nudges my shoulder. "Did you see who just showed up?"

My head swivels to the front door and there's Sergei in a sports coat holding a bouquet of yellow flowers, his eyes pinned to Trudy. Goosebumps break out on my arms. "I thought I saw a spark between them."

Penny chuckles. "Me, too."

Sergei runs a hand through his hair, takes a deep breath, then marches in Trudy's direction. My gaze swivels to Trudy, who has headphones on and is focused on her knitting project in front of her. It looks like she might be making a hat, but it could just as easily be a sock. I don't know anything about yarn crafts.

Sergei stops in front of Trudy and thrusts out the flowers. She looks up and drops her needles, surprise and pleasure flitting across her face. She removes her headphones and takes the flowers, bringing them to her nose and inhaling. She gives Sergei a brilliant smile and motions for him to sit in the chair next to her.

Penny turns to me. We clasp hands and squeal like little girls. Watching two people connect in real life stirs up a longing deep in my soul for my own special person.

"I didn't know Sergei had such strong game," Penny says, making me laugh.

"I know. How can I find my Sergei?" My smile dims a bit, which, of course, Penny catches.

She puts a hand on my shoulder. "Hey, you'll find your perfect match. Just don't settle."

"I won't."

"Good." She gives me a wink. "So, think we'll be invited to their wedding?" She motions over to Sergei and Trudy who are now holding hands.

"We better be!"

4

Anna

THE BELL OVER the door chimes merrily when I open it, and I smile. Book club is my favorite Thursday of the month. I definitely love the books, but the members of the Book Babes are truly the best part. It started with Rachel, Deb, Lori, Susan, and me. Rachel works at Page Turner Books where our meetings are held. I met Deb at the library and found we share similar tastes in books despite the nearly forty-year age difference between us. She told me about Rachel's new book club and we spent the better part of a year reading through Jane Austen's catalog. We moved on to other classics, but started adding in contemporary titles as well. It's why we went from calling ourselves the Classic Chicks to the Book Babes.

With the name change, we also added a few new members. First, there was Abbie, Rachel's sister, who moved to town for work. Then Julie, Rachel's sister-in-law, joined us and brought free chocolate. Our newest member is Meredith. She's married to Brett

Jacobs, who is also an employee at Page Turner Books. I asked Penny once if she'd like to come, but she prefers to pick her own reads. I definitely understand that sentiment. We've read a few books I didn't particularly enjoy, but, like I said, it's the people I show up for. Well, and the delicious chocolates Julie makes. Rachel's got us all addicted to the truffles from Little Shop of Sugar.

When I reach the meeting room at the back of the store, I find I'm the last to arrive today. It doesn't happen very often since I work just up the street from the bookstore, but I wanted to get some dinner and it took longer to get my order at Haywood Street Market than I expected. The lamb gyro I bought was worth it, though. Of course, I'm going to be tasting garlic from the tzatziki sauce all evening.

"Hey, ladies. Great to see everyone."

Deb comes over and gives me a hug. "Hey, Anna. So glad to see you."

"Same. What'd you think of *Lessons in Chemistry*?"

She grins. "I thought it was great. The treatment of women was hard to stomach at times, but I was glad to see how Elizabeth persevered and stayed true to herself."

I nod. "It makes me appreciate more what my mom and other women before me have done to change things for my and future generations."

Deb squeezes my shoulder. "Just keep moving us forward however you can."

Her words make me pause. Do I have the power to positively influence future generations of women? I suppose I have a little sway in library programming and the books we add to our collection. Not a lot, but I should use what I have.

Rachel claps her hands and instructs us to grab a snack and

take a seat. When we're all situated, she dives into a discussion of the book. The consensus seems to be surprise that the book wasn't a contemporary romance like the cover led us to believe, but was thoroughly enjoyable in its own right.

After a long, and occasionally heated discussion, we throw out ideas for next month's book before deciding on *Dear Edward*. It's one I've had on my to-be-read pile for a while, so I'm looking forward to it.

"Hey, Anna," Lori says. "Have any more date disasters to share from MeetCute?"

My eyes light up at her question. Even though it's sort of depressing not finding anyone I'm compatible with on the app, it's entertaining and a little soothing to hear the disbelief and outrage on my behalf. "You know it, Lori."

I launch into a detailed description of my escape room experience with Josh. Lori bristles when she hears about his mansplaining and Susan scoffs in disbelief when she hears he pushed me out of the way while I was working on the lock.

"Well, he definitely wasn't right for you," Deb says, shaking her head. "He's obviously a dummy, since he couldn't see how amazing you are. Doesn't he know brains are better than beauty any day? Not that you aren't beautiful, Anna. You know you are, but men who are worth pursuing are those who know that it's good to have a partner who challenges them and helps them grow. Lord knows Scott could be stubborn as all get out, but he appreciated I wasn't a pushover." She wipes her eye and my heart squeezes with sympathy. She rarely talks about her late husband, but I know she wishes he were still here to love on all of their grandbabies with her.

I lean over and wrap an arm around Deb's shoulder. "I appreciate your wisdom. I'll keep that in mind."

"So," Abbie says. "Have any more dates lined up on the app?"

"No. I closed my account after that last disaster, but I'm not sure how else to meet a nice, normal man. Not that I've found one of those on MeetCute, anyway."

Lori straightens up and waves her hand in the air. "Ooh! I could set you up. Our landscaper is *quite* attractive and in excellent shape. He owns his own business, too, so you know he's got ambition."

My nose wrinkles. "I appreciate the sentiment, but wouldn't it be awkward if things didn't work out between us? You might have to find someone else to mow your grass."

Lori shrugs. "Eh, Dave's the one who interacts with him. Guys seem to be able to compartmentalize stuff like that, so I doubt he'd quit or anything."

I appreciate she wants to help, but I just don't know. "I'd hate for things to be weird between you and me if I don't like the guy you set me up with."

She waves away my concern. "It's not like he's part of my family. Now, setting you up with my *son* might be awkward since he's already married."

"Well, thanks," I say, chuckling, "but I'll pass for now. I'll try to connect with guys in person first."

Who would that be? I'd never get involved with a co-worker, but our patrons are a variety of ages. Maybe I should look more closely at the men who come into the library. I suppose it might be a little awkward to see someone again after a failed date, but I've run that same risk with guys from MeetCute. Of course, I haven't been on a date with anyone who actually has a library card. That could be one of my problems. Maybe I need a fellow reader.

I might also find guys around town at places I frequent. Perhaps looking for a date in my everyday life would yield more success than what I've had so far online. There's only one way to find out.

5

Brody

I STARE AT the screen, willing words to flow from my fingers onto the page. After a few productive sessions in a row, I was confident scenes would continue to spill easily from my mind, helping me really get into the story and giving me a shot at hitting my deadline. However, my creative flow turned out to be a trickle that has dried up once again.

I'd hoped spending the weekend outdoors doing things I loved would help fill the inspiration reservoir. Two days of hiking, camping by a river, and taking in the beauty of nature breathed life into my soul, but seems to have done nothing to give me ideas for Ciara's next journey.

Hey, wait. Maybe she needs to go on a heroine's quest—a danger-filled trek through unknown territory to reach some fabled temple or wise hermit where she can figure out how to outsmart the group who wants to overthrow her as leader of the community.

My fingers itch to run with the idea, but first I pick up my phone to double check I've got an alarm set for fifteen minutes before closing time at the library. I will not be caught unaware like last time. While I didn't mind the opportunity to get another look at Anna's beautiful blue eyes, the surprise of her appearance did nothing to make me look cool or smooth. I was a stuttering fool. Definitely not the impression you want to make with someone you have a crush on.

And I do have a crush on the beautiful, kind librarian. I didn't plan for it to happen. I'd been visiting different libraries in the county, trying to find one that would be a suitable workplace. Most of them had been fairly small, just one large room that allows one to hear everything that's happening in the library, including the loud and screamy children's story times. I don't mind kids, but their unpredictability and random sounds are not conducive to the focus I need when I'm writing. I often use noise-canceling headphones, but sometimes I like the quiet murmur of folks, the soft rustle of pages turning, and the occasional opportunity to overhear snippets of conversation. It's amazing the things people talk about in the library.

When I visited Pack Memorial Library the first time, I was pleased to learn there's a separate children's library in the basement. The main floor is all adult content and where the cubicles are located. I spent the first hour there wandering through the shelves and scouting the seating options for the ideal location. And boy, did I find it. It's tucked into a corner far from the entrance, but has a view of both the entrance and the circulation desk, which I found was a plus when I noticed the spunky librarian with shortish pink hair. It's grown out since my first visit and she's dyed it a lovely red shade, which somehow makes her blue eyes pop even more.

I approached her a year ago, summoning all my courage to

talk to her and see if her personality was as attractive as her appearance. It was a disaster. I hadn't practiced what I was going to say—my first mistake. I don't know why I thought I could wing it. After walking confidently up to the circulation desk where she was standing, I froze when she smiled at me. Sweat broke out across my forehead and her smile wobbled a bit as a crease furrowed her brow. My hands were shaking, and I shoved them into my pockets so she wouldn't notice.

As the silence stretched longer and her smile disappeared, I searched my brain for something coherent to say. "F-f-fantasy b-b-books," was what I came up with, even though I'd never read a fantasy novel in my life.

"Are you looking for recommendations?" she asked.

I nodded stiffly, because it was the only thing I could do.

She took me over to fiction, apologizing that there wasn't a specific fantasy section, but to look for spines with unicorn stickers on them.

"I promise they all don't have unicorns in them," she said. "It's the standard sticker."

Once again, nodding was my only method of response.

"What do you like about fantasy? I don't read this genre, but perhaps the blurbs can help us find something you like."

Her kindness toward me, even in my incredibly awkward state, amazed me. I fumbled for something to say and finally managed to spit out a response. "R-reluctant heroes."

That made her smile. She turned back toward the shelf, scanning the spines. She pulled out a book, her eyes glancing over the back cover, then put it back. She grabbed another one, read the cover, then passed it over to me. "What do you think of this one?"

I took the hefty volume in my hands, my eyes roving over the cover. Two people stood on opposite cliffs, weapons in their hands, separated by a large chasm. The red rocks reminded me of some of the national parks I'd visited out west in college. The back sounded intriguing. I looked up and saw her watching me. I nodded and tucked it under my arm. The smile that broke out across her face and the delighted twinkle in her eyes punched me in the chest. I wanted to see more of those smiles.

She turned away, moving down the aisle in search of other fantasy books. She spent half an hour walking me through the shelves until I had a dozen books that would take me several months to get through with their two- and three-inch-thick spines.

"Do you want me to check you out?"

I would have loved for her to check me out, maybe even agree to a date with me, but there was no way I had enough courage to make a flirty joke like that. I glanced down, mortified to realize I was wearing my oldest jeans with holes in the knees and a faded Royals T-shirt. Had I even remembered to brush my hair that morning? I ran a hand down my face, realizing I hadn't shaved in over a week. I met her eyes and saw a strange look on her face. Could she read my thoughts? I panicked, trying to work out what to do.

She pointed at the books cradled between my left arm and my side. "Or are you looking for more books?"

Ooooohhhh, right. She'd asked me a question. Inside, I was dying of embarrassment, but I probably just looked stoic. I managed to nod. She motioned for me to follow her to the desk. The books landed with a thud and I dug out my wallet and handed over my library card for her to scan.

"Hello, Matthew Cooper," she said. "I'm Anna. Nice to meet you."

I wanted to tell her my preferred name, but it was taking all of my strength to stand there and not bolt out the front door. I'd already acted weird enough for one interaction, so I did my best to keep it together. Anna scanned the barcode of each book, stuck the return date receipt in the cover of the top one, and slid the stack over to me.

"Here you go. Enjoy."

I nodded and tried to smile, though it probably looked more like a grimace, then picked up the foot and a half stack of books, tucked them under my arm, and hurried out the door. And that was the worst first impression ever.

That day has probably never crossed her mind again, but it's etched in mine after many, many replays. Even though I'd decided Pack Memorial Library was the prime spot for work, it took me a couple of weeks to gather the courage to go back. And when I did, I made sure to look professional. Hence the slacks, button downs, and clean-shaven face most days. If she does remember me, I'm hoping to wipe out that first memory with a more polished, put together persona. Of course, stuttering out one- and two-word answers really isn't helping. I should probably talk to my therapist about my issue so we can role-play potential scenarios. I've found that going through the motions within the safety of Gabi's office really helps reduce the anxiety I feel in the moment when the situation occurs. It's mostly been work-related scenarios, but perhaps it's time to expand into social situations. Particularly, romantic social situations.

I cringe at the memory of my awkwardness, but something good came out of the interaction. I ended up really enjoying the books she picked out. Fantasy is quite a bit different from science fiction, but in both genres, an author creates worlds. Sci-fi is more technology based and scientific principles while fantasy contains more magic and monsters. I wonder if writing something a little different from sci-fi would help me get back on track with my book. But what would I write about?

My mind floats back to that first interaction with Anna. What if she were a witch and used magic to float the books off the shelves? What if I possessed undiscovered magical abilities? Perhaps I had been born into a magical family, but was given to a regular human family and raised with no knowledge of how to use magic? Perhaps to protect me from some evil force?

My heart thuds with excitement as ideas flood my brain about a magical world and a prince who's been hidden away since birth. I hunch over my laptop, my fingers flying across the keys as this new world unfurls on the page. I don't censor my thoughts, but write everything that pops into my head. I'm deep into the story when my phone buzzes beside me. It's my alarm, letting me know it's time to pack up and go home. I stop the buzzing, then glance down at the bottom of the screen.

Whoa. I just wrote four thousand words about a fantasy meet cute. I don't write fantasy or romance, but this was a fun exercise. Was it because I was writing about Anna? I look back at the screen, amazed at how well the words flowed. Is the story any good? I won't know until I reread it, but it felt good just to be in the zone again. I chuckle, realizing the writer in me subconsciously changed the names to protect the innocent. Or guilty, as the case may be, as I'd be horrified if Anna found out I wrote a romantic scene involving the two of us. But there's no way she would know who Aurelia Runeld and Beorn Daevon represent. Not that it matters. This whole thing is fantasy in the highest order. There's no way Anna sees me in any kind of romantic light. She doesn't even know who I am. To her, I'm probably just some weird, random guy who comes into the library every week. It's not how I want her to see me, but I'm not sure how to change things. Or if I even can.

I don't have a lot of dating experience precisely because I get nervous when I realize I like someone and then clam up whenever I'm around them. I know I put too much pressure on myself, but having the spotlight on me is terrifying. And that's what dating feels like—having one person focused solely on you, close enough to see your rough edges and all your faults. That kind of attention puts all my senses on high alert and it's really hard to get over that mental hurdle of feeling trapped and exposed. Once again, maybe it's time to see my therapist regularly. There's no guarantee of anything happening with Anna, but I would eventually like to find someone to share my life with and it's not going to happen if I can't get further than a first date with a woman.

I gather my things from the cubicle, stand up, and make my way to the parking garage. I don't see Anna on my way out. My eyes have a mind of their own when I'm in the library, using every opportunity to seek her out. It's like my brain has a browser window continuously open and searching for signs of her and cataloging any new information it discovers.

For instance, today Anna was wearing skinny jeans, black low top Converse shoes, and a flowy green shirt. She had swirly gold earrings that reminded me of a double helix and matched her curled hair. She looked very sexy, though I would probably choke on my tongue if I ever tried to say that out loud to her.

I slump into the front seat of my car with a sigh. I'm frustrated at my lack of progress on my sci-fi novel and at my inability to have a normal conversation with a beautiful woman. Something's got to change.

January 18

Dear Anna,

Thank you for the plant suggestions and the cute little pet rock. Did you paint the mouth and hair yourself? I love that it has googly eyes. I've named him Dwayne. He sits on my desk and stares at me while I try to write. I think maybe he's a little judgy of my lack of words lately. I may have to move him to the living room so I won't feel his accusing eyes on me.

I'm sorry you haven't had success on your dating app. I applaud you for putting yourself out there. It's not easy. I think your optimism and openness will lead you to the right person for you. Not that I think we have only one soulmate or anything. I believe a person could be happy with multiple people. Wait, that didn't come out right. I'm not a proponent of polygamy, just saying you shouldn't worry about missing "the one" when there are probably a number of people who would be a good fit as your romantic partner. Not that you're worried about that. Perhaps you agree with me, in which case, ignore this whole tangent.

I will check out the book you sent (it was delivered today). I'm desperate enough that any potential aid is welcome. You'd think a writer would look for books to help with an issue like writer's block, but it didn't even cross my mind. Thank goodness I have a librarian friend who is smarter than me.

I recently finished A Gentleman in Moscow *and found it quite interesting. It's hard to imagine being stuck in a hotel for most of one's adult life. I'd go mad if I couldn't get out of the house and immerse myself in nature on a regular basis. What about you? Think you could stay indoors indefinitely? It's certainly possible to survive since you can have just about anything delivered to your door these days. Of course, your job isn't exactly work-from-home friendly, so I don't know how you'd support yourself. What do you think you'd do if you couldn't be a librarian anymore?*

Sincerely, Winston

6

Anna

STANDING IN LINE at Hill of Beans, I debate between getting the blueberry muffin and the veggie breakfast burrito to go with my latte. My heart wants the comforting sweetness of the muffin, but my head reminds me I need energy for the day's shift. Saturdays are usually the library's busy days since most people are off work.

The library doesn't open for another few hours, but I thought I'd try my hand at meeting men in my everyday life, so I've devoted this morning to seeing if there are any attractive, single men at my favorite coffee spot.

The guy in front of me looks to be about my age. He has a full head of black hair and is wearing dark wash jeans and a black T-shirt. It's a nice look that's casual but not sloppy. When he turns his head to peruse the pastry case, I take in his profile, admiring his straight nose, square jaw, and long, dark eyelashes. I definitely could get used to looking at that face. Time to do something to get his attention.

I point at an item in the case. "The blueberry muffins are delicious."

He turns, flashing me a boyish grin. "Yeah?"

I nod, intrigued by the dimples that have appeared in both cheeks. "Yes, but honestly, everything they serve here is fantastic. You really can't go wrong."

He turns completely around so we're facing each other. "Sounds like you're a regular."

"Sure am. Is this your first time visiting Hill of Beans?"

"I just moved here and am trying to get the lay of the land."

It's my turn to smile. "Well, you've found the best coffee shop in town, so I'd say you're doing pretty good."

He gives me a once over, which I don't mind when his smile widens. "I'd say so, yeah. What are your opinions on their drinks here?"

I think he's flirting with me. That's a good sign. Maybe meeting someone in person won't be as difficult as I imagined. "They make great smoothies and the baristas do an excellent job with lattes and cappuccinos. The only thing I can't vouch for is their tea, because it all tastes like hot water to me."

I scrunch up my face in disgust, and he laughs. It's deep, rich, and invites me to chuckle with him. I love guys who have a sense of humor.

"I'm not a tea drinker either. So, what are you ordering this morning? It may help me with my decision."

"Probably a latte and a veggie breakfast burrito."

"Are you a vegetarian?"

I'm not, but I don't know why this would concern him. I hope he's not one of those people who looks down on others who think and live differently. That'd be a real bummer.

"Why do you ask?"

He shrugs. "My sister is, and she's coming to visit. I was going to ask if you knew of any good restaurants I could take her to."

Oh. My cheeks warm from the realization that I was just judging him, even though I hate when people do it to me. That's what I get for jumping to conclusions. "I'm not, but there's a great Indian restaurant a few blocks over that has tons of delicious vegetarian options."

"Cool. Maybe I could get your number and you can text me about where to eat and fun things to do with visitors?"

He wants my number? Does this mean he's interested? I should suggest that I give him a tour myself and show him all the fun things. You know, like go on a date. I take a deep breath, steadying myself for making a bold proclamation that we should go out, when a woman comes rushing up to us and wraps her arms around the guy's neck. She pushes up on tiptoe and kisses him firmly on the mouth.

What's happening here? This isn't his sister, is it? Surely not, because there's no way his sister would be running her hand up and down his chest or pressing kisses along his neck. Yeesh, you're in public, lady.

Okay, so I guess he wasn't asking me out. No biggie. It's his turn to order, so I hang back. Thankfully, once they've gotten their stuff, they head out of the store, so I don't have to worry about him asking for my number again. What if he was one of those guys who likes to keep his options open and he was flirting with me even though he's obviously seeing someone? Maybe I dodged a bullet. Still, I was hopeful this attempt to meet someone in person would be successful.

Latte and burrito in hand, I take a seat at the last open table in the café. I take the lid off my coffee to let it cool and unwrap one end of my burrito. Taking a bite, I look around me. There's a guy about my age on his laptop in the corner. He's also talking loudly to someone, but I don't see a phone. Must be using bluetooth. I don't understand why people don't take their phone calls outside to not bother other patrons. He's getting more than a few dirty looks from the people sitting around him, but doesn't seem to notice. Or maybe he just doesn't care. I like a guy who's considerate of those around him, so he's not for me.

There's a younger guy with a backward ball cap on, eating a muffin and typing furiously on his laptop. He could be a college or grad student working on an assignment. While cute, he's definitely too young for me. I've been out of my twenties for some time and am not eager to return to those years of figuring out who I am and what I want with my life. Plus, if I'm remembering correctly, guys that age are still having fun and not looking for anything serious, whereas I'm ready for love, marriage, and kids.

At thirty-seven, I know my fertility window is closing. Not that I'll feel incomplete if I don't experience pregnancy, but I would like to raise kids and I don't want to be retirement age with a kid in elementary school. No way do I want to be confused for someone's grandparent. Of course, just because I'm ready for that stuff, it doesn't mean I'm going to rush into anything. I've waited long enough that I'm not settling for just anyone. I want a guy who will love everything about me, quirks included. I want someone who reads and will discuss books with me. Someone who loves the outdoors like I do and is settled in Asheville. I love it here and don't see myself living anywhere else. I've got my routines, my favorite restaurants, a wonderful job, and great friends. Plus, being in the mountains lets me access my adventurous side that likes long hikes, kayaking, and stargazing. I'd love to have a significant other to do all those things with, plus it'd be nice to have a built-in travel buddy.

I met a guy in my late twenties who I thought could be the one. I was living in Tennessee at the time. We took adventures to various hiking and kayaking spots nearly every weekend, sometimes venturing into North Carolina, Virginia, and Georgia for our excursions. We'd talked about taking trips to kayak the Amazon and Glacier Bay in Alaska. He read a lot of nonfiction, mostly books pertaining to gorgeous locations around the world. He wanted to visit as many places as he could, which I don't begrudge him because the world is a beautiful place. After we'd been dating about six months, he told me he was quitting his job to go backpacking throughout Europe and Asia for as long as his money would last. He invited me to go with him, but I'd just gotten a job as a children's librarian and didn't want to give up the opportunity. We parted on good terms, but his wanderlust has kept him out of the States all this time. Last I heard, he was exploring the Australian Outback with a small group of people he'd met in his travels. I don't regret the relationship, but have yet to find someone else I could see myself building a life with.

A touch to my shoulder brings me back to the present. I look up into a pair of bright blue eyes and my stomach clenches. The blond hair and scruff across his face make me suck in a breath. He looks just like Trevor Donovan, the actor in all those Hallmark Christmas movies I watch in December. I blink and realize he's asked me something.

"I'm sorry, what?"

He smiles, and I realize he's not the actor, but could pass for a brother or cousin. "Do you mind if I sit here?"

My heart speeds up. This hot guy is asking to sit with me? Yes, please. I motion to the chair across from me. "Be my guest."

I wince internally. Did I really just quote a children's movie?

Well, the guy does kind of look like the Beast after he's transformed. Of course, that guy had long red hair, but the eye color is the same.

"Thanks."

I straighten up, excited to start a conversation with this handsome stranger. My enthusiasm is snuffed out when he plops down, sticks earbuds in each ear, and focuses on the phone in his hands. Well, sugar waffles. I'm zero for two on connecting with a real person. One more strike and I'll be out. Except this isn't baseball, so I can play this game as long as I need to. Alas, there aren't any other obviously single guys in here that pique my interest. And none that are as attractive as the man in front of me. I can at least enjoy the view.

I stare unabashedly at him while I finish my breakfast. He's got high cheekbones, thick expressive eyebrows that remind me of the brother in *While You Were Sleeping,* and hair that flops over his forehead in a cute way. Too bad he's obviously not interested in me.

I push back from the table and grab my drink. I'm halfway out of the seat when the guy grabs my arm with his hand. His fingers are cool to the touch, but they still make my heart race. Maybe he realized he's about to miss his chance of getting to know me. I pause in an awkward, crouched position, mesmerized when his eyes meet mine. He pulls one of the ear buds out and gives me a lopsided grin that makes my heart squeeze a little. Is he going to apologize for ignoring me and ask me to stay?

"That's my drink."

What? I look down at the cup in my hand and realize the lid is still on. On the other side of the table is my latte, which has probably cooled enough to drink.

"Oops." I shoot him an embarrassed smile. "Sorry about

that.”

I set his drink back down, and he pulls his hand back to his side of the table. I snap the lid back on my drink, then exit Hill of Beans as quickly and gracefully as I can manage. I'm tempted to look back and see if he's watching me, but restrain myself. Would it be worse if he *was* looking or if he'd already forgotten me and gone back to whatever was on his phone?

Outside on the sidewalk, I look at my watch. I still have half an hour before I have to be at work. Might as well take a leisurely stroll around town to get a few steps in, finish my coffee, and replay my failure at executing an in-person meet cute. Who knew these things were so difficult to recreate in real life?

7

Anna

PENNY'S DOUBLED OVER with laughter listening to me recount my epic fails from Hill of Beans this morning.

"I can't believe you almost stole Beast's drink!"

She practically shrieks the last word, and I put my hand over her mouth. "Shhh."

It seems kind of ironic that I'm shushing a librarian in a library, though we can get pretty rowdy when we're together. Plus, I can't help chuckling a little at how weird my morning was. It was embarrassing in the moment, but already I can see the humor in it. I try not to let things get me down for long. It's kind of a gift of mine—the ability to move on quickly from awkward situations. I'll probably head back to Hill of Beans on Tuesday before work and not feel any trepidation about possibly running into Fake Trevor. I like that name a lot more than Penny's moniker of Beast. It just sounds nicer.

"At least I'm making an effort. Why is it so hard to meet a

nice guy in real life?"

Penny shrugs. She's been married to her husband, Michael, for a decade. They met working at an animal shelter, fell in love with each other and a five-year-old Bichon Frise named Muffy. She died a few years ago, but they've adopted more dogs from the shelter over the years and their house occupancy is up to six at last count. Their dogs are an adorable, wild bunch, but it's too much chaos for me. I'm a one pet at a time kind of person. Not that I have any creatures in my home right now. Maybe I should get a plant like I'd advised Winston. I can watch something grow under my care without the astronomical vet bills or being heartbroken if it fails to thrive in my apartment.

"I don't envy you in this dating environment," she says. "Since Hill of Beans was a bust, have you scoped out potential hotties here at the library? They're likely to read, which I know is one of your preferences."

My eyes scan the room. Sergei and Trudy are seated side by side in chairs next to the audio books. Half a dozen women have taken over one of the rectangle tables and are in deep discussion about something. A teenage couple rifles through magazines while holding hands. There are a few patrons with their backs to us at the computer stations. "Um, do you see any hotties?"

Penny does her own perusal of the room. "What about George?"

My gaze swings over to our security guard seated behind a desk near the entrance. I'd guess him to be in his mid-forties, so not out of my age range. He's a little taller than me and participates in cycling races, so I know he cares about fitness, but I'm not interested. "I thought he was seeing a yoga instructor who works at the YMCA."

Penny's eyebrows raise and she nods. "Oh, yeah, that's right.

My bad." She looks behind me toward the computers. "What about that guy?"

I turn around. "Which one?"

"The one with the black hoodie. Javier, I think? He's cute and in here almost every weekend."

I snort. "Yeah, to chat with his girlfriend, who lives in Sweden. I don't think he's used his card for anything apart from the computers."

"Oh. Hmmm. You're right. It *is* tough to meet someone in person nowadays."

"Told ya. I'm doomed to be single."

"Wait!" Penny hisses. "What about that guy that always uses the cubicle in the corner?"

My brow crinkles in thought. "Which guy?"

"You know…the professor."

Realizing who she's talking about, my head swivels over to the cubicle in the back of the room. I turn back to Penny. "There's no one there."

She releases a breath. "I know that, but what about that guy? He dresses nicely, is never a problem in the library, and is attractive."

"He's also very standoffish. When I approached him to let him know the library was closing the other week, he barely said one word before bolting out of the place."

"Maybe he's shy. A lot of introverts visit the library."

I suppose that could be true. His one word was an apology, and he looked pretty distressed. Plus, he came to my aid in the parking garage. Our interaction was awkward, but not everyone would do what he did. If he's shy, his odd behavior makes sense. I'm so used to my outgoing personality that I don't always stop to think about the fact that not everyone relates to the world like I do.

I don't know enough about him to judge him. Still, it feels a little unprofessional to be looking for dates where I work. Most of these people don't want to be bothered by a boisterous librarian. They want to show up, get their books and movies or use the computer, and get out. Unless you're that group at the table who is definitely enjoying their socializing. And I can't dismiss the romance blooming between two of our regulars. Still, that's different. The adage about not trying to mix business with pleasure pops into my head and it's famous for a reason—probably because it's good advice.

"Well, whatever. I think I'll stick to looking in places I frequent that don't provide me with a paycheck."

Penny shrugs a shoulder. "Suit yourself. Hey, Michael has a cousin who's single. Want me to set you up?"

I shake my head. "No, thanks. That sounds like a whole lot of awkward waiting to happen if it doesn't work out."

A few people come up to the desk to check out items and our conversation ends, but the idea of having other people help me find someone is becoming more and more appealing. It's rough out here in the dating world. I probably should ask other people to help me expand my potential dating circle. It couldn't be worse than how I've been doing on my own, right?

8

Brody

WHEN I STEP into The Palm Room, a cute name for a local plant store, the flora's soothing green color invites me to take a deep breath and let it out. My shoulders relax and a sense of calm invades me. Huh. I didn't know plants had this effect on me. Of course, this store reminds me of being out on a hike or paddling down the New River with all the lush vegetation surrounding me. Maybe that's why I feel more serene—it's like the outdoors, only inside.

I've never thought about adding plants to my home, but I'm wondering if there are more benefits to it than I assumed. I was just joking when I asked Anna if I should get a plant instead of a pet, but the more I've thought about it, the more appealing it's become. Now that I'm here, it seems inevitable that I'll head home with at least one living green thing to take care of. It might not be good company like a dog or cat would be, but I won't have to worry about it not getting enough attention or destroying any of my furniture.

Despite being a writer, I don't spend as much time at home as one would think. I've made the library my primary work station which allows me to keep to a schedule. When I show up, I put my phone in airplane mode and get to work. It's easy to tune out the other patrons, and most are respectful enough to speak in low voices. Sure, my attention occasionally gets snagged by a certain librarian, but my social anxiety keeps me from wasting time in conversation, so I suppose that's one plus to the racing heart, sweating, and blank mind I experience in specific situations.

Walking down the aisles, I'm overwhelmed by the options. Anna gave me a list of plants to consider, but I don't know what they look like. I see a guy wearing a shirt that says *I WET MY PLANTS* standing behind the register. He gives me a friendly smile as I approach.

"Can I help you?"

"I'm looking for a houseplant and my friend gave me a list of options, but I don't know what they look like or where to find them."

His smile widens. "Let me see the list. I can tell you which ones we have."

I pull up the Notes app on my phone and hand it over. Joey, according to his name tag, reads it, then hands it back.

"We've got most of those and I'll show you a few others that are similar. Follow me."

He leads me to a section in the back labeled *Indoor Plants*.

"This vine with the heart-shaped leaves is called a Pothos. It can survive just about anywhere."

It's a plant. Not much personality. Do plants have personalities? I don't know.

"I kind of want something that's cool to look at."

Joey nods. "Okay. How about this Chinese Evergreen?"

He points to a plant with pink and green speckled leaves. Definitely more interesting than the other one. Am I a pink plant person? Maybe.

"It has potential. What else?"

"This one over here is called a Flaming Katy."

What's flaming about a small, dark green plant with tiny buds? Joey must see my skepticism.

"It doesn't look like much at the moment, but it'll produce bright red flowers soon."

A flowering plant sounds kind of nice.

"Will you show me the rest of the ones on my list? I'd like to see all my options together."

He smiles. "Sure. I'll grab one of everything and line them up."

He darts around the area, grabbing various pots and placing them on the ground in front of me. Besides the plants he's already shown me, there's a tall plant with shiny green leaves, a plant with long green and light yellow leaves that reach straight up from the pot, one with a spiky yellow section in the middle that looks like a cross between leaves and a flower, a tiny green and white striped plant whose leaves all point up like it's reaching out to me, a plant with serrated-edged leaves and small red buds on the ends, and a large leafy plant that looks like something I'd see in an office. He sets down a small bulbous cactus with yellow spikes covering it like hair and puts his hands on his hips.

"Okay," he says. "You've got the Pothos, the Evergreen, the Katy, a Rubber Plant." He points to the tall one with shiny leaves. "Snake Plant, Bromeliad, Zebra Haworthia, Christmas Cactus, Cast Iron Plant, and another cactus."

It's cool seeing the variety all lined up. What would I like to see when I'm walking around my house? I have plenty of space for all of them. Is it too ambitious for a beginner plant parent to consider multiple dependents at once? Well, the odds of at least one of them staying alive are good this way. My eye pauses on the Cast Iron Plant. It reminds me too much of waiting rooms. I don't want my house to feel like an office. Sure, I have an office in my house, but I try to keep it on the playful side to stoke my imagination.

"I'd like to get everything but that one." I point at the offending plant.

"Sounds good, man. I'll grab a wagon and wheel everything to the front."

"Thanks."

Joey rings me up, and I pull the wagon to my car. Opening the trunk, I wonder if it's going to be filled with soil when the pots tip over on the ride home, but then remember my tent gear is in the back seat. I grab the tarp I use to keep dew from seeping into the bottom of my tent and spread it out across the trunk. It's large enough that I can tuck it in between the various pots, which will hopefully keep them secure while I drive.

When I get home, I carry everything into the kitchen, setting the plants on the island. Then I turn and survey my open living area, wondering where each plant should go. I stick the spiky bulbous cactus and the Flaming Katy in the window over the kitchen sink. The viney Pothos is set on top of one of my bookshelves in the front room. Joey said they can get long, so this position gives it plenty of room to trail down toward the floor. The Rubber Plant goes into one corner of my living room and the Chinese Evergreen goes in another.

I carry the Zebra Haworthia and Bromeliad into my office and look around for places to set them down. The office has a small cutout with a large window in the middle and two smaller ones on the angled sides that face the woods in my backyard. I had a desk custom made to fit in the spot so it spans the entire trapezoidal area. I set the smaller zebra striped plant down on a corner of the desk. The wall to the right of my desk has the door leading in and several filing cabinets I use for book stuff, bills, and financials. On top is a collection of photographs I took at various national parks. The gorgeous sandstone arch from Arches, Grand Prismatic Spring in Yellowstone, a beautiful ice-blue lake with a snow-covered mountain in the background from Glacier, the yawning chasm of the breathtaking Grand Canyon, Zion's steep red cliffs, Sequoia's General Sherman Tree, El Capitan in Yosemite, and the sharp-edged Grand Teton mountain range.

The opposite wall has a closet where I usually store my camping and travel gear. I haven't used my gear as much as I'd like in recent months. I've been too busy stressing about this latest book. Maybe spending more time outdoors would actually help this writer's block I've had for months. Sure, my last weekend away didn't help bust me out of my rut, but it can't hurt to go somewhere for a week or two. Long trips have historically helped ideas break loose.

The back wall of my office is all bookshelves. It has copies of my books in various formats and languages. There are also business and craft books, a few souvenirs from my travels, and books I've read written by other authors in my genre. There are a few toys and miscellaneous items strewn about. A pendulum that draws in sand sits on a shelf next to a liquid motion sandscape. On another shelf is a wooden bowl of items to fidget with—magnets, brain teasers, and a stress ball, to name a few. A magnetic dart board is on the wall next to the closet. I find a place for the Bromeliad on the bookshelves. I like the splash of color on the white shelves.

The Snake plant ends up in my bathroom and the Christmas cactus on the dresser in my bedroom. Satisfied with the new arrangement, I fill a pitcher with water and give a little to each of my new housemates.

I have too much energy to sit and focus on writing, which is fine because the library's closed today. Returning to my bedroom, I lace up my sneakers, head out of the house, and down to the neighborhood greenway. I start with a leisurely walk, but quickly realize I want to sweat and pick up the pace. My feet carry me along the familiar loop that traverses a good portion of the neighborhood before I finally end up back at my front walkway, panting, sweaty, and feeling suitably tired. My watch tells me I completed six miles. I check the mailbox, my pulse jumping when I see a letter from Anna.

Shucking my shoes just inside the door, I drop the rest of the mail onto the side table in the foyer and carry Anna's letter into the kitchen, slicing through the envelope with my llama letter opener I received from a friend as a joke.

In college, we went to this zoo of sorts that had many exotic animals—zebras, giraffes, wallabies, lemurs, tigers, sloths, and the like. We wandered over to the llama enclosure with food pellets. I held my hand out, and the llama gobbled up the food. Another llama stuck its head over the top of the chest-high gate, trying to get at the cup in my hand, but I pulled it back. And then the llama I'd just fed spit on me. A nearby worker assured me it was probably trying to warn off the other one, who was also seeking food, but that didn't change the fact that my shirt was doused in a yellowish liquid that smelled terrible. I had to rip my shirt off and throw it in the trash because I was dry heaving from the stench. Not my favorite memory, but I can laugh about it now.

The card inside the envelope has a bright rainbow splashed

across the front, which makes me smile. The inside is blank except for Anna's writing.

January 23

Dear Winston,

As you know, I'm no longer taking part in online dating, however I still want to meet someone, so I thought I'd try my hand at meeting people in person. I struck up a conversation with a guy in line, and he seemed flirty and open until his girlfriend came up and kissed him. Obviously, that won't work because I'm not into sharing boyfriends. Later, a cute guy sat at my table, but then ignored me the entire time. I almost stole his coffee, which was embarrassing. Alas, no love connection at Hill of Beans. Well, except for my love affair with their lattes and blueberry muffins. My book club has offered to set me up on blind dates and I'm seriously thinking about accepting.

My heart tugs with sympathy, but there's also a feeling of relief at her lack of success. I'm not sure why she started telling me about her search for a partner and I have mixed feelings about it. I like her and want her to be happy. But also, I like her and would like to be the one who makes her happy.

You'd think it'd be easy to walk up to someone you're interested in and have a normal, pleasant conversation, but that's not how I work. I've had anxiety since I was a kid, but I've been through therapy and gotten better at managing it. There are a few particular situations where I still have work to do. The idea of being in a large crowd and having all the focus on me is still terrifying. I don't have too much trouble avoiding that scenario. However, my other rough spot is talking to someone I'm interested in romantically. It wasn't as much of an issue in college, but I had one girlfriend who embarrassed me in front of a crowd and I've been gun shy ever since. The thought that, once again, I could be ridiculed and rejected in front of an audience puts all my senses in overdrive whenever I'm near a potential romantic partner.

Of course, Anna is so sweet that I doubt the thought of publicly embarrassing someone would even cross her mind. But her outgoing nature probably wouldn't enjoy being with someone like me who prefers quiet nights in and hiking into the wilderness where I'm more likely to meet a bear than a person. She seems to thrive on relationships and community, which is one reason I have done little to engage her in conversation and let my true feelings about her be known.

I'm quite enjoying being her pen pal, though. The pressure of performance and fear of humiliation are mitigated through the page. That, and the fact she doesn't realize it's me she's writing. She thinks she's writing an author, which she is, but I write under a pen name and it was what I used when I wrote her a thank you note after our first meeting. I was still a little raw from our terrible interaction and thought hiding behind my pen name would be fun. And it was, except now that we've been corresponding for so long, I feel a little bad about the deception. I've thought about coming clean, but we're not friends in person, so it would be super awkward. Plus, I bet she'd be disappointed to find out it's been me writing her this whole time. She doesn't even know my name. There's no real reason to come clean except to clear my conscience. If we became close in person, then I'd reveal myself, but that's never going to happen since I can't act normal around her.

Still, knowing she's serious about finding love has me questioning everything—my need to hide behind an alternate identity, my reluctance to seek additional help for my situational anxiety, and whether I actually like Anna in a romantic capacity or am just casting infatuation on a safe person, one I know won't go anywhere but also won't hurt me. Not wanting to delve further into these thoughts, I return my attention to the letter in my hands.

I'm sorry I sent you such a critical pet rock. He didn't seem nearly so self-righteous when I picked him out. It must have been the spiky hair I added that made him so prickly. (I know you're only joking, so don't fret that I'm actually freaking out. It's just a rock.) But don't let him add to the guilt you already seem to feel about being stuck in your writing. I wish I had something useful to share with you. Though, perhaps you've already started writing again and your block is in the past. I hope that's true. You're such a brilliant writer and I can't wait to see what story you share next.

I can't imagine being stuck in my apartment indefinitely. I don't even have a fire escape or a roof garden to visit when I need fresh air. Just a couple of windows. I'd probably be forced to create a book club for my apartment complex and who knows what such an eclectic group of people likes to read? Though, maybe my neighbors would surprise me and we'd form a tight-knit community that's truly wonderful.

I liked your question about what I'd do if I couldn't be a librarian. There are actually virtual librarians that help patrons search for materials, provide resources, and request electronic books. Of course, that's sort of cheating the question. Probably, I would do something like proofread, edit, or review books. It'd still keep me around books, which is a must. Thankfully, ebooks exist so I could still check out those from the library. I might get more into audiobooks if I was home all the time, just to hear other people talk. I think I'd miss that regular connection with new people I get at the library if I was stuck in my building. Now you're making me want to read the book and see how the character copes. I'm going to add it to my TBR list (which is already over a hundred books long, but since the recommendation is from you, I'll put it at the top).

Have you gotten a plant yet?

Sincerely, Anna

I've learned a lot about her through our correspondence. I know she reads a lot of romance and cozy mysteries. She had a white long-haired cat named Sparkles growing up, but doesn't have a pet now. Her favorite hiking spot is Little Bradley Falls. She has two younger sisters who are both married, but she doesn't have any nieces or nephews yet. She lives alone in her apartment, which I know is in South Asheville, not too far from my house. I now also know she frequents Hill of Beans and likes their lattes and blueberry muffins. That information gets stored in my Anna vault, though what I'll do with it, I don't know.

While I know some personal information about Anna, I've been much more tight-lipped. She knows I'm an author and live in the area. I have a PO Box that I use for all of my author correspondence, which I have forwarded to my physical address. My agent insisted on this in case I acquired any fans with stalker tendencies. Anna and I have talked a lot about books, so she knows my favorite, Ken Follett's *The Pillars of the Earth*. You'd think being drawn in by historical fiction would make me want to write it, but I don't want to see how the sausage is made, so to speak. I'd rather leave that as my fun, leisure reading and write something different.

I haven't told Anna about how I ended up an author. To be fair, she hasn't asked, but I should be more forthcoming about myself.

Moving from the kitchen to my office, I sit down at my desk and pull a piece of stationery from a lower drawer. I tap my pen on the desk as I ponder my reply. My gaze flits around the room until it lands on the plant at the corner of my desk. What's Anna going to think of the fact that I purchased nine plants today? Her smiling face pops into my head and I grin, then set pen to paper.

9

Anna

"SET ME UP."

Half a dozen heads swivel in my direction.

"What's that, Anna?" Rachel says.

I drop into a chair, let my tote bag hit the floor, and cross my arms. "I need help with my dating life. The app didn't work. Trying to meet people in person was a veritable disaster. Maybe I don't know what to look for in a potential mate. You all have had success finding a spouse, so you must know something I don't. What am I doing wrong?"

Susan, who's in the seat to my left, places a comforting hand on my arm. "Oh, sweetie. I doubt it's you."

"I'd like to say it's the guys, but I'm the common denominator. Perhaps my radar for compatibility is broken. The app guys seemed perfect on screen, but we were like oil and water in real life."

Susan raises an eyebrow and tilts her head. "Did I ever tell you how Roger and I got together?"

I straighten up at her tone, intrigued. "No."

She smiles. "I was taking a statistics class in college and one day noticed some guy staring at me. It felt a little creepy, so I actively avoided him as much as I could. One day, on the way out of class, he held the door open for me, but I ignored him and hurried to my next class. Later that week, he caught up to me on the way to class and asked to sit with me. I told him I had a boyfriend, but that didn't deter him."

A few women chuckle at Susan's sly smile.

"He chatted with me in class and, over the course of the semester, we became friends. Eventually, I broke up with my boyfriend, and Roger and I were solid friends by then. I didn't start thinking about us becoming something more until my ex told me he could tell Roger liked me as more than a friend.

"I realized Roger was kind, fun, and respectful of me—all desirable qualities. We'd gone to a concert together and to dinner a few times and, after the conversation with my ex, I realized Roger really was someone I would be interested in dating and my feelings toward him changed. I took him to dinner, told him I was interested in moving beyond friendship if he was, and that was it. I think the months of friendship really helped lay a solid foundation for our relationship."

Rachel clasps her hands together. "Oh, Susan, that's so sweet. You and Roger are so adorable together, too. Thanks for sharing."

Susan nods, then turns her focus back to me. "No one has the same story, but I think patience and being open to all possibilities is your best bet for finding someone on your wavelength."

I place my hand on hers and give it a grateful squeeze. "Thanks, Susan. I appreciate the reminder that true love takes time and relational attention. I can't expect to fall instantly in love.

Instant attraction, maybe, but I want more than that." I turn my attention around the circle. "Which is where, I hope, you all come in. If you're still open to arranging dates for me, I'm game."

Abbie grins and rubs her hands together. "Excellent. I've been thinking about this and have an idea to make this fun for everyone."

Rachel rolls her eyes. "You have to make everything a competition, don't you?"

"Not *everything*. Just listen to my suggestion before you diss it."

"Fine." Rachel extends her hand, motioning the floor to Abbie.

Abbie bows in her seat. "Thank you. Okay, so I thought each of us could find an eligible bachelor who isn't related to us to avoid awkwardness if things don't work out." She looks at me, and I give her an appreciative nod.

"At the same time, we also pick a book for a potential future group read. *But* we wrap the book in brown paper and list a few enticing clues about the book. We let Anna choose which book sounds most interesting, we read that book, and she goes on a date with the person whose book is chosen."

"I'm sorry for doubting you, Abbie," Rachel says. "I really like that idea."

Meredith leans forward, her eyes shining. "I have one little additional suggestion. What if we each plan a date and have the book clues allude to the type of adventure Anna will have if she chooses it?"

Abbie claps her hands and laughs. "Oooh, I like that. I bet it'll make it easier to convince the guy to go on a blind date if all he has to do is show up."

I narrow my eyes. "Are you insinuating that you're going to have to bribe guys to go on a date with me?"

Abbie waves a hand in front of her. "Not at all. I just know a lot of guys have trouble coming up with something other than going to a restaurant. Plus, since we know you, we can tailor the dates to your interests and you can see if the guy enjoys doing things you like."

My shoulders relax. "Oh, okay. I like the sound of that. What does everyone else think?"

Lori, Deb, Susan, Rachel, and Meredith all nod.

"Excellent," Abbie says. "It's settled."

"What's settled?" Julie says, rushing in the door. "Sorry I'm late, but I brought chocolate."

She sets a large tray on the table next to the coffeepot and removes the foil with a flourish.

A chorus of *oohs* and *aahs* comes from the circle of chairs as we take in the beautiful display of chocolates. They're arranged in some sort of shape I can't quite figure out.

"Oh, it's a plane!" Lori says.

Julie smiles. "Glad you get it. The wings are made from special truffles just for tonight. They're imitation Twix."

"Just like in the story," Deb says.

"Yep. Help yourselves. And somebody tell me what I missed."

Abbie grins. "Anna's ready for us to set her up and we've decided we'll plan the date. She'll pick a blind date book with clues about what she'll be doing, and we'll read the book for the next meeting."

Julie's eyes widen. "Wow, I missed a lot, but that sounds like fun. Are we starting next month?"

All eyes swing to me. After a moment, I nod.

"Great," Rachel says. "It's all settled. Everyone is responsible for finding a single guy they think Anna would like to agree to a date, figure out what they'll do, and wrap a book with clues related to the date. I have one more thought, though. What if, for this project, we meet every two weeks or after Anna goes on a date, whichever is longer? That way, Anna doesn't have to wait so long if a date doesn't work out."

"I don't mind reading more books," Deb says.

"Me either," Meredith says. "Do you have any stipulations, Anna?"

My brow furrows. "What do you mean?"

"Like, does age difference matter? Do they need to live in Asheville or can they be from a surrounding area? Any deal breakers like if he vapes or has mutton chops?"

"Oh. Um, probably at least out of college, but not older than my parents. Someone within an hour's drive. Definitely not a smoker or someone who is super judgy about diets or exercise habits. Other than that, I guess I'm open. Oh, preferably someone who likes to be active and do things. I don't want to spend every night and weekend on the couch."

"That's helpful, thanks."

Having to discuss my dating preferences is making this feel very real. I could have seven dates with seven strangers. The idea is both exciting and a little terrifying. I might be forced to endure seven terrible dates, but there's also the possibility of meeting someone I really click with. This raises a question in my mind.

"Hey, I just had a thought. What if I really like the first guy I meet through this? Do I still have to go on the other dates?"

The group is quiet for a minute before Abbie shakes her head. "No. This isn't *The Bachelorette*. If you find someone you really connect with, I think you should continue to pursue it and see where it goes. We can always circle back if we need to."

She looks around the circle for agreement and is met with

unanimous head nods. "Great. Now that that's settled, I want to try the Twix truffle. Can we start our book club now?"

I chuckle. "Yes, let's get back to business. Thanks for all your help, ladies. I look forward to selecting a book date next month."

After everyone has grabbed a drink and a few chocolates, we settle back into our chairs and Julie facilitates our discussion of *Dear Edward*.

"You know," Lori says as the end of the meeting nears, "the author has a new book out that has been getting rave reviews. I'd be interested in reading it soon."

"Make it your blind date pick," Abbie says.

"Actually," Rachel says, "we still need a book for next month. Anna won't be selecting a read today. I'm game for reading *Hello Beautiful* if everyone else is. Otherwise, someone else make a suggestion."

"Sounds good to me," says Susan. "I hope it's just as good as this one was. Maybe a little less heartbreaking, though."

Lori shrugs. "I can't guarantee anything."

Susan waves a hand. "It's fine. What does everyone else think?"

"Works for me," says Deb.

The rest of the ladies nod.

"Then it's settled," Rachel says. "I don't think we've read an author back-to-back since we read through all of Jane Austen's books. And that was before Meredith, Julie, and Abbie joined us. Alright, everyone. Have a great month and happy reading!"

"And take some chocolates home with you," Julie adds.

10

Anna

WHEN I GET home, I drop my mail on the counter on my way to the bedroom to change into my favorite pair of pajamas—a super soft sage green T-shirt with a mountain landscape and the words *Get Outdoors* scrawled below and gray leggings with pockets. After washing my face and brushing my teeth, I head back to the kitchen for a drink of water before bed.

A light blue envelope half-buried under bills and junk mail catches my eye and I stop, sliding it out from among the mail stack. Impulsively, I bring it to my nose and sniff, surprised to catch a hint of something woodsy. Is Winston's stationery scented, or did he spray some cologne on it? Has it always had a smell? Curiosity carries me to my nightstand. I open the bottom drawer and grab a small stack of blue envelopes and sniff them. My lips twist to the side. They don't smell like anything. They've either lost their smell or this one is different. Maybe the envelope got mixed in with a leaking fragrance box?

I head back to the kitchen to smell the rest of my mail. Nothing else has the same scent. Huh. Maybe I'm imagining it. I grab the unopened letter and inhale deeply again. Definitely an eau de tree of some kind. I slip my finger under the flap and slide, leaving a jagged tear in the envelope. Pulling out the paper, I run my fingers over the raised monogram and inspect the paper for a water stain that will prove my cologne theory. The top and bottom left corners look a little grayish. I pick up the envelope and see the bottom corner looks smudged. Another sniff confirms it's the source of the pleasant odor. It looks like an accidental occurrence, but gives me an idea for my response. Who wouldn't enjoy receiving a scented letter? But before I get carried away, I should find out what Winston's letter says.

January 30

Dear Anna,

I experienced second-hand embarrassment on your behalf reading about your encounters in the coffee shop. However, I hope you know you shouldn't worry about guys who don't recognize how incredible you are. It only took meeting you once and staring into your bright blue eyes for me to want to make your acquaintance and spend more time getting to know you. I've enjoyed our regular correspondence. When I receive a letter from you, it's the highlight of my day.

I took your advice on choosing a plant over an animal, but was a little overwhelmed in the store and ended up bringing nine home with me. I think the zebra haworthia is my favorite. It sits on my writing desk next to Dwayne (yes, he's still in my office; I put a small top hat over his spikes and it seems to have calmed him down) and I think of you whenever it catches my eye.

I'm still struggling with my sci-fi sequel, though I have started a fun side project that has given me some inspiration. I doubt my agent or editor would be happy to hear I'm working on something else, but I'm hoping the creativity will bleed over. The deadline feels like a guillotine hanging over my head, but there's nothing more to be done other than what I'm doing. Maybe I need to add some fantastical sci-fi element like a time machine to move the plot forward. What do you think of time travel as a plot device?

Sometimes being outside helps me think clearly about my projects. I may have to take a long trek through Pisgah or DuPont sometime soon and take in some fresh air. Do you like hiking? It's one of my favorite things in the world.

I've been using this letter as an excuse to avoid writing, but I probably should get back to it. Thanks for helping me take a break from this infuriating block.

Sincerely, Winston

P.S.-I read the book you sent. It had a few ideas I've tried out. I managed to get a few hundred words, but it's still like pulling teeth—slow and painful. Maybe it's just something I have to keep pushing against until I finally break through.

I hug the note against me, warmth blooming in my chest from Winston's words. My letters are the highlight of his day? He wants to get to know me better? Have I ever told him how much I enjoy his letters? Probably not, but those little blue envelopes are a bright spot in my days as well.

I hate that he's struggling with his writing project, but there's nothing I can do other than wish him well.

I love that he now has nine plants in his house. Do they all make him think of me? Is that something I hope for? Perhaps the conversation from book club tonight has me thinking about relationships a little too much. I don't know very much personal information about him, though I have learned he likes hiking just like I do. We now have two things in common—hiking and books, which is more than I've found with the guys from the MeetCute app.

Maybe I should have been more specific about my requirements for the book club dates, but I didn't want to exclude some potential matches by being too picky. I'm a little wary about how that will go, but the group assured me they wouldn't be offended if I didn't click with their picks. Perhaps shaking things up in my dating life will be just what I need. Because if Blind Date and a Book doesn't work, I'm not sure what else to do.

February 16

Dear Winston,

I love that you gave Dwayne a hat. I can picture him with a monocle and tuxedo jacket with tails, though how he can wear a jacket without a body, I don't know. Does he look like he's going to the opera?

Were you able to get to DuPont or Pisgah? I enjoy hiking both of those places. Wintergreen Falls in DuPont is one of my favorite waterfalls. Most people don't hike back far enough to see it, so I can often take in the views all alone. It makes me feel like some seventeenth century explorer stumbling upon a natural wonder for the first time.

As far as your book goes, time travel can make a story interesting, depending on how you use it. I feel like it adds an element of danger when the characters can risk altering the future in detrimental ways. It reminds me of an episode of The Simpsons *when Homer tries to fix a toaster and ends up in the time of dinosaurs. The Treehouse of Horror episodes are some of my favorites. Especially The Shinning. I've never read the book or seen the movie (horror is not my thing), but I've seen enough clips of Jack Nicholson busting through the door that it feels like I've watched it. I got off on a tangent. Do you watch* The Simpsons? *My gut tells me it's not your thing, but people are surprised to hear I enjoy it, so who knows?*

Sincerely, Anna

11

Brody

I RAKE A hand through my hair, pushing back from my desk. My head plops against the back of the chair as I slump against the leather. Releasing a frustrated breath, I grab the green foam ball out of the bowl of toys and toss it into the air. It thunks back into my hand and I throw it up again. The rhythm soothes me and the stress knotting my shoulders eases slightly.

After a few more tosses and catches, I drop the ball back into the bowl and return to my computer screen. I've not made much progress with Ciara's dilemma. Even adding in a time travel element hasn't shaken inspiration loose. I still feel like I'm as doomed as the kingdom of Mephilus is against the duplicitous advisors. My agent wants to see a completed draft by the end of the month, so he and I have time to tweak it before sending it on to the publisher, but I need another fifty thousand words to finish the story. Ideally, words filled with suspense and surprises and a satisfying resolution. No big deal.

The telltale buzzing of my cell phone has me rifling through the papers spread all over my desk until I find it wedged like an oversized bookmark in the middle of my ideas notebook. A groan escapes me when I see it's my agent.

Reluctantly, I accept the call. "Hey, Mark."

"Brody, my man!"

I close my eyes at his enthusiastic greeting. This call is not going to go as he hopes.

"Tell me you're just running through an edit and will have the manuscript to me by the end of the week." His heavy breath makes me wonder if he's jogging right now.

"I wish."

"What's the holdup?"

I blow out a long breath through my lips. "I just can't get into the story. Everything wrapped up so nicely in the first one, I kind of put the world behind me."

"I know, Bro. But the pros think a sequel would sell. And it might get you back into the game as a true player."

My eyes roll of their own accord. Mark's always been about trying to get me to be a big name, which I can't fault him too much. It's a big reason I picked him to be my agent. Who wants someone who doesn't care what happens with your career? But the downside is I feel pressure to help him achieve his vision for me and it's only adding to the stress of my looming deadline.

"I hear you, and I'm trying."

The short fantasy story I created pops into my head. It was so much fun to write. The words just flowed out of my brain and onto the screen. Sure, it was only a couple thousand words, but it reminded me a little of when I wrote *Into the Unknown*. I hadn't expected it to be such a big hit, but I'm sure my enthusiasm for the project showed through the story.

"Why don't you send me over what you've got so far," Mark says. "We can brainstorm together like we did for your other two books."

He seems to have forgotten that my last two books didn't do half as well as my debut, but I'm sure he's just trying to stay positive. Which, honestly, is probably what I need more of—positivity. I'm not exactly optimistic I'm going to get this book finished in time. At least, not in a form that draws people in and has them binging chapters and ignoring all their other duties until they've turned the last page. *Excellent positivity, Brody.*

"What's that?"

Did I say that last bit out loud? "Oh, nothing. Sure, I can send what I have. Perhaps you can see through the weeds and help me find the right direction."

"Great. I've got some time this afternoon. Just email it to me and I'll send you my thoughts by tomorrow at the latest."

It's an excuse to take a break from beating my head against the wall. Perhaps I should find something fun to do. Refill the creative well, so to speak. I turn toward the window and get a glimpse of trees through the window. A hike is just what I need right now to clear my head and get some perspective.

"Sure, Mark. I appreciate your willingness to help."

"That's what I'm here for. But you know…" He trails off and my body tightens, bracing for whatever he's going to say. Whenever he starts that sentence, I know it's something I won't enjoy hearing.

"What?"

"It'd go a long way with the publisher if you'd agree to do a small book signing tour. Just five or six stops where you read a snippet of the book and answer a few questions from the audience. Consider it a token of good faith that lets them know you're all in."

"No." I shake my head vehemently, even though no one can see it. "Not going to happen. I can't do it."

Mark sighs through the phone. "I know it makes you uncomfortable, but they asked me to float the idea by you. Being an enigmatic author appeals to some fans, but many more want to connect with the person who brought them joy through some words on a page. If you were willing to do this, I bet they'd be more open to anything new you might like to write."

I grab the green ball from the bowl and squeeze it firmly. Letting my fingers pulse against it does nothing to quell the anxiety rising in my chest. Just the thought of being the center of attention in a room where we discuss personal things, like my motivation and inspiration behind the books, has my pulse spiking. My desire for anonymity is the reason I initially refused a book tour. The publisher didn't care when I was a debut author, not wanting to spend too many resources on an unknown, but they pushed pretty hard with the second and third books. They probably blame some of the other books' lackluster response on my refusal to engage with readers.

The stories were well-written with engaging plots and did better than a lot of other books, but paled compared to the juggernaut of my first so much that they felt like flops. I think readers wanted the books to be in the same world as *Into the Unknown* and were disappointed they weren't. Which is, apparently, what my publisher also thinks, as they are only accepting a sequel. The dangling carrot is that they'll seriously entertain other ideas once I produce this one, but I wonder if they'll try to coerce me to turn this potential duology into an entire series. Why put money on an unknown when you can continue to squeeze money out of a current hit?

I don't want to be a one-hit wonder, though. Nor do I want to be pigeon-holed into only writing about one world I created. Ideally, I'd write stories that readers love indefinitely, but I know there's nothing else open to me with my current publisher until I satisfy their demands. Perhaps I could pitch my new ideas elsewhere, but I'm technically on the hook for one more book with them. Not that they have to publish it, but I have to at least produce a finished manuscript of some sort. And I know if it's not what they want, they won't even consider other stories from me. Would other publishers consider me if my current one rejects this manuscript?

"I know you're just doing your job, but it's still a no go. Let's hope I can produce a story they're satisfied with."

"You know I'm on your side, Brody. I want what you want and I'm pretty sure you want to keep writing and publishing books, which you can only do if you actually write and submit a completed story."

"Message received. I'll email it over now."

We hang up and I grimace as I attach what I've got so far and send it through space to my eager agent. I should be glad he's hungry for success and wants me to continue to pursue my writing dreams. Obviously, he makes money when I make money, but he is a genuinely good guy. I'm just in a funk and it's coloring everything around me.

I glance out the window again, light glinting off the bare trees outside my window. Pushing up out of my chair, I head to the bedroom to change into hiking clothes, before stuffing snacks, water, and a jacket into my backpack and hopping into my SUV. I drive to the entrance to the Blue Ridge Parkway next to the Arboretum and head south on the parkway for twenty-five miles before turning right into the parking lot for Graveyard Fields.

Hoisting my backpack onto my shoulders, I start the trek,

visiting the lower falls first, before hiking out to the upper falls. Enjoying the view, I eat a snack while thinking about the direction I want to take with the story. The falling water pulls me into a trance. I forget everything and just stare at the natural beauty. Breathing deeply, I let my abdomen fill with air, hold it for a bit, then slowly release it. I repeat these slow breaths until a peacefulness envelops me. My eyes feel heavy and I lean back against the rock I'm sitting on. Sliding my backpack under my head, I close my eyes and enjoy the tickle of a soft breeze against my face.

Awareness comes back to me slowly until I hear rushing water off to my left. Batting my eyes open, I'm surprised by the shadows around me. I sit up, rubbing my eyes. The sun is gone, dropped behind one of the surrounding hills. Checking my watch, I realize I slept for several hours. Guess the stress was getting to me more than I thought. Now, though, I feel quite refreshed. Maybe I really needed to just be in nature for a bit.

Digging through my front pocket, I find my headlamp and strap it over my hat. It's only twilight, but I still have to hike back out to the parking lot and darkness descends quickly in the mountains. I take a long drink of water, shrug on my backpack, and make my way along the trail back to my vehicle. The parking lot is empty except for my car.

Settling into the driver's seat, my stomach rumbles with hunger. My phone vibrates in my pants pocket. A look at the screen shows me I have a new email. Probably Mark's notes on my manuscript. Not ready to lose all the peace I gained on my hike, I decide to wait until I get home to open it.

The drive back is silent, except for the sound of the wind rushing in my open windows. I love driving on the parkway with the windows down even in the winter. It sometimes makes me wish I had a dog who could enjoy the outdoors with me, but I spend so much time indoors at a desk that I'd feel guilty not giving it more attention. A cat is more independent, but I doubt it'd like going on car rides and hiking through the forest. I've seen videos of people with cats in baby carriers and backpacks, so I suppose it's not out of the realm of possibilities. Still, let's see how things go with my plants. So far, they all look alive and well. And they make me smile and think of Anna, both good things.

My mind mulls over thoughts of Anna, focusing on her bubbly personality and kind eyes, the humor in her letters, and her openness to life and experiences. She is so amazing. I hope she finds someone who cherishes her the way she deserves and appreciates all of her uniqueness. *That could be you*, my mind interjects. It seems to have forgotten that I can barely get one word out when I'm around her. *So change that*, it says. Yeah, that's easy to say, but much harder to put into practice. *But I bet it'd be worth it. She's worth it.* Arg. There's nothing quite like having a fight with yourself and realizing your subconscious is smarter than you. Fine, self. I'll think about it.

12

Anna

MY FIRST DATE with a Blind Date and a Book candidate has arrived. Everyone in the group showed up with books wrapped in brown paper and a few descriptive sentences to intrigue me. They all sounded interesting, but I chose the most enigmatic one (and maybe also because of the word romance).

A menagerie of characters! A competition of unbelievable feats. One night only—a romance that's simply magical.

The book is *The Night Circus*, chosen by Susan. It's a book I've heard good things about, so I look forward to diving into it. The good thing about this setup is that even though I'm technically choosing the book, I won't feel bad if people don't like it because it wasn't really my selection. And I don't have to facilitate the discussion, though I do have to dissect my date (or dates, if we hit it off) with the group.

Susan arranged for me and my date to attend the show of a magician passing through town. I haven't heard of the guy, but he made it to the finals of *America's Got Talent,* so I watched a few of his appearances on the internet. I think I figured out one of his illusions, but the one with the playing cards has me stumped. Maybe he'll do it at the show and I can pay closer attention.

My date's name is Benjamin, and he's someone who works at Roger's accounting office. The knowledge that he's an accountant has me picturing a skinny guy with glasses. I know I'm stereotyping, but Benjamin even sounds a little nerdy to me. I'm a little wary about how the date will go, but am hoping to be pleasantly surprised.

We're meeting for dinner beforehand at Haywood Street Market since the show's at the Thomas Wolfe Auditorium, which is just up the street from the food hall. Susan got us front row seats, so we will see everything the magician does up close.

When I open the doors to the food hall, I look around for a guy wearing a blue sports coat. A navy blazer is in line at a local brewery, but it's on a very tall guy with broad shoulders, so I keep looking. Seeing no one else, I decide to approach the oversized human.

"Excuse me," I say, when I'm right behind the guy. "Are you Benjamin?"

The behemoth turns and gives me a brilliant white smile. "Please call me Ben. You must be Anna."

He extends his hand, and it dwarfs mine, but his grip is surprisingly gentle.

"Wow, you're tall."

He chuckles. "I get that a lot."

I still can't believe this giant of a man is an accountant. He should be playing a pro sport or something. I shake my head, trying to dislodge my judgmental thoughts. "Sorry, I just didn't expect an accountant to be built like you." I motion up and down with my hands before realizing how rude I'm being. I quickly tuck my hands into my jacket pockets. "Sorry, again. I don't mean to stereotype."

Ben gives me an amiable smile. "It's fine. I played tight end in college. Might have made it pro, except I blew out my knee senior year."

"Oh, I'm sorry."

He shrugs. "Good thing I like numbers so much. Doesn't pay as much as the NFL, but I'm much less likely to get a concussion or tear a ligament."

He gives me a wink and I laugh, delighted he's got a sense of humor. I may end up with a crick in my neck from looking up at him all night, but that's okay because he's very nice to look at. His short brown hair is gelled on top, he's got two dimples that pop when he smiles, a square jaw, and dazzling golden brown eyes. I can tell from his fitted sports coat he's still in great physical shape. If he does any running, maybe we can work out together. I know I'll never match him in weight lifting, but I've got a decent mile pace.

"So true." I motion toward the beer menu. "What are you ordering?"

"I was thinking about the Pie in the Face from Flying Circus Brewery to get me in the mood for this evening."

My eyes light up at his playfulness. This is great. Maybe I'll be one and done with these blind dates, though I'd still like to read all the books. *Don't get ahead of yourself, Anna.* "You definitely should." I scan the menu. "Perhaps I'll try the Ace Up the Sleeve."

Ben grins at me, then orders for both of us when it's our turn. When he hands me my beer, he says, "What were you thinking about eating?"

Looking over the shops in the corridor to our left, my attention stops at Curry in a Hurry. "I think I'm in the mood for Indian food."

I look at Ben and see his nose wrinkle. "No thanks. I'm not a fan of spicy food."

"They have non-spicy options."

He shakes his head. "Nah, don't want to risk it. Think I'll get a burger from B4s."

Well, there's the first strike against him. I like an adventurous eater. Someone who won't venture out of their culinary comfort zone would be tough to travel with, and I want to travel. I have yet to leave the United States, but I haven't really had a travel buddy. I guess that's something I'm looking for in a potential partner. Of course, American fast food exists all across the globe, so maybe Ben would still be willing to travel.

After we've gotten our food, we settle in across from each other at one of the long tables in the center of the hall. "So, Ben. Do you like to travel?"

He nods, chewing quickly. "Yes, I do. One of my goals is to make it to all fifty states. So far I'm at forty-two."

"Wow, that's great. What do you have left?"

He ticks them off on his fingers. "Alaska, Arizona, New Mexico, Utah, Oklahoma, Rhode Island, Connecticut, and Maine. What about you?"

"I'm interested in travel, but haven't been many places. I'd probably have forty states still to see. But I'd really like to travel internationally."

He tilts his head from side to side. "As long as I don't have to learn a new language or eat something I can't identify, I'm game. Though, what I'd really like to do is go to one of those all-inclusives with the bright blue water. I'd spend all day swimming, drinking, and napping in the sun. I wouldn't have to leave the resort."

While that sounds wonderful, my desire to travel is to experience the culture. Sure, an occasional tropical vacation might be nice, but it's not all I'd want to do. "I'm more of an explore where you are kind of person. I like seeing the history and culture of a place."

Ben waves a hand. "Eh. I suppose some of that might be okay."

Not exactly glowing agreement, but it's something I can work with.

"How's your beer?" I've noticed he hasn't touched the glass since we sat down.

"It's alright. A little too sweet for me, though I should have suspected with pie in the name. How's yours?"

"I like it. It's a little sour with some sort of citrus kick to it."

Ben reaches across the table and picks up my glass. He takes a drink and sets it back down, my glass now nearly empty. "Yeah, that's pretty good."

My forehead furrows as I try to process exactly what just happened. I cannot believe this stranger just drank my beer without even asking. And now it's almost gone. The only good thing is that he paid for it, but his actions are still rude in my book. There's his second strike.

Am I a food snob for docking him points for his food preferences and behavior? Maybe, but if we were in a relationship, his tendency to take food or drink from me without asking would slowly wear away at my patience until I exploded.

I had a boyfriend in college who would pick at my food. Once, I had a big, juicy strawberry on my plate. He picked it up, took a big bite out of the end, then *put it back on my plate*. Who does that? That was just one of several red flags in the relationship. He taught me not to let too many little things slide because they're often an indicator of bigger things like narcissism, lack of boundaries, and general disregard for me as a person.

Not sure how to respond to Ben's inappropriate actions, I focus back on my chicken tikka masala, thankful that I at least know he won't be pilfering any. Our end of the table is silent until we're both finished with dinner. Ben gets up, takes our plates and glasses, and puts them in the bins near the trash cans. I suppose that's a positive point for him.

I try to let the drink thing go, knowing I'm not a perfect person either. I'm sure I have quirks that bother the people I date. For instance, I prefer reading to television, so when I agree to "watch a show" with someone, more often than not I lose interest quickly and turn to the kindle I always carry in my purse. And, when I'm reading, I tend to lose track of what's around me and can end up ignoring someone who's trying to talk to me.

When Ben returns to the table and puts his coat back on, I do the same. We head out front and walk up the street to the theater. There's a line at the door, but the ticket scanners are efficient and we're inside and in our seats within a few minutes. There's still half an hour before the show starts and I search for something to say.

"What kinds of things do you like to read?"

"I have subscriptions to Sports Illustrated and ESPN. Does that count?"

Technically, yes, but that's not what I'm looking for. I want to see what genres interest him. "Sure. Do you have a favorite book or author? Or a series you read recently and enjoyed?"

Ben twists his lips while he thinks. "I read the Fox and O'Hare series by Janet Evanovich and Lee Goldberg a while back. It was fun with its cat-and-mouse chases and crazy heists."

Okay, that's something. "I haven't read those. I'm more into cozy mysteries and romance than action and adventure."

He rolls his eyes. "Are you one of those girls who swoons over hand flexes and over-the-top romantic gestures?"

His blatant dismissal of romance readers makes my hackles rise. I suddenly feel less guilty about stereotyping him.

"What if I am? Is there something wrong with positive portrayals of love?"

"No, but, come on. Most of those plots are so outlandish. Fake marriages? Secret royalty? That isn't realistic."

I'm surprised he's knowledgeable about the genre, but it seems like that's only so he can ridicule it. I cross my arms over my chest. "And I'm sure a guy taking down an international drug ring all by himself with just his smarts and a hand gun happens all the time in real life."

Ben puts his hands up in front of him. "Hey, we can like what we like. I'm just saying, I'm not expecting to be called into action to rescue the president's kidnapped daughter, while I'm sure there are plenty of women who disregard regular guys because they're waiting for a literal knight on a white horse to confess his love and whisk her away to a fabulous life."

I clamp my lips together, afraid of what might come out. We still have a magic show to get through and I promised the group I'd give the guy a fair shot, but Ben has just about walked himself off a cliff into an ocean of *Never Going to Work*. Needing some space, I stand up.

"I'm going to use the restroom and get a bottle of water. Would you like one?"

"I'm good."

Not even a *Thanks for offering*? Okay, I'm probably just being nitpicky now, but I don't see this evening ending with a second date request or acceptance. At least not on my part. Ben didn't seem too concerned with my defensiveness over romance books. Perhaps he enjoys sparring. I don't mind a little verbal back and forth when it's something trivial or impersonal, but this feels like a sticking point to me.

I spend long enough in the lobby that the lights are dimming when I reach my seat again. My dawdling successfully prevents me from having to speak to Ben again until the show's over. I sure hope this magician dazzles us with his tricks. I need something to make this night worthwhile.

13

Brody

RELEASING A FRUSTRATED breath, I pick up the stress ball I brought with me and squeeze it tightly in my fist for a few seconds before letting my fingers go slack. Tossing the ball back and forth between my hands, my head drops back, wishing inspiration could be found in the drop tile ceiling, but alas, I'm not writing about a zoo, so the lion, giraffe, and hippo water stains are no use. I drop the ball onto the cubicle's flat surface and remove the over ear headphones that have been piping soundtrack music into my ears. I'd chosen a playlist composed of songs from epic adventures like *Lord of the Rings* and *The Matrix*, hoping to pry ideas loose, but I haven't gotten very far in—I look at the time on my phone—the three hours I've been here. I groan at my lack of progress.

A voice nearby perks me up and I swivel my head around. I don't see anyone, but I hold still and close my eyes, focusing on the surrounding sounds. I hear fingers on keyboards from the computer stations a few rows up. Someone coughs twice. The overhead fluorescent hum steadily lights. And then words ring clear again from somewhere off to my right.

"He really said that about romance readers?"

I recognize the voice of the dark-haired librarian.

"Can you believe it? I knew that was the death knell of anything happening between us, but it actually got worse."

That's Anna. My heart stirs at the awareness of her proximity. The two must be somewhere among the nonfiction shelves.

"What's worse than having one of your passions belittled?"

Anna breathes out a laugh. "Okay, maybe not *worse*, but still pretty bad."

"I'm listening."

Me too.

"Okay," Anna says, "so my friend got us front row seats to see this illusionist, which sounded kind of neat. I'm not really into magic, but I like unique experiences. I guess *Benjamin* wasn't very impressed by the guy's performance, because he kept whispering snide comments to me throughout the show."

"Ugh," her friend says. "I hate guys who disparage others' pleasures."

"Same. But that wasn't all. His voice got louder as the show progressed and by the end I know the illusionist could hear him. He glared our direction at the end of the show. It was so embarrassing. I made sure to stand and clap loudly once it was over so he'd know I didn't share the same opinion."

I'm embarrassed on Anna's behalf. She'd never act ugly toward someone, so I'm sure her date's behavior mortified her. I feel only a twinge of guilt about being pleased her date went poorly. It's hard to imagine someone being so rude at a show, but I know there are people who lack self-awareness and proper etiquette.

"Yeesh. Did you have to endure an awkward car ride home?"

"Thankfully, no. We met at the food hall so I waved goodbye, ducked his attempt at a goodnight kiss, and rushed to my car without looking back."

"He tried to kiss you? Was he that oblivious?"

"I guess so. Or maybe he's just used to people focusing on his good looks and ignoring his poor behavior."

I've known guys like that who have their behavior excused because they're attractive, athletic, rich, or have some sort of exceptional quality. They make things harder for the rest of the male population because we then have to work hard to prove we're not like them.

"Ick," her friend says. "I'm sorry your first Blind Date and a Book didn't work out."

She's going on blind dates now? When did this happen? Who's setting her up?

"Yeah, but I have six more to choose from, so who knows what will happen?"

My blood runs cold. She's really serious about finding someone. I have to do something if I want to even have a chance with her. I met with my therapist last week and told her about Anna and my desire to have conversations with her that don't make me drip with sweat and bring on a panic attack. We role-played a little in the office with Gabi pretending to be Anna. My homework before the next meeting is to ask Anna something library-related just to work on starting a normal conversation before I even think about bringing up the fact that I would love to take her on a date.

The reminder that part of the reason I came to the library was to complete my therapy homework makes my heart speed up. I'm getting hot underneath my button-down and sweater combo. I quickly remove the sweater and stuff it into my bag.

I realize I don't hear Anna or the other librarian talking anymore. I look around and spot Anna scanning books into the computer at the circulation desk. Her friend is nowhere to be seen, so it's the perfect time to approach. What was I going to ask her again?

My mind is suddenly blank, sweat beading under my shirt collar. Come on, Brody, think! You can ask her anything. What new release would she recommend? Does she have any sci-fi book recommendations? Yeah, that's the one. I've wondered if I should immerse myself back into the science fiction world, hoping it'll spark new ideas about the story I'm working on. I've been reading more fantasy lately, which is probably part of the reason I wrote that short story so quickly.

I've been thinking a lot about that Anna-inspired work. Maybe I should continue to work on it and see if it could become a future novel. I can use what I just heard about her date as a setting for Beorn to insert himself into Aurelia's path. Perhaps they're both at a wizard's competition and she's with some annoying fairy and Beorn uses his ingenuity to draw her away from the situation. He might make her laugh and help her forget her embarrassment from the fairy.

Part of me knows I'm stalling on talking to Anna, but another part is really excited about this idea. I set an alarm for an hour from now, making a deal with myself that I'll talk to Anna when it goes off. Satisfied with the bargain, and relieved that I don't have to face her right this second, I replace my earphones, pull up the fantasy document—currently titled *Daydream*—and get to work.

The buzz of my phone startles me. I'm right in the middle of a scene and set another alarm for thirty minutes from now. I rush to capture my thoughts quickly. Twenty minutes later, my hands lift from my laptop's keyboard. Stretching my back and neck, I smile at the screen, satisfied with what I've accomplished. I save my work and shut down my computer. After everything is in my bag, I stand up and take a deep breath, running through my monologue in my head. *Hi, Anna. Can you give me a recommendation for a few good science fiction books?* Easy enough. Do I need to say *Hi, Anna* though? Is it creepy to point out that I know her name? She wears a name tag so it wouldn't be weird for me to address her by name. My skin tingles, my heart already pounding in my chest.

Noticing she's not at the circulation desk, I look around the room to see if I can spot her. She's not at the computers. Walking along the end of the aisles of the nonfiction section yields nothing. Perhaps she's in fiction or gone to the restroom? My heart squeezes when I consider the possibility that she's gone home for the day. Did I miss my opportunity? The thought is a mixture of disappointment and relief. I really do want to find a way to cut through my anxiety and have a normal interaction with her, but given my less than stellar history of our interactions, I know it won't be easy.

The only thing I can think to do is ask the other librarian, who's currently stationed at the circulation desk. She would probably know where Anna is. I'm not thrilled about potentially revealing my interest in Anna to her friend, but if I don't make this interaction happen today, I might not have the courage to try again for another week.

I stroll toward the front, hoping Anna will reveal herself along the way. Thirty seconds later, I'm staring into the smiling face of her friend.

"Hi. Can I help you?"

I glance down at her name tag.

"Hi, Penny. Is Anna still around?"

Her smile widens, making me frown slightly. Why does my question seem to delight her?

"She just ran down to the children's section. She should be back shortly."

Penny turns toward the stairwell that leads down to the basement and I follow suit just in time to see Anna's head pop up, followed by the rest of her. She smiles in my direction, but I quickly realize she's looking at Penny and instruct my heart to calm down.

"Anna," Penny says. "This gentleman wanted to see you."

This time, her smile is aimed at me. "Hi, how can I help?"

My eyes dart from her to Penny. When I'd imagined this scenario, I hadn't pictured an audience. A lump forms in my throat and sweat prickles my forehead. I swallow down the lump, trying to remember what I was going to ask her. Something about books. What's her favorite book? No, that's not it. *Think, man.*

Anna gives me a questioning look and I force myself to spit something out.

"B-book recs."

Oh, Brody. That was terrible.

"Okaaaay. I might be able to help. What kind of books? Bestsellers? Action? Horror?"

She winces at that last word. Does she not like to be scared? Me neither, but right now I'm terrified. Still, I have to muddle through this conversation no matter how awkward it feels or how stilted my words.

"Sci-fi?"

I didn't mean for that to come out as a question, but at least I didn't stutter this time.

"Science fiction?"

I nod, afraid to say anything else. I can feel Penny's eyes on me and I force myself not to look at her, afraid of what her expression might be. Anna's probably also looking at me, but I dare not meet her gaze for fear I'll give up on this inquiry and run away like a frightened dog with my tail between my legs. Figuratively, of course.

If only I were more like Beorn. He's not afraid of talking to women. He knows what he wants and goes after it. Of course, he's also a made up character so he can be as brave and chivalrous and muscled as I want him to be.

Anna motions for me to follow her and leads me back down the stairs, talking over her shoulder. "I don't read a lot of science fiction, but there is one author whose work I enjoy. Are you open to reading young adult novels?"

My heart thumps so hard against my sternum I'm surprised Anna can't hear it. I nod, beginning to feel a little lightheaded. I take a deep breath and try to focus on grounding myself while we descend to the basement. *Five things I can see. Off-white cinderblock walls, Anna's wavy hair, Anna's cream-colored blouse, Anna's fitted blue jeans, Anna's short black boots.* I can't tell if it's helping, but I continue on with four things I can touch. *The cool walls, the nylon material of my backpack, the smooth cotton of my shirt, the skin on the back of my hand. I can hear our steps echoing off the walls, someone flushing a toilet, the ping of the elevator as it reaches the basement.* The only thing I can smell is some light floral scent that seems to come from Anna's hair. I nestle my chin into my chest and smell the cologne I sprayed on my shirt before I left my house this morning. By the time I've finished my grounding practice with the minty taste of my gum and no longer feel like I might pass out, we're inside the children's library and standing in front of the YA section.

Anna runs her fingers along the spines on the far right shelf before pulling out a book. She hands it over to me and I almost laugh when I see the cover of *Into the Unknown*, my debut book.

"This book is amazing. It's about a teenage girl who doesn't know she's part of a powerful dynasty and must save her country from imminent doom."

She must read my astounded expression as skepticism, because she quickly adds. "That may not sound very interesting to you, but I can assure you it's a worthwhile read."

I can't remember when I last read through the book. Maybe it would help me see the best way for the story to proceed. I really should have reread this before I began the sequel. It seems so obvious now that the book's in my hands that this is a good idea. I have a shelf full of copies at home, but she doesn't know that, so I will check out this copy to keep up appearances. The cover is quite worn. I guess people really do like this book.

"Thanks." I try to meet her eyes and smile, but I'm afraid it's more of a sneer.

"Sorry I can't be more help. Winston, the author, has two others that are also good, though they didn't get as much hype as this one."

Her voice is filled with warmth when she says *Winston,* and it does something to my chest. Does she *like* the guy? Her letters have been warm, but she's the friendly type. The thought that there might be something more than friendship between us is obviously appealing, but probably just a fantasy I'm making up in my head because I want her to want more. Of course, she doesn't know the truth, so even if she has an affection for the author, it doesn't mean it'd translate into something real between us. Not unless I can get over my awkwardness and calm my anxiety.

Keeping my eyes trained on the book, I take another deep breath, hoping my next words will sound normal. "T-this is perfect. Thank you, Anna."

Well, not terrible at least. She shifts beside me, but I'm still afraid to look her straight in the face.

"You're welcome. I'm going to head back upstairs, but you can check out down here. Maybe browse through the shelves and see if any other books catch your eye. Look for the stickers with the spaceship on the spine, though that doesn't necessarily mean there are aliens. That book," she points at the one in my hand, "is alien-free."

I chuckle and force myself to meet her gaze. "I-I'll keep that in mind."

She hits me with her devastating smile before heading back upstairs.

I decide it can't hurt to browse other YA sci-fi novels, so I grab a couple more before checking out. I'm relieved I can truthfully tell Gabi I completed her homework. I didn't knock the conversation out of the park, but I made it through several minutes of interaction without running away, which is a step forward. And I managed to navigate myself through a panic attack, which was not easy. There's hope for me yet.

14

Anna

AT BOOK CLUB last week, I shared about the failure that was my date with Benjamin. Susan was mortified he had acted so terribly. Though she'd only met him once before at a work function of Roger's and he'd seemed like a complete gentleman. Of course, people can have work personas that reveal nothing about their true nature. I soothed her the best I could, promising I didn't hold it against her.

After our discussion of *The Night Circus,* it was time for me to choose a new book from the remaining selections. My pick sounded quite interesting.

A music superstar, an adrenaline-chasing gold-medal athlete, a Michelin-starred chef, a renowned detective, and a state senator all walk into a possibly haunted house…and someone dies.

I don't normally go for scary books, but it sounds Agatha

Christie-like and I enjoy a good murder mystery. Having read the first few chapters of *The Guests*, it's a little creepier than I usually like, but I've already been sucked in trying to figure out who's going to die and why. I flipped through the front a bit and am excited the story switches characters each chapter. There's one perspective titled "The Murderer" which I think will be an interesting addition.

Of course, I was wondering if Lori, who picked the book, was going to make me go to a Haunted House or something. Thankfully, her idea went in a different direction. My date with Tyler, her landscaper, is a day at Dollywood. She combined the music superstar and adrenaline junkie parts for a theme park date.

Pigeon Forge is about two hours from Asheville and I was a little worried I wouldn't have anything to talk to Tyler about, but we filled the time without too many awkward pauses. He talked about his landscaping business and how it was a continuation of his high school gig of mowing neighbors' lawns. He went to college and studied business, so he'd be prepared to make a full-time career out of his love of being outdoors.

It turns out we both enjoy hiking in the mountains. Tyler actually hiked part of the Appalachian Trail one summer during college. I always thought that would be a fun adventure, but didn't want to hike it alone as a single woman and couldn't ever find someone to go with me. I know Cheryl Strayed hiked alone, but I can't imagine what I'd do if I came face-to-face with a bear on a trail all by myself.

Tyler asked me about my job as a librarian and indulged me while I gushed about my coworkers, my love of books, and the wonderful programs we offer through the library. He was surprised to learn about our Zoom program that gives patrons free passes for local things like the Nature Center, Arboretum, and Lake Julian paddle boats. I've used passes to visit the Art Museum and the Aquarium down in Hendersonville.

Once inside the park, we take the Dollywood Express train through the park to get the lay of the land, as it's the first visit for both of us. I haven't been to a theme park in ages. Probably because I'm not really an adrenaline junkie. I suppose kayaking can be pretty exciting if you find some fast, choppy water, but I'm not into dropping down waterfalls or doing barrel rolls. I prefer a sit-on-top kayak and miles of nature watching without worrying whether I'm going to get dumped out by some whitewater.

"Which of these rides looks like something you'd like to do?" Tyler says.

I smile at him, appreciating his handsome face with his square Superman-like jaw. Actually, with his black hair and blue eyes, he kind of reminds me of Clark Kent. He's not wearing glasses, but that's just because he's chosen contacts today. I only know that because he told me a crazy story earlier about his glasses falling off and getting obliterated by the lawn mower one summer in high school. After he ran home to get his replacement pair so he could actually see again, he spent hours making sure he got every piece of his destroyed glasses out of the family's lawn, for fear their dog or toddler might find some of it.

I don't know if it's the fact that he was so conscientious of the vulnerable members of that family or that he was willing to share an embarrassing story about himself, but it endeared him to me. Not that I thought it was all that embarrassing. It's nothing like walking around school with your dress half tucked into your underwear. Not that I've told him this story about myself. Definitely not first date material.

"I will ride just about anything you might find at a state fair, but I don't ride roller coasters." I give him an apologetic look.

"Sorry."

He smiles. "No worries. I don't ride them either."

"You don't? I thought all guys liked high octane thrills."

Tyler shrugs. "Not *all* guys."

I grin at him. Yet another thing we have in common. So far, this date is going great. "Sorry for assuming. What types of rides do you like?"

"Anything that doesn't go upside down. That's the part that freaks me out about roller coasters."

"For me it's the enormous drops. I feel like I'd faint in terror if I ever tried to ride one."

"Well, we can't have you fainting on our date," he says, giving me a wink that makes my stomach swoop. "I'd hate to cut our day short."

I feign turning my attention to the map on my phone so I can hide the wide smile blooming on my lips. I'm definitely feeling some chemistry between us. "Let's start in The Village and check out the rides there since that's where we'll be at the end of this train ride."

"Sure." When I look at him, he holds my gaze, a sly look on his face. "Or we could take another lap on the train and see what happens." He wiggles his eyebrows suggestively.

My mouth drops open in surprise. Even though I'm feeling attraction, it's way too early for me to act on it. Though, maybe if today continues to go well, I may drop my "no kissing on first dates" rule. Tyler has very kissable-looking lips. "Uh, maybe later."

He leans back, a smile on his face. He doesn't seem to be as flustered as I feel. Guess he's just confident and not afraid to go after what he wants. That's not a bad thing.

The train returns to the station, and we disembark. Our first stop is the carousel. It'll give me time for my fluttering emotions to settle. I'm concerned Tyler will find it too juvenile, but he happily jumps aboard and straddles a white horse with brown mane and a red bridle, patting the seat of the black-maned horse next to him. Our horses gently pulse up and down, though Tyler pretends he's on a bucking bronco, practically falling off the back and making me laugh, until the attendant yells at him to settle down. That only makes me laugh harder.

After that, we ride The Waltzing Swinger, The Scrambler, Sky Rider, Dizzy Disk, Lemon Twist, and finish with Demolition Derby. I choose a shiny blue car and Tyler picks a green one. He spends the whole time trying to get away from me while I chase him down and bump him with all my might. Even though he claimed to have mechanical failure, I know he stopped sometimes on purpose so I could catch up. Especially since I kept getting hit from the side by other drivers. I suppose everyone's fair game in bumper cars.

When our time is up, I climb out of my car and make my way to Tyler. He's wincing and holding his neck. "Oh no, Tyler. Are you okay?"

"I think I may need to dial all 9s and report whiplash from the beating I just took."

My forehead creases in concern, but at the reference to those annoying injury lawyer commercials, my eyes narrow suspiciously.

He laughs and pulls me into a side hug. "Just kidding, Anna. I'm fine."

I give him a mock scowl before smiling. "I don't know about you, but I am getting a little hungry."

His eyes flash with delight. "My buddy told me one thing we *have* to eat while we're here. Can I see your phone?"

I hand it over and he scrolls around a bit before handing it back.

"Come with me," he says, grabbing my hand and pulling me along. When we reach an old-looking wooden building with a water wheel on the side, he slows down and leads me to a queue that's a dozen people deep outside the door.

"Whoa, what are they serving in there? Steak tartar?"

Tyler wrinkles his nose. "Steak tartar?"

I shrug. "I don't know, just trying to think of something fancy. Would caviar have been a better choice?"

He smiles and nods toward the building. "Does it look like a place that serves fancy food?"

"No, you're right."

"I probably should have asked this sooner, but do you have any food allergies?"

No one has ever asked me that on a date. It's kind of weird, but also surprisingly thoughtful. I shake my head. "Do you?"

"Nope, just wanted to make sure you didn't have celiac disease like my sister because then we'd have to figure something else out."

"I'm good, though I'm sorry about your sister."

He quirks a shoulder. "She's fine. I'm just glad they figured out why she was having so many issues. We were all very worried there for a bit."

The line moves quickly, and when we step inside the building, I'm assaulted with the fragrance of fresh bread and cinnamon. I groan. "Tyler, this smells heavenly."

"I agree."

After we've gotten our Cinnamon Bread with sides of icing and apple butter, we head outside and find a free table. Tyler motions to me. "Ladies first."

"If you insist."

I pull off a piece, hesitating on which cup to dip it into before going for the sugar rush of icing. I push the whole thing into my mouth, closing my eyes to fully experience the flavors.

"Oh my gosh," I say, holding my hand over my mouth to hide the food inside, "this is so good. You have to try it, Tyler."

He tears off a piece, dips it into the icing, and pops it into his mouth. His eyes brighten and he nods vigorously, chewing quickly.

"That's so amazing," he says after swallowing. "I wonder how it is with the apple butter."

I wave my hand, inviting him to try it out while I finish chewing my piece.

"So?" I ask, after he's finished chewing his second piece.

"I don't want to give my opinion until you've tried it."

He doesn't want to color my assessment? He's so thoughtful. I dip my second piece into the apple butter and chew, considering the added cinnamon and apples. I bet the bread by itself would be enough, but the dipping sauces give it that extra oomph.

"Okay," I say. "They're both fantastic. I don't know if I can pick a favorite."

Tyler nods. "I feel the same way. I bet the bread without the toppings would be equally fantastic."

Did he just read my mind? Maybe we're just that in sync today. There's still a small undercurrent of nerves running through me, but that's only because we're getting to know each other and I think there's potential for a second date. So far, he hasn't been turned off by anything I've shared with him. And everything I'm learning about him just makes me want to know more.

We finish the rest of the bread, then walk through the shops at Craftsman Valley before deciding to check out the Birds of Prey show. We see demonstrations with eagles, hawks, falcons, owls, and vultures. The adorable owls are my favorite.

"Don't you think it'd be pretty cool to fly like an eagle?" I ask

Tyler as we leave the show.

"I suppose if I wasn't afraid of heights, it might be cool."

I turn to face him. "You're afraid of heights?"

"Yeah. I fell off a small cliff as a kid and refuse to get on anything taller than a stepladder."

"Don't you have to trim trees as a landscaper?"

"Sometimes, but I have my crew do those parts of the job. Does that bother you?"

I quickly shake my head. "No. I appreciate your honesty. I guess that's another reason not to like roller coasters."

He frowns, his forehead creasing, but somehow he's still very attractive. He looks broody, which I didn't think I'd be into, but it really works on Tyler.

"I hadn't ever thought about that, but I suppose you're right. Hey, what if we rode a roller coaster together? Maybe it'd help us both and it could even be fun. Lots of people seem to enjoy the thrill."

I really like the idea of being next to strong, thoughtful Tyler while experiencing something new and scary. Am I ready to face my fear? At least if I faint, I know Tyler will be able to carry me off the ride in his muscular arms. My heart rate picks up, but I think I want to do it. "Yeah, okay. Which one should we ride?"

Tyler glances around. We're near three different coasters—Wild Eagle, FireChaser Express, and Tennessee Tornado. "Uh, let's do the one that looks most traditional. That eagle one looks too crazy, and the express sounds like it'll be super fast."

That just leaves the tornado, which also sounds a little crazy, but he decided quickly, which is probably for the best. The longer I think about doing this, the more likely I am to lose my nerve. Looking at Tyler's slightly pale face, I think he's feeling the same way. "Tennessee Tornado it is."

The line is surprisingly short and we're at the front in less than five minutes. My heart is hammering in my chest. I cannot believe I'm about to ride my first roller coaster. The brown cars come to a stop in front of us, the shoulder harnesses lift, and the guests depart down the stairs on the opposite side. The white gate in front of us opens and Tyler walks to the left side of our car in the middle of the group. I sit down next to him and glance over, startled at how much paler his face has become. His hands are shaking slightly.

"Tyler, are you okay? We don't have to do this. We can leave now."

He shakes his head and swallows. "No, it's okay."

I don't know him well enough to abort on his behalf, so I pull the harness down until it locks into place. I wiggle left to right, making sure I feel secure in my seat. The attendant comes by and pushes down on the harness, which clicks a little tighter. Now I'm really not going to move. I might not be able to breathe easily either.

"Sir, please lower your harness," she says before moving behind me to the next person.

I look over at Tyler. He's white as a ghost, his forehead beaded with sweat. His hands are gripping his thighs and he's staring straight ahead like he's in a trance.

"Tyler?" I reach over with my left hand and touch his forearm.

He startles and jumps straight up, hitting his head on the shoulder harness. "I'm sorry, I can't do this. I'm sorry. So sorry."

He steps out of the car and bolts down the stairwell without even glancing back. My heart, which was already beating loudly, kicks up even higher. Did he just leave me to ride this thing alone?

What in the world?

I don't have much time to feel the betrayal of his exit because the attendant pushes down the harness to my left and the cars start moving. Oh no. This is happening. My only consolation in this whole thing is that the drops usually come right at the beginning, so I don't have to endure the torture for too long. However, the slow tick, tick, tick of the cars up the incline feels like it takes two years. The anticipation is excruciating.

The first few cars tip over the apex, bringing the rest of us with them. I open my mouth to scream, feeling my heart in my throat, but there isn't a long drop like I expected. It's short and the track curves right quickly, which doesn't bother my stomach at all. However, it turns out to be a decoy, because we then drop almost straight down into a tunnel and I scream my lungs out. We come out of the tunnel straight into a loop, which is exhilarating, and I wonder at the upside-down world. We curve around the track into another loop, which I surprisingly enjoy before returning to the building where the ride started.

The coaster stops and the harness releases. I push mine up and step across the empty seat onto the platform. I feel a little jittery but also incredible. That was nothing like I expected and I kind of want to do it again. I feel like I'm riding a high all the way down the stairs until I come face-to-face with a contrite-looking Tyler.

"Anna, I'm so, so sorry. I panicked. I pictured the huge drop, and while we were waiting, the video showed several loops. I didn't know this coaster went upside down. It was just too much. I'm sorry."

Part of me has compassion for his dilemma, but another part is annoyed he stranded me on my first roller coaster after I'd shared my fear. He didn't even try to help me get out of going alone; he was totally focused on himself. And I get the whole flight-fight-freeze thing, but it doesn't feel good to be the person left behind. "It was too much for you, I get it. But it hurt a little that you left me all alone to do something that was really scary."

He grabs my hands in his, his eyes boring into mine. "I know. I get it. I messed up. Please don't let this one thing ruin what I think has been a great date so far."

His earnestness appeals to my softer side, but I'm still stung. However, I don't want the rest of the evening to be soured. Especially since we still have a long ride back to Asheville.

"Let's go see the Chasing Rainbows Museum. I want to see which of Dolly's outfits they have inside."

Tyler lets out an audible breath, his shoulders relaxing. He lets go of my hands.

"Sure, that sounds good. Then maybe we can catch a music show and get some food."

We spend the rest of the afternoon in the park, enjoying more of the non-roller coaster rides, before Tyler drives us back to Asheville. It's quiet for the first few minutes and I look out the side window while trying to come up with conversation.

"Have you been to Great Smoky Mountains National Park?"

I turn to Tyler, surprised by his question. "Once. I came to see the synchronized fireflies."

"Oh, cool. I haven't seen that. My focus when I come is to hike the trails. I've seen a few bears up there."

"That must have been scary."

He shakes his head. "Not really. I always carry bear spray with me and hang my food in a tree at night."

"Smart." Reminding me we have a mutual enjoyment of the outdoors, I decide to find out if we share my other great love. "What are some of your favorite books?"

"I, uh, don't really read much. That must sound crazy to a librarian like you."

I tilt my head back and forth. "A little. Is there a reason?"

"Staring at pages of words makes me feel like I'm back in school. I barely made it through college, but I focused on my goal and that's what helped me finish my degree. I promised myself I wouldn't have to read another book after I graduated."

My heart drops. Someone who doesn't read at all? Is that a deal-breaker for me? "Have you?"

"Have I what?"

"Read another book since you graduated?"

His lips screw up in thought.

"No, I don't think so. Unless magazines count. I have a subscription to Garden Designs for client ideas."

"Technically, that's reading."

I spend the rest of the car ride trying to figure out what life between a reader and non-reader would be like.

"I had fun today," Tyler says, when we pull up to my apartment.

"I did, too."

"Again, I'm sorry about abandoning you. It was an awful thing to do."

I nod, not sure what to say. It felt like a big deal at the time, though I wasn't in any real danger. Still, I didn't enjoy being abandoned. I suppose he was a good sport for at least trying to overcome his fear. Should I give him another chance? We do have a shared enjoyment of the outdoors and there was some physical chemistry between us. If he calls, I'll probably say yes.

"I forgive you. Thanks for the ride and for introducing me to the amazing cinnamon bread."

"You're welcome. Goodnight, Anna."

He makes sure I'm inside my building before he pulls away. Definitely another mark in the positive column for his show of chivalry. I feel a bit of hope that this Blind Date and a Book scheme may actually result in a love connection.

15

Brody

SURPRISINGLY, I'VE BEEN making progress on my sequel. Anna handing me a copy of my first book turned out to be one of the best things that could have happened. I spent a day reading through it and making notes about potential tangents that could be followed in this new book. I'd forgotten some of the minor plot points, but now think I have a better handle on what might come next. I've scrapped everything I'd previously worked on, which I'm sure Mark won't mind. His comments on the chapters I sent him were less than enthusiastic.

After finishing my reread of *Into the Unknown*, I spent the better part of a day figuring out which characters from the first book should continue in the sequel and what their roles will be. I found a logical way to add time travel to the story and still like the idea of a helper named Rylan, who may or may not turn into a love interest, so those elements will stay. I hadn't originally thought about introducing a romance subplot, but after the fun I've been having with my fantasy story, I decided to go for it. I may be writing a sequel, but I need some fresh elements to make the book engaging to readers, even if I'm keeping some things the same for familiarity and nostalgia.

Having done a bunch of pre-work, I'm back at the library and making good headway on this new version of the sequel. Of course, starting with a zero word count again has anxiety buzzing around in my chest, but I've got my outline and plenty of caffeine in my veins after a stop at Hill of Beans for an espresso before the library opened. I'm an intrepid explorer, diving back into a world I created years ago, but finding it's much more fun now.

I knocked out three thousand words in my two hours. If I can keep this pace up, I will definitely have a first draft finished in a week and a half, maybe less, which would give me a few days to tweak it with Mark before submitting it to the publisher. I'll be cutting it close, but at this point, they'll just be happy to see a novel's worth of coherent words about Ciara's saga.

I dive back into the story after consulting my notes. I've never outlined before, but must admit I'm seeing the benefit of having an idea of where the story is going. It's different from my usual pantsing method, but that only seems to work if I don't have a deadline. It's hard to hear the characters when I'm worried about getting the book finished on time. It's probably why my first book was so well-liked. I worked on it for two years, taking months between writing chapters as I waited for the characters to tell me what happened next. But that process won't work if I'm expected to produce a new book every year or two. Just look at the two disasters that were my follow-ups.

Okay, they weren't actually bad. They just didn't have that same sparkle and magic as *Into the Unknown*. I've received a few fan letters from people who enjoyed them, but nothing like the deluge

I'd received for Ciara's story. It was all the requests for more of her world that had the publishers seeing dollar signs. Obviously, I'd like this new book to do well, but I really want to continue trying new things and see what other stories I enjoy writing.

After another few hours of work, I remove my headphones. The tips of my ears are a little sore from being squished by the foam of the ear pads for so long. I massage them to help the tingly sensation abate. Realizing I've been sedentary for a solid five hours, I decide it's time to move. I save my work, stick everything in my bag, and stand up. I'll be back, but I don't feel comfortable leaving my stuff unattended in a public location. Pushing in my chair, I take long strides to stretch my leg muscles on the way to the restrooms in the building's basement. When I return upstairs, I decide a little fresh air is also called for and exit the library onto Haywood Road.

Delicious smells assault my nose and my stomach rumbles in response. Might as well turn this into a food break. I walk down the street and pull open the door to the Haywood Street Market, buying myself a chicken wrap, which I carry back outside to eat while I walk around the downtown area. My eyes snag on the display window of Page Turner Books. They've got a few new releases right up front whose covers intrigue me. Maybe when I finish my draft, I'll treat myself to a little book therapy. I continue strolling until I reach Pritchard Park, a tiny triangle of trees, boulders, and brick. One side of the park has a row of chess boards and two older men are in the middle of a game. Sometimes on weekends, there's a drum circle and people play and dance while the scent of patchouli and other things float through the air. Right now it's empty. I perch on a boulder and people watch while I finish my sandwich.

Wandering up the other side of Haywood on my way back to

the library, I peek into Little Shop of Sugar. The chocolate inside always looks appealing, but there's no food allowed in the library and I'd hate for it to melt in my bag. Maybe I'll stop by before I go home and get something to reward myself for a productive day. I wonder if Anna likes chocolate. I could ask her in a letter and then leave her some at the circulation desk.

When I return to the library, my shirt is warm to the touch from the sun and I feel ready to do more writing. On my way to my favorite back corner, I notice a young man with curly blond hair occupying the cubicle. I freeze in place, stunned that I've not previously experienced this situation. No one ever sits in my cube. The guy looks up at me with a quizzical look. I turn away quickly, not wanting him to think I'm weird, and take a lap around the library in search of an alternate seating arrangement. There's an empty table between periodicals and nonfiction and I sit down, noting that the chair lacks the comfort of the one I'm used to occupying.

Not wanting to lose the momentum I'd gathered before my break, I put on my headphones, open my laptop, and skim the last few paragraphs of the story. After consulting my outline, I place my fingers on my keyboard and get back to it. I manage another few thousand words before a loud noise breaks into the music playing on my headphones. I remove them from one ear and look around. I hear another thump and quickly stand up, worried. Moving quickly toward the sound, I peer around the end of a bookshelf and see a figure bent down, struggling to pick up three huge volumes from the floor. Making my way to her, I crouch down, grab the books into my arms, and stand back up.

The woman also stands, and I realize it's Penny. She's giving me a confused look.

"It sounded like you were struggling," I say. "Where do you

want these?"

Her brow clears, and she smiles. "Would you mind carrying them to the circulation desk for me?"

"Sure. Anything else I can do?"

"No, but thank you for your help."

I walk across the floor and set them all on the counter, giving Penny a nod and a smile, then return to my table in the middle of the library. Now that I'm not wearing my headphones, I can hear noises all around me. Even with my headphones back on, there's still a low drone of noise. I definitely prefer my quiet corner. Maybe I should see if it's open now. I gather all of my stuff up again, and start toward the far corner, but halt when I hear Anna's voice nearby.

"Things were going really well until we tried to be brave and ride our first roller coaster together."

"Did you throw up?" Penny's voice. "Did *he* throw up? On you?"

Anna laughs. "No, that would have been awful. He didn't have the opportunity to throw up on me because he bailed at the last minute, leaving me to ride all by myself. I was already nervous, but losing my seatmate ratcheted everything up to terrifying."

There's a sharp intake of breath. "Oh, Anna, no! How rude. I can't believe he did that to you."

"He was terrified, which I understand, so I'm not holding it against him. However, he hasn't responded to any of the texts I sent him after our date, so I guess he wasn't feeling it."

My heart lurches. They must be talking about another one of Anna's dates. How could someone abandon sweet Anna like that? He sounds like a snake. One whose neck I'd like to wring. Do snakes even have necks? Maybe they're one long neck? Okay, not the best simile. He's more like a dragon, one who I'd slay with my sword, dodging his fiery breath and ignoring my fear because I'm fighting for my love.

Okay, so I don't have a love, per se, but I feel all my protective instincts well up just thinking about someone hurting Anna. Can't they see how wonderful she is? I certainly can. If only I could get out of my head long enough to have a normal conversation with her. Perhaps then I could ask her out, show her that there is someone who recognizes her awesomeness and wants to provide her with all the joy and goodness she deserves.

My phone chimes in my pocket, and my body tenses. I thought I'd turned it off. Anna's and Penny's faces appear around the corner, with identical stern faces facing my direction. I quickly pull out my phone and flip the button to silence it, mouthing "sorry" in their direction before hurrying back to my favorite corner. Thankfully, it's empty, so I slouch down into the seat, embarrassed to have made noise in the library.

Unlocking my phone, I click on the new text message. It's from my best friend, Levi.

Levi: Hey, man. I'm going to be in AVL in a few weeks for work. Can I crash with you?

I grin. I haven't seen him since his wedding a couple years ago. He and Elizah got married at Red Rocks and it was incredible. Their honeymoon involved a week of hiking and camping at various national parks in the state, which I'm sure wouldn't be the ideal vacation for most women, but Levi and Elizah are perfect for each other. It probably helps that they met whitewater rafting through the Grand Canyon. She was a visitor, there with a group of college friends. Levi and I were boat guides, and I could tell he was falling for her right away.

Brody: Of course. You don't even have to ask.

Levi: Thanks. I'll email you my itinerary. Find something awesome
for us to do.

By awesome, he means adrenaline-filled. It's still a little chilly
for water adventures, but there's always hiking. I haven't taken him
to Looking Glass Rock yet. We could go zip lining at The Gorge.
I've heard good things about it and know he'd love it.

Levi and I met the summer after my freshman year. Both of
us worked at a Jeep tour place in Colorado Springs that visited the
Pikes Peak foothills and Garden of the Gods. We became thick as
thieves, stayed in touch after we returned to our respective colleges,
and spent our remaining summers working together at various
outdoor adventure locations.

After our senior year of college, Levi convinced me to do one
more summer job with him before we embarked on real careers.
He wanted to do something unforgettable and so we signed up to
be whitewater rafting guides through the Grand Canyon. It was the
best summer of my life. He met Elizah at the end of the summer
and followed her back to Boulder.

I had no idea what I wanted to do after graduation. I had a
degree in accounting, though spending my days in a cubicle didn't
sound appealing. Which is kind of ironic, given how I spend a lot
of my days now. But I run my own schedule, which feels different
from having a regular nine-to-five job.

That was the summer I started writing. Staring at the walls of
the Grand Canyon day after day got me thinking about how
strange it would be if it had been man made instead of carved from
glaciers. I wrote a story about people making these crazy machines
to carve a huge depression through the middle of the country, then

diverting water to make the river.

I thought it was funny and shared it with him. He said I should submit it somewhere. I didn't know where to begin, but thought I'd give it a try. I sent a few stories out to various publications. Receiving fifty dollars for my first published story felt like winning the lottery. It was a high that was almost as heady as successfully maneuvering through the class four and five rapids on the Colorado River.

After a few more publications of short stories, I attempted to write a full-length novel. By this time, I was working at an accounting firm, because fifty dollars here or there didn't pay the bills. I wrote in the evenings and on weekends and *Into the Unknown* slowly revealed itself. I submitted it to a competition, and that's how I ended up with my agent. He loved the book, helped me tweak it a bit, and the rest is history.

When *Into the Unknown* took off, it was more than anyone expected from a debut author and I was offered an additional three-book deal, which is where I am now, trying to wrestle this last one into something readable.

I should be working on it right now. Sliding my phone back into my pants pocket, I pull out my laptop and headphones. I stare at my work in progress for a few minutes, but my mind wanders back to my earlier daydream of fighting a dragon for Anna. It seems like something Beorn would do for Aurelia. My fingers itch to turn my thoughts into a scene in that story, but my conscience tells me I really need to work on the sequel.

Maybe if I get this one scene down, I'll be able to refocus on the sci-fi book. It's good to take breaks and refresh, right? It's a weak excuse to work on the fun project, but it's enough for me to open the other document and start typing.

I'm startled when my phone buzzes against my thigh. It

continues buzzing, letting me know it's not a text message. Who would be calling me? *My agent*, I think with a groan. I pull it out, relieved when it's only my alarm, letting me know the library's closing soon. Looking at my laptop screen, I'm embarrassed to realize I spent the rest of the afternoon working on my fantasy idea. Well, I got a decent start on the sequel. I'll work on it a little more after I get home. *And*, I promise myself, *I won't open Beorn's story again until I have a finished draft of the YA sci-fi*. Yeah, right.

16

Anna

TONIGHT'S DATE IS courtesy of Abbie. Her book selection, *Swing Time*, means I'll be having dinner and going to a shag club with one of the assistant basketball coaches at UNC Asheville. Abbie is the athletic trainer for the team, which is how she knows Howard.

With a name belonging to an eighty-year-old, I'm prepared for a retiree with a receding hairline, so I'm startled when I exit my apartment building and see a baby-faced guy with a thick head of blond hair.

"Howard?"

He gives a self-deprecating grin. "I know. What were my parents thinking? I go by Howie, actually, but Abbie prefers to use my full name because she enjoys getting under my skin."

I smile, charmed. "Of course she does. Nice to meet you, Howie. I'm Anna."

When I stick out my hand, he bypasses it for a bear hug. I

stiffen, belatedly double tapping his back with one hand, as the other arm is pinned to my side. Thankfully, he quickly releases me and takes a step back.

"I was excited when Abbie asked me to go on a date with you. I think it's awesome you're a librarian. You get first dibs on all the new releases."

"Do you enjoy reading?"

He nods, turning to open the passenger door and ushering me into his car. "I always carry a book with me, just in case I have some free time."

Settling into the seat, I smile up at him. "Me too."

Our commute to Table, the restaurant Abbie picked for us, takes about five minutes, enough time to suss out Howie's reading preferences. He enjoys nonfiction, specifically basketball-themed, as well as literary fiction and murder mysteries. I like a well-rounded reader.

"How long have you been an assistant coach at UNCA?" I ask, after we're seated.

"This is my second year. It was my first job after graduation."

Oh, my gosh. This kid is at least a decade younger than me. I suddenly feel ancient. There's no way this guy is even remotely looking for a serious relationship. Though, if Abbie picked him, I could be wrong. She knows I'm looking for love, so I might as well be honest with him.

"What do you think of my whole Blind Date and a Book adventure? Does it seem pathetic I'm using friends to find a serious relationship?"

He shakes his head. "It's not pathetic. I think it's great you know what you're looking for and are willing to go after it. I tired of the games women played in college. It's fine that some people want to have fun, but I'm not a serial dater. I want to find my one person and settle down."

I'm shocked, but also pleasantly surprised.

"And our age difference doesn't bother you? You're what, like twenty-four?"

He smiles good-naturedly. "Actually, I'm twenty-eight. I spent four years in the military before attending college. I wasn't sure what I wanted to do with my life and thought some extra time might help me out."

"Oh, you certainly look much younger."

"I get that a lot." He winks at me and I can't help but smile at how casually he's handling my pointed questions.

"I'm sorry for being so blunt, but like you said, I'm not here to mess around."

"Totally cool. Ask me whatever you like. Should we look at the menu and order?"

I nod, picking up the piece of paper on the table in front of me. There are a variety of options, each of which has at least one ingredient I'm not familiar with. I pull out my phone and use it to look up the things I don't know.

"What do you think you're going to get?" Howie asks.

"I think I'll try the swordfish with cauliflower and avocado. You?"

He wrinkles his nose. "This all sounds a bit fancy for me. I'm going to stick with the burger and fries."

Another nonadventurous eater. You'd think living in Asheville would change that, but I guess people like what they like.

The server appears and takes our orders. Howie asks for the bread appetizer as well.

"My buddy came here and said Heidi's Bread is a must-try. Though, for that price, it better be amazing."

I frown. Nine dollars for some bread does sound like a lot,

but I thought Abbie was paying for our fun tonight. Even though Howie's older than I assumed, he's still fairly fresh out of college, so maybe he still has that scrimp and save mindset of most students.

"I guess we'll see."

Howie tells me about the guys on this year's basketball team and what he thinks their chances are of winning the conference. I share about upcoming programs for the library. Other than books, we struggle to find common ground, though we both bond over how out of this world the bread is. The first bite is so buttery and delicious, I groan when it hits my tongue. Thankfully, Howie has the same reaction, so I don't feel self-conscious about it.

The rest of the food is good, though our conversation stalls. Luckily, the second half of our date won't require much talking, though I suppose we will communicate with our bodies.

We arrive at the shag club a few minutes before the lesson starts. Howie goes to the bar and brings back two bottles of water.

"It's important to stay hydrated whatever exercise you're doing."

"Thanks," I say, taking one. His serious concern softens my heart a little.

There are a dozen other couples milling around. I don't recognize anyone else here. Most of them look like college students or recent graduates, but there's also a middle-aged couple. I'd hate to be the oldest person here. I feel better knowing the age gap between me and Howie isn't as large as I'd assumed, but it's still close to a decade. A lot happens to a person in one's twenties. I didn't really start feeling like I knew who I was until the last few years. It gives me pause about a potential future with him. Who knows the type of person he might become over the next decade?

The instructors, a man and a woman, take the center of the

dance floor and split us up, women on one side and men on the other. Howie looks at me and shrugs before moving to his side of the floor. I line up across from him. We spend almost an hour learning the steps of shagging on our own, then we're invited to get together with our partner and try them out as a couple.

Howie and I work the steps and get into a pleasant rhythm. Then Howie starts improvising and I realize how well he leads. I follow his movements and soon we're spinning and doing all kinds of crazy convoluted moves. When the song ends, the instructor tells us the real dancing will begin in fifteen minutes.

I'm grateful for the break because I'm sweating and still amazed at Howie's skills. He takes my hand and leads me to the table where our waters are resting. I slump down in my chair and take a long swig of water. "Whew, that was fun. You are an excellent dancer."

He shrugs, drinking from his own water bottle. "My parents made me take lessons as a teenager. Guess I haven't forgotten how."

I set my elbows on the small round table between us and lean in. "I bet you were a very popular prom date."

He leans forward, grinning. "You know it. My dance card was full the whole night."

"I'd probably have signed my name on it a time or two."

"I would let you have every dance if you wanted."

There's a beat of silence as his words sink in. Then he's leaning forward across the table and I realize he's about to kiss me. I jerk back, feeling my face flush.

He blinks, stunned, then straightens, running a hand through his hair and looking everywhere but at me.

I feel bad for causing him discomfort. "I'm sorry, Howie. I know we had some flirty banter going on there, but I'm not comfortable kissing in public." Maybe a first kiss across a table in the middle of a dance hall might be romantic for some, but it's not my ideal situation.

"Hey, no problem. That's cool." He's still avoiding my gaze. "You want another water?"

I look at the half-full water in my hand. "No, I'm good, thanks."

He stands. "I'm going to grab another one for myself, then."

"Okay."

While he's gone, I look at the other couples nearby. They're in various states of cuddling. The couple closest to my table is sitting shoulder to shoulder, looking at something on the woman's phone. At another table, a man and woman have their arms around each other and are actually kissing. A few others are holding hands or snuggled up together. Am I wrong to want to avoid PDA? Just because it's all these people's thing, doesn't mean it has to be mine. I believe physical intimacy comes from having an emotional connection with someone and I don't yet feel a strong connection with Howie. We could definitely get there, though.

The music starts up, and many of the couples make their way to the floor. Other people have shown up during the break and the floor is mostly full. I don't see Howie at the bar. Maybe he had to visit the restroom after all that water.

When he still hasn't returned after another fifteen minutes, I grow concerned. I ask someone coming out of the men's room if there's a guy in there with a red checkered shirt, but he looks at me weirdly and shakes his head. I can't see him anywhere. Did he go outside to cool down?

Out front, there are a few people smoking, but no Howie. I head toward his car before realizing his black sedan is conspicuously absent. Surely, he didn't leave without telling me. He seems too considerate to strand me without transportation. I walk through the rows of cars just to make sure I didn't misremember where we parked, but reality soon settles on me. Did I embarrass him so much that he couldn't face me anymore? Guess he wasn't as mature as I thought. Sighing, I pull out my phone and schedule a ride share. I rub my arms, noticing the drop in temperature since we went inside almost two hours ago. I hope my car gets here quickly.

17

Brody

THE WOMAN SLIDES into the back seat of my vehicle, shutting the door and rubbing her arms. I crank the heat, hoping she'll warm up quickly. A glance in my rear-view mirror sets my heartbeat soaring. *Anna's in my car!* I knew the destination address looked familiar, but assumed it was because it's near where I live. It's just now clicked that it's the address I put on every one of my pen pal letters.

I quickly look away, tugging my baseball cap farther down over my forehead. *Just be cool, man. You've been practicing with Gabi.* Except not one single made-up scenario involved picking her up in my car. I bet she was on a date. Another peek in the mirror tells me she doesn't look happy. It could just be from the cool temperature, but it's only her leaving this dance club, so that's not a promising sign for how it went. A promising sign for me, yes.

Okay, Brody. Just pretend she's like any other passenger. She probably won't even recognize you. She definitely would not expect you to be her ride share driver. That last thought helps calm me. I sometimes find it hard to believe I voluntarily pick people up in my car and take them to wherever they need to go. I don't do it for the money, though. I drive for the conversations I hear and the body language descriptions that come from watching different people in my mirror. Not in a creepy way. It's book research for me. Maybe if I pretend she's just another passenger I'm observing, all will be well. Okay, what would I normally do when I pick someone up?

"Hello. I'm Brody, your driver. Do you prefer music, conversation, or silence?"

Her eyes catch mine in the mirror, and I quickly dart my eyes to the road.

"You like the Royals?"

Her question surprises me. I nod, then pull out of the parking lot and begin following my GPS direction.

"I hate to tell you this, but I pull for the Cards."

My eyes automatically return to the mirror and find her grinning.

"Those are fighting words," I say, unable to stop myself from smiling.

She chuckles. "It's not my fault you pull for the wrong Missouri team."

My smile grows. She seems to have chosen the conversation option, so I'll do my best to oblige.

"Nice car," she says. "I have a Subaru, too."

"I know," I say under my breath.

"What?"

"That's cool." I search for a new subject. "So, you like to shag?"

There's a long silence, which gives me time to hear what I just said.

"I mean… No, not… Dance! Shag *dance*. I wasn't asking…" I shut my mouth, realizing I'm only digging a deeper hole for myself.

A laugh from the back seat eases the tension in my shoulders. "I know what you meant, Brody, but thanks for the laugh. I needed it."

I stay quiet, unsure how to respond. Thankfully, she continues.

"This was my first time trying shag dancing," she says. "It was fun, but the date didn't end well. Hence the ride share."

"I'm sorry to hear that." Am I really though? Obviously, I want Anna to be happy, but I also don't exactly relish the thought of her falling for another guy. The fact that she can joke about it lets me know she's not too bruised by whatever happened this evening.

"Eh, it's fine. He wasn't right for me and it's better to know that before we get too far down the road."

It's silent in the car for a bit and I search for safer ground. I decide to comment on her earlier statement. "How did you end up a Cards fan?"

"I grew up near Saint Louis."

She's from Missouri? What a cool coincidence. "I'm from Kansas City."

I see her straighten in the back seat through the mirror. "Really? Small world. How did you end up in Asheville?"

"Work brought me here."

Now is the perfect time to go into specifics, but I'm afraid if I reveal myself I'll turn into a stuttering fool again. I don't want to mess up this fairly normal conversation with my awkwardness.

"Same," she says. "Did you ever visit the Gateway Arch?"

I shake my head. "No. My family preferred the western part of the country. We went to the Omaha Zoo and out to Mount

Rushmore and Yellowstone. What about you? Ever get some KC barbecue or visit the giant shuttlecocks?"

"The giant…whats?"

I wince. Wow, where is my head tonight? Certainly not on thinking before I speak. "Badminton birdies might be the more familiar name. It's an interesting art installation."

I study her face, noting the hint of amusement that tips the corners of her lips up slightly. "Ah. No, we vacationed in Chicago and Michigan."

We're both quiet after that until Anna speaks again. "I just can't believe my ride share driver is a Missourian like me. Poor choice in sports teams aside, that's pretty cool."

"Hey! Who won the World Series most recently?"

She quirks a challenging eyebrow at me. "Who has the most World Series wins?"

Anna's got me there, but I have to say something so she doesn't think she's won. "Well, neither of us, because we don't play baseball."

She smiles. "True. You're lucky we haven't played each other yet this season, or I'd really get into it with you."

"I appreciate your passion. What else are you passionate about?"

She leans forward, her eyes sparkling. "Books."

I grin. "Me too. Favorite author?"

She scowls. "You can't ask me that. How am I supposed to pick? Do *you* have a favorite author?"

"Ken Follett."

"Oh. Well, then, if I *have* to choose…I'd say it's a tie between Jane Austen and Agatha Christie."

I take a right, realizing we're close to her place and torn between wanting to keep her talking and anxious to drop her off so

I can go home and rehash this night in my mind.

"Solid choices. Do you prefer to read authors who are already dead or are you into contemporary stuff as well?"

"I enjoy plenty of contemporary authors. Richard Osman, Fredrik Backman, Katherine Center, Elle Cosimano, Christina Lauren, Abbi Waxman—"

"Okay, thanks," I interrupt, chuckling. She sounded like she was just getting started.

Anna laughs. "It's probably good you stopped me. I could talk about books forever."

I pull up to the curb. "As nice as that sounds, I must regretfully inform you we have arrived at your destination."

She looks out the window. "Oh, I wasn't even paying attention. Thanks for the ride, Brody. You're getting five stars."

"Thanks. Have a safe rest of your evening."

"I'll do my best."

She gets out of the car and I wait until she's inside the building before I pull away to head home. Well, that went way better than I could have imagined. Maybe that's why the pen pal thing doesn't cause me any discomfort. When I pretend to be someone else, there's no pressure. Of course, that's no way to have a genuine relationship. Eventually, I'm going to have to let her know who I am and that I like her. However, this feels like a step in the right direction. Maybe if I keep practicing with Gabi, I'll eventually be comfortable around Anna. Practice makes perfect, right?

18

Anna

I'VE GOT A song stuck in my head. It was playing on the radio during my car ride home on Saturday. I don't know the title, but the chorus was catchy enough I've found myself humming it several times this morning: while I was brushing my hair, on the car ride into work, even while standing in line at Hill of Beans for my coffee and muffin. Something about seeing with new eyes what was always in front of me. I can't place the voice and I'm usually pretty good at recognizing a singer's voice, so it must be a new artist. Maybe I'll ask Penny when she comes in.

I'm the first one at the library, despite my pit stop for caffeine, so I take the cart out to the book depository and load up the volumes that were returned while the library was closed over the weekend. Back inside the library, I scan them all in, rifling through the pages to make sure there isn't any obvious damage to them or forgotten treasures.

I've found many unique things among the pages of returned

books. Birthday cards, grocery receipts, to-do lists, pressed flowers, a train ticket, pictures, even an apology note. Once I found a squished taco which required a book replacement. When I called the person who'd last checked it out, they said they didn't know how a taco ended up in the book since they didn't care for Mexican food, but still sent the money for us to purchase a new copy.

Today's books have nothing interesting. Just a couple of scraps of paper for bookmarks. A few books have holds at other libraries, so I set them aside to put them in the proper bins that will be sent out later in the week. Some are children's books that belong on the lower level, so they go on their own special cart. The rest I stick onto another book cart to be reshelved.

When everything is checked in and I've performed the rest of my pre-opening tasks, I wheel a cart onto the floor toward the fiction section. I straighten the shelves as I add the returned books, enjoying the quiet of the library. Taking a deep breath, I smile at the familiar library smell—a mix of paper and dust. There's also a faint odor of fried chicken. Someone devoured a bucket of KFC in the fiction stacks a week ago, the only evidence the red and white tub of bones pressed into the shelves next to Liane Moriarty's books. I'm surprised they snuck it in with no one noticing. I suppose that's what backpacks are for.

"What song are you humming?"

I jump, clasping a hand to my now racing heart. "Penny, you scared me. When did you get here?"

She grins. "Just a minute ago. Sorry to startle you."

I smile back. "It's my fault. I was lost in my own world."

"Yeah, I noticed. What were you humming?"

I shrug. "I heard it on the radio the other night, but don't know what it's called. The chorus is something like, 'my future was always right in front of me, but I didn't see you until that night.'

Do you know who sings that?"

Penny shakes her head. "That doesn't sound familiar. It must be new. I bet we could look it up. Anyway, just wanted to say 'hey.' I'm going to unlock the doors and then start on the interlibrary loans, so I'll staff the circulation desk until you're finished with shelving."

"Okay, thanks." I motion to the cart, which is half empty. "I shouldn't be too much longer and then I'll switch with you so you can pull books."

She nods, then heads back out of the stacks toward the front. I return my focus to the task at hand. Patrons file in and I say hi to all who pass by me on their way to whichever part of the library they prefer. When I finish the nonfiction reshelving, I notice the professor is in his favorite cubicle, typing away. I wonder if he's researching something or working on a paper or book. Whatever he's doing, he's quite focused.

When I reach Penny at the desk, I tilt my head toward the cubicle in the back. "What do you think he teaches? It looks like he's working on a paper or something academic."

Penny studies the man for a minute. "He gives me Indiana Jones vibes. Nerdy, but in good physical shape and kinda hot. So archaeology, maybe?"

I shake my head. "He doesn't have that two-day stubble Harrison Ford sported. Wouldn't he be gone a lot on research trips or digs or something? Or is that just in the movies and real archaeologists do their research on computers? "

She shrugs a shoulder. "No idea. What's your guess?"

I narrow my eyes to see him better. From this distance, it's hard to really see much detail. "He's fairly clean cut and looks like he's always going to meetings in his khakis and checkered dress shirts. Maybe something with finance or accounting? Perhaps he's in here doing people's taxes or financial reports. Or writing articles about the country's fiscal irresponsibility."

Penny grins. "Why don't you ask him? Whoever is closest to the truth wins a coffee."

I eye her skeptically. "Um, no. I try not to bother patrons and he seems to enjoy keeping to himself."

"Fine. New topic. What's got you humming and smiling this morning? Did your date go that well on Saturday?"

I roll my eyes and release a forceful breath through my nose. "Nope, quite the opposite. The dude tried to kiss me and then stranded me at the shag club."

"What?" Penny's eyes light with fire and I chuckle at her protectiveness. I hold up a hand to stop her from the rant building on her tongue.

"It's fine. He was almost a decade younger than me, so we really didn't have a future."

"Then what's with your buoyant mood?"

I try to suppress a grin, but finally give up. "I kind of hit it off with my ride share driver Saturday night."

Penny's eyes widen in surprise. "You what?"

"The guy who picked me up at the club was really nice. I commented on his Royals hat and found out we're both from Missouri. And we both like books, which is apparently harder to have in common than I expected. I don't think we like the same genres, but at least he reads. And he made me laugh after my terrible date, which also isn't nothing."

She perks up. "Ooh, he sounds better than all of your dates so far. Did you exchange numbers?"

"No. He was completely professional."

"Did you mark him as a favorite driver?"

My brow furrows in confusion. "Did I what?"

Penny sighs, like I'm a lost cause. "If you rate a driver with five stars, you can star them as a favorite and request them for future rides."

"Huh. Didn't know that. I did give him five stars."

"Was he cute, too?"

I shrug. "He was wearing a hat, and I sat in the back, so I didn't get a good look at his face."

"Not helpful. I need more details, Anna!"

I laugh at my friend's frustrated face. "He was just my driver."

"Yeah, but it sounds like you had a connection. You should explore that if you can."

"Maybe. Oh! I also got a letter from Winston yesterday."

Penny groans. "Not this again."

"What do you mean *again*?"

She holds up a hand, ticking off fingers as she talks. "First, you don't know anything about him. Second, you have no idea what he looks like or how old he is. Third, you don't even really know if it's a man."

I open my mouth to make a retort, but she silences me with her hand. I cross my arms across my chest and slump back against the desk, knowing Penny's on her high horse and I have to wait until she runs out of steam.

"Fourth, even if he *or she* is honest about who they are, you'll probably never actually meet them. You like the mystery of Winston too much to ask to meet in person. It's the romantic in you. You can keep the illusion of this smart, mysterious, handsome writer alive as long as you never come face to face with reality, which is that he might be a lonely old lady."

When she drops her hand, I take that as a sign she's finished.

"I highly doubt my pen pal is who you're suggesting, but I obviously have no actual proof other than Winston's words. Still, I have to tell you what he wrote in his letter."

"What he *or* she said, you mean?"

"Whatever. Let me read it to you. I'll never get it exactly right."

I bend down and open the desk drawer containing my purse and pull out the sky blue envelope. I push it toward Penny's face.

"What does this smell like to you?"

Penny gives me a weird look, but then closes her eyes and inhales.

"Ooh, that smells nice. Outdoorsy, like cedarwood or something."

I nod. "That's exactly what I think. The last couple of letters have smelled like this. One reason to think he's a man. Do you think he's putting cologne on them? On purpose?"

She shrugs a shoulder. "I don't know the person, so I suppose that's plausible. Or maybe they spilled room deodorizer on the stationery."

I frown, realizing it's not out of the realm of possibilities. Still, I prefer my theory. I know I'm romanticizing my correspondence with Winston and probably reading more into his words and stationery than is probably there, but it makes me feel like I'm living in my own Jane Austen novel and, frankly, I could use some romance in my life even if it's imaginary. I'm certainly not getting it from going out on dates with real-life men.

"Anyway, listen to this." I pull the paper from inside the envelope and open it up.

April 12

Dear Anna,

I'm sorry for the long delay in writing, but I hope you'll forgive me when you find out why. I'm happy to report I've found some inspiration at last for the newest novel, and have nearly finished it. Will it be as well received as its predecessor? That's a hard bar to hit, but hopefully the fans will be satisfied. You've helped me a great deal, more than you could possibly know.

I have a confession to make. I've also been working on a secret writing project. It's not science fiction, but a new genre entirely. I don't know if it will turn into something publishable, but it's been fun and was inspired by you. I think you've become my muse.

I pause my reading to look up at Penny, whose eyes are wide just like mine were the first time I read that last line. I grin, then continue reading because even though that set my heart aflutter, it isn't my favorite part of the letter. I flip over to the back.

I've been thinking about you a great deal and a question popped into my head the other day. Do you like chocolate? If so, what kind? Do you have one absolute favorite chocolate brand? I walked past Little Shop of Sugar recently and thought about getting you something, but wasn't sure what you might enjoy. Which made me wonder if chocolate is even something you eat. I must admit I have a bit of a sweet tooth, so it baffles my mind that there are people out there who can pass up brownies and cookies and truffles (though I've heard of people who are allergic to chocolate which just makes me feel bad for them). Since I've asked this question, I will answer it myself. I love good milk chocolate that's creamy and melts on the tongue. I really like the Parisian and Peanut Butter Explosion truffles from Little Shop of Sugar. The milk chocolate ganache is so good!

I'm almost out of space, so I must stop, but just wanted to tell you that these letters back and forth have meant so much to me. Each envelope I receive with your name on it is like a warm hug, reminding me that there are good people in the world and that one of those people is my friend. I cherish our relationship. I cherish you, Anna.

Sincerely, Winston

P.S.-Yes, I'm a Simpsons fan. My favorite episode is "The Devil and

Homer Simpson" when he sells his soul for a donut. The Treehouses are so funny!

When I finish reading, I take a beat, enjoying the warm sensations swirling around in my chest. Winston cherishes me! He thinks about me a lot.

"Wow," Penny says, bringing me out of my thoughts. "Winston."

"I know, right?"

I look up at my best friend and am surprised to see a concerned look on her face. "What?"

"It's just…" She twists her lips to the side, indecision written in the creases of her brow. "I don't want to see you get hurt, Anna. This person sounds sweet, but what if they're not who they appear to be?"

I sigh. I know she's trying to protect me, but I feel like I am really getting to know Winston through our letters, and I highly doubt he's pretending. "I appreciate your concern, but I think his words are true. And did you see he mentioned my favorite chocolate shop? More proof that he's local."

"I suppose. It still seems a little weird to me."

I wave away her concern. "I think it's sweet, like an old-fashioned romance. Though, until recently, it's been more friendly than romantic. But this last letter…"

Penny nods. "Yeah, their feelings toward you seem more than friendly. I mean, cherish? That's an emotions-driven word."

"I think so, too."

"Well, I don't want to be a Debbie Downer, so I'll just say I hope Winston's intentions are true."

I give her a hug. "I appreciate your concern. I promise I'll balance my joy with pragmatism and not allow myself to get too swept away."

She hugs me back. "Believe me when I say that I hope you are properly swept away sometime soon."

I squeeze her once more before letting go. "Thanks, friend."

After I return the letter to its envelope and inhale the cedarwood scent one more time, I put it away in my purse and return to work, Winston's words circling through my head, making my heart float with happiness. I so hope he isn't too good to be true.

April 17

Dear Winston,

I'm so glad to learn we have a shared enjoyment of Homer's antics. I must admit, sometimes I feel juvenile for laughing at the jokes, but we all need outlets where we can let go and experience joy, right? You obviously understand that. I watched Treehouse of Horror IV after receiving your last letter and laughed out loud at Homer exasperating the devil's minion with his voracious appetite.

I'm happy you've exited your writing slump and are almost finished with your novel. I'm sure your true fans will enjoy the book. I look forward to reading it. I can't believe you're working on TWO projects at once! I don't know how you keep it all straight in your brain. I'd get them all confused and it would turn into a mess. What I'm trying to say is I'm impressed and awed by your abilities.

Do I like chocolate? No. I LOVE IT!!! I have tried just about everything at Little Shop of Sugar (mainly because the owner is a member of my book club and brings dessert every month for us to enjoy) and it's all fabulous. My favorites are the white chocolate truffles like the Taj Mahal and Lemon Haze, but I won't turn down any I'm offered.

I've been meaning to ask you where you got your stationery. I love that it has your initials embossed on the top. The blue color is pretty too. Is blue your favorite color? My favorite color is purple. Lavender especially, but all hues are great. Related, I'm curious about your pen name. I know it's not your real name because there's no information online about you other than your books. You don't even have a social media account! I'm not asking you to tell me your real name, but does M.B. stand for something or are they two random letters you thought sounded good together? Did you even choose your pen name? Maybe your publisher chose it for you. I just now had that thought.

I look forward to hearing from you again.

Sincerely, Anna

19

Brody

AFTER AN HOUR of hiking up Looking Glass Rock, Levi and I finally crest the top and start the short descent down to the vantage point. When I exit the copse of trees onto the bald granite overlook, I stop to take in the view. Levi stops next to me and I hear a sharp intake of breath. Smiling, I look over at his awed face. Turning back, I take in the valley before us and the mountains sprawling away from us in all directions. It's a gorgeous, cloudless day with a brilliant blue sky.

After a few deep breaths of fresh mountain air, I walk forward to the knob of rock on the otherwise smooth surface and have a seat. I feel Levi settle in beside me.

"Wow, Brody. This view is incredible."

"Yeah, I know. Makes the long, uphill climb worth it, huh?"

"Sure does. And it was pretty cool to see those white squirrels, too."

I grin. "Did you know the original white squirrels escaped

from a traveling carnival?"

He shakes his head.

"In the mid-nineteen hundreds, a Brevard resident gave them to his niece, who wanted to breed them. She was unsuccessful, but when one of the squirrels escaped, the other was released and they successfully added to the squirrel population without human interference."

He chuckles. "That's crazy. Have you seen them before?"

I nod. "There are white squirrels near my house."

"Whoa. Your house is like twenty miles from here. How in the world?"

"I don't know. Nature finds a way, I guess."

Levi rolls his eyes. "Okay, Doctor Malcolm."

"What? *Jurassic Park* is a classic movie."

"I agree. Just messing with you."

We quiet, both turning our attention to the rolling hills of trees, which is all we can see from our perch on the side of the mountain. The sun warms my face and I turn it up, closing my eyes.

Laughter breaks the peaceful atmosphere, and I turn. A group of high schoolers emerges from the end of the trail and spread out across the rock like a swarm of ants. Our solitude is over, but we continue to sit and enjoy our remarkable view of nature until all the chatter becomes impossible to ignore. I turn to Levi, who's looking back at me with raised eyebrows. I nod and we stand up in perfect synchronization. We hike up over the peak of the mountain, then begin our long descent to the bottom.

"Hey, Levi," I say when we're about halfway down, "how did you know Elizah was the person for you?"

When I glance over, he's grinning at me, his eyes sparkling. "I think I kind of knew she was someone special shortly after our rafting trip started. There was just something about her that kept drawing me. It's like she was true north and my heart was a compass that kept pointing to her."

My eyes widen as the information slots into place. "That's where your compass tattoo came from."

He smiles at me, patting his chest. "Yeah, I got it right after she accepted my proposal. But, really, I think I knew for sure we were meant to be when she surprised me with skydiving passes for my thirtieth birthday. Anyone who'd jump out of a plane with me is someone I can count on no matter what happens."

I nod. Of course, it'd be Elizah's mutual love of adrenaline highs that would seal the deal. Though, I suppose it's beneficial to have some things in common. And having similar ideas on how to spend leisure time is probably important. I think it'd be challenging to have a satisfying relationship if one person wanted to travel the world while the other preferred to live and die in the town they grew up in and stay home playing video games every weekend. Though, I suppose people have probably made that work as well. Who am I to judge others' relationships? Especially when I don't have one of my own.

"Where'd that question come from?" Levi raises an eyebrow. "Are you seeing someone?"

"No."

"But…?"

My lips curl up in one corner and I shake my head. Levi knows me so well. "There's someone I'm interested in, but whenever I've tried to talk to her, I'm either mute or stuttering two-word answers."

"Oh, man. I'm sorry. Have you thought about seeing someone again to help you work through this new situation?"

"I'm seeing my therapist weekly and we've been role-playing.

She's given me homework, and it seems like it's helping." My shoulders straighten at a memory. "The woman was actually a ride share client recently, and we had a normal conversation while I drove her home."

Levi smacks my shoulder. "See there? That sounds like progress."

I tilt my head back and forth. "Yeah, but we didn't make eye contact except in the mirror. Plus, I don't think she knew who I was, so there wasn't that pressure."

"Still." He's quiet for a minute and, when I glance over, I can tell he's mulling something over. I wait, knowing he'll fill me in when he's solidified his thoughts.

"What if…" he says slowly, "it's an environment thing. You're most relaxed outdoors, right?"

"Yes."

"Ask her to do an outdoor activity, like a hike or something. Maybe being in nature will help keep you out of your head."

I let his words settle into my brain and my gut. There's logic in what he's saying, but there's still an obstacle to address. "That might work, but I still have to be face-to-face with her when I ask her to do something. And there's the real chance I'll be so awkward she'll decline. Even if I'm not awkward, she still might not be interested."

Levi shakes his head. "No way, man. Girls think you're hot. I see heads turn your direction when we're out together. She's gotta at least be intrigued enough to give you one date."

My forehead wrinkles. "Are you sure they're not looking at you? I remember all your summer girlfriends in college."

He grins, knowing I've got him there. "Yeah, but now I'm an old married man."

I scoff. "We're the same age. Does that just make me an old

man?"

Laughing, he shakes his head. "You really know how to twist my words. Guess that's why you're the writer, huh, name twin?"

Shaking my head, I try to smother my smile. "Not this again. We are not name twins."

"Of course we are. Mine is the Hebrew version, and yours is the Christian one. Milk and leche are the same thing, just different languages, right?"

"Whatever you say, man."

Levi grabs my shoulder. "Hey! What if you wrote her a letter? Ask her out in writing. Then you don't have to worry about stuttering or anything like that."

I chuckle. "It's funny you say that, because we're actually pen pals." I hold up a hand when he opens his mouth. "However, I've been using my pen name, so she doesn't know it's me."

"Why would you do that?"

"I used my fancy stationery and figured, since those were the initials at the top, might as well go along with it. When I wrote the first note, I didn't know it'd turn into anything significant. I mean, sure, I had a crush on her, but I didn't really know her. Now I do, and everything I've learned about her has only made me more infatuated."

Levi twists his lips to the side in thought.

"That's tough. Sounds like you've gotten yourself into a bit of a pickle. I'm not really sure what to say other than you have to decide if you like her enough to risk feeling anxious and appearing awkward. If not, leave her be. But if your feelings are deeper than infatuation, which I suspect they are since you're talking to me about her, then you know what you have to do."

I sigh. He's so good at getting right to the heart of things. Which is really where I am—trying to decide if I'm ready to risk my heart for someone I feel drawn to.

April 24

Dear Anna,

Your enthusiasm for chocolate made me smile. I think it's great you find joy in so many things. It's cool you're friends with the Little Shop of Sugar owner. Are there any other interesting people in your book club I might have seen around town?

I must admit it feels good to have moved past my writer's block. It was like nothing I'd experienced before. The words just seemed to flow with my other books. I guess it was all the pressure I'm feeling to write a book people will love. It also feels like my last chance with my publisher. I'd hate for my writing career to be over so soon.

My stationery was a gift from a family member after I published Into the Unknown. *I use it for all of my author correspondence. Though, I don't have any other stationery, which is why I'm continuing to use it with you. Perhaps I should buy something new to distinguish work letters from personal ones.*

I use a pen name to protect my real identity, obviously. I suffered a major trauma in childhood and didn't want to risk it coming up in interviews when people Googled my real name. The surname Winston comes from a small town in Oregon. My parents took me there one summer when I was a child. We visited the Wildlife Safari and spent a week hiking and camping in Umpqua National Forest. We had the best time. Less than a year later, my parents passed away suddenly. My pen name reminds me of the wonderful times I had with them and makes me think they might be proud of me if they were still alive.

I've never told anyone about my pen name, but I feel like I can trust you with things close to my heart. Thanks for being a good friend.

Sincerely, Winston

20

Anna

April 24

Dear Winston,

Thank you for trusting me with sensitive information. I promise it is safe with me. I can imagine your parents being proud of the person you've become. I'm sorry you lost your parents at all, but that it happened at a young age breaks my heart. Obviously, I'm curious about who your guardians were for the rest of your adolescence, but I know that's rude and don't expect you to answer. Whoever they are, they must be amazing to have helped you become the talented author you are. Of course, I'm just speculating. Perhaps you have had even more obstacles to overcome than I can fathom, and I now have both feet wedged firmly in my mouth.

I pause, wincing at my words. Should I just toss this card and start over? I flip it closed, smiling at the adorable hedgehog on the front under the words *Sending you hedge-hugs*. I don't have a second hedgehog card and it's too cute to discard, so I decide to push ahead and hope Winston understands what I'm trying to say, albeit rather inelegantly.

I'm not sure whether to say anything about his confession of being afraid of his writing career being over. That's something I want to mull over for a bit. In the meantime, I should talk about something more lighthearted.

I had another terrible date this week. I feel bad not hitting it off with any of the guys my book club has set me up with thus far. I doubt my friend, Julie (Little Shop of Sugar owner), will be too concerned that it wasn't a love match with one of her husband's rec league teammates. Travis was nice, and quite tall, but he only wanted to talk about basketball and some truck he's restoring. Neither are subjects that interest me. I suppose that might make me a snob, but I think some common ground is necessary. At least this one didn't involve me being left at a dance club or being patted on the head like a dog.

We went to one of those Paint and Sip places and attempted to create the same picture from the example at the front of the studio. It was a night sky with two owls on a branch. Mine didn't turn out half bad. My date, however, thought the picture was too feminine and freehanded a monster truck crushing a line of cars. At least, that's what he said it was. I just saw some colorful rectangular blobs. The activity was fun; the company was tolerable. At least our book club book is enjoyable. It's about a painter who acquires face blindness right when she's in the middle of a portrait competition. I'm curious to find out if she can overcome her deficit and win. It's also a romance, so we'll see who she ends up with. I love a good happily-ever-after story.

I lift the pen from the card, wondering if I'll ever get my own happily ever after. Optimism is still my prevailing emotion, though, I'm halfway through my Blind Date and a Book men and have yet to go on a second date with any of them. If only they could be sweet and sensitive like Winston. At least, that's how he appears through his letters. Not having met him, I don't know if this is just a persona or the real thing. There's only one accurate way to find out. Would he be up for meeting in person? I know he wants to keep his identity a secret, but surely he knows he can trust me by now. I'd gladly take the secret to the grave, especially if he turns out to be as genuine as he seems. I feel like he's someone I could fall in love with. We like books and the outdoors. He's been very complimentary of me lately, which makes me wonder if perhaps his feelings toward me are shifting into romantic territory. Of course, I could just be projecting my own hopes. There's no harm in asking, right?

I was wondering…would you like to meet? We've been corresponding for quite a while and I feel a strong connection with you. It'd be so wonderful to put a face to your letters. If not, it won't hurt my feelings, but I thought I'd check in case it's something you've been thinking about, too. Regardless, I love receiving a letter from you and hope that we can continue to correspond. There's just something special about finding an actual letter from a real person in my mailbox. It tells me I'm seen and cared for. That may sound silly, but it's how your letters make me feel. I must get to work, so I'll wrap this up. Take care, my friend.

Sincerely, Anna

P.S.-Another book club member is also a local author. Her name is Rachel Price. Her last name is Haynes now, but she goes by Price for her books. She also works at Page Turner Books.

I wasn't lying about needing to get to work. I scribble Winston's address on the envelope, stuff the card inside, slap on a stamp, and drop it in the mailbox on my way out the door. Thankfully, traffic's light and I park in the garage with five minutes to spare. No time for a Hill of Beans stop, but I'll survive. I'm all ratcheted up on excitement from extending a meetup invitation to Winston. I don't know what he'll say, but, until he responds, there's a mountain of possibility. Even if he says no, I suspect he'll willingly continue to correspond. But, if he feels the same connection I do, I hope he'll choose to explore it in person with me.

Walking down the corridor toward the main library entrance, I see Penny pushing a full book cart through the front doors. I open the library door for her and she smiles in thanks, wincing when one of the cart wheels emits a piercing screech.

"We've got to get that fixed," I say, letting the door shut behind us with a solid clunk.

"This is the first time I've heard it," Penny says.

"Yeah, but it's just going to get worse if we don't do something about it now. Let me see if I can find the can of lubricant we used last time."

After dropping my stuff in the desk drawer, I walk back to the storage closet. Reading the labels, I find ant spray, several cans of compressed air, various bathroom cleaners, furniture polish, and a few microfiber dusting cloths. I bend down, pulling out a bin of old rags. I hear a thunk inside and remove the pieces of cloth until I uncover a rusted can of lubricant. Giving it a dubious look, I grab it and shake it, the ball inside rattling. I guess we'll see if it still works.

Back behind the circulation desk, I crouch down, but quickly realize I can't tell which wheel is the complainer just by looking. I push and pull the cart a little, but hear nothing. Penny is scanning all the books back in, making several piles on the desk.

"I'm going to leave this can under the desk. If you hear it squeak again and can figure out which wheel, please take care of it."

She pauses in her scanning to look at me. "Why don't you just spray all the wheels? Maybe that'll take care of the problem."

Duh, Anna. "Yeah, great idea."

I get three of the wheels coated before the can makes a spraying sound without emitting any liquid. "Uh, oh. Looks like we're out. Let's hope I've already gotten the squeaky wheel."

"Would you mind shelving the stack on the right?" Penny says. "I'll make sure the rest of these get into the proper boxes."

"No problem."

There are probably thirty books on the stack, so I stick them back on the cart. Guess we'll find out about that wheel. I shelve all the books without the cart making unpleasant noises. Must have sprayed the squeaky wheel. I feel satisfaction from having fixed an issue, even though it was fairly minor. "What else can I do?"

Penny looks up from the computer. "Want to pull holds from the shelves? We've got quite a list today."

"Sure."

I pick up the page, grab the cart, and head back out to the floor. After gathering all the fiction holds, I move over to the nonfiction shelves. Glancing over at the cubicles, I see someone in jeans, a sweatshirt, and a baseball cap occupies the professor's seat. I wonder if it bothers him when he shows up and his regular space is taken. He seems to like his routine, but I suppose that doesn't mean he can't also be flexible. I turn back toward the task at hand, but the guy moves and the KC on his hat catches my eye. Could this be the ride share guy or is there another Royals fan in Asheville? It'd be a weird coincidence to find him here in my library. Curiosity gets the better of me and I head his way.

Stopping beside the cubicle, the guy is busy typing on a laptop. Perhaps he's hard at work on the next great American novel. I feel bad about interrupting his work, but it's just so rare to see a reference to the Midwest that I just can't help myself. "Are you a Royals fan, or did you just find that hat in a thrift store bin?"

"You sound like a true Cardinals fan."

My jaw drops. How does he know that? He lifts his head, and something about his eyes is immediately familiar. My gaze drops to his lips, which form a small smile. "How did you know that?"

He presses his lips together and his Adam's apple bob as he swallows. "I-I'm Brody."

My eyes snap up to his and they're exactly the same shade of green I saw in the rearview mirror not too long ago. "You were my ride share driver." He nods. No wonder he felt familiar. "How did you end up here in my library?"

He frowns slightly. "I'm h-here all the time."

My confusion must be written on my face, because he lifts his hat and runs a hand through his hair.

"This," he says, gesturing to the cubicle in front of him, "is kind of my spot."

I look from his hair, to the table, to his jeans, and back to his face, which has a day's worth of stubble. "Professor?"

It comes out as a question because, even though it's obvious now, it's a little hard to believe. The professor has been quiet and nervous whenever we've talked. The ride share driver was friendly, has a sense of humor, and didn't stutter once during our twenty-minute ride.

His brow furrows, and he tugs the hat down over his head. "Brody."

I shake my head, still trying to reconcile all this information. "Yes, I realize that now. Sorry."

Does he do anything besides pick people up and drop them off? I would assume so based on the business casual clothing he normally wears. Maybe he has the day off from his daytime job. Everyone's entitled to a few personal days, and it's none of my business if he chooses to spend it at the library. For all I know, he could still be working today, but just in more comfortable attire. "Are you working today?" I ask.

He tilts his head toward the computer. "Yep."

"Ah." I still can't believe the guy in front of me is the same one who's always in here. He seems different somehow. He's not as outgoing as he was in the car. If he's shy, then maybe the environment plays a role in his demeanor. You don't really make much eye contact when you drive and your brain has the distraction of driving.

"Is there something you wanted?"

I blink twice, my brain trying to filter his words and all this new information. "What?"

"Was there a reason you came over, or did you just want to insult my baseball team?"

My face warms. I did insult his team, didn't I? Oops. "Sorry about that. It's just I so rarely see sports team paraphernalia from the Midwest. I thought it was strange to see two Kansas City hats in a matter of weeks, but I guess I've only seen the one."

He nods, but says nothing. His phone buzzes on the table in front of him and I realize how awkward it is to be standing over him in his chair. *Jeez, Anna. You're at the top of your game today.*

"Aaaaaanyway…" I'm suddenly mortified by my behavior. "I'll let you get back to it Prof…er, I mean Brody. I guess I'll see you around." I wave my hand in the air, indicating the surrounding library, but quickly pull it down when it feels like I'm twirling a fake lasso.

He nods. "Um, before you go, I have something for you."

"You do?"

He reaches into his backpack and pulls out a small blue gift bag. I take it from him, feeling all kinds of confused. Why would this guy give me a gift? It's not my birthday or anything. I reach in, recognizing the feel and shape of the item inside. When I pull out the coffee mug, I nearly drop it when I see it's a replica of the one I shattered in the parking garage.

"What in the world?" I'm not looking at him, still stunned by such a thoughtful gift. Pink cellophane paper is stuffed inside. When I pull it out, I realize it's a bag of truffles from Little Shop of Sugar. My jaw drops open, and my gaze swings back to his face. "Where did you find this?"

He cuts his gaze away, his hand massaging the back of his neck. "I saw it in a store and thought you might like it."

"Oh, my gosh. This is amazing. Thank you so much!" I'm tempted to bend down and hug him, but he looks like a skittish rabbit, plus I don't know him that well. I just can't believe I'm receiving such a thoughtful gift from a practical stranger.

"Y-you're welcome."

Not sure what else to say, I thank Brody again before making a beeline for Penny at the circulation desk. "Penny! You'll never guess what just happened."

"Someone proposed marriage to you in the periodical section."

"What? No. But I wouldn't mind a proposal in the library from the right person."

She smirks, amused. "Then I give up."

"The guy that's always at the same cubicle—"

"The Professor," Penny cuts in.

"Yes, him. He's that ride share driver I told you about."

Her expression sobers. "Five-stars guy?"

"Yeah! And look what he just gave me."

I set the mug on top of the desk. Penny picks it up, inspecting its contents. "Ooh, chocolate. Hey, don't you already have this mug?"

I shake my head. "I did, but it broke. I'd completely forgotten, but Profess—, I mean Brody, was the one who took care of my cut that night."

"Brody, huh? I kind of enjoy calling him Professor better."

I throw my hands up, exasperated. "Why are you so hung up on what to call him? Do you not get that this guy I've interacted with a handful of times got me a super thoughtful gift?"

"Oh, yeah, I suppose that *is* more important. What does it mean?"

I sigh. "I don't know. Maybe nothing. But…maybe something?"

"Well, you're the one who has to figure it out. Speaking of figuring it out, where did he go?"

I spin around to face the cubicles. They're all empty, but I spot my abandoned book cart. How did we miss him leaving? Placing the mug back in the bag, I set it in the drawer with my purse before returning to work. My mind stays stuck on the fact that my chatty ride share driver and the guy who gave me such an amazing gift are also the person who bolted at closing and could barely ask me for book recommendations. He was still pretty serious this afternoon, but something about him has caught my attention. Maybe it's the knowledge that he can be open and funny in the right circumstances. I'd love to see that side of him again. I wonder if I could make that happen.

May 4

Dear Anna,

I suppose it shouldn't be surprising that a librarian knows several authors, but it suddenly makes me feel less special. Now I know I'm just one of several writer friends you have. Not that I'm jealous or anything (okay, maybe just a little). I checked out your friend's book and thought purchasing it where she works would be the best way to support her. She wasn't working the day I was in, so I didn't meet her. However, since her picture's on the back cover, I'll look for her the next time I'm in the store. I'm a few chapters in and enjoying it. Thanks for the recommendation!

I'm sorry you're striking out on your blind dates. At least you got a cute picture out of it. You strike me as someone who is naturally talented and would have skill with artistic pursuits. I do not. My paint by number pictures even look pitiful. I can appreciate art, however. There's a local artist who makes these really neat metal sculptures. He also paints and does some glass blowing. His name escapes me at the moment, but his business is called Double Rainbow Designs, which I don't quite understand because none of his art contains rainbows. You should check out his stuff, though. He's got a booth at Woolworth's down the street from your library if you get some free time on a lunch break one day.

I appreciate your kind sentiment toward my family. My aunt and uncle took me in after my parents died and they are amazing. They didn't have any children of their own, so adding me to their family was a big adjustment, but I think we all appreciated being together after our devastating loss (my aunt is my mom's sister). Anyway, they were very supportive of me and encouraged me to explore my passions and find a career I loved.

I spent my college summers working for various outdoor travel companies out west and they were the best experiences. I met my best friend, Levi, my first summer in Colorado and we worked together the remaining three summers after that. He now lives in Boulder with his wife, Elizah. If my writing hadn't taken off, I would probably still work in accounting. Definitely not my passion, but I've got a good head for numbers and finance. Though, if this sequel doesn't do well, I may have to go back to it. Gotta eat, right? Let's hope it doesn't come to that.

I, too, feel a strong connection with you. I've enjoyed our regular correspondence and am interested in putting a face to your wonderful words as well. Let's meet on the seventeenth at Hill of Beans at nine a.m. If that doesn't work for you, there's plenty of time to respond and give me an alternate day and time.

Sincerely, Winston

May 10

Dear Winston,

The seventeenth at nine a.m. at Hill of Beans is perfect. I can introduce you to their blueberry muffins, unless you're already enamored with them as well. I'll be wearing a bright green cardigan so you can't miss me. Looking forward to it!

Yours truly, Anna

P.S.-Carlos Vega is the mastermind behind Double Rainbow Designs. His company name is a tribute to his wife, Abbie, who's also a member of my book club. I have one of Carlos's glass vases in my living room.

21

Brody

RUSHING TOWARD THE elevator in the parking deck, I see the stairs off to the left and decide it's the faster route. My nose scrunches up at the foul smell in the stairwell, so I pinch my nose shut and breathe through my mouth until I'm out onto the street. I'm late for my meeting with Anna. I woke up with plenty of time to get ready, but then hit unexpected traffic on I-26 which had me crawling across the Jeff Bowen Bridge. Frustrated, I got off on Patton, but only found more traffic as I made my way to the Rankin Avenue parking deck.

Out on the street, I look both ways before dashing across the road to Hill of Beans. My T-shirt is sticky with sweat, but luckily it's hidden under a light jacket. Outside the door, I readjust the hat on my head and peek inside. She's already here and standing in line. My body has been awash with anxiety since I agreed to meet her and she confirmed the time and location. I want her to know it's me, but am nervous she'll be disappointed to learn I'm M.B.

Winston. What if she laughs at me? What if everyone inside hears her reject me and looks at me with pitying faces? Sweat breaks out across my forehead at the thought and my breathing becomes shallow. My heart is pounding in my throat and my stomach twists ominously. Stepping away from the window, I press my hands up against the wall of the building. *Come on, Brody. Not now. What can you see?* White-painted brick. My fingers pressing into the bricks and turning white to match. Blue sky above. The gray sidewalk. My blue sneakers. *Remember to breathe. In and out. What can you feel?* I can feel the rough texture of the brick, my fingers aching from pressing so hard on the wall, a breeze on my face, solid ground beneath my feet. I hear the whoosh of a door opening, the sound of people talking…I can't do this. It's too much. *You have to. You can't leave Anna hanging. You practiced with Gabi. What else do you hear?* Does the whoosh of blood in my ears count? No, wait. There's a crow overhead. Okay, what do I smell? Coffee. Rich, delicious coffee. And something sweet, like a cinnamon roll or doughnut. What can I taste? A little bile in my throat. I shake my head. Not pleasant or ideal. Name something else. The hot, bitter flavor of the coffee I'm about to purchase.

Still sensing my body on alert, I practice some deep breathing while I close my eyes and run through the scenarios I worked on in therapy yesterday. I walk in, smile at Anna, and say hi. I tell her I'm Winston and she looks surprised, but then accepts this information gracefully. We get coffees and muffins, I pay, and we sit down. I admit to her I struggle with anxiety, and that's the reason behind this ruse. She accepts my apology and we have a pleasant conversation, just like in our letters.

There's a slight breeze as I feel someone pass behind me. I'm facing the building, so I'm sure this looks awkward. Running my fingers along the wall, I feel the divots of the mortar between the bricks. The slight roughness is a welcome contrast to the smoother bricks. I continue this soothing motion until my heart rate feels normal and my stomach has settled.

Yes, there is the possibility of rejection, but if I know Anna like I think I do, that won't happen. She's a kind, generous person who probably gives others the benefit of the doubt. Pulling out my phone, I silently curse myself that it's already nine thirty. I'm very late for our meeting. Walking over to the entrance, I open the door, step inside, and search for Anna. I see the back of a redhead wearing a bright green sweater, the same one I saw on her when I first looked in. Relief courses through me that she hasn't left yet, but then my gaze swings to a man sitting in the chair across from her. He has dark hair and eyes and an athletic build. She says something, and he throws his head back and laughs. Who is this guy? Did someone come in and is now pretending to be me? I'm frozen in place as I watch him talk to her, the wide grin still on his face. She laughs, the sound of her pleasure making my heart sink. How can I compete with this guy?

She must have already given up on me. I bet she met the guy while she was standing in line. They hit it off, and now they're on a date that's obviously going well. It's my fault, really. I can't be a normal, easy-going guy. Sure, I pulled the illusion off at our last meeting, but that was with a few pep talks from both my therapist and Levi. He was the one who suggested I wear the baseball cap because it might help me feel more comfortable, and it worked, which is why I am wearing it now, though the magic must have worn off because my stomach is roiling with anxiety at the sight before me.

"What can I get you?"

Startled, I realize I've somehow entered the queue and am now at the front. *Quick, order something so you don't draw attention to yourself. Make your purchase like a normal person and then you can leave when it's ready.* "Tall black coffee and a blueberry muffin, please."

She takes my name, then spins the tablet around so I can pay. I move off to the side, trying and failing not to stare at Anna and her new man. She probably wants someone who is as outgoing and fun as she is. Someone who won't be late because he's having a panic attack. If nothing else, maybe I can take credit for helping Anna find her happiness.

"Brody."

My head snaps to the counter. My order's ready. I forgot to make my order to go, so my coffee's in a white porcelain mug with Hill of Beans stamped on the side. Guess I'm drinking it here. Maybe there's a free table near the front. I pick up my order, but only take three steps before I hear my name again.

"Brody?"

I stop, closing my eyes. A mixture of emotions washes over me. Pleasure at the sound of my name coming from Anna's mouth and dread that I now have to go over and see this meet cute close up. Slowly, I turn, fixing what I hope is a smile on my lips. "H-hey, Anna."

I reach the table way too quickly, nodding first at Anna and then at the guy across from her. Thankfully, both my hands are full, so I don't have to shake his hand.

"Come here often?" Anna says with a smile.

"Uh, no. Not really."

"What a fun coincidence. Care to join us?"

"Oh, I don't want to intrude. I'll look for a free table."

My head swivels around the room, but every table is occupied. Just my luck.

"You're not intruding and we have a free seat," Anna says. "This is my friend, Tom. He's a photographer. Tom, this is Brody.

He's a regular at the library."

So she already knows this guy who makes her laugh. I'm so jealous. And doomed. I lift my chin in acknowledgment. "You two look like you're in the middle of something. I'll just…" I've forgotten what I was going to say.

Tom stands up. "I have to get going, anyway. I told Rachel I'd be back with breakfast and, if I don't go soon, our burritos will be cold."

He picks up the brown bag from the table, gives Anna a quick hug, then leaves.

"Sit down," Anna says.

Realizing I'm staring at the door, I do as she says, setting my coffee and muffin down in front of me.

"Oooh, you got a blueberry muffin. Aren't they the best?"

Wow, a lot just happened. Obviously, Anna was not on a date because the guy was wearing a wedding band and mentioned another woman. I feel a wisp of relief, but it's gone a second later, replaced by my good friend anxiety.

"I, uh, I haven't had one before, actually."

She grins at me, her eyes sparkling. "You're in for a treat, then." She motions to the empty plate in front of her. "Mine's already gone, but it was delicious."

I nod absently, my mind trying to figure out what to do. Do I reveal myself and apologize for being late? I feel too amped up to risk another panic attack when she finds out who Winston really is and shows her disappointment, so I take the coward's way out.

"Do you come here often?"

She nods, her smile fading. "Yes, but today I'm meeting someone. Or, at least, I was supposed to meet someone." She picks up her phone. "He's almost an hour late."

My gut twists with the knowledge I'm responsible for her

disheartened expression. "I'm sorry."

"It's not your fault. I wish I had his number so I could call him."

Guilt washes over me. I never wanted to hurt her. Stupid anxiety. I should tell her. But how do I even start? *Hey, by the way, I'm M.B. Winston. Small world, right?* That just sounds dumb. Plus, I seriously doubt she'd think someone as awkward as me wrote those letters.

Anna suddenly straightens, her eyes wide. "What if he took one look at me and left?"

"N-no way. You're so beautiful."

Her gaze lifts from the table and there's a note of surprise in her eyes. "That's a nice thing to say."

I swallow hard, my brain buzzing loudly with the admission. *Come on, Brody. The least you can do is make her feel better.* "It's t-true. You have a wonderful smile and are so kind."

This gets one side of her mouth to quirk up and she quickly looks away, tucking a strand of hair behind one ear.

"Thank you, Brody. I appreciate your sweet words. I'm honestly a little bummed right now. I thought I'd made a real connection with this guy, but maybe it was only one sided."

I shake my head quickly. "Not possible. You're awesome."

She fixes me with a skeptical look. "You barely know me."

"I've seen you at the library. You charm every patron who comes in. I bet there are people who visit Pack Library just so you can brighten their day."

I clamp my mouth shut, realizing I'm getting too personal. I hope she doesn't read between the lines, because this could get awkward quickly.

Her smile is now genuine, and she reaches across the table and sets her hand on my forearm. The physical connection makes my arm tingle. Her eyes widen slightly and I wonder if she feels something, too. She pulls back quickly. "You're too kind."

There's an awkward pause and I break off a sizeable chunk of muffin and stuff it in my mouth. I'm delightfully surprised at the rich, buttery taste in my mouth. I'm used to muffins being dry and crumbly, but this one is anything but.

"Oh, man," I say, after swallowing. "That is good!"

Anna chuckles. "I know."

Impulsively, I split the rest of my muffin and put half on her plate.

"Oh, no, Brody. I couldn't possibly."

I give her a small smile. "Of course you can. You can't let it go to waste."

She scrunches her eyebrows and mouth, I guess trying to look put out, but she just looks cute.

"Fine," she huffs out, a smile breaking across her face. "Thanks."

"You're welcome. So, Tom is a friend of yours?"

She lifts a shoulder. "Kinda. His wife started the book club I'm in, so I know him through her."

Another book club connection. Wait a minute…suddenly everything connects. Book club. Rachel. Page Turner Books.

"He's married to the author!"

Her brow furrows. "Yes. How did you know Rachel's an author?"

My mind spins with thoughts. She told *Winston* about Rachel's book. How would I know? She doesn't even know I'm an author. *Think, Brody, think.*

"Oh, uh. I think I saw a flier in the library about a signing or something."

Weak, Brody. You really think she's going to buy that?

"We did host her book signing. Did you go?"

"No. How's her book?"

She smiles, and relief courses through me that I seemed to have dodged a bullet. "I really liked it. I know you're more of a fantasy and sci-fi guy, but it's got a lot of action that I think you might enjoy."

"It's cool you know a local author."

Her expression darkens. "I actually know two."

My skin prickles, anxiety beginning to well up again. I've hurt her by my deception. *You're better than this. Tell her the truth.*

I take a gulp of coffee, wincing when I realize it's now lukewarm. Tepid coffee is as enjoyable as this moment, but I'm responsible for the awkwardness. I rub my fingers up and down the fabric of my pants and take a deep breath. "Anna, there's something—"

Her phone blares music from its spot next to her cup.

"I'm so sorry. That's rude. It's my sister. She never calls. Let me just make sure everything's okay."

"Yes, of course."

"Hey, Heather. Can I call you ba—"

Her brow furrows, and then her eyes widen. With each second, her face grows more and more concerned. "Oh no! Just a second, Heather."

She takes the phone away from her face and looks up at me. "My mom's in the hospital. I need to go."

"Oh no, I'm so sorry. Yes, go. I'll clean up everything."

She gives me a small smile. "Thanks, Brody."

She's out of her chair and through the door in a flash. I clear the table and head out to my car. I'm not sure how to feel about being granted a reprieve on confessing who I am, but I have a feeling it's only going to be worse the longer I wait.

I try to convince myself it's okay because she and I are not really in-person friends yet. She likes Winston, but I really don't know how she feels about Brody. She seemed pleased to see me today, but she's a friendly person. She's probably excited when she sees any of her library patrons out and about. I really need to know we have a solid friendship foundation because, if not, I have a whole lot to lose.

May 18

Dear Winston,

What happened? I was so looking forward to talking to you in person, but now all I have are scenarios for why you didn't show. It doesn't seem like something you would do deliberately, so you must have a reasonable explanation. Please share it with me so that I can set aside the doubts that have been creeping in.

I consider you a dear friend and cherish our regular correspondence, but perhaps you don't feel the same way. If that's the case, please put me out of my misery.

Sincerely, Anna

22

Anna

I PACE AROUND my living room, eying the light blue envelope lying on the coffee table. It arrived three days ago, but I've put off opening it. Most likely, it explains Winston's no-show at our meetup, but I'm not sure I want to read what he has to say. I was hurt he didn't show up. Intellectually, I know he had no way of contacting me to say he couldn't make it, but that doesn't diminish the sting I felt at the coffee shop. I guess that's the downside of old-fashioned snail mail.

My mind has gone wild with possible reasons for Winston's absence. The first thing that popped into my head was that he was injured or ill, which twisted my heart with concern. Then it was that he had changed his mind and didn't want to break this comfortable correspondence bubble we're in. Perhaps he was afraid of shattering the glass that is our idealized versions of one another. I'd had that thought before I suggested we get together, but have been so disillusioned by my dates that I was desperate to reach for something that felt positive and might have real potential.

I told Penny about his no-show performance and we brainstormed explanations for his absence. An aging relative fell ill, and he had to rush to their aid. He had terrible food poisoning and felt like he was at death's door. Someone broke into his house, and he was waiting for the police to make a report. His publisher summoned him about his latest book and he had to fly to New York overnight.

We both scrupulously avoided the idea it might have something to do with me. I had the thought that he showed up, saw me through the window, didn't like what he saw, and left. I blurted this out to Penny just so it wouldn't stay trapped in my head. She vehemently denied this idea, saying I'm a hottie and reminding me he already knows what I look like because our letters started after I helped him in the library. Somehow, I'd forgotten that because I only know Winston through letters. I really wish I could remember our face-to-face meeting. How was I to know it would become so significant?

When Winston's letter appeared in my mailbox, I was relieved to know that whatever happened, he's still alive. While the idea seems a little morbid and extreme, it couldn't be ruled out. But, now that I have proof of life, I'm not sure I'm ready to find out what really happened. What if he says he's through with our relationship? It's been one of my highlights and I'd be very disappointed if it were to end. I really like the pick me up I get when I see a letter from him in my mailbox. *Just do it, Anna.*

I take a deep breath, releasing it slowly, then lunge toward the letter, ripping the envelope open and taking out the paper inside. Bringing it to my nose, I'm delighted to find it has that cedarwood smell I've grown accustomed to.

Unfolding the note, my eyes pour over the words.

May 22

Dear Anna,

I'm so sorry about what happened. I was temporarily detained but did eventually make it. I am overcome with remorse that I wasn't able to officially introduce myself to you. If I had a real time machine, I'd go back and change things so that we had the meeting you anticipated. I hope you'll forgive me. I, too, have truly come to consider you a dear friend, and the thought of losing you terrifies me. Please tell me I haven't ruined everything.

Hoping against hope for a response, Winston

I'm relieved this isn't a goodbye letter, but I don't feel completely satisfied with his explanation. Did he show up after I left to finish my call with my sister? It's a possibility because I really wasn't thinking straight after I heard the words "Mom" and "hospital" in the same sentence. Thankfully, it ended up only being a broken ankle. When Heather called crying, my mind jumped to the worst-case scenario.

Really needing to discuss this letter with someone, I grab my phone and call Penny.

"What's up, chica?"

I smile at her warm greeting. "I finally opened the letter."

"Ooooohhh! Why wasn't he there?"

I sigh. "He said he showed up late. We must have missed each other."

"Whaaaaat?"

My sentiments exactly. I read her every word of the note and give her a few seconds to digest its contents. "So what do you think, Pen?"

"It sounds like an unfortunate situation. He seems sad about it. Either that or he actually chickened out and is lying to you."

Chickened out? He doesn't seem like someone who's easily intimidated. He comes across as confident and self-assured in his letters. Still, Penny is known for her insight into other people. She reads me like a book most of the time. "Why would he do that?"

"You two obviously hit it off on paper. He could have been worried he'd disappoint you in person. He's built you up as this amazing person, which you are, and had last second concerns that maybe you'd done the same with him and the reality wouldn't match your idealization of him."

I know I've gotten some ideas about what a relationship with Winston might look like from our correspondence, so why wouldn't he have done the same? I hadn't worried that he would be turned off by the real me until after I'd been stood up, but I can believe the thought might have crossed his mind as well.

"You really think that might be it?"

"I certainly think it's a possibility. You could always ask him when you write him back?"

"You think I should respond?"

"I know you're going to. It's obvious you like him." From the sound of her voice, I can tell she's smirking at me through the phone.

I cross my arms over my chest even though she can't see me, a little annoyed she knows me so well. "Maybe so, but his no-show felt like rejection. I'm not sure I want to risk that again."

"You're continuing to do the blind dates thing even though it hasn't yet worked out. It's the same reason you're going to see where this thing with Winston goes. You should explore every potential avenue in search of your one true love."

She's got me there. I do want to find love. A man won't complete me, but I've watched my parents' relationship and their example of care, support, love, and companionship is something I envy and hope for myself one day. I'm sure their relationship isn't perfect, but it's beautiful. They lift one another up and have encouraged each other to pursue their passions. I want someone who believes in me and supports me. So, yeah, I'm going to keep looking for it.

"I don't believe there's just one person out there for me. Winston and I have actually had this conversation about soulmates."

"Oh, you and Winston have talked about true loves, huh?" Penny's teasing voice makes me smile.

"Yeah. So what?"

"Nothing. It just further proves my point. You're going to keep writing to him. *And,*" she adds, clearly sensing my objection, "I think you should. He sounds like a nice guy."

Penny's support means a lot to me. Even if she thinks writing letters is a little archaic, she loves me and just wants me to be happy. "Thanks, Penny. I appreciate you."

"You're welcome. I love you, Anna. You know, this wasn't why I thought you were calling."

"What else would I call for?"

"I thought maybe you wanted advice on what to wear on your date today."

I roll my eyes. "We're just hiking. I'm wearing my normal gear—yoga pants with pockets for my phone and keys and my waterproof boots."

"I hope you're also wearing a shirt. Otherwise, you might be a little chilly. Though it might get you a second date with whomever you're seeing."

I roll my eyes. "His name is Zach. It's someone Meredith knows."

"Which one's Meredith again?"

"She's the newest member. Works at the Arboretum. Married to Brett, who works at Page Turner Books with Rachel."

"Right. The Christmas Queen."

I laugh. "That would be a perfect name for her Crafty store if she was ever looking for a change."

"Thanks. Have fun with Zach and call me after to tell me how it goes."

"Will do. Thanks, Pen."

After I hang up, I realize I need to leave in five minutes if I want to be on time for my date. We're meeting in DuPont to do the four and a half-mile hike to all the waterfalls, and it's going to take me about forty minutes to get there. I'm still dubious about car rides with people I haven't met before after what happened at the dance hall. It'd be awful to be stranded in a state park. Though maybe Brody would rescue me again. Of course, with the spotty reception in the park, I doubt I'd be able to pull up the app.

I can't believe Brody was at Hill of Beans last week. Now that I know who he is, I feel like I see him everywhere. It helps that he's been wearing his Royals hat. It's probably the only one in the entire city. I wonder why he's wearing it so much now. Maybe I just never noticed before.

It really was nice seeing two familiar faces while I waited for Winston. Tom had me laughing with stories from his latest trip with Rachel. They've been going all over the place. She claims it's all book research, but it sounds like extra honeymoons to me. They've been married for four years, but you wouldn't know from watching them when they're together. Their mutual infatuation would be nauseating if I didn't like them so much. Not even having a kid has dimmed their romance. Honestly, I hope I'm just like them when I finally find my person.

I really wish Winston and I had been able to connect last

week. My gut tells me we'd have fun together in person. I'm very curious to find out if our paper connection translates into a face-to-face one. Penny's right, I am going to reply. We've built up over a year's worth of kindness and connection. I'm not ready to just throw that away over one hiccup. However, I can't reply now because I've got to go.

When I arrive at the parking lot, I'm relieved to see it's only half full. These waterfalls are notoriously busy, but I guess today is our lucky day. Grabbing my hiking pack from the passenger seat, I exit my car, lock it, and stick my keys in my pocket. I've got water, a few snacks, a small towel, tissues, hand sanitizer, and a first aid kit. You never know what you're going to encounter on a trail. Sometimes I carry bear spray, but this area has so many visitors, there have been no reports of that kind of wildlife.

"Anna?"

I peer over the hood of my car and see a guy sitting in a tall truck. His window is rolled down, and he has a tentative smile on his face. He's wearing a hat and has a full beard and mustache, so I can't really tell what he looks like, but the mountain man thing suits him.

"Zach?"

His smile stretches to reveal straight white teeth. He rolls up his window and gets out of his vehicle. We meet around the back of my car and I realize he's got the same hiking backpack I do, just in a different color. I motion to mine. "Great minds."

"I guess so," he says. "I've got a first aid kit, snacks, extra water, some sunscreen, insect repellent, two emergency ponchos, a flashlight, some paracord, bear spray, and a pocket knife. I doubt we'll need the bear spray, but I'm an Eagle Scout, so I like to be covered."

I grin. I like him already. Who knew emergency preparedness was sexy? Certainly not this girl. I'm quickly warming up to this rugged guy. Who, I notice, appears to be in great shape. His shirt stretches tight across his muscular chest, fitting snuggly against his strong shoulders and defined arms. An image of him chopping wood flashes through my mind. Do I have a thing for lumberjacks?

"Awesome. I have a lot of the same gear, so we're doubly prepared."

He nods. "You ready to experience nature with me?"

"Yes, I am."

We walk down to Hooker Falls first. Zach motions me over to a rock and we sit together for a few minutes, staring at the cascading water.

"I know it's not as impressive as what we'll see next, but I kind of have a soft spot for this one. The rush of water soothes me. Sometimes, when I'm feeling stressed, I come out here with a blanket and lie on the ground with my eyes closed, just listening."

"That actually sounds heavenly."

He smiles at me and we sit a little longer, before he stands and offers me his hand. I take it, noticing the calluses on his palm and fingers. Maybe he does chop his own wood. Or works with his hands. I don't think Meredith told me what he does.

"So Zach," I say while we hike to the next waterfall, "what's your job? I know you help with Winter Lights, but that's seasonal work, right?"

"Yes, I work the s'mores station when I'm there, but my regular job is making hand-crafted furniture."

I laugh, pressing my lips together when Zach turns a quizzical look my way.

"Sorry. When I first saw your beard and strong arms, my mind decided you were a sexy lumberjack. To find out you actually work with wood made me laugh."

Zach smiles. "You think I'm sexy, huh?"

I can't believe I actually said that out loud. Is there any way to save face? Probably not. Just lean into it. "You certainly are very fit and have a great smile."

"Thank you. I do it to attract the ladies."

My mouth drops open. "You do?"

He chuckles. "No, but I'm not mad that you like what you see."

My cheeks flame with embarrassment at his frank assessment. I'm suddenly fascinated by the sight of the path in front of me.

Zach gently knocks his shoulder into mine. "Hey, I'm sorry if my teasing made you feel uncomfortable. It's not every day that a beautiful woman hits on me and I'm honestly quite flattered. I tend to joke at inappropriate times."

I look up into his warm, kind eyes and feel my discomfort dissolve. Oh man, is this guy for real? He's hot and kind and has a sense of humor. How in the world is he still single? When he laughs, I realize I said that last bit out loud.

"I don't know if that's supposed to be a joke, but the truth is, I've been very focused on growing my business and it's sort of taken over my life. I have customers all over the south and plenty of custom orders. I realized recently I wasn't doing very well at the whole work-life balance thing, so when Meredith asked if she could set me up on a date, I agreed. And boy am I glad I did."

His warmth diffuses the last of my shame, and I give him a bright smile. "I'm glad you did too."

We spend the rest of the hike talking about jobs we had

before we found our respective passions. Everything I learn about him just makes me like him more. Especially when he patiently helps an older woman make it safely down the long staircase to the overlook at Triple Falls and then supports her trek back up to the top. I bet he'd make an attentive and loving husband.

When we make it back to the parking lot, I'm a little disappointed our time together's nearly over. This was the best date I've had in a long time. Possibly ever. There's only one question I haven't yet asked that I'm afraid might cast a pallor over this lovely day. But, I'm in it to win it, so I want to know now whether we're compatible on an issue dear to my heart.

"This is going to sound random, but it's important to me, so I have to ask. Do you like to read?"

Zach grins. "I kind of assumed this would be one of the first questions you'd ask, since you're a librarian. Yes, I read."

A small sense of relief creeps in, but I need more details. "What do you read?"

"A lot of books on woodworking, of course. I want to continue to hone my craft. But I also like books that involve adventure and travel. Anything about surviving in the wilderness intrigues me—real or fiction. Occasionally, I'll read murder mystery. What about you?"

We don't read the same things, but it sounds like he reads regularly, which makes me happy. "I read a lot of the new stuff that comes into the library, but my comfort reads are romance and cozy mysteries. I remember reading *Hatchet* in elementary school and being enthralled by the boy's harrowing journey to rescue."

Zach's eyes light up. "Yes! That was the book that ignited my passion for survival books. I read every other Paulsen book I could find. I re-read those books from time to time just to remember how I felt the first time I read it."

Oooh, he's a re-reader? Definitely a good sign.

"I have to admit I've probably read *Pride and Prejudice* a good two dozen times. It's my very favorite novel."

"Haven't read that one, but I saw the movie."

This surprises me. "Which one?"

His brow furrows. "There's more than one?"

"Oh, yes. I need to know if you've seen the best one."

"Um, the one I saw had Keira Knightley in it."

I nod. "That one's not bad, but the BBC series with Colin Firth is by far the best. Probably because it's five and a half hours, so they were able to put more into it."

"Maybe we could watch it together. Seeing as how it's the best version and all."

My eyes widen. He would watch half a day's worth of television with me? I'm floored. Who is this guy and where did he come from? "Yeah, that would be fun."

He rubs the back of his neck, looking down at the ground, before returning his gaze to mine.

"Speaking of fun, would you like to go hiking with me again?"

He wants to see me again! "Yes, of course."

Zach drops his hand and straightens his shoulders, his smile wide. "Awesome. I'll text you later this week and we can set something up."

He opens my door for me, then waves as I drive out of the parking lot. I've got a second date! The first one in what feels like forever. I feel a twitch of guilt as Winston comes to mind.

I like him, but after the letdown of our non-meetup, I'm not sure what's going to happen. I can't keep my life on standstill while I try to figure out what he wants, especially if that turns out to just be pen pals. That would be fine, but I also want someone I can see regularly and do things with. And what if Penny's right and it's a lonely old man instead of someone my age like I've been imagining? I can't put all my eggs into Winston's basket when there are so many unknowns. Especially if I really do want to find someone to share my life with.

Still, I really hope Winston is the man I think he is. Maybe, I allow myself to think, if he wants something more, the knowledge that I've met someone who has real potential might get him to reveal his true feelings. Am I saying I hope he's a little jealous? Maybe. But he might just be happy for me, in which case, there's no reason to feel guilty.

If he likes me back, great. If he doesn't, then maybe something will work out with Zach. Either way, I have a potential avenue for my happily ever after. I'm feeling optimistic and can't help singing along to the radio all the way home.

June 2

Dear Winston,

You haven't lost me, though I wish things would have worked out. Perhaps we should have planned better, maybe exchanged numbers or something. I'm not one to hold someone accountable for something they couldn't control, so I forgive you and hope our letters can continue to be honest.

There is some good news to be shared. I went on another blind date and had a great time! My date was fun, considerate, and we connected on several levels. In fact, I'm seeing him again this coming weekend! I can't tell you how long it's been since I've been on a second date. Our first date was a hike through DuPont State Park to see the waterfalls. I'm sure you're quite familiar with the location. We had the place nearly to ourselves, which was nice. We're going on another hike, but we haven't yet decided on the trail. I'm just so excited! I hope you're happy for me as well. You know how much of a struggle dating has been for me.

What's the latest with your writing? I know you said the words were finally flowing. I believe your official deadline has passed. Were you able to turn it in on time or did you get an extension? Have you heard from your publisher? I hope they like it because I, for one, want to read more stories from you. Hopefully, you can find someone else to publish your work if your current publisher passes. It'd be a tragedy not to find out what happened to Ciara. I thought she was a spunky underdog that everyone could relate to.

How are your NINE plants doing? All still alive? And what about Dwayne? I made him a new hat. I bet it'll look great on him!

Sincerely, Anna

23

Brody

I TYPE ONE last sentence and lean back, satisfied with my work. After the disaster of my meeting with Anna the other week, I holed up in my house, avoiding the library, and searched for some way to fix the awkward situation I'd created. The letter felt like grasping at straws, so I was glad when a note from her arrived in my mailbox. Unlike her usual cards with bright pictures on the front and cute sayings, this one was plain yellow. It felt like a message—that she was holding me at arm's length, worried about getting close enough to be hurt.

And I do think I hurt her by not being truthful in the coffee shop. I've run through alternate scenarios since I watched her walk out of Hill of Beans. For instance, what if I'd just walked in, apologized for being late, and said, "Hi, I'm Winston." Would she have even believed me? There's no other explanation for how I'd know who she was supposed to be meeting, so probably. But the panic attack combined with seeing her sitting with another guy depleted my rational thinking and I focused on just surviving.

I'm grateful she's forgiven me, but I realize it'll take time and intention to rebuild the trust and openness from before. I felt gutted when I read her "good news." As her friend, I should be excited she's finally had a positive dating experience. As someone who wants to be her date, it's devastating. I'd go hiking with her. And what does connecting on "several levels" mean? Did they kiss? Not that I have any right to be jealous.

But I am. I want her to be happy, but deep down, *I* want to be the one who makes her happy. I can't keep letting my anxiety win. I'm going to have to really push my comfort zone if I want to have any chance of showing my true self to Anna. Of course, if she's seriously dating someone, I can't in good conscience try to steal her away. I know she's only been on one date with the guy, but Anna's looking for love, so when she finds it, she's going to be all in. The thought twists my insides.

I was delighted to see some playfulness from her with Dwayne's hat. Of course, she sent a tiny red ball cap with a cardinal on it. There's no way he's going to wear it, but it made me smile and even felt a little flirty. Though, I haven't told her Winston's a Royals fan. It's *Brody* who wears the Kansas City ball cap. Things are getting muddled in my mind now that I've had a few in-person interactions with her that weren't completely awkward.

My eyes skim over the words on my screen. I sent my sci-fi book off to my agent two weeks past my deadline, which I'll take as a win considering I didn't think I'd ever get it finished. The publisher came back with some edits for me, but overall they're satisfied with the book. I've continued working on the fantasy romance and have had a lot of ideas about how that should go. My failure with Anna in real life had me imagining all kinds of scenarios where I was successful at wooing her and revealing my true feelings. Beorn did a much better job of showing Aurelia how much he cares for her. He created a beautiful verdant forest from his magic, where he serenaded her with poetry he'd written and confessed his deep feelings for her. To his delight, she admitted she felt the same, and they lived happily ever after. Yes, he'd screwed up earlier by pushing her away because he feared for her safety, but all was revealed and mended, which gives me hope that all is not lost with Anna. Sure, what I'm writing is pure fiction, but sometimes it holds a little truth for real life.

There's a wrench in my plan with this new guy, but there's nothing I can do about that. I just have to be patient and trust that fate is on my side. And, if not, I'll at least hope that this guy makes her immensely happy. I'll push my feelings down and share her joy as her beloved pen pal. If that turns out to be the case, I won't ever reveal my true identity. It'd just make things awkward, and I'd have to give up my favorite writing spot at Pack Memorial Library.

I'm proud of this new novel, though. The story flowed out of me, reminiscent of my previous books. It could just be the fun of imagining me and Anna together, but it feels like something worthwhile. On a whim, I send it to my agent with the words, *What do you think?*

I'm still riding the high of finishing a project and feel the need to celebrate my accomplishment. Even if it doesn't turn into anything, I needed the reminder that writing is supposed to be fun. What else is fun? Being out in nature and moving my body through the forest. Where should I go? My mind swings to Anna and I remember her favorite place is Little Bradley Falls. I haven't been there in years. I just wrote a book about her, so why not celebrate by going somewhere she'd appreciate? It's late morning, so I pack a small picnic, change into swim trunks, and head out.

When I arrive, there aren't any cars in the parking area, which is surprising on such a gorgeous day. I walk along the water, climbing over rocks and using tree roots to swing around more challenging sections. I'm technically not on the trail, but this way is more fun, and enough people travel along the creek that there's a well-worn path. When I reach the waterfall, I pull a blanket out of my backpack and set it on a rock. Wanting to take advantage of the solitude, I decide to take a swim in the pool below the falls. Removing my shoes, socks, shirt, and hat, I venture down to the edge. The water's still a little chilly, but cold water doesn't bother me. After moving around the perimeter of the pool and treading water for a bit in the middle, I tip onto my back and float. The sound of voices breaks the tranquility of the moment. I keep my eyes closed until I hear them pass by, then straighten up, climb back out, and dry off.

A couple sits on a rock near the side of the waterfall. The guy hands a water bottle to a woman in black yoga pants, a gray T-shirt, and a red baseball hat. A short red ponytail sticks out of the hole in the back of the hat. When she turns to look at the waterfall, I catch her face in profile and realize it's Anna. I freeze, my mind trying to process what I'm seeing. Is she on a date? Is this the guy she told me about? My gaze swings to the guy. He's smiling at Anna in a way that makes my teeth clench with jealousy.

It's one thing to read about a situation in a letter. It's quite another to come face-to-face with reality. I quickly turn away, digging into my bag for a sandwich. I sit down on the blanket with my back to the couple. Of course, this means I'm facing the trail I came in on so my view is trees and rocks. Who comes to a waterfall and stares at the trees? I turn my body enough to see the left side of the falls, but it means I can also see Anna out of the corner of my eye. Their voices carry across the water between us.

"Let's climb up the side and take a picture," the guy says.

"I don't know, Zach. Is it safe?"

The guy's name is Zach. I'm not sure whether I'm happy to have additional information about my new nemesis. Not that he knows we're in competition. It feels ridiculous to have instant animosity toward a stranger, but here we are.

"I've done it several times. There are little notches in the rock from everyone climbing it so you'll have no trouble finding purchase for your feet."

"Okay, I guess it'll be fun."

In my peripheral vision, I see them stand and make their way over to the side of the falls.

"You go first," Zach says. "If you slip, I'll be able to catch you."

Okay, I can't be mad at him for being concerned about her safety. I turn my head to watch Anna climb, narrowing my eyes at Zach when I realize he's appreciating the view of Anna's backside. She reaches the top safely, and Zach is not far behind. I want to look away, but some part of me feels compelled to be tortured by watching Anna on a date with another guy.

He leads her to a spot near the upper falls, wraps an arm around her waist, then leans his head against hers and snaps a selfie. He takes another one, this time pressing a kiss to her cheek. My fists clench at his boldness. Am I going to have to watch her kiss another guy? My stomach roils uneasily.

They're now too far away to eavesdrop on their conversation, but Zach motions to another part of the falls. When Anna nods, he takes her hand and guides her along the ledge. What happens next takes only a second, but I see it all happen in slow motion.

One of Anna's feet slips out from under her and she releases Zach's hand, her arms swinging up in the air. Then she's falling backward and I hear a thud as she hits the rock ledge and goes still.

Before my brain can fully process everything, I've grabbed my backpack and am racing toward the side of the waterfall.

178

24

Anna

MY FIRST THOUGHT is how embarrassed I am for being such a klutz on my date with Zach. He'd warned me that the rocks were slippery, but I hadn't had any problems yet. I was distracted because he'd just kissed me on the cheek and was holding my hand, so I missed the algae coating the rocks in front of me.

The second thought in my mind is actually a question. Who is this shirtless guy standing over me? His hands are in my hair, gently probing my scalp, so all I see is a muscular chest and rock hard abs. I know this isn't Zach because this magnificent torso is wearing navy swim shorts with red crabs on to them and Zach has on olive-colored shorts. It's certainly not an unpleasant view, but it feels wrong to be appreciating a male form that doesn't belong to my date. Though I'm human, so I don't close my eyes and am rewarded with the sight of toned muscles rippling under his skin as he moves.

"Tell me if anything hurts," he says, continuing his

examination.

One hand slides down my neck, causing goosebumps to pebble on my skin. Probably just because I'm sitting in a puddle of water. His hands run down my shoulders and arms, along my torso, and to my legs. I wince when he touches a spot near my calf.

"I'm going to roll up your pant leg so I can see what we're working with."

I suck in a pained breath when my yoga pants rub against the sore spot.

"Sorry."

"I'm the one who should be sorry," I say. "You're just being a good Samaritan."

His back is to me while he examines my leg, so I see the gentle raise of his shoulders. He pulls some antiseptic out of a bag. "This may sting a little."

I feel the medicine touch the wound and fist my hands so I don't make any noise. Still, my leg jerks a little at the unpleasant sensation. He reaches back over into his bag, giving me a view of the gash on my leg. It doesn't look too deep. He uses a clean cloth to dab away the blood, then gently spreads some antibacterial ointment over it before covering it with a bandage.

Nodding at his first aid work, he zips his bag, then turns to face me. My eyes widen when recognition hits me. What's Brody doing here? And why has he been hiding that ripped body under khakis and dress shirts? That thing should be on display in a museum or something. I realize my mouth is hanging open and quickly shut it. Remembering the feel of his gentle hands as he checked me for injury, I break eye contact, embarrassed that I was having more-than-friendly thoughts about a library patron.

"Thanks for your help," I say, staring at the bandage on my leg.

"You're welcome," he says. "I don't think you have a concussion. Can I help you back down to the ground?"

A throat clears behind me and I turn to see Zach, a weird look on his face as he stares at Brody. "I can help her." His gaze swings to me. "We should probably have you checked out by an *actual* doctor, just to be on the safe side."

I look down at my leg again. "He seems to know what he's doing." Remembering my manners, I say, "Zach, this is Brody. Brody, this is Zach." They nod in acknowledgment. A question pops into my head. "Are you an Eagle Scout, too, Brody?"

He glances over at Zach before returning his gaze to me. "No. My summer jobs required extensive first aid training. After seeing some terrible accidents occur far from civilization, I never go anywhere without my kit."

What kind of summer jobs did he have? Maybe life guarding? Or camp counselor. Though, with a body as fit as his, perhaps he had more extreme jobs like rock climbing guide or survivalist school. There is more than meets the eye with this man. I'm itching to ask more, but it would be poor form to show interest in another man while I'm on a date. I glance over at Zach, who's frowning. Especially when your date looks like he might be jealous.

"Well, I'm certainly glad for your preparedness."

"Anytime." He hesitates, like he doesn't want to leave me, but then he looks behind me, nods, and makes his way back down the side of the waterfall.

I push up off the ground to stand, thankful the movement doesn't bother my leg. Superficial wounds sure can bleed a lot, making them appear more serious than they are. I turn to Zach so my eyes don't accidentally follow Brody.

By the time Zach and I are back down at the base of the waterfall, Brody's nowhere to be seen. There's a tug of disappointment in my stomach that surprises me. I've been having a great time with Zach. I shouldn't let one heroic moment by someone I barely know derail this good thing that's started between us.

Zach stuffs our picnic items back in his backpack.

"Are we leaving so soon?"

He looks at me, a frown on his lips. "I'm serious about taking you to a doctor."

I give him a confident smile. "I'm fine, Zach. My rear took most of the impact. I promise I didn't hit my head. Everything feels fine."

His look is skeptical, but then his shoulders drop, and he gives me a small smile. "If you're sure you're okay, I have some cookies I brought for dessert."

I nod. "Yes, I'm sure. Cookies would be great, though. I could use a little chocolate."

He pulls them out, giving me a sheepish smile. "Sorry to disappoint. These are oatmeal raisin."

Ugh. The worst type of cookie. I don't even consider it a cookie. It's more like a granola bar. "Oh. I don't really care for those, but you go ahead."

I sit down on the rock, turning my gaze to the waterfall. The multiple cascades are so beautiful. Sometimes I like to swim in the pool below, but my soaked rear tells me it's a little chilly for my taste. I'm surprised Brody took a dip. I still can't believe he was here and came to my rescue. Zach has a first aid kit as well, so I would have been fine either way, but my mind recalls the tenderness with which Brody checked me for injury. There's a lot more to him than just library patron, ride share driver, and possible professor. What else is he hiding?

After Zach polishes off the cookies, we hike back out to our cars. He gives me a hug, which is warm and comforting. He presses a kiss to my temple before pulling back and grasping my hand with his. He stares into my eyes for a few long moments. Is he going to kiss me? I'm not entirely opposed to the idea.

"Are you sure you're okay? If you feel the least bit woozy, tell me and I'll drive. I can come back with a friend and get your car later."

I smile, appreciative of his concern. "Yes, I promise I'm fine."

"I'm going to drive behind you to your apartment, just in case."

His sweetness softens my heart. What a thoughtful thing to do. "I'm really fine, but if it'll make you feel better, go ahead."

"Thanks. I enjoyed our hike until you slipped. I'm sorry I placed you in danger."

I wave away his concern. "I enjoyed my time up on the ledge. I like being adventurous."

His crinkled brow smooths out as his concern melts into relief. "Well, okay. Would you like to go out again? Maybe do something a little different next time?"

I pause, considering his request. Do I want a third date with Zach? Other than his terrible taste in cookies, things are good. "Yes, that would be wonderful."

He grins widely and pulls me in for another hug.

"Great! I'll call you and we'll set something up."

He opens my door for me, then follows me back to my apartment building like the gentleman he is. I'm excited to see what we'll do on our next date. I'm also thrilled to be going on a third date with someone. This is practically uncharted water for me.

When I get inside my apartment, I strip off my wet clothes and take a hot shower. The water warms me and rinses away the dirt from my embarrassing fall. My mind drifts to Brody's gentle hands and the confident way he took charge of the situation. That's the second time he's come to my rescue, and I can't help but feel a spark of affection for him. Who is this guy? All this new information is blasting away my preconceived notions of him and making me want to learn more.

June 7

Dear Anna,

I appreciate your willingness to think the best of me. Your kind heart is one of the things I love about you.

I suppose congratulations are in order regarding your second date. I assume he treats you with the kindness, consideration, and respect you deserve. You shouldn't settle for anyone who doesn't make you feel as special as you are or who isn't your champion. You are an incredible woman deserving of all the love in the world.

You may be shocked to hear all of my plants are thriving. Though no one told me you have to dust plants. Some were looking a little dull, but, after a swipe with a microfiber rag, they're back to their vibrant green selves.

Dwayne says thank you for thinking of him, but regrets to inform you that red is not really his color. It clashes a bit with his gray pallor. He looks better in cooler colors. I apologize for his snootiness. I don't know where it comes from. I certainly didn't raise him to behave so rudely.

I'm also happy to report that my sci-fi sequel was sent off to my publisher several weeks ago. They accepted it with some edits, so you'll get to read Ciara's story after all. I appreciate your confidence in my abilities. I, too, related to Ciara's underdog qualities.

I also finished the fun project I was working on. I sent it off to my agent, who really liked it, despite it being nothing like my previous novels. We'll see if it goes anywhere. In the meantime, I feel like I should start on something new. No ideas spring to mind. What's something you'd like to see me write?

Grateful for you, Winston

25

Brody

IM IN THE library in my usual location, hoping the routine will spark a new idea for a project. I thoroughly enjoyed my fun project and Mark thinks it has potential. Perhaps I should try another new genre and see if I can get some purchase. What would be fun? Murder mystery? Maybe, but that one would require some planning. Like motive, red herrings, and a plausible but subtle reason a character would kill someone.

What about a thriller where a guy was on a first date with someone and really clicking with them and they're kidnapped? He then has to figure out why and learns it's someone who's seeking revenge on him for something that happened years ago. I like that idea. Not a first date, though. He should really be into the person. They could have been together for a year and he was getting ready to propose. Yes, those stakes are higher already. Okay, but who is his nemesis? And why?

My head tips back and I stare at the water spots on the ceiling.

There's a new one starting near the giraffe. It looks kind of like a penguin. Not helpful unless somebody was an animal smuggler and the main character thwarted him somehow. No, that's too out there. I swing my gaze around the room and land on the computers. Perhaps the character was an undercover agent monitoring the dark web and helped capture some nefarious person who spent a few years in prison, but escaped and is now bent on exacting revenge. The reader (and character) wouldn't know it was an escaped convict, so that could be gradually revealed as he digs deeper into things. I like it.

My eyes flick over to the circulation desk. Anna's smiling at a woman while checking out a stack of books for her. I stare at her, my mind remembering my favorite features—her warm sparkling eyes that set a person at ease and invite them to share their deepest secrets, her infectious smile that makes you feel like you're always welcome in her presence. Her hair is half up in a ponytail, giving me an unobstructed view of her lovely face.

I want to go over and ask how her leg is, but don't know what I'd say after that. Obviously, I'm not asking about her date. I already know what's happening there, but I don't actually know her well enough to mention something so forward like that. *Winston* could ask her that, but she and Brody are practically strangers. I'm seriously beginning to regret not telling her at Hill of Beans. Things are getting more complicated than I'd like.

However, it doesn't seem to matter that I've been waiting until I had a fully fleshed out plan to approach her, because she's headed my way right now. She gives a wave and a smile, continuing toward me. *Well, Brody, you're just going to have to wing it.* Excellent. I'm so good at on-the-fly conversations with people I'm interested in. *Just say something nice about her shirt. Compliment her hair. Easy enough.*

She stops, her smile instantly making my lips curve up in

response. Are my eyes as warm as hers or do they show some of the panic bouncing around inside my chest?

"Hi, Brody."

I swallow, willing my brain to get in gear.

"H-hi Anna. Your hair looks nice."

See? Not too hard.

She brings her hand up and touches the barrette clipping her hair back.

"Oh. Thanks. And also, thanks for taking care of me the other day. You were quick on your feet at the waterfall."

"You're welcome. H-how's your leg feeling?"

She lifts her leg and kicks it lightly back and forth.

"Right as rain."

"Good."

She looks at me expectantly, but for the life of me, I'm not sure what's supposed to happen now.

"Well," she says. "I don't want to bother you. Just wanted to express my appreciation for your help."

After a few seconds of silence, me desperately searching for something to say to keep her smiling at me, she turns away. Come on, Brody. Say something. *Anything!*

"Wouldyouliketogohiking?"

It comes out in such a rush, even I have a hard time understanding what I just said.

Anna spins around to face me. "I'm sorry?"

I clear my throat and take a deep breath, hoping it will slow the pounding of my heart. "I-I was wondering if you'd like to go hiking sometime. W-with me."

Her brows raise before knitting together. "Oh. Um. I'm kind of seeing someone."

"Not as a date. Just…friends. Just a friendly hike. I like hiking.

You seem to enjoy hiking. I know a bunch of great waterfall hikes. Many without ledges to fall off of."

I clamp my mouth shut, realizing my babbling sounds a little manic. And, also, I think I just insulted her.

She's pensive for a second. "A hike as friends?"

I nod. "I know we don't know each other very well," I start, wondering what I can say to convince her to say yes, "but sometimes it feels a little lonely hiking on my own. I-I wouldn't mind having someone to talk to."

This seems to dissolve her reservations, because she smiles and gives me a small nod.

"Yeah, okay. I'm free on Monday if that works for you."

My head quickly moves up and down. "Monday is great. Do you want me to pick you up or meet somewhere?"

She taps her chin.

"Uh, let me think about that. Why don't you give me your number and we can work out the details later this week?"

I quickly scribble my number on a piece of notebook paper, tear it out of my book, and hand it to her.

"Thanks, Brody."

She folds it up and sticks it in her pants pocket, then gives me a smile and a nod before walking back over to the circulation desk.

I duck my head, afraid my wide grin might make her change her mind about the hike. I have a non-date activity with Anna. If nothing else, it's an opportunity to let her get to know the real me a little more. I better make a call to Gabi to see if we can do some more practicing this week. I've been feeling a lot better about interacting with Anna, but this is going to be a lot of one-on-one time, and I want to be as prepared as possible. This is my big chance to see if I can flip the switch from friend to potentially more. Yes, she's seeing someone and I don't want to be "that guy", but there's no guarantee he's the one. Is there really harm in laying a little groundwork just in case something changes? I can't give up completely just because there's a new obstacle.

My eyes refocus on my laptop. I should funnel these giddy, excited feelings into the character who's in love with his girlfriend. How is he feeling, knowing he's on the cusp of proposing to the woman of his dreams? Inspiration slams into me and my fingers fly over the keyboard.

June 12

Dear Winston,

Congratulations on getting your sequel finished and off to your editor. I can't wait to hear when it'll be published. (But not soon enough for my liking, because I'm dying to find out what challenges befall Ciara and how she'll overcome them. At least, I assume she overcomes them. It'd be a pretty disappointing follow up if she is defeated or killed. If this is the case, give me a heads up and I'll keep the confident, victorious Ciara in my head and not mar it with any other versions. On second thought, don't tell me anything. I'm sure however her story has changed, it's still wonderful. I have no doubt in your abilities to craft an amazing, engaging story.)

I'm intrigued about this new project of yours. Can you give me any additional hints or details about it? Is it a similar genre? Same genre but new world? Something way different, like a murder mystery? I've always been in awe of people who can craft a story that keeps me guessing about the murderer until it is revealed. Of course, maybe I'm just bad about seeing the nefariousness of the characters and assume everyone is who they say they are. My friend Penny says I'm too trusting of others, but I don't see it as a liability. I'd rather be optimistic and see the good in others than go around being suspicious of everyone. Sounds like a miserable way to live. But I digress. I think it's great you've found a passion project.

Regarding what you should write next, I don't think I'm much help. I think you should write the things that excite you because it'll come through in your story. If I give you a type of story that falls flat in your mind, there won't be the proper passion and inspiration behind it. I'd be interested to hear what you start on next. Will it be more of this new project or something in the sci-fi realm? Or maybe still YA, but a different genre or sub-genre? I wish I could give you some truly valuable advice.

As for Dwayne, perhaps he's reached his adolescent phase and is trying to become his own person. I know I was a little cantankerous when I was in my teens. I'd pick fights with my parents some days just because. I wasn't upset at them or anything. There was just something in me that needed to exert my autonomy. I've included a blue pageboy cap, which I hope will suit Dwayne's preferences.

It's still too early to know if the guy I'm seeing has long-term potential, but we've arranged for a third date to see Two Left Feet at The Xcape this weekend. I'm not familiar with the band, but am open to new experiences. I'll let you know what I think of the band in my next reply. If you like this band, please spare me a potential foot-in-mouth situation by letting me know. I'd hate to excoriate something you love. What kind of music do you like? I mostly listen to pop and Top 40, but I also enjoy the symphony. Especially when they play Christmas music.

I'm nearly out of white space on this card, so I'll wrap this up. Maybe I should switch to paper for next time to have more writing room. Looking forward to your reply!

Sincerely, Anna

26

Anna

LOOKING AROUND THE crowd gathered outside, it looks like Two Left Feet is a popular band. Several people are wearing shirts with the band's name on them. I've been here for ten minutes waiting for Zach to arrive and find me. A familiar face breaks free from the crowd, hurrying toward me. Julie throws her arms around me, giving me a tight squeeze.

"Anna, are you going to the TLF concert, too?"

She releases me, and I smile. "I am." Motioning to her shirt, I add, "You must be a big fan."

"The biggest! I've even gotten Jayson hooked."

I turn my head to smile at her husband, noting he's also got a band shirt on. "Nice. I'm actually meeting Zach here for a third date."

"Oooh, how exciting! Glad to hear things are going well between you two. We're going to head inside so we can be near the front. Want us to save room for you?"

I shake my head. "Nah, I'll let Zach choose where we stand. He's the fan. I'm just along for the ride."

"You're gonna love it, I promise."

They head inside and I start a game on my phone. I've beaten four levels, and the crowd has thinned out significantly—probably all inside, because the show has already started—when Zach reaches my side, slightly breathless.

"I'm so sorry, Anna. A friend broke down on the side of the road and asked for a ride. I didn't think it'd take so long."

The hint of annoyance I was feeling at being kept waiting melts away. "That's okay. It was nice of you to help your friend."

"I'm just glad I made it in time. Let's go in."

"Technically, you're late."

He waves a hand in dismissal. "It's just the opening band."

The guy out front scans the tickets on Zach's phone and we walk through the lobby into the concert area. The crowd is obviously enjoying the band, dancing and waving arms in sync with the music. He grabs my hand, pulling me through the crowd until we're near the front. I get a few dirty looks from people as we slide up to a prime spot, but because it's so loud, all I can do is apologize with my facial expressions.

I've never cared where I saw a show from, since it's easy enough to hear the music from anywhere in a venue. Zach turns a bright smile on me and I see he's got both a hat and a shirt with the band's logo on it. He might give Julie a run for her money for the title of biggest fan. He gives me a quizzical look, tilting his head toward the stage and I interpret him as asking what I think of the opening act. It's loud, because we're right next to a wall of speakers, but the beat of the song is catchy. I smile and nod, which seems to satisfy him.

After a couple of songs, he leans close and motions taking a drink with his hand. I nod and he pulls out his phone, typing something before handing it over to me. I smile when I see he's asked what I want. I type a response. He nods and heads back through the crowd, which seems to swallow him whole.

When the band finishes up, Zach still hasn't returned. The lights go up while the instruments on stage are set up for the next band. I could use a bathroom break, but don't want to lose our spot. Glancing around, I recognize another face in the crowd.

"Brody!" I yell it to be heard over the din of the crowd. His head snaps around, his eyes widening in recognition. I wave and beckon him over.

"Anna, hey. You like Two Left Feet?"

"No, I'm here for Sauren's Revenge."

Surprise flits across his face. "I'd never heard them before. You must really be into indie rock music."

I chuckle. "No, actually. I was just kidding. My date brought me here because he loves TLF."

"Whoa, you're already using the acronym. You're destined to be a fan."

I roll my eyes. "We'll see about that." I quickly pinch my lips together, concerned I might have offended him. He's not wearing any band merchandise, just a plain gray T-shirt and his Royals hat. "I mean, there's nothing wrong with being a fan, but based on the opening band, I don't think this will be my kind of music."

He smiles. "You might be surprised. TLF plays lots of covers. And their original stuff is pretty good, too."

"They're a cover band? I didn't know that."

Brody nods, then looks away. I search for something else to say to break the awkward silence building between us.

"Are you a big fan?"

"Where's your date?"

Our questions come out simultaneously, making us laugh.

"You first," he says.

"No, it's nothing. I've actually been wondering where Zach is." I look around, but still don't see him anywhere. "Um, would you mind holding this spot? I really need to run to the restroom."

"Yeah, no problem."

After finding the bathroom, I search the lobby for Zach, but there's no sign of him. Unsure of what else to do, I head back inside and weave through people toward the speakers on the right. When I'm almost to my destination, I see Zach in conversation with Brody. I pause, taking in the scene. Both men are about the same height and build. His light brown beard obscures the lower half of Zach's face, but his piercing blue eyes have an enticing sparkle to them. Brody's light stubble gives full view of his handsome features, one of which are his warm green eyes.

I shake my head. Why am I comparing them to each other right now? They're both nice guys I know who like hiking. I'm going adventuring with Brody tomorrow. He made it quite clear it's just an outing between friends, which is appropriate since Zach's the one I'm dating. We haven't talked about being exclusive or anything, but I don't usually date more than one person at a time. Not that it's ever really been an option for me.

I continue my route, stopping in front of the men just as Zach tips his head back and laughs. A glance at Brody's amused smile makes me think I just missed something good.

"There you are, Zach."

He turns to face me, holding out a bottle of water. "Sorry that took so long. I ran into a guy I know who also makes furniture. We got to talking in the drinks line and I got distracted."

Can I really be mad at someone for getting distracted by their passion? Probably not. How many times have I let time get away from me because I was in a heated discussion about books? More than I'd like to admit.

"Anyway," he continues, "Brody here was just telling me about a runaway raft and a stowaway lizard that happened one summer while he was working at the Grand Canyon."

There are all kinds of interesting things in that sentence and I'm about to ask for more details when the crowd cheers. I turn my head in time to see the band walk out and grab their instruments. Guess I'll have to wait for the story. A touch to my shoulder has me turning, and Brody leans close, talking loudly over the noise.

"See you tomorrow?"

I nod. We're going hiking somewhere, though he hasn't given me a destination. It doesn't much matter since he's driving. I initially hesitated when he offered to pick me up, but since this is not an actual date, I feel okay with it.

He turns, disappearing into the excited crowd. My eyes follow him before turning back to Zach, whose face is full of excitement. He grabs my hand, giving it a light squeeze, before letting go and turning toward the stage. The music starts up and the cheers grow in volume.

I'm pleasantly surprised to realize I know the first song. It turns out I know quite a few of them. Getting into the spirit, I sing and dance along with everyone else. When the show's over after two encores, we head out into the night, a mass of sweaty, giddy people.

"Are you sure you don't want me to take you home?" Zach says.

"Yes, but thank you. And thanks for the ticket. This was a fun time. I see why you like TLF."

He grins at my use of the acronym. "I told you. Thanks for being open to something new."

My phone dings, and I hold it out to Zach. "My ride's here."

"I had a great time with you, Anna," he says. "I'll text you about doing something else together, yeah?"

I smile. "Yeah, that sounds nice."

He gives me a brief hug and kisses my cheek. "Great. Text me when you get home, so I know you're safe."

I nod, then get into the car. My thoughts are all over the place on the ride home, thinking about Zach. He kissed my cheek, but I kind of wish he'd aimed for my lips so I could see if we've got a physical spark to match our relational one.

I can't believe Brody was there. He's showing up everywhere these days. And that Royals hat has become as conspicuous to me as a neon yellow vest in a crowd of goth teenagers. He must be wearing it more frequently than he used to because I'm sure I would have noticed it long before now if he wore it every time he was in the library. Plus, I wouldn't have referred to him as The Professor if he always wore a hat.

When I'm in my apartment, I text Zach, then hop in the shower to rinse off the sweat from the concert. I set an alarm so I have time to eat breakfast and get dressed before Brody picks me up. There's a feeling of anticipation in my gut that's confusing. Probably just some leftover adrenaline from tonight's show. However, when I wake up the next morning, the feeling's still there.

27

Brody

AFTER DROPPING A package for Anna off at the post office, I drive over to her apartment complex, while mentally rehearsing potential scenarios that may come up throughout the day. I sent a text early this morning to let her know the place we're going has a pool for swimming in case she is interested in that.

I park in a space, then walk up to the call box and press the button next to her name. It rings twice before she answers.

"Is that you, Brody?"

I smile at the sound of my name on her lips. I wonder if she gets a little thrill when I say her name. Probably not. She's friendly to everyone, so I'm probably imagining any potential chemistry between us.

"Yes. Hello, Anna."

"Hey! I'll be right down."

I take a few steps down to the sidewalk so as not to crowd the front door. A minute later, she bounces out the door and hops down the steps. I'm speechless, taking her in. She's wearing a pink tank top and black shorts. I haven't seen her reveal so much skin since…well, ever. Anna's work uniform is jeans and sweaters, with the occasional dress and leggings thrown in. It is well air-conditioned, so her long pants and sleeves for work make sense. I say a silent prayer of thanks for the warmer weather.

"Where are we going?"

She looks up at me with bright, curious eyes and my lips tip up of their own accord. "To a waterfall."

She tilts her head, puts a hand on her hip, and rolls her eyes. "Duh. Which one?"

Her sassiness causes warmth to pulse in my chest. Does this small show of attitude mean she feels comfortable enough with me to show new sides of her personality? I sure hope so. "Patience, grasshopper."

"Grasshopper?"

I shrug. "You did sort of hop out of your apartment building and down the steps."

She fixes me with a challenging gaze. "And?"

"And I thought it was cute."

As soon as the words are out of my mouth, I regret them. *Wrangle your feelings, Brody. She doesn't think of you like that. Quick, change the subject.* "It's a bit of a drive and then a longish, but mostly flat hike with just a little altitude change, but nothing strenuous. Is that okay?"

"A mostly flat hike to a waterfall? That seems incongruous."

"Nice word, Ms. Librarian, but it's true."

"Well, now I'm intrigued. Take me to this miracle of nature."

I laugh, then motion her toward the car. After setting the GPS on my phone, I back out and head toward the Blue Ridge Parkway. After a long, scenic drive during which we make small talk about the concert and favorite hiking places off the parkway, I exit and take a few turns until we're on a gravel road. I park at the barricade, turn off the car, and climb out. Grabbing my backpack from the trunk, I shut the door and come face to face with a bright red abomination on Anna's head. I groan without thinking, which makes Anna laugh.

"I can't believe you're going to make me look at that thing."

She adjusts the Cardinals baseball cap, then points at me. "I've seen that hideous thing on multiple occasions, so it's only right for your eyes to be assaulted as well."

I chuckle at her mischievous grin. "Here I thought you were all sweetness and sunshine. Who knew there was a sly devil hiding inside?"

She shrugs, her grin widening. "I'm a complex individual."

I don't have a response, so I incline my head to the barrier. "The road washed out a while ago, so the hike is longer than it used to be and not particularly scenic for a large swath of it."

"That's okay."

We pass the barrier and start walking at a decent clip. With each step, I feel my body tense a little more. For some reason, being together in the car was comfortable. Probably because I do it so much driving ride shares. Now, however, I'm acutely aware of the gorgeous woman next to me, and my desire to impress her and make her like me only adds to my nervousness. I try to swallow down the sudden lump in my throat. I swipe at the sweat beading on the back of my neck. Gabi and I did a little role playing a couple days ago, and I thought I'd be fine, but I feel a pressure to impress or, at least not make a fool out of myself, and being in nature actually makes me feel more exposed rather than comforted. My heart pounds against my ribs and my peripheral vision dims. I grab the straps of my backpack and run my hands up and down them, focusing on the feel of the canvas fabric against my skin. I listen to the crunch of gravel under my shoes and the birds chirping in the trees. I hear a Carolina Chickadee, an Eastern Towhee, and the rhythmic tapping of some kind of woodpecker. Gradually, my pulse slows, my vision clears, and I can breathe comfortably again.

I chance a glance over at Anna. She's looking at me with a concerned look.

"Are you okay?" I ask.

"That's what I just asked you."

"Oh, uh, yeah, kinda."

"You sure? Because you were looking quite pale for a minute and I don't think you heard what I was saying."

I've been caught. Might as well fess up. "Sorry. I struggle with anxiety and sometimes I get a little overwhelmed."

Her face softens. "Do you need to stop and rest? If I'm talking too much for you, I can stop."

"No, you're fine. I'm feeling better. It just creeps up on me sometimes. What were you saying?"

"I was just wondering what the name of the falls is."

I don't know how I was expecting Anna to react to my news, but it certainly wasn't that she'd take it in stride, which is actually the perfect response. She just seemed to accept this facet of me and move on after acknowledging her initial concern. Huh. Maybe it's not as monumental of an issue as I've been making it out to be. I know I'll ruminate on this later, but right now, I want to focus on being in the moment. "Courthouse Falls."

"Where did the name come from? Is there a rock that looks like a judge's bench?"

I shrug. "It's part of Courthouse Creek, but the etymology is unknown to me."

"Ooh, good word. Were you an English major in college?"

"No, my degree is in finance and accounting."

"A numbers guy."

I don't know what to say to that, so I stay silent. Thankfully, Anna continues the conversation without my help.

"I didn't take any of those classes in school. Speaking of college, you mentioned receiving extensive first aid training for your summer jobs. What did you do?"

Have I mentioned my summer jobs in my letters to her? If so, I can't remember exactly what I said. I don't want to lie to her. Well, explicitly lie. I'm obviously lying by omission, but if it seems like she might like me without knowing my full identity, I will tell her who I am. Resolved to be truthful, I swallow down the unease.

"One summer I was a whitewater rafting guide at the Grand Canyon."

"Wow, that sounds amazing. Was it dangerous?"

I tilt my head back and forth. "There are some pretty strong rapids, but if everyone listens to their boat guide, it's usually fine. More people got hurt while we were camping for the night. They'd wander off in the dark and trip over a rock and scrape up their hands and knees. Though there was one client who had a severe allergic reaction. We had to use an EpiPen and call a helicopter to evac him out." Seeing the worried crease between her eyes, I quickly add, "He made a full recovery."

"I can't imagine what I'd do in that situation. I'd probably freeze or panic."

"It's really hard to say until you're in that situation. If you have the proper training, it's likely to take over when the need arises."

She gives me a wry look. "Like when someone slips on a rock?"

I smile. "Yes. I'm glad you're okay, by the way."

She lifts a shoulder. "Just me being clumsy. I appreciate your concern, though."

"What kinds of summer jobs did you have in college?"

Anna smiles sheepishly. "I worked at a local bookstore and volunteered at the library."

"Does that mean you've always known you wanted to be a librarian?"

"My elementary school librarian was instrumental in fostering my love of books. Knowing how influential she was for me, I'd love to help others in the same way."

"But not children?" She gives me a questioning look and I clarify my statement. "You work upstairs at Pack, which is the adult section. Why not the children's wing in the lower level?"

"When I moved to Asheville, the only opening was for adult circulation. If the head children's librarian position ever opens up, I'm definitely applying. However, if that doesn't happen, I'm okay with it. I really love helping patrons of all ages fall in love with books."

"I've enjoyed your recommendations."

She gives me a grateful smile. "Thanks. By the way, what did you think of that YA sci-fi? It won't hurt my feelings if you didn't like it. I was reluctant to try the genre, but the author spun a very engaging story."

Goosebumps rise on my arm. I didn't expect our conversation to bring us here. It's an opportunity to unburden myself of my secret, but what will she think? Will she feel betrayed? I'm terrified of hurting her. Delaying probably won't make much difference, but maybe I can find some way to explain myself that blunts any sting of pain. I need more time to figure it out. I swallow down my guilt.

"It was interesting."

She makes a face. "In other words, you hated it."

"No, no. I liked it. It was unexpected, is all."

"I can see that. It took me a bit to get into it myself. I hear there will be a sequel. I, for one, am interested in reading more of the story."

I feel surrounded by ticking time bombs. We need a new topic. Thankfully, we're almost at the falls. The trail slopes down for a few yards and then I step onto a path to the left that will take us down to the base of the falls. "We're here."

"But the trail keeps going."

"Yeah, that's the Summey Cove Trail and is another way to get here, but it has some steep inclines. I like our gentle journey better."

I motion for Anna to precede me down the path. We cross a small bridge and then come to a set of steep stairs that will take us the rest of the way down. Anna pauses at the top of the stairs and sucks in a breath. We stand next to each other and stare at the forty-five-foot waterfall dropping into a large, deep pool in a cove surrounded by trees, boulders, and bushes.

"Brody, this is beautiful."

I turn my head, smiling at the look of awe on her face. "I know."

"Are we going swimming?"

"We can. Or we can jump off the top of the falls."

She turns to me, her eyebrows sky high. "We can do what?"

I nod to the falls. "The pool's pretty deep and people do it all the time."

"Have you done it?"

"Several times."

She presses her lips together, her eyes assessing the pool and the top of the falls. "Where do you jump from? Don't you worry about slipping in the water?"

"You actually jump from the side, so it's not quite from the top. It's still fun. What do you think?"

She's silent for a long minute, then puts a hand to her chest. "I think my heart's about to beat out of my chest at the thought."

"We don't have to do it. We can just swim in the water below if you prefer."

I usher her down the stairs, around the large tree trunk that blocks our direct path to the falls, and lead her to a rock big enough for both of us to sit on. Removing my backpack, I take a drink from my water bottle.

"Let's do it."

Her words surprise me. "You sure?"

"Yeah, let's go for it. But can we do it now before I lose my nerve?"

"Sure."

She drops her pack next to mine. We remove our hats, shoes, socks, and outer clothing until we're just in our swimsuits. I can't help but notice how amazing she looks in her sunshine yellow one piece. I avert my eyes when I realize I'm staring, hoping she didn't notice. I lead her up the path to the overlook. She peers over the edge, keeping her feet a healthy distance from the edge of the cliff. She straightens up and takes a step back, her eyes wide like saucers.

"You don't have to do it if you don't want to."

She swallows, panic and fear etched on her face. "N-no, I'd like to. But…will you go first?"

I nod, giving her a reassuring smile. "No problem. But if you decide it's too much, just take the trail back down and we'll swim in the pool."

She gives me a grateful look, but then narrows her eyes like she's trying to screw up the courage to take the leap.

I walk over to the edge and look down, deciding where I want to leap from. Finding a suitable spot, I turn back to look at Anna. "See you down below."

I face forward again, bend down, and leap with arms and legs out wide. The air rushes over my body and I squeeze my legs and arms to my sides just before my feet break the surface. The cool water is a slight shock to my body. I kick back up to the surface, swim over to the shallow part, turn, and look up at the top of the cliff. Anna's face is just visible. I wave up at her, a giant smile on my face.

"You can do it!" I shout.

Her face disappears, and I wonder if she's decided against taking the leap. But then a flash of yellow flies into view, arms and legs askew. Her shocked scream pierces the quiet air, and she grabs her nose just before sinking beneath the water. When her head bobs up, her smile is as bright as her swimsuit.

"That. Was. Awesome!"

I grin. "You were amazing. Is your heart still beating a mile a minute from adrenaline?"

She nods, then swims over toward me, until we're both standing knee-deep in the water. Without warning, she wraps me in a tight hug. I'm so caught off guard by the feel of her body against mine that she's pulled away before I can even think of putting my arms around her. *Snap out of it, Brody. This doesn't mean anything. She just sees you as a friend.*

"Thanks for bringing me here," she says, a million-watt smile still on her face. "I feel so powerful now. Like I could do anything."

"You *can* do anything."

She shivers. I rush to my bag, pulling out the towels I'd packed. I hand her one before wrapping the other around myself. "Are you hungry?"

She nods, and I drape my towel over a flat rock before pulling out the food I'd packed. A shadow falls over the blanket and I realize Anna's standing right behind me.

"Wow, Brody. You sure came prepared."

I shrug, trying to appear calm, even though my heart's beating wildly at Anna's closeness. I feel a mix of anxiety and happiness. This day is going better than I'd hoped.

Planting myself on a rock, I motion for her to do the same. She chooses the one next to mine and I try not to read too much into her positioning. I hand her one of the plastic boxes.

"I hope you're okay with turkey, cheese, lettuce, and mayo."

She gives me a bright, heart-stopping smile. "Sounds perfect. I'm starving all of a sudden."

"An adrenaline spike has a tendency to make one ravenous."

Her warm eyes shine with something that looks like pride. She should feel good about what she just did. Even Levi had to build up his courage when I brought him here and he isn't afraid of much.

Anna's expression shifts to one I can't quite read. "Do you bring lots of people here to see if they're brave enough to jump?"

"Other than my best friend, you're the first. And he hesitated for a long time before jumping. I'm very impressed by your courage. You are an amazing woman."

Her expression shifts, going from slightly concerned to pleased before finally settling on surprised. Is she not used to being complimented? I find that hard to believe. Our eyes meet and I'm startled by the intensity with which she looks at me. There's something new in her gaze I haven't seen before. Her tongue darts out, running over her bottom lip, drawing my eyes down to her mouth. The air around us feels heady and charged. Is it just me or has something shifted between us? I force my eyes up to Anna's, but her gaze seems fixed on the lower half of my face. My throat is suddenly tight. My pulse feels like there's a jackhammer in my neck. I swallow thickly, my thoughts jumping between wondering if Anna feels the same heat I do or if this is the beginning of another panic attack. Sweat pops out on my forehead and I swipe it away, my eyes never leaving her face.

My body leans forward slightly, the desire to get closer to her growing with every second. My stomach heaves with uncertainty and I briefly close my eyes, willing my body not to revolt. When I open them again, Anna's still looking at me, her expression serious but also somehow inviting. Surely this isn't all in my imagination, but how do I know for sure we're on the same page? My eyes move down to her lips in time to see them part slightly, a sigh escaping from her mouth. A desire to capture her lips with mine flares in my chest. Anna's eyelids close and the sight of her vulnerable position makes my chest tighten with awe at her demonstration of trust. I take a deep breath, gathering the courage to make the move I desperately want to make and hoping my anxiety won't ruin the moment. I lean forward to close the remaining distance between us.

28

Anna

THE SOUNDS OF a branch snapping and voices nearby make my eyes fly open. Brody's head snaps back from its position less than a foot from my face, his eyes wide and wild. His head whips around to the trail behind him. My eyes follow in time to see a group of people step into the clearing. Their conversation pauses as they stare at the waterfall. *Whelp, that sure killed whatever vibe was going on between me and Brody.*

What was the deal with that, anyway? We're just friends, but I don't know. After jumping off that ledge, I was flying high, feeling invincible. And then Brody said such nice things to me and, well, with the soothing sound of the waterfall and the idyllic scenery around us, plus the fact that he brought me a towel and fixed lunch for us. It just seemed so romantic there for a minute.

You're dating Zach, I remind myself. *This is just an outing with a friend.* Though his heated gaze looked way more than friendly. I'm probably just imagining things. He hasn't done anything untoward.

He knows I'm dating someone and seems like the kind of guy who respects boundaries. I just got wrapped up in his kind words and actions, that's all. Besides, even if this was a date, it would be our *first* date, and nothing happens on my first dates.

But I can't not notice how hot he is, especially with his shirt off, his muscles on display throughout lunch. Not that he's purposefully showing off. We did just jump into a pool. I can't reasonably expect him to wear a shirt just because I think his body is nice to look at. I'm just glad whatever was happening between us got interrupted before we did something we'd regret.

Would you regret it, though? I scowl at my wayward thoughts. Of course, I'd regret it. I'm not a cheater. Zach is the one I'm seeing. Even if it's still early and we're not officially a couple or anything, he's the first person I've really felt a connection with in a long time and I want to see where it goes.

What about Winston? I sigh. My inner conscience is not pulling any punches today. Sure, I'll admit it. I've thought maybe I could have something real with my pen pal, but that was before he stood me up. Our on-paper communication has recovered from that blip, but I'm still trying to guard myself from thinking it could actually turn into an in-person relationship. I haven't quite regained contentment for how things are, but I'll get there.

"Shall we head back?"

I meet Brody's gaze, disappointed to find the heat from earlier gone. *Get yourself together, Anna. You're. Just. Friends. He doesn't see you as anything more.* "Sure."

We put our clothes and shoes back on, gather up the towels and trash, and head back out to the trail. After a few minutes, the only sound is our feet stomping along the dirt path.

"How does a librarian get from Missouri to North Carolina for work?"

The question comes out of nowhere, but I'm grateful for something to talk about.

"Via Tennessee, actually." At his questioning face, I explain. "I've always wanted to travel. After college, I looked for librarian jobs in other states. I interviewed for several, and was offered a position in Chattanooga. I worked there almost ten years before it occurred to me I still wasn't traveling like I wanted. Sure, I'd been to Atlanta, Nashville, and the Great Smoky Mountains, but those were all road trips, not real travel, so I looked around for another position. I visited Asheville after applying for a job at Pack Memorial Library. I fell in love with the town and gladly accepted the offer. Unfortunately, I still haven't taken a real vacation. Not even to the Atlantic Ocean." I sigh. "Maybe traveling far and wide just isn't in the cards for me."

"Anything's possible. You seem like a person who can do anything she puts her mind to. I mean, you've lived in three states. That's not nothing."

"Yeah, but it isn't the world."

"If you were given a free plane ticket anywhere—"

"Costa Rica."

He laughs. "Okay, no hesitation. Why there?"

I grin. "Bioluminescent kayaking."

Brody's eyes light up. "Yeah, that's awesome."

"You've been?"

"Not yet, but it's on my bucket list."

I perk up, pleased to learn we have a common desire. "What else is on your bucket list?"

"Hike the Appalachian Trail from start to finish, sky dive, see a space shuttle launch in person, become a dad, and see the Northern Lights."

My heart melts a little at his admission that he wants to be a dad. I don't hear a lot of guys excited about fatherhood. "That's an eclectic list."

He shrugs. "I have a lot of interests. Do you have a bucket list?"

"I hadn't really thought about it. Maybe I should make one. How did you end up in Asheville from Missouri?"

A scowl creases his forehead before disappearing. What was that about? He releases a deep sigh that feels heavy with meaning.

"I had a rough childhood, so I kind of looked for opportunities to get away. It's one reason I worked out west during my college summers. I felt so free out there that I looked for locations where I could feel the same sense of openness. When I visited Asheville, it just felt right, so here I am."

I understand the feeling of freedom living here. Curiosity about his past gets the best of me. "Please forgive me if I'm overstepping, but what happened when you were a kid?"

He's quiet for a long time and I wonder if I've offended him.

"My parents died in a car accident when I was eight years old. I was in the car and survived with only minor physical injuries, but it was pretty awful seeing my parents like that."

My heart twists in sympathy. I place a hand on his arm and give it a gentle squeeze. "I'm so sorry, Brody. I didn't know."

He gives me a wry smile. "You couldn't know. Being the only survivor, the media took an especially keen interest in the story. I felt like I was hounded everywhere I went. After a while, I was afraid to leave the house. I felt anxious all the time. I'd beg not to have to go to school for fear of cameras taking my picture and microphones being shoved in my face. That's when the panic attacks began. My relatives moved me from St. Joseph to Kansas City, hoping a bigger city would give me anonymity again."

I can just imagine a small, scared Brody, eyes darting around every time he was in public, searching for danger. To have to deal with that on top of losing one's parents is unfathomable. My heart breaks for what he endured. "Did you get anonymity?"

He nods his head. "I did. And also a lot of therapy to help me deal with everything."

The memory of Brody's panicked face in the library when I told him it was closing comes to mind.

"Do you still get panic attacks?"

"Sometimes. Mainly when I feel like everybody's looking at me or when I make a mistake and fear judgment. Sometimes large crowds trigger it. But I've been going to therapy to help manage it."

I give him a sympathetic smile. "That sounds tough. I'm sorry."

He shrugs. "You didn't do anything. It's just how my life has gone. I'm sure your life isn't perfect either."

He's right. "No, it's not perfect. I have two sisters and they're both excruciatingly in love with their husbands. As are my parents."

His brow knits together. "Their love hurts you?"

"Yes." I sigh. "No. Actually, I'm just jealous. I want so much to find someone who loves me as well as their spouses do, and whom I can love back just as fiercely. I've been trying for so long but keep coming up empty. What's wrong with me that I'm so unlovable?"

Brody's hand on my arm stops me. He gently presses his hands to my shoulders, bending down to meet my eyes. "You are *not* unlovable. You are an incredible person. I'm sad that you feel that way. You're so special. You're kind, thoughtful, encouraging, and so generous. You make each person you meet feel appreciated and seen. It's an amazing gift you possess. Someone will see how incredible you are and sweep you off your feet."

I'm stunned at the passion with which he delivers his speech. Warmth curls through my body with each kind word he speaks, buoying my spirit. The earnestness in his gaze has my heart squeezing with hope. Could what he's saying be true? Could my forever person be closer than I've imagined? I search his eyes, wondering if his words are optimistic hope on my behalf or coming from a deeper well of emotions. We don't know each other enough to have real feelings for each other, but perhaps there's some potential there.

He releases my shoulders, taking a step back. "Sorry. I got a little intense, huh? I didn't freak you out, did I?"

I blink a few times, my mind still swirling with all the wonderful things he just said. I wish I could write them all down so I don't forget anything. Would that be weird? "No, you're fine."

Needing time to sort through my thoughts, I start walking again. Brody falls into step beside me. From my periphery, I can see him cast occasional glances in my direction, but the silence between us doesn't feel uncomfortable. I'm relieved he's giving me space to reflect on everything that's happened today. This non-date has been way more emotional and intimate than most of my actual dates through book club. I'm not sure what that means.

When we reach the car, I decide to set aside my thoughts and get this adventure back on more solid footing. "Courthouse Falls was pretty amazing. What other secretly awesome places do you know about?"

Brody smiles. "I wouldn't say it was a secret, just one of the less frequented places. Have you been to Glen Falls? It's a pretty unique place, though not as secluded as today's location."

I shake my head. "Haven't heard of it. Will you take me sometime?"

It feels weird being so forward, but it's what friends do, right?

"Sure," he says. "We could also go kayaking if you'd like. I know a few good spots."

"I love kayaking! Though, I have to admit, I prefer gentler waters. I don't know how to roll a kayak and the idea of traversing whitewater makes me nervous."

He grins. "It's not too hard to learn. I could teach you, but I know plenty of places where that skill isn't needed."

My heart picks up speed at the idea of being upside down in the kayak, but I'm also a little excited about the possibility of learning how to get out of the situation. And the possibility of doing it with Brody is quite enticing. "Let's just start with getting on the water first."

"Sure thing."

He shoots me an amused smile that makes my stomach flip. I'm finding this confident, fun Brody very appealing. It seems like a stark contrast to the shy, stuttering professor of the past, but maybe that was just me painting him in the wrong light. I probably caught him in situations that made his anxiety flair. Knowing it's an issue for him and understanding its origins has really softened me toward him. He's had so much pain and suffering. My whining over not having a boyfriend seems so dumb by comparison.

I can't believe I said all that stuff out loud to him, either. No guy wants to hear about a girl pining for true love. I roll my eyes at my patheticness. I should be fortunate to have had such wonderful examples of solid love in my family. It's proof it can be found, and even if I don't end up with a romantic partner, at least I have the love and support of my family. Brody will never see his parents again, and it doesn't sound like he has any siblings to lean on. At least he had some extended family who did their best to care for him.

Our drive back to Asheville seems much shorter than the drive to the falls, probably because we talk a lot about books. When we reach my apartment, Brody gets out like he's going to walk me to my door.

"You don't have to see me all the way to the door."

"I don't mind."

In front of my apartment building, I unlock the door and push it open before turning to Brody. "Thanks for an adventurous day. I still can't believe I jumped."

He grins. "I'm proud of you. I know it was a little scary."

His praise warms me from my head to my toes. "Thanks. And I'm sorry for complaining about my love life. I know it's dumb compared to your heartache."

Brody shakes his head. "Don't apologize. It's not dumb. You're allowed to want to be in love. It's one of the greatest feelings in the world."

Has he been in love? Why do I feel a stab of jealousy at this prospect?

"Besides," he says. "I think your openness will lead you to the love you seek."

My forehead wrinkles in thought. Something about Brody's words strikes me funny. I feel like I've heard something similar before. Am I experiencing déjà vu? Shaking my head, I let go of the thought. "Thanks. I hope you're able to cross everything off your bucket list."

He gives me a serious, penetrating gaze. "Me too."

Impulsively, I lean in and give him a hug. Friends hug, right? I didn't just do it because I enjoyed the feel of his chest earlier in the day after my big jump. Okay, maybe part of the reason was because I appreciate the sensation of his firm muscles against my body. Unlike earlier, Brody wraps his strong arms around me, pulling me tightly against him. My face leans against his chest, and I sigh at how nice this feels.

His arms loosen around me, and I reluctantly let go. He takes a step back, one hand reaching to clasp the back of his neck and the other shoving into the pocket of his swim shorts. The memory of his toned calves and tight backside as he climbed the steep slope in front of me earlier in the day flashes through my mind. I'm so glad Brody can't read my mind or I'd be so embarrassed.

"See you around," he says, turning on his heels and bounding down the stairs.

"Bye," I whisper to his retreating figure.

Closing the door to my apartment, I lean against it, my mind thoroughly disheveled with the day. I'd just expected a nice day outside getting to know someone I've seen around the library for over a year. There was no way to anticipate how things actually went and all the tension I felt between us. My thoughts are tumbling over themselves, trying to reconcile this Brody with the one in the library. I might be wildly misreading the situation, but I'm pretty sure he wanted to kiss me earlier. I can't deny I'm feeling quite a few more-than-friendly feelings for him at the moment.

But Zach! My heart stutters at the unbidden thought. I'd completely forgotten about him over the course of the day. Guilt douses the giddiness I felt only moments earlier. Am I cheating on Zach? No. I did nothing wrong. This was just a friendly hike. But maybe I shouldn't do anything else with Brody. At least, not while I'm dating someone else. I'm so confused. What do I want? And, more importantly, who do I want?

June 17

Dear Anna,

I appreciate your kind words about Ciara's story. I hope you find it to your liking. While you say you don't want any details, I will do my best to send you an advance reader copy from the publisher so you can read it early.

Regarding my secret project, I'm venturing into a mashup of two genres. I don't know if it's any good or if it was just a fun diversion that will turn out to be a throwaway project.

While waiting to hear from you and itching to occupy my mind with a new story, I started trying to write a thriller, but my mind kept wandering back to the secret project's characters. I then wondered if I could work on a sequel, but add in thriller elements to it in their world. Yes, I did some world building in my fun project, which may be a hint as to its genre.

Regarding advice, here's a pointed question for you that may help you uncover the other genre. If someone you loved was kidnapped, what would you be willing to do to ensure their safety? How would you keep going in the face of the possibility that someone you truly care about is suffering because of you? I'm sincerely interested in hearing your response.

Dwayne loved the blue hat. He thinks it suits his complexion fantastically. I can't believe you'd still provide him with a gift, even after his backhanded appreciation. That just proves how kind and grace-filled you are. I am in awe of your magnanimity.

I'm a big fan of Two Left Feet, actually. I find the shows to be a great way to let go and have fun. I rarely feel comfortable letting loose, but something about the noise and vibrant crowd frees my inner child. It won't hurt my feelings if you didn't care for them, but I hope you had a good time.

I've enclosed a little something for you. It's a thank you for the gift of your friendship. Your kindness and acceptance of me have meant so much more than you can imagine.

Sincerely, Winston

29

Brody

I'VE BEEN RIDING high after my date with Anna last week. Okay, so it wasn't technically a date, but it sure felt like it. At one point, it almost seemed like we might kiss. But maybe that's just what my imagination wants to believe. At least she indicated she would like to hang out again. Even if it's only as friends, that's better than her telling me to get lost.

I'm still impressed she jumped off that cliff. It would have been fine if she didn't, but seeing her willingness to push her comfort zone gives me hope that we'd be compatible if we were to date for real. Of course, I'd have to get the courage to officially ask her out, and I'm certainly not going to do that while she's seeing someone else. I can't interfere, no matter how much I want to. I was serious when I asked Anna to hike as friends. Nothing I did crossed any lines, even though we came a little close for comfort before those other hikers appeared. Adrenaline highs can lead to impulsive decisions, like considering kissing the beautiful woman sitting next to you. I tried to be a perfect friend. I didn't even initiate a hug or a second hangout, even though I really wanted to do both. I have to admit I'm walking pretty close to said line, though. I just can't help myself because Anna is so amazing.

We haven't talked since I dropped her off and I'm wondering if I scared her off somehow. I've done some work in the library—our time together gave me some fodder for the new story I'm working on. However, I keep picturing Anna as the protagonist. Should I turn this new story into a sequel of my fantasy romance with an added thriller element? Since Beorn did all the rescuing in book one, this could be her chance to rescue him right back and prove that they're perfect for one another. Ooh, I like that thought.

Wanting to capitalize on this bit of inspiration, I jump up the hammock in my backyard where I've been thinking and rush into the house. When I reach my computer, I drop into the desk chair, pull up my outline and type in the idea, then lean back, trying to figure out what that scene might look like. My phone buzzes in my pocket, breaking my concentration. My agent's name flashes on the screen and I answer it.

"Brody, my man! I've got some news."

I pull the phone away from my ear, his boisterous voice a shock to my eardrum. "Hey, Mark. What's up?"

"Petrocius Publishing loves your new fantasy romance book. They want to rush it to print for the next cycle."

My heart speeds up at the surprising news. "That sounds great, but what are they offering for it? And what does that mean for *Time and Time Again*?"

Mark laughs. "You cut right to the chase, don't you? You fulfilled your contract with them when you submitted the sci-fi sequel. They're offering you a new three book deal, seeking two more fantasy books to start a new series."

They must like my most recent manuscripts if they're offering to front me for more books, but do I want to be on the hook for writing a series? I'm enjoying writing whatever sparks my fancy. What if I sign a contract and then lose motivation to continue writing fantasy? Right now, I'm being driven forward by my interactions with Anna, but what if she falls in love with the guy she's seeing? Will my ideas dry up? Would heartbreak kill my muse?

"I don't know, Mark. The idea of having to produce two more books on deadline isn't all that appealing to me. Is there a way to take it a book at a time?"

"The contract is guaranteed money, Bro. You can write terrible stories and you'd still have gotten paid. If you only get paid for this book, there's no guarantee they'll publish future books."

"It's nice to know you have so much faith in my writing."

Mark blows out a breath. "That's not what I meant."

"I know, but listen. I'm actually already working on a second fantasy book, but I think the fact that I'm doing it simply because I want to and not because I have to is the reason it's flowing so well. It's a risk not taking money up front, I get that, but I think I'll produce a better product without the pressure of a deadline."

My agent is silent for a few beats. "Okay. I understand what you're saying. I'll talk to the publisher about just buying this book, but can I at least tell them you're working on another one already?"

"Sure. And if they're not interested, maybe someone else will be."

He chuckles. "Oh, no doubt. I sent the manuscript to a few places and they're all willing to publish it if Petrocius passes."

This news stuns me. "Mark, you should have led with that. Why not allow it to go to auction in the first place?"

"I thought it'd be considerate to give your current publisher first shot, but I can definitely mention the fact that others are interested. That should get them amenable to your proposal. If it's as big a hit as I expect it to be, it should drive up the advance you'll receive for the next one."

I smile. "Now you sound like my agent."

Mark laughs. "I'm just glad to have such great news to share with you. I'll return to Petrocius with your counteroffer and let you know what they say."

We hang up and I lean back in my chair, thrilled at the news. I'm so glad my new book has so much interest. I had a blast writing it and I guess it's shown through in the story. I hadn't expected the publisher to want to get the book out so soon. Well, we'll see what they say to my terms. If they're that excited about it, there shouldn't be a problem.

My first impulse is to tell Anna about it. Unfortunately, I can only do so as Winston, and I sent her a note the other day, so I will have to wait until I hear from her again. I suppose I could send her back-to-back letters, but what if she's already responded to the previous one? I could receive a letter tomorrow from her and then will have to decide if I send one back immediately or wait to see if she responds again, and it'd get confusing and then what if the letters stopped as we each waited to hear from one another? No, better to just wait until she writes back and then respond. Even if my fingers are itching to share my good news with her right this second.

Tempering my urge, I turn back to my laptop. Perhaps I can funnel this excitement into my current project. There's nothing particularly joyful going on right now with the lovers being chased by dangerous people, but perhaps I can fit a few light-hearted, tender moments between the two into their escape. I grab a stress ball from my bowl of toys and squeeze it while working out what to write next.

It's a struggle to keep my mind from wandering off topic and imagining what Anna's face would look like if I told her my news in person. I'm sure she'd squeal with excitement and wrap me in a tight hug. My chest squeezes with longing for a real-life reenactment. It can only happen if I figure out how to reveal my dual identities to her in a way that doesn't make her feel like she's been duped.

I toss the ball into the air and catch it, repeating this action several times, hoping the repetitive movement will dislodge a plausible idea for either the book or my real-life conundrum.

June 26

Dear Winston,

OH. MY. GOODNESS. Winston, you didn't. The lavender stationery is amazing! It's just like yours, only it has my initials on it. You're probably wondering why I'm not using it for this note, but I just can't bring myself to sully one page or envelope yet.

By the way, how did you know my middle initial? The paper is so pretty. I promise my next letter to you will be on the stationery. Thank you so much! You are so thoughtful. I just can't believe you'd send me such a wonderful gift. Okay, that came out wrong. You are a kind person, so I can believe it, but it just hadn't occurred to me I'd be the recipient of such a thoughtful gesture. Thank you. You are a wonderful friend. I'd say you're the best, but my real life best friend, Penny, might get offended. Enough gushing. Let's move on to more important stuff.

Based on the clues, I'm going to guess that you wrote a fantasy romance. Is it YA like your sci-fi novels? And now you're working on a thriller fantasy romance?! I don't know that I've ever heard of that. Sounds interesting for sure.

What would I do if someone I loved was kidnapped? Whatever it took to get them back. I would gather up whatever amount of ransom money was asked.

I'd go to the police, try to hire someone to go after them (are there mercenary type people you can pay to track down a loved one or is that the CIA?), offer myself as an exchange. Anything and everything.

I can't even imagine how to get through a day when someone is suffering because of me. Honestly, I'd be paralyzed with horror and sadness. I guess it's good you're only asking hypothetically. I'd hate to be in that position, though I know it happens all the time around the world. How people face another day not knowing what's happening to their friend or family member, I don't know. It's truly heartbreaking to think about.

Wow, this letter took a bleak turn. I'm not sure how to come back from that, other than to be glad Dwayne has a fondness for the color blue. He's a real conundrum. Who knew a rock could have such a complex personality? Plants certainly aren't this difficult. Maybe I should make my own rock and see what he or she is like. Any suggestions for a name (please don't say Kid)?

I really enjoyed the TLF show. They played quite a few songs I knew the words to. Their original stuff wasn't bad, but since it was the first time I'd heard it, I can't say whether I really like it. Maybe I'll listen to it again. Regardless, I'd definitely be down for seeing them again.

I would love an advance copy of Ciara's story if you can swing it. I won't hold my breath, though, because I know how these things work. Sometimes my friend, Rachel, who works at PTB, gives me an ARC she's read and liked. Publishers send ARCs to the store all the time hoping to have their book promoted in the window. I'll tell her to keep an eye out. Let me know if you hear anything about your special project. I'm very intrigued!

Sincerely, Anna

30

Anna

STEPPING INSIDE GLI Amanti, my eyes scan the room in search of Zach. He waves at me from the bar and I make my way over.

"The hostess said our table should be ready in a few minutes. Would you like something to drink while we wait?"

"A glass of wine would be great."

Zach gets the bartender's attention and orders two glasses of Chianti. We've just gotten our drinks when the hostess calls Zach's name. We follow her to a small booth in a back corner of the restaurant. The lights are low and instrumental music plays throughout the restaurant, making this quite an inviting and intimate place to eat. Does Zach have romance on the brain this evening? I wouldn't mind that at all.

We make small talk about our workweeks until we've placed our orders. Then Zach takes my hand and looks deep into my eyes, his expression serious. My stomach flips at the intensity.

"Anna, these few weeks, getting to know you have been so much fun. I like that we've been able to hike and see one of my favorite bands. Every time I learn something new about you, I like you even more."

My heart warms at his positive words. It almost feels like he's leading to a proposal or something. My eyes widen briefly that this might be *the* proposal, but I toss that thought away. We barely know each other. We haven't even *kissed*, for goodness' sake. I mentally chastise myself and refocus on the cute, sincere guy across from me.

"I haven't felt this comfortable with a woman in a long time. I was looking forward to seeing if this thing developing between us might go the distance."

Was? Uh oh. Might as well get it out in the open, so I don't spend time catastrophizing in my mind.

"But…?"

He flashes me a small smile. "I just found out my mom has cancer."

Compassion wells up in my chest. "Oh, Zach. Oh no, that's terrible."

"Yeah. The doctors have said it's early enough that they should be able to get rid of it with surgery and chemo."

I squeeze his hand and give him a reassuring look. "Well, that's something."

He nods. "It is. And I'm sure you're wondering what that has to do with us."

I mean, yeah, but I didn't want to be rude and shift the conversation away from the real concern. I sit still, waiting.

"I'm an only child and my dad left when I was a kid, so it's just the two of us. She lives in Charleston and I'm going to move down there so I can help her with treatment and anything else that comes up. I know a four-hour drive might not seem like much, but I know myself. I'll be so focused on Mom that I'll end up neglecting you and you don't deserve that, which is why I wanted to be honest up front."

Zach is such a great guy. He obviously loves his mom, and he's been very respectful of me. I'm disappointed things between us are ending, but it's certainly nothing that could be helped.

"I understand. I can't say I'm not disappointed because I have also enjoyed our time together, but you need to do what is best for your family. You're a wonderful son and have been a fun date."

He gives me a grateful smile. "Thanks for being so understanding, Anna. I wish things could be different, but…"

"I know."

A server sets a basket of garlic knots between us, and he releases my hand. At least I hadn't yet fully invested myself in the relationship. Of course, if I'm honest, it's because part of me is still holding out hope that Winston might be the real deal. I mean, he sent me monogrammed stationery in my favorite color. And, thanks to an internet search, I know it's *expensive* stationery. I should have known by the thickness of the paper and embellishments around the monogram, but still. Who spends three hundred dollars on some paper and envelopes?! Certainly not me. Most of my correspondence materials come from the dollar store.

"So," I say, hoping to avoid any awkwardness between us. "Are you taking all your furniture-making stuff with you?"

"Yes. I'm taking everything that will fit in my truck and giving up my apartment. I don't know if I'll come back to Asheville once she's cancer-free. Charleston may end up being a great place for my business. All those fancy old houses must need some one-of-a-kind pieces for their sitting rooms."

He gives me a conspiratorial grin, which I can't help but

respond to. My heart pangs with regret that I probably won't see his lovely smiles after tonight. "I'm sure you'll do great."

"If you ever visit the area for vacation or whatever, please give me a call. It'd be nice to see you and catch up."

"Sure thing. I've heard great things about the city but never been."

Our food comes and Zach shares all the must-see places and a long list of great restaurants. I tease him by giving him my own play-by-play of everything to do, see, and eat in St. Louis if he ever heads to the Midwest. I haven't been home for two years and my mom is on me to come for either Thanksgiving or Christmas this year. I'll probably go over Thanksgiving just because I miss Mom's famous stuffing and cranberry salad. Attempts to recreate them last year were unsuccessful.

When dinner is finished, Zach pays despite my attempt to cover my half, then walks me to my car. "Take care of yourself, Anna."

"I will. Let me know how things go with your mom. I'll be thinking about you both."

He pulls me in for a hug. "See, that's one of the many reasons I like you. You genuinely care about other people."

When he steps back, he gives me a sad smile, then opens my door for me. I see him waving in the rear-view mirror as I drive away. That was definitely not how I thought this date would go when I was getting ready earlier this evening. I'm definitely bummed things didn't work out. I groan, realizing this probably means I have to return to Blind Date and a Book. I'm so tired of first dates. Can't I just find "the one" and settle down in a love cocoon already?

Okay, so I don't truly believe in "the one," but I'd like to find someone who loves me well and who I can love back. Maybe I should be more forthcoming about my feelings with Winston. At least then I can find out if he possibly feels the same and if we might actually try a real-life relationship. I realize this means potentially ruining our very wonderful pen pal relationship, but I need more. I have enough friends; I want love. And I'm going to use my super amazing new stationery when I tell him. This thought is both exciting and terrifying. I'm definitely on the edge of a precipice, like I was with Brody the other day. There's no telling what will happen when I jump, but I can't stand still any longer. It's time to make a move and deal with the consequences.

June 29

Dear Winston,

I know I just wrote to you, and there's a chance I may receive a letter from you before you receive this one, but there's something I have to say. I like you. These letters between us have been more open and honest than some of my in-person relationships, so I figured why stop now?

I realize you may not feel the same way as I do and, if so, that's fine. I'm prepared to continue our friendly correspondence, but I would be doing myself a disservice if I didn't at least tell you the truth and find out whether my feelings are reciprocated.

It might sound crazy to you that someone could develop feelings simply through correspondence, but I know how I feel. Though I must admit, I've had fearful thoughts that somehow I've gotten you all wrong. Some of my friends think you could be a woman or that there might be a huge age gap between us. I must admit that those two things would quickly put a damper on my feelings.

BUT, if you are indeed a mean between thirty and fifty years old, like I believe, then I'd really like the opportunity to see if we could have more than just a letter correspondence.

I'm tempted to ball this up and throw it away out of fear I'm screwing everything up between us, but I must know. Also, this stationery is way too pretty to throw in the trash. I even went out and bought a fancy pen because my usual blue Bic just didn't seem right.

Desperately awaiting a response, Anna

*   P.S.-Even if it's a "no," please write back. Not hearing from you ever again would be agony.*

31

Brody

I'VE RETURNED TO the library to work on my newest project. I enjoyed hearing Anna's thoughts on what to do in such a desperate situation as having a loved one kidnapped. Aurelia, my main character, has cycled through the emotions of despair, devastation, helplessness, and has landed firmly in anger and a desire for vengeance. Since it's become a fantasy thriller, there aren't police or a CIA to help return her beloved Beorn, but there is a secret guild of mercenary magicians she's now on the hunt to find. Of course, there's a risk of being killed for even attempting to locate them, but she has no other options.

I've really enjoyed making my own twists on the usual fantasy story and hope my audience will love it as well. I don't actually have an audience yet for my fantasy romance, but Mark and Petrocius are both convinced I will and are putting resources into marketing it. They've scrambled to get it through editing and are already sending out ARCs. They were serious about getting it out quickly. Mark got the publisher to agree to a one-book deal, though they've requested first look at whatever else I create. I can live with that. Especially since they've given me a lucrative contract.

Leaning back against the chair, I clasp my hands and lift them over my head to stretch out my back and shoulders. I tilt my head side-to-side and around in circles to work out any kinks in my neck and remove my headphones to give my ears a break from being squished for so long. The noise of the library rushes into my ears, giving me a bit of a start: the clacking of the keyboards at the computers, someone laughing softly, the thud of a book being dropped on a table. My ears focus in on one voice in particular somewhere to my right in the nonfiction stacks.

"…since we met at Gli Amanti. But it didn't end up being romantic at all."

"Oh no, what happened?"

It's Anna and Penny.

"Zach's mom has cancer, and he's moving to Charleston to be with her."

"That's terrible, but so sweet of him."

Anna chuckles, but there's a note of bitterness in it. "Yeah, it is. But it also means he broke up with me."

"Oh, Anna. I'm so sorry."

I hate that Anna got dumped, but am relieved to realize I've been given a new chance to express my feelings for her. I can ask her out on an actual date now, instead of pretending I just want to be friends. Though, should I give her some space first, time to heal any heartache or something like that? I don't want to risk taking too much time, but I don't want to be insensitive.

"Well, yeah, but at least I wasn't over the moon for him or anything. My feelings weren't nearly as invested as they are with Winston."

I hear a deep sigh.

"Seriously, Anna? You're still clinging to this mystery pen pal?"

"Look, I took your advice, okay? I wrote him a letter and told him how I felt. The next time I hear from him, I'll know if we have a chance or if it was all in my head."

She's telling Winston she likes him?! Oh man, this is big. What am I going to do? It's great that she likes him, but what if she doesn't like *me* as him? If I can get her to go on an actual date with me, it might help her see my potential. Or do the complete opposite and cement me firmly in the friendship zone. Either way, I have to do something soon. But how do I do it without looking like a jerk?

She told me she was seeing someone, which I said I respected. I can't ask her out now unless I admit I overheard her conversation. And even then, she was *just* dumped. I feel like I'm stuck between a rock and a hard place.

"Did you also ask him if he's really a man?"

"Yes. And how old he is. You happy, Pen?"

It hadn't even occurred to me she wouldn't know those details about me. The lack of information about M.B. Winston online means the author could be anyone. I will clear that up when I write Anna back, though it sounds like I'm going to have to wait for this newest letter to arrive.

"Honestly, I just want you to be happy. If this Winston person turns out to be the real deal, then great. But what if it doesn't work out?"

"I know you do. I still have two Blind Date and a Book options left. Who knows? Maybe one of those guys will be the man of my dreams."

"Zach certainly had potential, so it's possible you'll find

another great guy."

"Let's hope. Deb and Rachel are the two members still unchosen. I'm a little worried about Deb's pick since she's in her seventies. I'm afraid she doesn't know any men my age."

Blind Date and a Book! That's my answer. Maybe I can somehow finagle my way into being one of their choices. I have no idea who Deb is, but I at least know where to find Rachel. Clinging to this tiny shred of possibility, I gather all my stuff together and make a hasty exit. I reach Page Turner Books in just under a minute, having sprinted down Haywood Street. At the front door to the store, I take a minute to brush down my hair and straighten my shirt. I should at least look presentable when I make my proposal.

The bell dings when I enter, and I head straight toward the checkout counter and the man I talked to last time I was in. "Hi, Brett. Is Rachel working today?"

He gives me a weird look. Must not remember me.

"I'm Brody. You helped me find a signed copy of her book last time I was in."

His gaze narrows suspiciously. "Why do you want to see Rachel?"

I'm embarrassed to admit what I'm scheming, but maybe he can help. "I wanted to talk to her about the Blind Date and a Book thing they're doing for one of her book club members."

Brett's mouth quirks up in a smirk and his eyes soften. "Yeah, that's a pretty crazy concept. You want them to set you up next? You know the group is called Book *Babes*, right?"

"No, I didn't know that, but I don't want to join the group. May I please talk to Rachel?"

He gives me an assessing look before clicking a button on his headset. "Rachel to the front, pronto."

We stand in awkward silence until a woman arrives wearing jeans, a shirt that says *SUPPORT YOUR LOCAL BOOKSTORE*, and brown hair in a bun on top of her head.

"This better not be some sort of prank, Brett. There's a lot of inventory in the back, and I won't be happy if I'm stuck here until ten o'clock."

Brett grins at her like the Cheshire Cat.

"Unfortunately, it's not, but thanks for the suggestion." She juts out her hip and looks like she's about to lay into him, when he holds up a hand and tilts his head in my direction. "This customer has a question about your book club."

She clamps her mouth shut, then turns to me with surprise in her eyes. "Hi," she says. "I'm Rachel."

I shake the hand she holds out to me. "Brody."

"We don't currently have any men in our club. It's not exclusively for women, but we read a lot of romance, which isn't generally men's cup of tea."

I glance over at Brett, who has his arms crossed and is blatantly listening to our conversation. Oh well. Guess I'm doing this with an audience.

"No, um. I heard about your Blind Date and a Book thing you're doing for Anna. And, uh, I was wondering…" My back feels sweaty and I have an urge to scratch my neck. I fist my hands to keep them from fidgeting. "Um, I know your book hasn't been picked and wanted to see if maybe I could be the guy she dates when she picks it?"

Rachel's eyes widen in surprise. Brett guffaws next to me, but I don't look in his direction. Rachel's the one with my fate in her hands.

"Oh! I see. Do you know Anna?"

I nod. "I see her in the library a lot and we've been hiking together."

She furrows her brow, thinking. "I suppose the rules don't say anything about the date having to be a complete stranger. However, I don't want to freak Anna out. Huh. This is an odd situation."

"Yeah. And I'm sure you already have a guy lined up. I hadn't really thought this whole thing through. Now that I'm thinking about it, this probably isn't a great plan. Sorry to waste your time."

I turn to go, but Rachel catches me by the wrist. "Hold on a second. I didn't say 'no.' I just need to think."

She releases my arm, looking out across the bookstore. I hold my breath, wondering what's going to happen. Finally, her gaze swings back to me.

"Tell me why you want to be set up on a date with Anna. Why not just ask her out?"

I take a deep breath, then blurt out my answer. "I'm afraid she only sees me as a friend. If we can go on an actual date, perhaps I can get shifted over to relationship material. Anna's such an amazing person. She's kind, generous, fun, and so smart. She helps everyone she can and truly sees each person she comes in contact with. She makes you feel known and special with the penetrating questions she asks. I look forward to seeing her in the library and find myself scanning the crowds whenever I'm out, hoping to catch a glimpse of her. Her warm, bubbly personality is so attractive to me. Not to mention she's gorgeous. I just want the opportunity to show her who I really am."

I've said too much. It's obvious by the way Rachel's mouth is hanging open in shock. A glance at Brett reveals a similar surprised expression. Swinging my head back to Rachel, it appears the co-workers are having a wordless conversation right in front of me. The silence is deafening. I'm tempted to slink away after such a raw confession, but this feels like my best bet, so I tough out the interminable wait. Finally, Rachel looks at me.

"Wow, okay. That's a lot, but in a good way. I believe you know her and care about her. However, I need to see if she'd be open to dating you."

My mouth opens, but she shakes her head, and I stay silent.

"I'm not going to tell her what you said. I'm just going to ask some feeler questions. Trust me. Give me your phone number and I'll call you and let you know if I'll help with your plan."

I deflate a little. It's not a yes, but it's not a no. I'll just have to be patient. Rachel seems genuine, so hopefully things will go my way.

I give her my number and thank her for her time, then head home, where I find a lavender envelope in my mailbox. My pulse picks up, knowing this contains world-changing words. There's a cardboard box on my front step that makes me grunt when I grab it. When I get to the living room, I set the box on the coffee table and tear open the envelope. My eyes scan the letter, my heart hammering in my throat. She likes me. Well, she likes *Winston*. I guess I haven't done enough sharing in my letters if she's doubting my own feelings, but that's definitely something I can remedy. I find a pair of scissors in my kitchen's junk drawer and slice through the tape holding the box closed. Inside are advance copies of the fantasy romance. There's a dragon silhouetted against a bright white moon on a blue background and *Dragons of Moon Kingdom* written on top in fancy gold lettering. It looks amazing.

Thumbing through the pages, an idea sparks in my mind. If Anna wants to know how Winston feels about her, he's going to show her in a way that will leave no doubt.

32

Anna

USUALLY, HANGING OUT with my book club is my favorite thing, but I'm dreading having to tell the group about Zach, even though this emergency book club meeting makes it pretty obvious what happened. They'll be sympathetic for sure, but then they'll encourage me to get right back on the horse, so to speak, and I just don't know if I'm ready to go out with someone new. Plus, I'm still waiting to hear from Winston. It's only been a couple of days since I sent the letter, but my stomach's been in knots, wondering what he's going to say. The waiting is the worst part of old school correspondence. I've gotten so used to texts and emails. It was a quaint concept when things weren't so complicated. Now, I just want to know if there's hope for something more or if the infatuation is one-sided.

I'm the last to arrive at book club. Not surprising since I dragged my feet getting over here. It's near the library, but I grabbed a burger at B4 first and may have been rooted to the table until Deb texted me, asking me where I was. She sees me first and rushes over to pull me into a hug.

"Everything okay?" she whispers into my ear. "You're missing your sparkle this evening."

I sigh, melting into her embrace. "Nothing catastrophic. Just feeling a little morose."

"Is this about Zach?"

I pull back from our hug. "Yes, but it'll be easier for me just to tell the story once."

She nods, then grabs my arm and leads me over to a seat. "You sit right here. I'll bring you some refreshments."

I give her a grateful smile. While she's busy at the table, Rachel plops down next to me. "Hey, Anna. How are you?"

I shrug. "I've been better."

She frowns. "Oh no. What happened?"

"I'll fill everyone in once we're all seated."

Rachel's pinched eyebrows fill me with gratitude at her concern. This is right where I need to be when I'm feeling sorry for myself. The Book Babes are such a wonderful, understanding group. By the time I leave tonight, there's a good chance I'll be feeling much better. She just nods and squeezes my arm affectionately before standing up. "Okay, gang. Get your goodies and then have a seat. Anna needs us."

There's a flurry of activity as everyone gets food and settles into the circle of chairs. Deb hands me a cup of coffee and a plate filled with truffles. There's no way I'm going to be able to eat all of them, but I appreciate the sentiment. Once everyone's in a chair, all eyes turn to Rachel.

"Great to see everyone. Don't worry if you haven't finished this month's pick yet because we're not talking about it tonight. Instead, Anna's going to tell us why we're here."

Seven pairs of eyes swing to me. "Hey, all. So, you know how things were going well with Zach?" A chorus of nods. "Well, his mom was just diagnosed with cancer, so he's moving to Charleston to focus on her and we broke up."

Everyone responds at once.

"Oh no."

"Poor Zach."

"Poor Anna."

"I'm sorry."

"That sucks."

Abbie's unvarnished assessment brings a small smile to my face. "Yeah, I'm obviously disappointed, but I can't be mad. I'd rush home, too, if it was my mom."

"So what now?" Susan asks.

I grimace. "I'm not sure. There are still two Blind Date and a Book options, but I don't know if I'm ready to jump into something else. I'm not sure if my heart can currently give a new person a fair chance, ya know?"

"I don't mean to sound callous," Rachel says carefully, "but did you have such strong feelings for Zach already that you're heartbroken?"

Wow, she got right to the heart of the matter.

"Truthfully, no. He definitely had long-term potential, but to be honest, I've kind of been into this other person."

"You've been seeing two people?" Meredith says, surprised.

I shake my head. "No." Brody flashes in my mind, but I quickly push the thought of him away. "Not really. I've been writing letters back and forth with someone."

Lori sighs wistfully. "Sounds so romantic."

I can't help grinning. "It kind of is. Except, I don't actually know who he is."

"What?" The circle of confused faces almost makes me laugh.

"Okay, bear with me as I try to explain this. I received a letter last year from someone named M.B. Winston."

Rachel's brow furrows. "That name sounds familiar."

"It should. He's an author who writes YA sci-fi books."

Her eyes round and her mouth drops open. *"Into the Unknown?"*

"That's the one."

"Wow! That's a crazy coincidence."

"Coincidence how?"

She shakes her head. "Nevermind."

Abbie turns toward me. "So, what does he look like?"

"I don't know."

Rachel notices the perplexed expressions around the circle and explains. "M.B. Winston is kind of a recluse. The author uses a pen name and has never done an in-person event. There has been lots of speculation in the book world that maybe it's someone famous who doesn't want their identity revealed, but, of course, they could very well be an octogenarian who lives in Nebraska."

I nod. "My friend Penny is worried I'm falling for a woman or a retiree."

"Let me get this straight," Lori says. "You've been writing letters to a stranger and have developed feelings for them, but you don't know their gender or age, let alone what they might look like?"

"Yeah. Not the most ideal situation, but I sent him a letter confessing my feelings and asking for those revealing details, so we'll see what he says. Yes, I think it's a man. Just the things he's said make me believe that. And I don't think he's old because we both like the same things, but I honestly don't know."

"Don't discount the possibility that he's a silver fox," Lori says. "Some older men are quite sexy."

"Anyway, I kind of feel like I'm waiting to see what happens with him before putting myself out there again."

"Have you talked to him about meeting in person? Does he live nearby?" Susan asks.

"We'd actually scheduled a meetup, but something came up and he wasn't able to make it. He lives in the area because he has an Asheville PO box and knows about Little Shop of Sugar."

"He does?" Julie looks pleased. "I sure wish we had more clues about his identity."

"You're telling me."

It's quiet while everyone considers the situation. Rachel's the first to break the silence.

"So, you're interested in your pen pal, whom you haven't yet met. Is there anyone you *have* met, besides Zach, who's caught your eye?"

I open my mouth to reply in the negative, but a man in a blue hat pops into my mind, making me pause. Rachel's eyes light up. "Oooh, tell us!"

I shake my head. "It's nothing, really. I went hiking once with a guy who frequents the library and have seen him around town a few times, but I don't know."

"Is he cute?"

Leave it to Lori to look for romance everywhere. Unfortunately, my answer is just going to egg her on.

"He is," I say reluctantly.

She claps her hands in delight. "Do you have a photo of him?"

I'm about to shake my head, but then I remember Brody texted me an image he snapped of us at the end of our hike. Pulling out my phone, I open our thread and click on the photo. "It really doesn't show much because he's wearing a hat and sunglasses."

Lori holds out her hand, and I pass the phone to her. She squeals when she sees it.

"He *is* quite handsome. I wish I could see his eyes, but his body language makes it clear he likes you."

"What?"

I make an impatient waving motion with my hand to get the phone back, but Lori ignores me. Instead, she shows it to Susan, who nods. "Yeah. I'd say he's interested."

The rest of the group gets up and crowds around Lori for their own view of the picture. All of them give me an amused look, making me feel flustered. I slump back in my chair, knowing there's nothing I can do to prevent the inevitable teasing.

"What's his name?" Abbie says.

"Brody."

"And do you think he has potential?"

I shrug. Since I was dating Zach, I hadn't allowed myself to think of Brody as anything other than a friend, but we did have fun together on the hike. And there was that one moment while we were sitting on the rocks, but that memory is just for me.

"Maybe. But there's still Winston."

"What if he says he just wants to be friends?" Meredith asks.

My heart twists painfully. "If he were to say that, then that's how it'd be. But until I hear, my emotions are in limbo."

"Do you really want to put all of your emotional eggs in one basket?" Abbie chimes in.

I scowl. She has a point, but it doesn't mean I have to like it. "I mean, yeah. I'd like to focus all my energy and emotions on one person, ideally."

"Fair point. But why not explore both and see where they lead?"

I suppose there's no reason I shouldn't do that, except... "Brody frequents the library a lot. It would be awkward to have to see him so much if we went on a date and it turned out to be a disaster."

"But what if it wasn't a disaster? Then you'd have even more reasons to enjoy going to work."

Abbie's words surprise me. I've been used to her being pessimistic about relationships and love. This turn about has me a little flustered. "When did you get to be such a hopeless romantic?"

She grins. "I guess that's what falling in love did to me."

I roll my eyes, then look around the room. Every woman in here is or has been in love. Deb lost her husband years ago, but has a gaggle of grandchildren to love now and seems quite content. Susan and Lori have been married for decades. Rachel, Julie, Meredith, and Abbie are more recently in love, but watching them meet their guys and fall in love has given me hope there's someone out there for me as well. So why am I reluctant to explore every avenue available to me? I sigh.

"I don't know about Brody, but I suppose it won't hurt to try another Blind Date and a Book."

Rachel's eyes spark with something I can't quite identify. Mischievousness maybe? She walks over to the bank of lockers and opens the one in the right corner, pulling out two brown paper packages. She comes back to the circle and sits down. The women who were crowded around Lori, take their seats as well. Lori hands me back my phone and I take a quick peek at the picture. Brody's got a wide, warm smile on his face. It's hard to imagine what he's thinking with his eyes hidden behind sunglasses, but I notice that he's leaning toward me, our shoulders touching. Is his body language revealing romantic interest? I can't tell.

"Alright," Rachel says. "I know you're waiting to hear from

your author friend, Anna, but you might as well try another face-to-face date. Who knows? Maybe one of these two books will lead you to love."

She passes the wrapped books around the circle to me. I read the first description.

An epic quest. An unlikely heroine. Confounding clues that must be deciphered or all will be lost.

I like the sound of that. I feel like an unlikely heroine in my quest for love. I scan the second one.

A secret buried in an ancient garden. Once uncovered, it has the potential to destroy the world as we know it. Two time travelers are our only hope.

That sounds interesting as well. I don't have any idea what kind of date that would be. I seriously doubt I'd be doing some time traveling. However, I'm in the mood to root for the underdog. "Both of these sound amazing, but I'm picking the epic quest."

Rachel pumps her fist in the air. "Yessss! That's my book." Her smile turns into a grimace. "Uh, I'm sorry in advance if it makes you uncomfortable. I had no idea when I picked it."

It's my turn to frown. What's she talking about? As soon as I remove the paper, my stomach drops with understanding. "*Into the Unknown.*"

"Yeah," she chuckles nervously. "I wanted to find something by a local writer and it sounded interesting. I had no idea you were connected to the author. I can pick another book if you want."

I take a deep breath. "No. It's fine. The story is really good. Let's just go with it."

"Okay. Give me some dates when you're free and I'll set

everything up."

My brow furrows. "Does this mean we're discussing two books at the next meeting?"

Rachel lifts a shoulder and looks around at the group. "What do you all think?"

Lori wrinkles her nose. "To be honest, I haven't really gotten into *Mr. Marple's Mortuary*."

"Me either," says Meredith.

Nodding heads around the circle shows a consensus. "Alright," Rachel says, "then let's abandon that one and read *Into the Unknown*."

We wrap up the meeting and head out. On the drive home, my stomach cycles between dread at what Winston's going to say and nervousness about agreeing to another blind date. I know I need to give the guy a fair chance. Who says he won't turn out to be the love of my life? *Highly unlikely*, my mind retorts. Still, I have to move forward. I can't wait around for a letter that may never come.

33

Brody

MY PHONE RINGS. The screen shows an unknown number, but it's got a local area code, so I answer.

"Hey, Brody, this is Rachel Price from Page Turner Books."

My pulse spikes. This is either good or bad news for me, but her calm, casual voice gives nothing away.

"Hi, Rachel. Are you calling with your verdict?"

"Yes. I've decided that you can be my blind date pick."

My shoulders sag with relief. One obstacle down. Now Anna just needs to pick her book.

"Thank you. I really appreciate your help. So what now? You'll call me back if she picks your book?"

Rachel chuckles. "That would be the case, except she chose my book tonight."

Whoa. We're just jumping right into this. I anticipated having some time to prepare for going on a real date with Anna.

"Okay…so when's the date?"

"Anna is free this Sunday. Would that work with your schedule?"

Three days from now? Not a lot of time to wrap my head around everything. But I've made great strides in feeling comfortable around her. This should be fine. "I can do Sunday. What did you have in mind for an activity?"

"You two are going to do an escape room together. There's a fun place downtown near Pritchard Park. And then I thought you two could go to dinner somewhere. Maybe sushi or tacos? She likes both of those."

Will the pressure of solving puzzles activate my anxiety? I haven't been to an escape room before, so there's no way to tell.

"How many people are in one of those rooms at once?"

"Usually four to ten."

Okay, so not too many people to worry about being the focus of attention. Though, having strange eyes watch me in a pressure-filled situation doesn't sound ideal.

"Do people feel trapped or squished together? Is it panic-inducing with the time limit?"

"I think it's just fun. It can feel a little crowded if there are ten people, but some rooms are actually two rooms which help spread things out. The group can ask for hints if they get stuck on a puzzle, so it's got a little excitement, but I wouldn't say there's pressure. If this sounds like too much, I can switch the date to Well Played Board Game Café as long as you agree to play Clue® while you're there."

I've been to Well Played. It's an expansive room that feels kind of like a cafeteria with walls of games to choose from. Definitely no chance of feeling claustrophobic, though there would be more people. Not that anyone pays attention to anyone else.

However, I want to challenge myself to get out of my comfort zone more. I don't want anxiety to rule my life anymore.

"An escape room sounds like a unique challenge. Plenty of people like them. We'll stick with your regular plan. Have you told her the date is with me?"

"No, I'd kind of like it to be a surprise. Can you tell me something you could wear that would make you easy to pick out?"

I grin, knowing just the thing. "My blue baseball cap. Anna will recognize it immediately."

"Great. I'll text you with the address and time."

"Thanks so much for helping me out, Rachel."

We hang up and I fist pump the air a few times. So far, things are working out like I'd hoped. The only thing I can't control is what she'll feel when she sees me, but I have to hope since Rachel okayed this plan, there's a good chance her feelings will be positive.

The next morning, I sit down with a copy of Aurelia and Beorn's book. I flip past the title page and copyright section to the dedication. All it says is "Dedication [TK]." I grab a pen, cross it out, and write my own. *To Anna, my inspiration.* I'm not completely satisfied. It sounds a little too simple, but it'll do for now. Besides, I'll be including a note, which will say a lot more.

I skim through the first chapter until I find Aurelia's name. I circle it, draw a line to the margin, and write: *She has the same first letter as you. Aurelia means 'the golden one', which is how I see you.* I'm tempted to note that Beorn also shares my initial, but don't want to give too much away. She'll probably figure it out on her own, anyway.

Continuing through the story, I make notes for the scenes that are inspired by hearing her bad date stories. She'll probably recognize them, but I like the idea of annotating the whole thing. It feels like sharing little pieces of me with her. When I get to the dragon scene, I admit to imagining being the hero who slayed all her bad dates and rescued her from having to encounter any more people who did not recognize her value.

It takes me all day to get through the story and, by the end, there are markings all over the book. On the last page, I pause, wondering how to phrase what I want to say. An idea pops into my head and I flip the page over so that I'm staring at the blank Acknowledgments section. My pen flies over the page.

When I'm finished, I close the cover, satisfied the message is clear. After wrapping the book in paper and finding a bubble mailer, I grab a sheet of stationery and her last two letters. I read through them to see if there's anything I need to respond to besides admitting how I feel. My heart is in my throat as I write my true feelings down, anticipating her reaction. I'm tempted to go all out and admit that I love her, but am afraid that might scare her off. It'll probably be obvious when she reads the story, but better to wait and make a confession like that in person.

When I finish, I seal everything up in the envelope and set it by the front door so I'll see it the next time I go out.

I'm so keyed up from the day that, despite the late hour, I need to decompress. It's too dark to go for a run, so I carry my laptop into the guest bedroom where I have a treadmill. Setting the laptop on the stand, I turn the treadmill on to a comfortable walking pace and spend an hour working on my newest story. I'm so excited to be sharing the first one with Anna. I hope she likes it because I think this next one might be even better.

The treadmill belt slows to a stop after the time's up. I save what I've written, then take a shower. Only one more day before my date with Anna. I hope she's as excited to see me as I am to see her.

34

Anna

I'M A LITTLE nervous to be going on another date to an escape room. The last one didn't turn out great. Plus, Rachel wouldn't tell me the name of my date. She just said to look for a blue hat and asked me what I would wear so she could pass along the same info. I decided it's hard to miss me in my book leggings. They have pockets for my keys and phone and look cute paired with a white shirt and gray cardigan. It's too casual to wear to work, but is frequently my outfit at home.

I've been to Breakout Games before. I told Rachel which rooms I've done so I could visit a new room this time. However, after the stress of working the room with Josh, maybe I should have asked for something familiar. Too late now.

When I step inside the front door, there's a group of people milling about. I don't see anyone in a blue hat. In fact, there aren't hats on any person in the room. Someone with a red Breakout shirt comes out from a door down the hall. "Who's here for Operation:

Casino?"

Most of the hands in the room go up.

"Come on back and we'll get started."

After they leave, there are only two other people standing in the lobby. A woman points toward a wall of photographs and a man follows her over to look at them, revealing a man sitting on a bench. He's staring down at his phone, a bright blue ball cap on his head. Something about his posture seems familiar. He must notice my approach because his head lifts and I see the letters K and C stitched across the front of the hat.

"Brody?"

He gives me a hesitant smile. "Hey, Anna. Nice pants. They're even better than I imagined." He squints, leaning closer. "Are there actually words printed on the pages?"

"No, just squiggles." I'm still processing what I'm seeing, so I speak my thoughts out loud to make sure I'm not misinterpreting things. "*You're* my blind date?"

"Yeah. I hope that's okay."

"How do you know Rachel?"

He presses his lips together, breaking eye contact. "Um, well. I don't." He shoves his phone into a pants pocket, then scratches his neck. "Not really, at least. I asked her if I could be her pick."

All thoughts screech to a halt in my brain. Brody finagled himself into a date with me? I can't even imagine what he might have said to Rachel to secure her agreement.

"Isn't that kind of cheating, though? I thought the whole point was for me to meet people I don't know?"

He tugs on the bill of his hat. "I, uh…maybe this wasn't a good idea. Do you want to cancel? We don't have to do this if it makes you uncomfortable."

He stands up, but I stop him by placing a hand on his chest.

His heart pounds against my fingertips. The wild look in his eyes reminds me of a deer about to bolt. His obvious distress concerns me. I don't want him to think he did anything wrong. I just need a minute to think.

He's frozen in place beneath my hand, his erratic heartbeat the only movement. Am I upset Brody's my date? No. I'm actually a little relieved it's someone I already know. He's got a comforting presence. I'm reminded of how in-charge he was when I fell at the waterfall with Zach, which is why it's so confusing whenever I see him acting skittish. Though, his admission of struggling with anxiety on our hike explains our varied interactions. An escape room is definitely a social situation. Maybe he's just really nervous. The thought softens something inside my chest. Is he worried I'm going to reject him? He apparently went to a lot of trouble to get me on a real date. Why didn't he just ask me out? He could be worried about messing up our friendship, which would be sweet. Or maybe he didn't know if I'd say yes otherwise. I was reluctant to go hiking with him, but that was partially because I was dating Zach. I should give him a chance. See if there might be something more than friendship between us. Realizing I've still got my hand pressed against Brody's body, I lower my arm and give him what I hope is a reassuring smile.

"Stay. I was just surprised to see a face I recognize, is all. It's actually kind of nice we're already familiar with one another."

His shoulders drop, and he gives me a grateful look. "Thanks, Anna. I knew I was taking a risk, but I didn't realize how scary it would be until right now."

Oh, my heart. What is it about displays of vulnerability? I guess it makes me feel like I'm safe to be myself with him, which is definitely something I'm looking for in a partner. I take a second to study Brody from his striking green eyes—have they always looked so bright and inviting?, to the bit of stubble on his chin—I wonder what it would feel like to rub my hand against it, his broad shoulders outlined through his plain black T-shirt—my fingers tingle from the memory of touching his chest only moments earlier, medium-wash jeans—a surprising change from khakis, and casual shoes. He looks like a regular guy. A regular, handsome, very in-shape man with kissable lips. *Get yourself together, Anna.*

Feeling a need to get back on less emotional ground, I wave my hand around the room. "Have you done an escape room before? Did Rachel tell you which one we're doing?"

"This will be my first time, but I believe with your outstanding intellect and my ability to follow commands, we'll be just fine. Though we're signed up for the Clue® game, which means we're trying to stop a murder."

The compliment he sandwiched in between his statements didn't fly over my head. I have to fight to keep my smile at a normal wattage. "That sounds like fun. Is it just you and me?"

Brody nods toward the couple on the other side of the room.

"They didn't have a reservation and our room can hold up to eight people, so I agreed to let them join us. I didn't think you'd mind, but I apologize if you do."

I shake my head. It's sweet he's willing to help them out. I'd have done the same. A Breakout employee comes down the hall, stopping once she reaches the foyer. "Is this everyone for Clue®?"

I step forward. "I think so." I turn toward the other couple. "I'm Anna. I think you've already met Brody."

"I'm Greg," the guy says, "and this is my sister Cat."

Now that he's said it, I can see a slight resemblance between the two.

"Follow me," the employee says.

She leads us into a room at the end of the hall, which looks almost exactly like the library in the movie. I wonder if it has a secret wall behind one of the shelves or something. There's an open doorway to the side that looks like it leads to a kitchen.

"Alright, everyone. If you've played the board game or seen the movie, you'll be familiar with your objectives: find out who's the murderer, what weapon was used, and in which room. This screen lists all your potential people, weapons, and rooms, which will help you keep track of the options you've ruled out based on clues you discover while you're playing the room. If you get stuck, you can ask for a hint by saying 'Oh, Butler!,' but everyone must be in agreement. After I shut the door, you'll have one hour to figure out all the clues. If you get it wrong, you'll have one more attempt to accuse the killer. Any questions?"

Everyone shakes their heads. I guess Brody's the only novice player. It gives me confidence we'll successfully complete the challenge.

As soon as the door thuds against the frame, Greg and Cat circle around the room in opposite directions, calling out what they see. They pull drawer handles, lift items on tables, and note lock locations. Brody and I just stand in the middle of the room. I catch his gaze and see he's as shocked as I am. We must be playing with professionals. He motions toward the doorway and I nod. We hurry into the kitchen and circle the room.

"Whoa, they're intense," Brody says. "Is there such a thing as speed escaping?"

I chuckle. "I'm sure there is. They definitely seem to be in a hurry."

Locating some random items that don't belong in the kitchen, we carry them back into the library and set them on a table where the other two have already set two opened locks.

"Wow, you guys must be super sleuths."

Cat nods. "Our best time is finishing with twenty-nine minutes left. We're hoping to get out with at least thirty today."

I'm suddenly not as excited that Brody was kind and let them join us. Are we going to get to do anything?

"I'm going to look at the kitchen again," Brody says, and I nod absently, trying to see if there's anything on the table that makes sense to me. It might if I checked out the library's walls. I turn toward the bookcase out of habit.

"I'll come with you," Cat says.

After a lap around the library, I'm confident I know what needs to be done with the books. There's a flash of movement through the kitchen doorway and I walk over there out of curiosity. Peeking my head in, I see Brody leaning against the kitchen counter, Cat's body pressing into his arm and her face angled up toward his. This looks more like flirting than playing a game. A spike of jealousy makes me narrow my eyes. I'm just about to turn away, afraid of experiencing déjà vu with my date flirting with another woman, when I register Brody's expression. His eyebrows are crinkled together, his lips turned down into a frown. His body is slowly leaning away from Cat. His eyes dart around the room, landing on mine. That look of panic from earlier is back. Okay, this is not what I thought it was. I knock on the door frame with my knuckles.

"Hey, Brody. I could use your help in the other room."

Relief flashes in his eyes. "O-okay, yeah. Coming, Anna."

He gently peels Cat off of him, then crosses to the doorway with two long strides. I lead him over to the bookshelf. When we stop moving, he takes a few deep breaths, releasing them slowly.

"You okay?"

"I am now, thanks. She just kind of snuck up on me and then I felt trapped."

I'm angry on his behalf, but also a little unnerved at the strong swell of emotion I felt when I saw them together. "You know, she is cute. It would be understandable if you were flirting."

He gives me a look like I'm suggesting something crazy. "N-no, Anna. Why would I flirt with her? I want to be with you."

I have to lock my knees to keep from being knocked down by that powerful declaration. Brody is not pulling any punches tonight. I guess he already admitted to orchestrating this set up. Well, he's definitely got me looking at him differently tonight. I'm not sure what to think about the man standing in front of me. However, now probably isn't the time to figure it out because we're on the clock. Which is reinforced by the sound of a latch releasing.

"Yessss!" Greg says, tossing the lock onto the table.

"We'd better get on it if we want to solve any of the puzzles ourselves," I say.

He nods, then walks over to the table to assess what's on top. He picks up a flashlight, then walks over to a print on the wall. Meanwhile, I scour the bookshelf, pulling off books with letters printed on the bottom of the spine.

Five of them look like they might be clues, so I search for a lock that needs five letters. It's securing the fridge in the kitchen. I work through a bunch of combinations before finally hearing a satisfying click. I grin, pulling the lock out and opening the latch. I gasp when I open the door and look inside.

"Guys!" I yell, shutting the door again.

"What is it?" Cat says, hands on her hips, her foot tapping impatiently.

Managing not to match her scowl, I swing the door open to reveal an opening into a room beyond.

"So cool!" Brody says, coming closer and holding his hand up for a high five. I slap it, pleased by his enthusiasm.

Cat ducks inside, quickly followed by Greg. Brody peers into the space after them, then motions me back into the library.

"I'm sorry about those two. Are you having fun anyway?"

"You didn't know what they'd be like. And, hey, I found a secret passageway. That's always cool."

He nods. "I think this print on the wall has a clue, but can't figure it out. Something seems off. Maybe you can help me?"

He hands me the flashlight and I shine it over the surface. Some of the letters do look a little weird. Like they're in a different font type, but it could just be my eyes playing tricks on me. Brody leans against the wall next to me, watching as I shine the flashlight around. The weight of his gaze on me makes my heart beat a little faster. Especially when my eyes dart to his lips, which are curved up into a warm smile. I swallow a sigh, imagining how they might feel against my own, and remind myself of the current objective to escape the room. But I can still have a little fun, right? We are playing a game, after all.

Summoning my flirty side, I look over at him and wink. His mouth drops open in surprise and he starts sliding down the wall. Suddenly, the room goes completely dark. My eyes blink rapidly, trying to adjust to the lack of light before noticing bright pink markings on the wall in front of me. It dawns on me that I'm holding a black light. The weird letters from before are now obviously numbers. Three of them. Well, five numbers actually, but in three separate combinations: seven, nineteen, and twenty-four.

I look over at Brody, who's now standing next to me, gaping at the wall. I swing the flashlight to the left, just making out a light switch. I lean forward and flip it up. The lights return. I don't think there have been light switches in other rooms I've played. I'll be sure to keep an eye out for them in the future.

"Good teamwork," I say, chuckling.

He smiles at me. I hear footsteps behind us. Turning, Greg is standing in the doorway to the kitchen.

"Hey, we're down to the last lock. I think it'll reveal the name of the murderer. Have you seen anything with three numbers?"

My gaze swings over to the electronic board. Sure enough, all the weapons have been crossed out except for the candlestick, and the only active location is the billiards room. The remaining suspects are Miss Scarlet and Professor Plum. When did they figure all of this out? At the top of the board is the running clock. We've been in here for twenty-five minutes. I look at Brody, who gives me a shrug.

"Maybe," I say, heading toward Greg. "Let's see what hides in the fridge."

Greg rolls his eyes, then gets down on all fours to crawl through the small space. Brody motions for me to follow Greg, and then enters behind me. With all four of us in the room, it's cramped. It just looks like a storage room with a broom, bucket, toolbox, and a wall of tools.

"Where's the lock?" I ask.

Cat motions to the toolbox, which is closed with a combination lock. I frown, remembering the last time I was faced with one of these. Despite my post-high school dreams about not being able to get into my locker before my trigonometry test, I'd never had issues with the locks at school. I think it was the pressure and stress of Josh that threw me for a loop. Looking at Cat and Greg, who are both sporting extremely serious looks, I feel my anxiety rising. A hand on my shoulder, turns my attention to Brody.

"What's going on in your head, Anna?"

How can he tell I'm freaking out? The gentle pressure of his hand is reassuring and I find myself wishing I could lean into his body for physical support. But that would be weird. I shake my head, trying to get myself to focus. "I don't want to let anyone down."

He gives me a reassuring smile. "Just do your best. This is supposed to be fun."

I give my body a little wiggle, shaking out my arms, hoping the motion will diffuse a little of my nerves. The movement knocks Brody's hand from my shoulder and I immediately feel the loss. Taking a deep breath, I turn toward the nemesis lock and spin it all the way around the dial, before focusing in. My first attempt is unsuccessful. Cat whistles through her teeth, impatient. I try again, but the lock still doesn't budge.

"What's the number?" Greg growls. I feel him looming over me and I shrink in on myself.

"She's got this," Brody says loudly, moving into Greg's space until he backs up away from me. "You've got this," he says gently to me, his body blocking me from the siblings.

I feel the warmth of his body and inhale deeply. A hint of something familiar catches my nose, but I'm too worked up about the lock to really analyze it.

"Come on, come on!" Cat says. "One minute left!"

I look over at her, but she's locked onto something over my head. Following her gaze, it's a clock with red numbers reading 31:17. We still have over half an hour. I roll my eyes, done with these crazed escape room people.

Spinning the lock to clear it, I turn the dial to the right until I reach seven. After a pause, I spin it left past seventeen and around until it stops on the number again. Finally, I turn it back right to twenty-four. Taking a deep breath, I close my eyes, then tug down on the lock.

It opens and I breathe a sigh of relief. Cat yanks the toolbox away from me, removing the lock and throwing it to the ground. She wrenches open the box and pulls out a pair of glasses and a smoking pipe.

"Professor Plum!" Greg and Cat yell in unison, practically diving through the hole. A few seconds later, the clock flashes above us: 30:01.

A door I hadn't noticed behind us opens and the woman from before ushers us out to the foyer. Cat and Greg are already there, rifling through the winner props for the photo. After they've made their selections, I choose one that says, "We did it!" Brody grabs one that says, "Genius." After the picture, the employee asks us if we'll stay for a second. The siblings leave and then the employee passes me a piece of paper. "This is for a free escape room. I saw what happened and am sorry you didn't get to fully enjoy the experience."

"Thanks," I say. "That's very kind of you."

"You're a very cute couple."

Her words surprise me. She thinks we're a couple? Do I correct her or let it be? Technically, we are a couple of people, and I'm not mad she thinks we're together. Of course, we're still on our first official date and haven't been able to talk much, although I've already learned some things about Brody in the past thirty minutes. He's shown himself to be patient, kind, reassuring, respectful, and protective. All good things in my mind. I smile at the woman, then grab Brody's arm and lead him out of the building.

35

Brody

OUT IN FRONT of Breakout Games, Anna drops her hand from my elbow and turns to face me.

"I was promised dinner this evening. Where are we going?"

I'm taken aback at her wording. She doesn't sound pleased to be spending more time with me, but I might as well see this whole thing through.

"Rachel suggested sushi or tacos, but I'm open to anything. Is there anywhere in particular you want to eat?"

Anna's eyes light up. "I haven't been to Blue Goose in a while. How does that sound?"

"Works for me."

I nod down the block behind her to indicate which way we need to go. She says nothing while we walk, her head swiveling back and forth, taking in the buildings and people around us. I use the time to analyze our escape room experience. Regret is too light a word for how I feel for inviting the siblings to join us. We'd probably still be in the room right now by ourselves if I'd said no. I'm sure it would have been much more enjoyable with just the two of us. I was trying to channel my inner-Anna when I agreed to let them play with us. It seemed like something she would have done. Regardless, I was not a fan of Greg or Cat. I felt like a trapped animal in that kitchen with Cat. If Anna hadn't asked for my help, I don't know what would have happened. Probably nothing too crazy, since there are cameras being monitored by staff. Still, I'd hate for our experience to have ended prematurely because I couldn't handle someone's overexuberant flirtation. Not that I wanted anyone to flirt with me except Anna.

Of course, our experience was shortened anyway by the two maniacs trying to beat their best time. I hated how Greg tried to take over the last lock from Anna. Putting my body between the two of them was the only thing I could think of to protect her. This is only our first official date, so the action could have seemed aggressive to Anna. Even though I feel emotionally connected to her, she doesn't know I'm the man behind the letters, so I have to remember not to let my deep feelings for her overflow into actions that are more intimate than is called for based on our real-life interactions.

I'm really struggling with this separation of my two halves. So far, things don't seem to be going as well as I'd hoped to feel confident enough to confess the truth to her. Maybe if our dinner conversation is more positive, this anxiety in my gut will ease. The knowledge that she has feelings for Winston should make me feel more hopeful, but she probably has this image in her head of what he looks like, and I'm afraid her imagination has drawn up a man who looks nothing like me.

When we reach the restaurant, I hold the door open for her. She smiles at me before walking through, which feels like a good sign. After ordering our tacos and some chips and queso, we grab drinks and find a table in the back part of the restaurant. There's a lot of noise with the music and conversations around us, making it hard for me to concentrate.

"What do you think about eating on the patio?" I ask, nodding toward the umbrella-covered tables through the windows.

"Sure," she says, grabbing her cup and our table number.

The door shuts behind us, muting the sounds from inside the restaurant. Music is still playing, but at a lower decibel. My body relaxes in the serene environment.

"Much better," I say.

"It was a bit noisy inside."

Might as well get the elephant in the room addressed. "I'm sorry about the escape room."

She waves away my apology. "It wasn't your fault. I'd probably have done the same thing. I'm sorry neither of us really got what we paid for."

"What Rachel paid for."

She chuckles. "Right. At least we've been given a do over."

Is she suggesting we have another escape room date? Together? "You can pick the room if you want."

It must be the right answer, because she gives me a bright smile. "How thoughtful. You know, Brody, I must admit I was surprised to find you as my date. What did you say to Rachel?"

Oh man, guess there was more than one elephant. My skin tingles. How much should I say? Well, the whole reason I'm doing this is to show her how I feel and see if my feelings could be returned. Why stop short now?

"I told her how much I admired you and that I thought you were awesome. I really enjoyed our hike to Courthouse Falls. Knowing you're adventurous and enjoy the outdoors like I do makes me want to share all my favorite spots with you. And, to be completely honest, I find you very attractive. You caught my attention the first time I saw you, and I immediately wanted to get to know you."

The startled expression on her face makes me wonder if I went a little too far. Too late to reel anything back in now.

"You say you wanted to get to know me when we first met, but you've been coming into the library for a long time and we're only becoming friends now."

I run my hands over my thighs, the roughness of the denim helping me stay grounded. It shouldn't surprise me she caught that confession. She pays close attention when someone else is talking.

"I told you I struggle with anxiety in certain situations. One that is particularly challenging for me is trying to talk to someone I'm interested in dating. I had a bad experience with a girlfriend who said some very unkind things while dumping me at a friend's party in front of a bunch of people I knew. Needless to say, I've been hesitant to put myself out there again."

I pause and take a deep breath. Might as well tell her the whole truth.

"And I overheard you talking to Penny about Blind Date and a Book. Hearing you're serious about finding love, I realized I'd better find a way to let you know how I felt soon, or you might find someone else." That sounds a little presumptuous to my ears, so I hastily add, "Of course, I realize you might not be interested in me, but I'd regret not telling you how I feel and at least opening up the possibility you might be able to develop feelings for me as well. Please don't feel any pressure. If you don't have romantic feelings for me, that's okay. I'll survive. I've been honest, which is all I can do."

Her eyes are deer-in-headlights wide now. I fear I've said too much, but the point of this date was to be open. I can't be any clearer than that.

A server appears with plastic baskets of food lined up one arm. She sets down the chips and queso, then Anna's chicken BLT tacos, and finally my fish tacos. They look amazing, but my stomach is so tied up in knots after my confession that I'm not sure I'll be able to eat until she says something.

"Wow," she finally says after a long beat of silence, during which my heart stutters several times. "I had no idea. I mean, the anxiety thing makes sense. You've definitely seemed like a different person recently. I assume it's a sign that you're more comfortable around me?"

"That and I've been doing a lot of practicing with my therapist."

Her brow furrows. "Practicing?"

"Role playing potential scenarios in a safe space can help reduce anxiety when they actually occur. You can't actually predict what will happen, but having a loose script is a tool I can work with. In addition to grounding practices."

"What are grounding practices?"

"There are physical things I can do like cross my arms and tap my shoulders, take deep breaths, perform clapping patterns. Actions that cause me to focus on things other than my spiraling thoughts. Sometimes it's a countdown of the senses—five things I see, four I can touch, three I hear, two I smell, one I taste. Most of the time, they work."

Her gaze softens. "Oh, Brody. That sounds tough. Have you struggled with anxiety your entire life?"

Okay, we're going into serious territory. I take a few deep breaths to stay under control, unsure if what I'm about to say will trigger an attack. Under the table, I tap my hands rhythmically against my thighs.

"No. It started after my parents died. I had nightmares about the experience for years. Thankfully, my new guardians put me in therapy. I took medicine for a few years until I developed strategies to help with the overwhelming panic and anxiety I felt. I manage pretty well these days, but there are still things that can trigger an attack."

I've been staring at my food while I talk, not able to meet her gaze, but now I'm curious about what she's thinking. Does she think I'm broken? I'll understand if this cancels out any feelings she might have been developing for me. Pressing my fingers into my legs, I force myself to look up into her face.

Her eyes are filled with kindness and compassion. "You mentioned some of that when we hiked together. I'm sorry for bringing it up again. It must be tough to think about."

"Sorry I'm such a downer on our date."

"Oh, no, you aren't. I feel honored that you're willing to share such sensitive information with me. I sense you don't talk about it with many people."

I shake my head. A lump in my throat from her tenderness keeps me from responding.

"I feel like I should be vulnerable in return," she says, "but the only thing I can think of is my yearning for someone to love me, which I've already told you about. Besides, it seems trivial in comparison. Especially because I have a gaggle of friends and family who do love me."

I clear my throat. "Your desire isn't trivial. I think it's great you know what you want and are pursuing it. You have a lot of courage that I envy."

Her face lights with a smile, her eyes crinkling at the corners. The way she's looking at me makes my stomach somersault.

"Thanks. That's a very sweet thing to say."

She grabs a chip, dips it in the queso, and takes a bite. The sharp crunch breaks the serious mood. I smile, glad that things seem to be going well despite the deep topics. I suppose it's good we're talking about things that matter. Wanting to keep the mood light for the moment, I choose a conversation starter that's sure to be a fan favorite.

"What book went along with this date?"

The smile drops from her face, and creases appear on her brow. "*Into the Unknown* by M.B. Winston."

My heart stutters inside my chest. Does she know? I didn't think I'd given away anything, but she is a smart woman. She definitely could have connected the dots. I need to find out. I'd hate to confess now, especially since I don't know if she's received the manuscript yet. "That's the book you recommended to me."

"Yeah."

She meets my eyes, and something in her expression makes my heart sink. Might as well go ahead and rip off the band-aid. "What's wrong?"

She sighs. "I've really enjoyed spending time with you, Brody. You've surprised me in a good way, but I need to be honest with you. I have feelings for another person. M.B. Winston, actually. I don't know if he feels the same way, but I've put myself out there and am waiting for his response. If there's a chance with him, I have to see where it goes."

My heart is beating rapidly in my chest. It's weird being jealous of yourself, but I definitely am right now. My fingers drum out a pattern on the table. "Oh. Okay."

She reaches across the table, grabbing my hand and giving it a light squeeze. "I'm sorry. I obviously didn't know I would be seeing you tonight. You're a really nice guy and, given different circumstances, I'd definitely be interested in exploring the possibility of you and me."

That's encouraging news, though what is it about my alter ego that she seems to enjoy more than in-person me? "Can I ask you something?"

"Sure."

"What is it about this M.B. Winston guy that you like so much? Is he super handsome? Is it because he's kind of famous or has money?"

She shakes her head. "I actually haven't met him yet, so I don't know what he looks like. And I don't care about fame or money. He doesn't seem to care about those things either, which impresses me. What I like is the way he makes me feel. He is kind, generous, funny, and a little zany like me. I can't really describe it exactly. All I know is that my days are better when I hear from him and I look forward to what he's going to say next."

"So it has nothing to do with him being an author?"

She thinks about it. "Actually, no. It's been fun talking to him about his writing, but I just genuinely like him. Whoever he is."

Her words fill me with hope that maybe everything will turn out okay. Will my extravagant gesture be enough to cushion the blow of my deception? It started out accidental, but it's definitely crossed a line somewhere and I'm not sure how to fix this mess I've made. "I guess I can't compete with that."

"I really am sorry, Brody. If things were different—"

"It's fine," I say quickly, not wanting her to continue to try to soothe me when I'm the one who's in the wrong by hiding who I am.

I pick up a taco and take a bite. The fish has gone cold, but I eat it anyway because I don't know what to say. My stomach twists with guilt that I'm the cause of Anna's conflicted emotions. My only comfort is the knowledge she likes both of us. I mean, both versions of me. It gives me hope she'll be okay with the two of us integrated into one. I only hope when the time comes she isn't furious I wasn't honest with her from the start.

July 12

Dear Anna,

You don't know what a joy it was to see a lavender envelope in my mailbox. I'm so happy you like the stationery. I must admit, part of me hopes that you'll think of me whenever you see it sitting on your desk. I hope this doesn't make me sound like a stalker, but I found your middle name on your social media profile.

That was very brave of you to be open about your feelings. You don't know how happy I am to hear my feelings for you are reciprocated. I've been trying to show you how much I like you through these letters, but was worried I wasn't being open enough, which you confirmed in your last letter. Believe me, I care deeply for you. I, too, was surprised at how much intimacy there can be in correspondence. To answer your questions, I am a forty-year-old man.

Yes, I wrote a fantasy romance. I'm still trying to get you an early copy of Ciara's story, but, in the meantime, I hope the attached will help you make do. I added a few things just for you (don't tell my publisher). I'm also including a pet rock I made. Can't wait to hear what you name it.

I feel relief finally getting our feelings out into the open. Especially since I know you care for me as well. Please let me know what you think of the new book.

Waiting with bated breath, Winston

36

Anna

AFTER A LONG day at work where patrons needing help was nonstop, I'm grateful to be pulling up in front of my apartment with nothing to do for the rest of the evening. I have four glorious hours to unwind before bedtime. Thankfully, I'm not working tomorrow so I can sleep in.

When I reach my apartment, there's a bubble mailer leaning against my door. I pick it up, and feel through the envelope. A firm, thick rectangle. It feels like a book, but I don't remember ordering one. I flip it over, my heart picking up speed when I see Winston's name on the return address. Did he send me an early copy of Ciara's sequel?

I quickly unlock the door, drop my bag in the kitchen, and tear into the envelope. I tip the contents onto the counter. There's a book, a light blue envelope, and a rock with drawn on eyes, nose, and a mouth. Aww, he sent me my own pet rock. I flip the book over. *Dragons of Moon Kingdom*, the cover reads. A giant full moon takes up most of the space, with dragon silhouettes inside the bright sphere. Curious, I flip it over to read the back cover. Who are Aurelia Runeld and Beorn Daevon? Is this Winston's secret project?

I'm itching to dive right in, but decide I should read his note first. I set down the book, running my hand lovingly over the cover. It's definitely fantasy and not sci-fi like his other books.

Lifting the envelope to my nose, I'm disappointed it doesn't smell woodsy like some of the others, but then feel silly. Pulling out the note, I unfold it and read, my surprise turning to warm delight when I discover Winston likes me too. And he's only a few years older than me! Ooh, a fantasy romance. I can't wait to see what happens in the story. I pick up the rock, moved by the fact that Winston made it for me. It's going to need a great name, though I have no idea what that might be at the moment.

I take a moment to savor the news that Winston has feelings for me. It seems crazy to think that two people can grow so emotionally attached through correspondence alone. Winston has seen me at least once, so he must also be physically attracted to me, but he's always focused on affirming who I am as a person, which feels really good.

Exchanging the note for the book, I flip it open to the title page. The next page is where the dedication is supposed to go and the words "To Anna, my inspiration" are written in Winston's familiar script. I nearly drop the book in surprise, but keep my hold, my heart thumping in my chest. He dedicated this book to me? His *romance* book? Wow! He isn't messing around in telling me how he feels.

I carry the book over to my favorite chair and get comfy, not even bothering to change out of my work clothes. I'm no longer bone tired like I felt when I arrived home. In fact, I feel excited, possibly even exhilarated. The goosebumps on my arm tell me I'm about to read something significant.

I turn to the first chapter, but am distracted from beginning the story when I see more of Winston's handwriting. He's circled the name Aurelia and drawn a line out to the margin where he's written *She has the same first letter as you. Aurelia means 'the golden one,' which is how I see you.* He named a character after me? Or is it just a thin covering of a story he's written *about* me? There's only one way to find out. I begin reading, immersing myself in the story and Winston's comments.

I don't move from the chair until I read the words *The End*, unable to put the book down. I'm amazed at how he wove pieces of my personal experience into the story. Some people might feel awkward about someone doing something like that, but I'm flattered he wanted to slay my dragons and protect me. For some reason, he didn't feel like he could do that in real life, so he did it in a made up world.

Now I want to meet him more than ever. Absently, I flip the last few pages wondering if there's an About the Author section already, though usually it isn't added to ARCs, same with the dedication. I pause when I spot Winston's handwriting again on the otherwise blank Acknowledgments page. My stomach flips when I see my name. He's thanking me! His words fill me with joy, but my mouth goes dry when my eyes find the word *love*. What exactly does he mean by that? Could I be reading more into this than is actually there? I need a second opinion, stat!

I reach for my phone, blanching when I realize it's three o'clock in the morning. Thankfully, I don't have to get up for work, but it's way too early to text or call anyone. I quickly brush my teeth and put on some pajamas, hoping I'm not too wired to get some sleep. I grab the book and carry it to bed with me, clutching it to my chest. Surprisingly, I fall asleep without much trouble.

When I wake up, I'm still on an emotional high, but am now ready to parse out the meaning of everything with trusted individuals. Time to rally the troops!

The doorbell rings, and I open the door wide, pulling Penny into a hug.

"Thanks for coming on such short notice."

She gives me one more squeeze before pulling away and looking over my shoulder into the living room beyond.

"You sounded a little desperate on the phone. What's this all about? Are you still trying to recruit me to your book club?"

I chuckle. "No. I just wanted as many friends here as possible."

Penny follows me into the apartment, taking a seat on the love seat next to Rachel. Julie, Abbie, and Meredith are sitting together on the couch. I plop down in the floral wingback chair.

"So, what's going on?" Abbie says, cutting straight to the chase.

"Okay, so you all know me well and have been part of my quest to find love."

Rachel's eyes brighten. "Did your date with Brody go that well?"

I scrunch up my nose, hating that he's gotten mixed up in my drama. He's a nice guy who obviously likes me. If I'd gotten to know him a few months before, we might have had a chance, but after the package I received from Winston, my heart no longer belongs to me.

"It did, but that's not what this is about. I heard back from Winston."

No one speaks, but their eyes are all trained on me.

"He sent me an ARC of a book he's been working on." I grab the novel from under my chair and hold it up. "He dedicated it to me and wrote notes about parts that were inspired by me."

Meredith clasps her hands together, her eyes twinkling with delight. "Oooh, Anna. That sounds so romantic."

"It definitely was, but he also thanked me in the acknowledgments."

"How sweet," Julie says. "What did he say?"

"See for yourself."

I hold the book out. Several hands reach for it, but Abbie snatches it first. She flips to the back, clears her throat, and reads.

"A huge thank you to Anna Hollingsworth for all her encouragement while I was struggling with writer's block. Her letters were a lifeline during a challenging time. Additionally, her generous and bubbly spirit gave me the courage to open myself up to love. I can't wait to see where the future takes us."

She looks up, her eyes round with wonder. My gaze travels around the circle of women, similar expressions on every face. I can't stop the smile that's blooming across my cheeks. I've read those sentences over a dozen times and they still don't seem real.

Rachel reaches over, grabbing the manuscript from Abbie and flipping through it, pausing to read things here and there. She looks up at me.

"Anna, Winston wrote you a love letter in novel form."

"I know."

"Wow," Meredith says. "I can't imagine someone writing a whole book for me. He spent days and weeks, maybe even months, thinking about you and trying to translate his love into an epic story. That's above and beyond."

"Says the woman who had a man create a bunch of questions for a trivia game just to ask her out," Abbie says, chuckling.

Meredith smiles, shrugging one shoulder. "You're one to talk. Carlos took a verbal beating from you just so he could spend time with you."

Abbie waves away the words. "It was a misunderstanding is all. I wasn't that hard on him."

Rachel rolls her eyes. "Is this what they call revisionist history?"

Abbie gives her sister a mock glare that quickly morphs into an amused grin.

"Let's focus back on Anna," Penny says. "That novel sounds like a crazy grand gesture, but how do you know Winston is who he says he is?"

I smile at my friend, grateful for her clear head.

"He said in his letter that he's a forty-year-old man." I hold up a hand to stop her rebuttal, even though she hasn't yet opened her mouth. "Yes, I realize it's just words, but I believe him."

"So, now what?" Rachel asks.

"That's the big question, which is why you all are here. What do you think I should do?"

"Meet him, obviously," Julie says. "Then you can see for yourself if he's been telling the truth."

Heads bob around the circle.

"But this time make it foolproof," says Abbie. "Exchange numbers so you can be in contact if something comes up."

"Yeah, that's probably a good idea," I concede.

"What happens if you see him and aren't attracted to him?" Penny says.

"I don't think that's possible. He may not look like Chris

Hemsworth, but I'm so attracted to his soul that his appearance really isn't a concern of mine."

Penny raises a skeptical eyebrow, but stays quiet. She obviously doesn't believe me, and there's no way I can prove my point until I meet him. Do I think he could be physically unattractive to me? Maybe, but I think love makes everyone beautiful.

"I'm happy for you," Rachel says, "but what about Brody?"

Oh, yeah. Him. I frown, discomfort lancing my gut at the thought of hurting him, but I've been honest with him so far, which is all I can do.

"I actually told him at the end of our date I was interested in another person. He said that whatever happened, he still wanted to be friends."

"And you believe him?"

I consider this for a few seconds. "I do. He seems like a straight up guy."

"Whew!" Julie says, using the book to fan herself. "That kiss at the end sure is steamy. He sounds like he knows what he's doing."

The group chuckles. Meredith grabs the book from Julie, flipping through the end pages.

"Three ninety-eight," Julie says.

Meredith's eyes grow big as she reads. She slaps the pages closed.

"Oh man! If I wasn't happily married...You've got to meet him, Anna, at least to see what he kisses like in real life."

I laugh, but sober suddenly. Will our on-paper chemistry translate into real-life? What if we have nothing to say to each other face-to-face? I shake my head at that thought. He's already seen me. It feels a little unfair to be at the disadvantage on that front, but if he's anything like I've built him up to be in my head, then everything is bound to work out. I just have to trust my gut that Winston is the same man as he presents himself to be.

"I'm not one to kiss on the first date, but after all this buildup, I may have to throw my rules out the window."

That gets a laugh from the group.

"Thanks, everyone, for coming. I appreciate your wisdom and support. I'm going to write him back and try to set up another meeting. Wish me luck!"

July 17

Dear Winston,

Oh. My. Word. Winston! I can't believe you wrote something as amazing as that. Okay, wait. Ignore my previous words. I CAN believe you wrote an amazing story because you're a professional author. I'm just blown away at how you were able to turn some of my dating mishaps into a fantasy novel. I mean, Aurelia having to face the twisted serpent alone after that one knight deserts her actually made me feel some of the same fear and frustration as when I was on the roller coaster by myself.

And when Beorn rescued and cared for Aurelia when she fell off that cliff and was concussed. She was so rude to him and didn't remember who he was and he still treated her so kindly and tenderly! I don't even remember telling you about that particular event, but obviously I must have. The lack of copies of both sides of our correspondence is a downside to paper letters, I suppose.

*You don't know how much reading this story affected me. I can't believe you took inspiration from our letters. And the acknowledgments! *heart eyes* Wow, Winston, I'm so flattered. One of my friends called it a love letter in novel form. Is that what it's meant to be? Okay, obviously it must be, and that's how I've interpreted it. Yes, I showed it to my book club, but they won't tell anyone.*

It's so wonderful to know we both care for one another. We absolutely must meet. Give me a time and place and your phone number. I don't want a repeat of last time. My number is 314-555-5683. I can't wait to finally see you face-to-face!

Yours truly, Anna

P.S.-Thank you for the rock. I named her Aurelia because she looks like a warrior princess.

July 21

Dear Anna,

So glad you enjoyed the book and appreciated all the transformed scenes from your dating escapades. It was fun thinking of ways to translate your mishaps into a fantasy setting. Yes, I suppose the book is one really long love letter to you.

Now that you've read it, perhaps you have more insights into the thriller sequel I'm working on? It's Beorn who's been kidnapped, and Aurelia must find a way to rescue him. It turns out she made an enemy while she was trying to find a spouse to fulfill her father's ultimatum of marrying within the year or forfeiting her spot in line for the throne. Remember Zyla, the sister of Caspian, one of Aurelia's suitors? She did not like seeing her brother heartbroken, so she now wants Aurelia to suffer heartache.

Exchanging numbers is a wonderful idea. Mine is 828-555-7323.

We definitely need to meet, though I can't set a date just yet. My best friend, Levi, has been hounding me to come see his new place (they just moved to a town near White River National Forest in Colorado). Since I don't have any impending deadlines, this seemed like the perfect time. How was I to know it'd turn out to be the same time as us expressing our feelings? I'll let you know when I'm back, but in the meantime, please text me so we can keep in touch.

I've enclosed a little something for Aurelia to help her fully embody her warrior princess mentality.

Yours, Winston

37

Brody

MY FLIGHT TO Colorado doesn't leave until this evening, so I couldn't resist the opportunity to see Anna one more time. Technically, I've been rejected, but I want to honor my word that we'd stay friends, so I've been showing up to my usual spot. We haven't done much interacting, but we've exchanged smiles and waves here and there.

Today, however, something's different. Every time I've looked around for Anna, I've caught her staring at me. There's no way to know what she's thinking, but I'm a little unnerved at the attention. Is she trying to puzzle things out? Part of me feels like it'd be a relief if she figured out the truth, but I've got a plan in motion that I'd really like to see through.

I've been trying to work on my book, but my emotions have distracted me, oscillating between excitement about spending time with Levi and Elizah and anxiety wondering whether Anna will feel duped when the truth is revealed. That's always a possibility, but I really hope when all is said and done that she's happy.

After another forty minutes of accomplishing nothing, I decide it's time to go home. Maybe I can get a little work done with fewer distractions. After packing everything up, I head toward the exit. Anna's at the circulation desk, her hands twisting the corner of her blue cardigan. I smile and nod.

"Bye, Anna."

"Brody, do you have a second?"

I pause, turning to face the desk. Her brows are pressed together, her mouth a firm line.

"Sure. What's up?"

"I've been wanting to talk to you, but haven't been sure how to say it."

"Say what?"

She looks to the side, chewing on her lip. Then she sucks in a deep breath and meets my eye. "I heard back from the other person I'm interested in. His feelings match mine, so we're going to meet and see where things go."

I try to look genuinely surprised. "Oh. Uh, okay. Well, congratulations."

"Thanks. I'm so sorry, Brody. I've really enjoyed spending time with you. I hope this won't keep you from continuing to use the library."

I wave away her concern. "It's fine. Like I said, we can still be friends."

Her shoulders drop in relief. "Thanks for being so understanding."

Had she really been anxious about officially rejecting me? Of course she was. She genuinely cares about all the people in her life. It's one of the many things I love about her. I shrug. If only she knew why I was so calm in the face of rejection. Soon she will.

"No problem. I'm going to go, unless you need to talk about anything else?"

"No, that was it. Would it be okay if I gave you a hug?"

I wasn't expecting this. But am I ever going to turn down a chance to be close to the woman I love? "Of course."

I meet her at the opening to the circulation table. She pushes up on her toes and wraps her arms around my neck. I circle her waist, gently pressing my hands into the small of her back. A breath in through my nose makes me feel like I'm standing in a field of lavender. Must be her shampoo.

"Mmm, Brody, you smell good."

"Uh, thanks."

She lets me go and steps back, an odd look on her face. "What kind of cologne do you wear?"

"Something woodsy. I don't remember the name. My friend gave it to me as sort of a joke, but I actually like it."

She smiles, but she's got a faraway look in her eye. "Yeah, it's nice."

"See ya, Anna."

She gives me a little wave and I head down the hall to my car. Not sure why she wanted a hug, but I'm not complaining. She felt so right in my arms. I hope to have many more opportunities to hold her close soon.

38

Anna: Hey Winston! How's Colorado?

Winston: Great to hear from you, Anna! Having a blast with Levi and Elizah.

Anna: Done any hiking?

Winston: Levi's had me on a new trail nearly every day. Yesterday we did the Trollstigen Trail. The attached photo is Isak Heartstone (aka the Breckenridge Troll).

Anna: That's so cool!

Winston: It's gorgeous out here. Makes me a little nostalgic for college and all the adventures Levi and I had in the summers.

Anna: Hopefully it's not enticing enough to make you move or I might never see you.

Winston: Nothing is going to stop me from meeting you. Well, other than this trip, but it's been planned for a while. Honestly, I kind of wish I'd delayed it so you and I could get together first.

Anna: I'm also eager to see and touch you. I'm a hugger, so be prepared for me to attach to you like a koala. *koala emoji*

Winston: Now I'm mentally kicking myself for taking this trip.

Anna: No. No regrets. Enjoy this time with your friend. I know how hard it is to get together with long-distance friends. When you get back, we'll have tons of time to enjoy one another's company.

Winston: You're so sweet. My arms are practically aching to hold you. To feel the warmth of your body against mine and smell your lavender shampoo in your hair.

Anna: How did you know my shampoo smells like lavender?

Winston: It's your favorite color. I thought it might also be your favorite scent?

Anna: Wow. Good guess, but it's actually not my favorite scent. More recently, I've become fond of whatever cologne you've been spraying on your letters. I'm guessing something with cedarwood?

Winston: You have a good nose. It's called Bravo Sierra. I hate to end this conversation, but Levi tells me it's time to lace up my hiking boots. Have a great day. Can't wait to see you!

Anna: Enjoy your hike. Let me know when you're headed back my way and we'll finally get our meetup on the books!

Winston: Will do. Know you're constantly on my mind. *heart emoji*

Anna: *heart eyes emoji*

39

Anna

"WHY ARE YOU staring at your phone with a moony expression?"

I jump, startled by Penny's sudden appearance. Where did she come from? Better yet, what have I been doing for the last twenty minutes? I can't account for the time, but I assume no one else has come up to the circulation desk to break me out of my daydreaming.

"Sorry," I say, pocketing my phone, suitably chastised for being on it at work. I know it's frowned upon, but I just can't help myself. I feel like a lovesick teenager. "Winston has been texting around this time, and I was hoping to hear from him."

She rolls her eyes. "Oh brother. You're really smitten with him."

There's no denying this accusation. I've been in a happy haze ever since Winston and I started texting. The instantaneous communication makes everything feel more real. I mean, he could send me a picture of himself and I'd know exactly what he looks like. For some reason, I've held out on asking him to do it. I think I really just want to take him in all at once. A photo would kind of be a letdown. Still, he's sent me a bunch of pictures of the gorgeous scenery from his trip.

Since I'm not going anywhere, I've been taking pictures of Aurelia and drawing fake adventures for her on paper. She looks perfect with the little crown and sword Winston sent. I know it's silly to be creating scenarios for a rock, but I've been imagining her escapades from the novel and recreating them to pass the time. I'm not even bothering to try to keep my mind off Winston, and this sort of makes me feel close to him. He's seemed to enjoy the pictures I've sent, cheering on my creativity.

"I am. I wish he'd come home already."

"How many more days is he out there?"

"I don't know. He hasn't purchased a return ticket. The perks of the job, I suppose."

"Sure, but I'd think he'd be desperate to get back to you. What's it been, two weeks?"

I sigh. "Nearly three. But he never gets to see his best friend. I can't begrudge him this time that he'd already planned before things between us reached this point. I mean, can you imagine how *we'd* survive living half a country apart?"

Penny gives me a horrified look. "Don't tell me you're thinking about moving?"

"No, of course not." I pause. "Though, if Winston told me he was moving and asked me to go with him, I might do it. After we've officially met, of course."

"You really like him that much?"

I shrug. "I know it seems ridiculous falling in love through words, but he makes me feel seen and accepted and loved. What more could I ask for?"

"I don't know…maybe someone who's physically present?"

It's my turn to roll my eyes. "Yes, for sure. And that's coming. When I see him for the first time, I'm not sure what I'll do. This man is the kindest, sweetest person I've ever been in contact with. If he turns out to be even half as good-looking as I've imagined, I'd be crazy not to turn my life upside down and marry him."

Her eyes soften, and she smiles. "Okay, this whole situation is actually pretty romantic. I really hope everything works out for you. You deserve to be happy."

"Thanks."

My eyes scan the library, stopping on the empty cubicle in the back corner. "Pen, have you seen Brody recently?"

She turns toward the back of the room. "No. Not for a week or two. Why?"

"It's nothing."

"That troubled look on your face is saying otherwise."

I huff out a breath. "Well…I don't know if I've seen him since I told him Winston and I are a thing."

She nods. "Makes sense. A lot of guys disappear when they find out you're not interested."

"Yeah, but he doesn't seem like that kind of guy. He was insistent we'd still be friends."

She shrugs. "I don't know. Maybe he just needs some time to get over his feelings for you."

My lips twist to the side as I absorb this thought. It still doesn't sit right, but it could be true.

"Do you have his number? If this is really bothering you, call and ask."

Reaching into my back pocket for my phone, I unlock it and scroll through my contacts until I see Brody Cooper. I click on the message button. Our previous conversation thread was about hiking and took place a few weeks ago. Not wanting to think too much, I send a quick text.

Anna: Hey Brody. Haven't seen you at the library in a while. Everything okay?

I turn my screen around to show Penny what I sent and she nods. After a minute, there's been no response, so I put my phone away, a little dejected. "Maybe he *is* avoiding me."

"Does he have any books due back soon?"

I hadn't thought about that. Stepping over to the computer, I type in Brody's name. I wouldn't normally go into a patron's history, but Penny's got me a little concerned, and I want to make sure he's okay. There aren't any matching results, which is weird. I know he's checked out books before. Switching tactics, I look up *Into the Unknown* to see the names of everyone who's borrowed it. No Brody, but there is a Matthew Cooper on the list. The name doesn't ring a bell, but he has the same last name as Brody. Perhaps they're related? Or could Brody prefer being called by his middle name? Returning to the search page, I type in "Matthew Cooper" and up pops a list of recently borrowed books.

Scrolling through the list, I see some fantasy at the top with *Into the Unknown* thrown in, along with a few thrillers. *This must be Brody's account.* I read the titles of more fantasy books, followed by a surprising number of young adult science fiction and a few nonfiction books on machines and time travel. A very eclectic mix. Remembering the whole reason I began searching, I return to the top of the page.

"He has nothing currently checked out."

"Oh, bummer."

My phone buzzes in my pocket, and I quickly grab it.

Brody: I had to go out of town. Miss me?

I chuckle, feeling pleased at his teasing tone. He really is a good guy.

Anna: Your cubicle is growing cobwebs. Just seeing how long I have before I need to dust them.
Brody: Not sure, but nice to know you're saving my spot for me.

Penny yanks the phone from me, reading through our brief exchange.

"He's flirting with you."

"What? No. He's just a nice guy."

"If that's what you want to believe."

Am I deluding myself? I mean, sure, he was definitely interested, but we haven't known each other that long. His feelings for me can't be more than surface level, though he went to a lot of trouble to secure a date with me through Rachel. Is that something a guy would do for someone he only liked a little? It's what I want to believe because the alternative is that I might be breaking some sweet guy's heart. Not that I'm doing anything intentionally. It's just unfortunate timing.

"Wow," Penny says next to me. "This guy has some interesting taste in books."

I look over to see her scrolling through Brody's patron history. "It's not any better or worse than my romance and cozy mystery log or your YA fantasy and regency romance one."

"No, though I bet he'd like your pal Winston's other books. Especially his new one coming out. Didn't you say it's fantasy?"

"Fantasy romance, technically."

I peer over her shoulder at the list again. I could imagine Winston's borrower history looking a lot like this as well. A sudden case of goosebumps makes me shudder. Something feels off. I look around, wondering if I'm being stared at. A patron approaches the desk with a small stack of books. I smile at her, then nudge Penny off the computer so I can check out the books. Right after her, I have another patron, then a steady stream of people with questions for the next hour.

When things finally settle down, my mind returns to Penny's observation. My brain is trying to make sense of something, but I feel like I'm missing a few pieces of a puzzle. My phone buzzes, startling me.

Winston: Hey, beautiful! I know you're probably at work, but just wanted to say I'm thinking about you.

I can't help the wide smile that sweeps across my face. Cradling the phone to my chest, I twirl in place, buoyed by his sweet words. It's going to kill me waiting to finally meet him face-to-face.

I'm pondering an appropriate response when someone rushes up to the desk from the library's entrance. I look up to find Rachel grinning at me with wild eyes.

"Anna, just the person I was looking for!"

I step back, surprised by the exuberance in her voice. "Hey, Rachel. What's up?"

"My boss, Sarah, just told us that M.B. Winston has decided to hold a signing for his new book in our store!"

My mouth drops open, my eyes as big as saucers. "He *what?!* He doesn't do public events."

"I know! His publisher called and said he agreed to do one, but only at Page Turner Books."

"Rach, that's awesome! When is it?"

"Next month."

I inhale so sharply; I start choking. Penny comes up behind me and rubs small, reassuring circles on my back until I'm breathing normally again.

"Wow," I say. "Rachel, you know you have to make sure I get a ticket to that event. Why didn't he tell me?"

"Maybe he doesn't know it's official yet. I mean, Sarah just got the call this morning."

My heart is beating fast from all the excitement. Winston's going to do a book signing? Why? It's going to obliterate the anonymity he's enjoyed so far. I don't get it. But maybe I can get some answers.

"Thanks for letting me know."

She smiles. "No problem. I had to tell you as soon as I found out. I've got to get back to work, though."

Before Rachel's even out the door, I've sent Winston a text.

Anna: You're doing a book signing at PTB?!

Winston: Yes. I'm a little nervous, but I hoped you'd come. Your presence would help anchor me, and I'm confident I could get through the event with you in the crowd.

Wow, he has a lot of faith in me. But I don't want to be the reason he's thrust into the spotlight. It is perfectly reasonable to want to be unknown after his earlier experience with fame.

Anna: But your anonymity will disappear. People might bring up the past.

Winston: That's true, but I'm tired of hiding. Hopefully, people will have some discretion, at least when talking to me directly. But, even if not, knowing I have you to help me through gives me all the courage and confidence I need.

My heart is beating rapidly now—both from excitement and from discomfort. When he's publicly unmasked, his fans will want to know everything about him. That will include who he's dating. Am I ready for a spotlight on me? Do I want people digging into my history? Not that I have any big secrets I'm keeping, but I did stupid things I wouldn't want millions of people talking about.

Of course, it's not like Winston's a famous actor or anything. Authors don't carry that much star power. I'm probably just worrying about nothing. If I'm tempted to drop my relationship with him over a hypothetical, maybe I'm not as into him as I thought. And if not, did I discard a perfectly good relationship with someone I know for a mere possibility? *Wow, Anna, you're spiraling.*

Winston: I'll be back in town for the book signing. You could meet me there and we could get dinner together afterward?

I don't love the idea of finding out who he is along with a hundred other people, but maybe it'd be better that way. I could see what he looks like and, if he seems like a different person at his event, we're in a public place and I can say it's not going to work out. Not that it's what I want to happen, but there's always a possibility we're only compatible on paper.

Anna: Sure, sounds great. Let me know the day and time.
Winston: Will do. Thanks for being so patient and flexible. You're the best!

If only he knew the thoughts that have been swirling around in my head. Hopefully, everything will work out and my worry will be for naught.

40

Brody

MY TIME IN Twin Lakes, Colorado with Levi and Elizah has been amazing. Every time I was standing on a peak or encountered something awe-inspiring, I wished Anna could have been here with me. It cemented the fact that I need to be with someone who appreciates the outdoors like I do. I realize Anna's job requires her to spend large parts of her days inside the walls of a building, but I would guess that just makes her enjoy her hiking and kayaking even more.

Maybe if this book is as successful as my publisher and agent think it'll be, we can get a weekend getaway house on a river where we can just drop our kayaks into the water from our backyard. Of course, in this imaginative scenario, Anna and I are together. Permanently. If our texts are any indication, I think the probability of that is quite high.

I've definitely enjoyed the faster mode of communication with Anna. Levi looked at me strangely when I had two phones sitting on my lap one afternoon. I explained the situation, and he just shook his head, muttering something about hoping it didn't come back to bite me. Truthfully, I do worry Anna will be upset at the deception. I mean, who uses his work phone to hide his identity from someone he cares about? I didn't go out and buy a new phone for the purpose, but I did pointedly give Anna my business line to communicate with Winston rather than my personal number. Initially, it was a self-preservation decision, but now it's dragged on so long that there really is no excuse. I can only hope love really can conquer all.

Today's my last day visiting and the three of us are going kayaking on a lake. Elizah drives us down to the access point. Levi and I carry the kayaks to the water's edge, and then wait for Elizah to park and join us. The hours slip away as we paddle around the lake. The sky is a gorgeous blue with a few fluffy white clouds floating lazily across the sky. When my shirt feels damp from sweat, I take it off and drape it across the back of the kayak to dry in the sun. Turning my face up to the sky, I enjoy the warm sun on my face and shoulders. It's a perfect day on the water. I glance to my left, where Levi and Elizah are paddling next to each other and talking. My chest thuds with longing for what they have. Love looks so easy with them and I think it's because they share many of the same interests.

Anna and I seem to have a lot that makes us compatible. We are outdoorsy book people, which sounds like an oxymoron. She has a silly side that helps pull me out of my seriousness, and I really appreciate that. We're both from the Midwest so we could see both of our families in one trip. It's only about a four-hour drive to cross the state, though I can afford for us to fly if we prefer. Though, I would be excited to see what a road trip with Anna is like. She likely brings car snacks and creates road trip playlists. I wouldn't be surprised if she has a whole cache of car games for when we get bored. I smile, imagining us striking out on an adventure together.

"What are you thinking about?"

I open my eyes and turn to see that Elizah's drifted over to my side. "Oh, nothing. Just enjoying the nice weather."

She smirks at me. "Yeah, I think you're lying. Spill."

I'm surprised she's able to read me so well. I haven't spent a lot of time with her since I moved out east. Maybe she has some sort of radar. "I was imagining what it might be like to road trip with Anna."

Elizah's eyes light up. "Road trips are the best! You learn a lot about a person when you travel with them." She turns to Levi. "Isn't that right, Teddy Weddy?"

My forehead crinkles. "What did you just call him?"

Levi chuckles. "When we met, I still carried around this tiny bear I'd had since I was a child. It was small enough to fit into one of my backpack pockets. When she and I took a trip to the Grand Tetons, she found him while looking for snacks." He gives Elizah an affectionate look so tender I feel like I'm witnessing something I shouldn't and avert my eyes. "But that was before I had a person to cuddle at night."

Elizah's warm laughter rings out across the lake. "Seeing that soft side of you was really endearing. It definitely is one of the things that made me fall in love with you."

As happy as I am that my best friend found such a great partner, it's just a stark reminder of what I hope for but don't yet have. *Soon,* I remind myself. The truth will be revealed in a couple of days and then we'll see what happens. I know what I hope happens. I hope Anna sees me and is thrilled. There's still a small part of me that expects catastrophe, but I keep forcing it down.

Worrying won't change whatever is going to happen, so there's no reason to cast a shadow over the amazing time I'm having right now with my friends.

41

Winston: Looking forward to seeing you tonight! I'll be the guy sitting at the book table. *winky emoji*

Anna: Me too! I'll be the woman fangirling over one of her favorite authors. *heart eyes emoji*

Winston: *thinking emoji* You may have to be more specific. There might be more than one fan present.

Anna: Oooh, confident are we?

Winston: The event is sold out, so I feel comfortable stating I have at least two fans.

Anna: Okay, you got me. I'll be the woman giving you actual heart eyes.

Winston: Hopefully, you'll be the only one. I've heard of overeager fans at book signings before which, I must admit, I'm a little nervous about.

Anna: Don't worry. I'll be your makeshift security. No one will get uncomfortably close to you.

Anna: Except maybe me. No promises.

Winston: You can get as close to me as you'd like. I promise I won't mind.

Anna: So excited for you and to finally put a face to all your words—both in print and just for my eyes.

Winston: If you want to arrive early so we can meet before the hullabaloo, I'd like that. It would really be nice to get a little second-hand courage and charisma from you to use for talking to readers.

Anna: I'll do my best, but the event starts at the same time as the library closes. I'll talk to my boss first thing and see if I can scoot out early.

Winston: It's okay if you can't. I'm just really excited to see you.

Anna: I know just how you feel. I'm practically jumping out of my skin with anticipation.

Anna: Okay, weird visual, sorry. Let's just say I'm buzzing like I've consumed a dozen lattes.

Winston: Have a great day at work and I'll see you later.

Anna: Thanks. You're going to be brilliant tonight!

42

Anna

"HEY ANNA," PENNY says, dropping her purse on the desk next to where I'm standing in front of the computer.

"Hey, Pen. Isn't it just a gorgeous day today?"

She furrows her brow. "It's raining," she says flatly.

"Yeah, but the soft patter of rain is so romantic."

"Whatever you say. Do we have a lot of holds to gather today?"

"Oh! Um, I'm not sure."

I started my morning work, but keep getting distracted by things. Or more accurately, by my thoughts. All I can think about is the fact that I'm meeting Winston tonight! I wonder if he'll tell me his real name. I'd feel awkward continuing to call him by his pen name, especially once we're officially a couple. Or are we already a couple? It doesn't feel right to say I'm dating someone I haven't laid eyes on, but that'll change in mere hours!

I didn't sleep well last night. Every time I fell asleep, I had the same dream where I walk into Page Turner Books and find out that Winston is actually Josh, that terrible escape room date. Sometimes he's Ben. His face keeps rotating between all the people I've been on dates with. The only ones that didn't make my heart sink were the times it was Zach or Brody.

I haven't heard from Zach since he moved to Charleston. Hopefully, his mom is doing well with her treatments. I should send him a text and check in. Maybe on my lunch break if I remember.

"Thinking about Winston, are you?"

"How did you know?"

"The fact that you haven't gotten past the log-in screen and you've been at work for half an hour is a pretty good indicator that your mind's not here today."

I give her a sheepish grin. "Sorry."

She smiles back. "Don't be. I'm excited for you. Which reminds me. I got you something."

She pulls a small rectangular box out of her purse. When she sets it in my hands, I'm surprised by the weight. "What is it?"

"Open it, silly."

I roll my eyes and tear into the paper. "You got me men's cologne?"

"I got you *Winston's* cologne."

"Oh!" I smile at her, then rip off the cellophane, open the lid, and take out the round black bottle. Unscrewing the lid, I put my finger over the opening and tip it to the side. I wipe my wet finger on a scrap piece of paper. Securing the lid again, I set it down, then pick up the paper and bring it to my nose, inhaling deeply. The familiar smell makes me smile, but also niggles something in my brain. I close my eyes and inhale again. A memory of hugging Brody pops into my head and my eyes fly open. "Brody wears this."

Penny's eyes widen. "Really? Are you sure?"

"I'm not positive, but I definitely smelled something similar to this when I gave him a hug the last time I saw him."

"Where has he been? I can't remember the last time I saw him."

I open my mouth to answer, but then pause. "I don't actually know. He said he had to go out of town, but I didn't ask any follow-up questions." My forehead crinkles. "Should I text him and see if he's okay?"

"Do you really care?"

My heart twists with regret. He's a nice guy with a kind heart. He deserves to be with someone who appreciates him. If I knew any single women I thought he might be compatible with, I'd set him up in a heartbeat. *Would you really, though?*

The unbidden thought catches me off guard. Okay, so maybe I was developing feelings for him. It might be a little weird seeing him with another person, but not if I'm happily with Winston. I probably should spend more time analyzing these feelings, but it'll have to be tomorrow because right now I can't do anything that requires any type of focus, as Penny so kindly pointed out.

"Maybe? I don't know. Let's not talk about this right now. What do *you* think Winston looks like?"

Penny grins. "I bet he's tall, with dark hair and a long, pale face. Like Edgar Allen Poe."

"What?!" I screech. "He's not a reclusive writer who stays out of the sun." At Penny's challenging look, I backtrack. "Okay, so maybe he's somewhat reclusive, but he's just spent the past month hiking in Colorado. He's probably got a bit of a tan, at least. And some nice leg muscles as well."

"You're not hoping for a skinny, long-haired emo guy who

only wears black?"

"Uh, no. I need a guy who can hike six miles without trouble and teach me to roll a kayak."

Her eyebrows shoot up. "That's pretty specific. Do you know anyone who can do that?"

I pinch my lips together when I realize who I'm thinking of.

Penny's eyes light up. "You do! Who is it?"

"Brody." I mumble the word quietly, but Penny still hears.

"Oh, man. Do you like *two* guys at the same time?"

"No." I slash my hand through the air for emphasis. "I care deeply for Winston. It's why I didn't go on a second date with Brody."

"But you wanted to."

It's not a question, and I glare at my friend's devastatingly correct insight. She narrows her eyes right back, and I sigh, knowing I won't win this staring contest.

"Yes, okay? I had a really good time, and he was the perfect gentleman. He ignored another woman's advances and protected me from an overbearing, slightly aggressive duo. Why wouldn't I respond positively to that?"

She nods. "Okay, you're right. I would too. But what happens if things don't work out with Winston?"

"I hope they will."

"But if they don't?"

"I don't know." I lift my shoulders to my ears and then drop them. I do it again just because it releases the tension in my neck. "I guess I'll be back to square one unless Brody is willing to give me a second chance."

I stare sullenly at the computer screen, but I don't actually see what's on it. Have I made a mistake pinning all my hopes for happiness on Winston? What if we turn out to be better pen pals than romantic partners? I'll have screwed everything up with everyone. Maybe that's what all my weird dreams were about last night.

A hand squeezes my shoulder, and I turn to Penny, who has a remorseful expression. "I'm sorry for putting doubt in your head. I love you and don't want to see my best friend get hurt. Everything will probably be fine. Winston will be exactly who you know him to be and you'll ride off happily into the sunset."

"Sunset?"

She shrugs. "I don't know. Maybe you'll stroll hand-in-hand down the block to your car and he'll hold the door for you and confess his love for you and all your dreams will come true. Is that better?"

I snicker, appreciating my friend's attempts to get me out of my head. "Thanks, Pen. Hey, will you come with me to the signing tonight?"

She chuckles. "A, I don't have a ticket; and B, I'm closing so you can scoot out early to go."

"I'm sure Rachel would let you in late. I can text and ask."

"As much as I'd like to see this mystery guy for myself, I'll let you have this night alone."

I roll my eyes. "Right. Me and ninety-nine other people."

"You know what I mean. Send me a picture, though, yeah?"

The idea that Winston and I will be able to take a photo together makes giddiness rise up inside me. "Sure thing."

"Good." She taps the computer screen. "Now get to work. I don't want to be stuck with a bunch of things to do before closing."

I laugh, but do my best to focus on my tasks. More than once my mind drifts to imagining what it will be like to walk into Page Turner Books and meet Winston. I'm so glad he suggested meeting early and that my boss agreed to let me skip out a few minutes early to make that possible. Everything is lining up perfectly!

304

43

Brody

MY EYES BOUNCE between the front door of Page Turner Books and the clock on the wall to my left. I slide my phone out of my pocket to double check the clock isn't off by fifteen minutes. Unlocking my phone, I check my texts. Nothing from Anna. Where is she? I'd gotten a text about thirty minutes ago saying she had to finish a couple of things at work but would be right over. She still isn't here, and the room is filling with people, some carrying well-worn copies of my previous books. The chairs are all full and people are lining up against the back wall.

My heart rate kicks up another notch. She wouldn't bail on me, would she? Did she peek in the door, see me, and turn right back around? No, there's nothing indicating I'm the person everyone's here to see. I could just be another fan, lounging around, waiting for the reclusive M.B. Winston to reveal himself.

Rachel was pretty shocked when Mark introduced me to her. Her surprise quickly turned to amusement. I asked her not to say anything to Anna before she arrived and she promised, though she asked if she could send her a text, encouraging her to get to the store as fast as possible. I certainly couldn't say no to that. It didn't help, though, because there's been no sign of Anna.

"Just a few more minutes," Mark says, slapping a hand on my shoulder. "I'm so glad you agreed to do this. I bet if you did a book tour, you'd sell a lot more books. Look at this crowd!"

His words only heighten the anxiety pulsing in my veins. It is suddenly hard to get enough air. My neck is slick with sweat and I look around for an exit. Seeing a doorway a few yards away, I quickly make my way to it and find myself in a hallway leading to the restrooms. Pushing the door to the men's room open, I lock it behind me when I realize it's single occupancy, then double over, my hands gripping my thighs tightly. Why is there not enough oxygen? What am I going to do? I can't go out there and face all those people. I was counting on Anna to help steady me and give me the courage I needed to do this. If I can't get myself under control, I'm going to have to cancel the event, which would definitely not endear me to my publisher or Mark. He flew from New York just to be here.

I'm trying to remember the various ways to ground myself, but all I can think about is the possibility that Anna rejected me and I just don't have confirmation yet. There's no way she'd just not show up. If nothing else, she'd text an apology or something. Radio silence is not her style. She let Brody down in person; I assume she'd do the same for Winston.

My brain stutters with the sudden thought that something bad has happened to her. What if she was in a terrible accident and that's why she's not here? She could have been robbed or accosted by someone with evil purposes. What if someone lured her to their vehicle, claiming to need help, and kidnapped her?

This is only accelerating my heart rate, but now I'm so far into the spiral, I don't know how to get out of it. Desperate for help, I call my therapist. Thankfully, she picks up on the first ring.

"Hello?"

"Gabi. It's. Brody." Each word comes out between shallow breaths.

"Brody, take some deep breaths with me. In two, three, four and out two, three, four. In two, three, four. Out two, three, four."

She continues to count out loud while I try to regulate my breathing with hers. It takes several minutes before it doesn't sound like I've been sprinting.

"Okay, Brody. Tell me five things you see."

My head jerks around the space, trying to focus on something. "Uh. Sink. Toilet. Mirror. Light. Blue tile."

"Great. Now four things you can touch. Please don't touch the toilet."

My smile at her humor attempt is more of a grimace, but it helps redirect my thoughts a little. I'm now very conscious that I'm hiding in the bathroom. After we finish the exercise, she has me do some tapping and walks me through a practice script of how the evening might go. A knock on the door reminds me that reality is waiting and I hang up after thanking Gabi for the impromptu session. She says she'll send me the bill and I'm not sure if she's joking. I'll gladly pay her for her time. I don't know anyone else who could help me recover from such an acute attack. I know I can't rely on her forever. Eventually, I'll have to figure out ways to handle stress without external intervention.

There's another knock, more insistent this time. I unlock the door and pull it open, surprised at the face I find on the other side.

"What are you doing here?"

Levi grins and pulls me into a hug. "I had to come support my main man at his first book signing. You didn't really think I wouldn't show, did you?"

"But I didn't actually invite you."

He gives me a wry smile. "Yeah, I noticed. Thanks for that, by the way."

"I meant I just saw you yesterday. I didn't expect you to fly out here so soon. Aren't you tired of me?"

"Of course not. Elizah sends her regards. She wanted to come support you as well, but had a big corporate group coming in she needed to be present for."

"I'm so glad you're here. I was just in the bathroom freaking out."

"I'm not sure whether that's better than a sudden stomach bug that Mark suspected was the reason for your quick disappearance."

I wrinkle my nose at the thought. "Ugh, probably better. At least it was something Gabi could help me with. If it was a bug, I'd be on my own."

"Is it the crowd that's got you so antsy?"

I tilt my head back and forth. "Partly that, but mostly the fact that Anna said she'd show up early, and we'd meet, but I haven't seen or heard from her. I've sent a few texts, but no response. I'm a little worried something happened to her."

Levi nods. "That's a valid reason to be anxious. I'm sure she'll show. Maybe something came up at work?"

"Yeah, maybe." I'm not convinced. I pull out my phone, hoping I somehow missed a text from her, but there's nothing. The time glares at me. "I'm late for my own signing."

"Oh, yeah. That's why Mark sent me. You ready to do this thing?"

"I guess I have to." I take a deep breath, rubbing my fingers against the seams of my pants. "Thanks for coming, Levi. I really need someone in my corner right now."

"Hey, no problem. You're going to do great."

He pats me on the shoulder, then guides me out front. When Mark sees me, he motions to someone. Brett stands up with a microphone and welcomes everyone to Page Turner Books. I look around the room, but still no sign of Anna. Rachel meets my gaze and shakes her head, letting me know she doesn't have any new information about Anna.

The reading goes well, and I make it through the question-and-answer time without too much discomfort. A few slow, deep breaths are needed, but no one seems to mind the delays in my responses. Someone asks about my pen name and lack of public appearances. I mention my parents and receive understanding nods and murmurs of sympathy, but don't divulge my real name. A super sleuth might eventually figure it out, but I'm not going to make it easy for them.

"Okay," Brett says. "We have time for one more question and then we'll move on to the signing portion of the event." A hand shoots up, and he carries the microphone over to the woman. She stands up.

"Hi, I'm Abbie. Can you tell me more about your inspiration for this new fantasy romance? Does it mirror a real-life romance?"

She's giving me a look like she already knows the answer, but that can't be right. The book isn't officially out. The publishers rushed to get copies available for tonight's event, so these are the first people to get their hands on the finished product. I don't even have final copies yet. My eyes scan the room once more, but come up empty with the person they seek.

"A friend of mine shared some of her dating disasters with me, which made it into the book in altered form. The character traits of Aurelia—the kindness, courage, generosity, and fun nature—all belong to my friend."

"Does Beorn possess many of your character traits?"

Wow, she doesn't pull any punches. How does she know the character's name? Maybe she's a plant from Mark. I wouldn't put it past him, but I didn't tell him about my true inspiration for the book. I doubt he's even read the dedication or acknowledgments to know about Anna.

"Um, not really. Beorn is a born warrior. He's more brave and daring than I am. I created him after thinking about who Aurelia deserves and traits I wish I had."

Someone yells, "I love you as you are, M.B.!" causing a wave of laughter through the crowd. I chuckle, nervously.

"Alright, that wraps up our questions," Brett says. "Let's give M.B. Winston some applause, and then we'll take a few minutes to get the signing table set up. Feel free to grab a cookie and a drink."

The crowd claps. I nod my head in acknowledgment, then stand up from my chair and walk over to Levi and Rachel, who are whispering to one another.

"Heard anything from Anna?"

Rachel gives me a regretful look and shakes her head. "Nothing. I even called a few times, but it went straight to voicemail. This has never happened with her before. I don't know what's going on."

"I'm worried something's wrong. Did you call her work?"

"Yes, but Penny said she left over an hour ago."

My anxiety is flaring again. "Should we call the police?"

Rachel bites her lip. "I don't know. Maybe?"

"Let's wait until after the event before we make any decisions," Levi says. "She may still show up."

I blow out a frustrated breath. "You're right. If she comes in, will someone let me know, please?"

"Of course," Rachel says.

Brett comes over. "Okay, M.B., we're ready for you at the table. I've got a couple of water bottles for you if you're thirsty."

"Thanks." I take one more longing glance toward the door, then turn and follow Brett.

44

Anna

MY WORK DAY passes smoothly, minus all the spacing out I've done imagining what my first meeting with Winston might look like. Penny teases me mercilessly throughout the day, but I expect nothing less from her. I know it's her way of showing her excitement for me. My boss even comes out of her office after lunch to tell me I can leave even earlier than we'd initially agreed on. And that time is now.

I grab my purse and rush to the bathroom to fix up my makeup and hair. Who wouldn't want to look their best when possibly meeting the love of their lives? I text Winston to let him know I'll be over to the bookstore even earlier than planned, but right after I hit send, the phone slips out of my hand and falls into the toilet. Plunging my hand into the water while stifling all thoughts of what might be in there, I grab the phone and wrap it in paper towels. It still works fine—thank goodness for water-resistant cell phones—but the battery is in the red. Too many checks of the time and random texts to Winston throughout the day, I guess.

Tapping the phone against my hand, a few drops of water release from the charging port, but a visual inspection shows some moisture still inside. A quick online search tells me not to charge my phone until it's completely dry, so I'll have to hope I have enough juice to hold me until I make it to Page Turner Books. It's only a two-minute walk, so I should be fine.

A look through my bag for a disinfectant wipe to clean the phone comes up empty. I'll have to stop back by the circulation desk and grab one. There's no way I'm sticking that phone anywhere near my face right now. Wrapping a clean paper towel around it, I drop it in my purse before washing my hands. One last check in the mirror with a smile to make sure there's nothing in between my teeth and I'm ready to go.

I find a container of wipes in one of the desk drawers and thoroughly wipe down my phone, even removing the case to clean underneath.

"What's up with your sudden fascination with phone cleanliness?" Penny asks, coming up next to me.

"I dropped it in the toilet."

She screws up her face in disgust. "Eww."

I shrug. "At least it still works."

As if to prove my point, my phone buzzes in my hand with an incoming text.

Rachel: OMG ANNA!!! GET OVER HERE ASAP! YOU'RE NOT GOING TO BELIEVE IT!!!!!! *surprised face emoji*

I turn the phone to show Penny.

"Oooh, I bet that means Winston is super hot!" she says.

My pulse kicks up at the thought. "You think?"

"Maybe. Whatever it is, it sounds like something really good."

I sure hope Penny's right. My legs are itching to dash over there, but first I have to visit my car. I type in a response, but before I can send it, my phone flashes a huge red outline of a battery and then the screen goes black.

"Uh oh. Phone's dead. Guess I'd better get over there before Rachel has a heart attack or something."

I practically skip down the hall and through the doors to the parking garage. This morning I put all my M.B. Winston books in my car so I can have him sign them tonight. Even the ARC he sent me is in there, though I purchased a finished copy from the bookstore for Winston to sign tonight.

Just as I reach my car, I hear a strangled sound, followed by a thud somewhere to my right. I peer around the back and see a heeled shoe lying on the ground. Concern wells up in my chest and I rush toward the shoe. On the way, a stockinged foot appears, followed by another shoe-clad foot, and a plaid skirt. The sight of curly white hair has me running the remaining distance. The woman is unconscious but breathing. Her purse has dislodged its contents. I grab my phone, then frustratingly toss it back in when I remember it's dead.

"Help! Can anyone hear me? Someone call 911!"

I stand up, looking around for another person. The elevator dings and a man steps off. I yell and wave my arms. "Sir! Help! Call 911!"

His head swivels toward me and he runs over, already pulling his phone out of his pocket and dialing.

"This woman is unconscious. She just fell or something. Please tell them to send an ambulance."

The guy talks into the phone, relaying our location. He keeps the phone to his ear, eyes darting between me and the woman next to me. "Their ETA is ten minutes."

"Great, thank you."

I get down onto my knees next to the woman, checking to make sure she's still alive. Unsure what else to do, I gather her scattered belongings and put them back into her purse.

"Should we move her?" the guy asks.

"I don't know. She's breathing and has a pulse. If she has any injuries we can't see, I don't want to risk aggravating them." The ground is chilly beneath my legs. I quickly stand up. "Will you stay here? I'm going to grab a blanket from my car."

Opening the trunk, I pull out a red plaid blanket, then push the tailgate closed, hitting the lock button on my keys. Returning to the woman, I drape it over her body, hoping to keep her warm on the cold concrete.

"Good thinking," the man says.

I meet his eye and notice how handsome he is. He's dressed in a business suit. The concern on his face probably matches mine. His compassion for a stranger touches my heart. If I wasn't already half in love with Winston, I might try to get to know him better. Of course, now that I'm happy, I'll probably meet lots of normal, kind men.

It feels a little awkward just standing around—or in my case, kneeling next to an unconscious stranger—but it also doesn't feel right trying to act like normal and have some inane conversation. Instead, I use the time to say a prayer for this woman and her family. I hope she's okay. Maybe she was dehydrated and passed out? I hope it's nothing serious.

Suit guy perks up, apparently receiving information from the emergency dispatcher. He moves the phone away from his mouth.

"The ambulance won't fit in the parking deck entrance.

They're parking and then will bring a bed and equipment up through the elevator."

I hadn't even thought about that. Thankfully, this parking deck has a functioning elevator at the moment. It's been spotty over the years. I can't imagine if they had to roll the bed up five levels.

A few minutes later, the doors leading to the library open and two paramedics rush over with a bed on wheels.

"Sorry for the delay," the medic says. "The bed was too big for the elevator. Where is the patient?"

I'd forgotten about the same-level access from Haywood Street. Guess I'm not thinking straight at the moment.

"She's right here." I stand up and move out of the way.

One paramedic crouches down with a bag and assesses her vitals. "Breathing. Slow pulse. No visible signs of trauma." Their gaze swings over to me and suit guy standing side-by-side. "What happened?"

I take a step forward. "I'm not sure. I was walking to my car and heard a muffled sound, followed by a thump. I hurried over and she was lying on the ground just like that. He," I nod to the man, "came out of the elevator and I asked him to call 911. Then I grabbed a blanket from my car to put over her."

The paramedic assesses us with shrewd eyes before appearing to believe me and turning back to the woman. "Let's start an IV and get her on the bed."

I stand back, watching the paramedics work. They roll her onto a board before transferring her from the ground to the bed. An oxygen mask is strapped to her face, and an IV inserted. One of them jots down our names and phone numbers.

"Where are you taking her?"

"To Mission Hospital."

I turn to the man. "Thanks so much for your help."

"It was the least I could do." He turns his wrist to glance at a shiny gold watch. Whatever his job, he appears to be successful at it. "Are you going to be okay? I have somewhere to be, but I can stay for a few more minutes."

Wow. Successful and compassionate. Why couldn't I have found *him* on MeetCute? Probably because he doesn't need an app to meet women, if I had to guess. "No, I'll be fine. Thanks, though."

He hesitates a second before nodding and walking away down the row of cars. The sound of a car door shutting reverberates around the deck. Shortly, a black Mercedes slowly rolls past, the guy waving before turning the corner and disappearing.

I feel the adrenaline rush out of me and I slump against the car, but quickly stand up when I realize it's not mine. Looking around for my purse, I grab my blanket from the garage floor and start folding it, spotting the handbag I cleaned up earlier lying on the ground. It must have been covered by the blanket. I pick it up, resigned to the fact that I'm going to have to deliver this to the hospital later. My gaze roams around the parking garage, but my purse is nowhere to be found.

I groan. The paramedics must have taken mine with the lady, thinking it was hers. Calling my phone won't do anything because it's dead. I straighten up, patting my pockets. I shut my eyes, dread settling like a stone in my gut when I realize I don't have my keys either. A thought gives me a shred of hope and I dash over to my car, grabbing the handle of my trunk. I pull, but it's locked tight. I drop my forehead against the cool metal of the car. There's a light film of dirt, which has probably been transferred to my skin, but who cares now? The night is ruined. I have no idea what time it is because my phone is dead. *I don't even have my phone.*

Maybe the woman has one. It doesn't feel right to be digging around in the bag of someone who's currently unconscious. Still, this is desperate times. I unzip the purse, relief coursing through me at the thin black rectangle inside. Tapping on the screen, I hang my head when the clock on the screen lets me know the event's already well underway. So much for meeting Winston beforehand. All the stress of the last hour wells up and it feels like a dam breaking as tears course down my cheeks. This is not how I wanted tonight to go. Perhaps this is the universe keeping me and Winston apart. I slide down to the ground, leaning against my bumper, my head resting on my knees, allowing my and frustration to leak out through my tear ducts.

 "Anna? Anna! What's wrong? Are you okay? Did something happen?"

Arms wrap around my shoulders and pull me into a tight hug. Even through my blurry vision, Penny is a welcome sight. One arm reaches out and grabs her, while the other tries in vain to wipe my face.

"Talk to me. Are you hurt?"

I shake my head, trying to get my sobbing under control so I can talk. I focus on taking a few deep breaths. Penny hands me a pack of tissues. It takes most of them to dry my cheeks.

"I'm physically okay," I finally manage to say.

Penny releases a breath. "That's good. What else?"

I wave my hand in the air, trying to figure out how to put my feelings into words, then tell her everything that happened in the parking garage. "Things keep going wrong. It feels like a sign."

She shakes her head. "Nuh uh. It's not a sign, just some bad luck. You're still in one piece." She looks at her phone. "The event is still going on. You can meet Winston. Just maybe not quite like you imagined."

I sigh. "I'm sure I look a mess. Would you want to meet someone you like looking like this?"

I wave a hand over my face. She purses her lips. "Nothing I can't fix."

She grabs one of the few remaining tissues and rubs it under my eyes and over my forehead. She pulls out a tube of lipstick and hands it over to me along with her phone, the camera in selfie mode. I don't look too disheveled, just red-rimmed eyes evidence of what I've been through. The lipstick helps me look more together. Still, I feel spent.

"I don't know, Pen. I'm already emotionally wrung out. Plus, I have to go to the hospital to exchange bags. Maybe I should just text Winston and reschedule." I smack my forehead. "Except I don't know his number."

"Look. It's never going to be a perfect time. Yes, this evening has been below average, but it can still be salvaged. When you look back on this evening, you can remember your mini disasters or you can think of it as the first night of the rest of your life with Winston. Which would you prefer?"

When she says it like that, do I really have a choice? "Will you come with me?"

She gives a beleaguered sigh. "Yes, of course."

I squeeze her to me. "Thanks. You're the best."

"I know. Let me tell Michael what's going on so he's not wondering where I am. I'll even drive you to the hospital after the event to get your bag."

I reward her with a sincere smile. "Thanks. Though maybe I

can get Winston to take me instead."

"Let's hope," she says, standing and pulling me to my feet.

"Oh, but my books…" I look longingly through the back window at the bag.

She rolls her eyes. "You *know* the author. I'm sure he'll sign them for you later."

"Yeah, you're probably right."

"I usually am." She gives me a teasing smile. "Now, let's go meet your perfect pen pal."

I nod, butterflies immediately swarming in my belly. This is really happening. I run a hand down my clothes, hoping they're not too wrinkled, then grab the bag off the ground and walk with Penny to the bookstore.

When we arrive, I try the door, but it's locked. I shake my head. Of course it is. I give Penny a "now what" look, but she's typing on her phone. She holds up a finger, then presses a button on her phone. The sound of a phone ringing comes through the speaker, then an out of breath voice.

"Page Turner Books, this is Rachel."

"Hi, Rachel," Penny says. "My name is Penny. I have Anna here with me out front of the store, but the door's locked."

"Oh! I've been trying to reach her. Be right there."

"Hey—"

But she's already hung up. Half a minute later, she's unlocking the door and smiling at me. "Yay, you're here! Want me to take you to Winston?"

I eye the line. "He's obviously busy. We'll just wait in line and meet him at the end."

"You sure?"

The excitement on her face gives me second thoughts, but this way I have time to get myself and my thoughts together.

"Yeah. I need a few minutes to prepare."

"Suit yourself." She turns to my friend. "Penny, right? Nice to see you again. I'd better get back to work. I'm manning the cookie station. Do either of you want one?"

"No, I'm good," I say.

Penny shakes her head, then turns to me once Rachel's gone. "Alright, tell me what you imagine happening when we get to the front of the line."

"Well, I'll obviously know what he looks like by then, because we'll see him at some point while we're moving our way up. Which is good, because it'll give me a minute to get used to that information. Then, I'd like to say something cute or flirty, but I'm drawing a blank. Maybe 'fancy meeting you here' or is that too dumb?"

She shrugs. "'Hi' has great success as a conversation opener. Or 'I love you; let's get married' can also be a crowd pleaser at times."

I narrow my eyes at her. There's no way I have the guts to just blurt out those three big words upon first meeting Winston. I'm not sure I even believe in love at first sight. Of course, while this will be the first time I'm laying eyes on him, he's already burrowed himself into my heart through his words. "Let's keep thinking."

"Fine, but I need to visit the ladies' room. Be right back."

While she's gone, I try to come up with something witty to say. The woman in front of me turns around and notices me twisting my fingers. "Nervous?"

"Yeah, a little."

"Me too. I had no idea he'd be so handsome. And that voice." She sighs. "It's like warm velvet."

Whoa. Now I'm really sorry I was so late. She's younger than me, fresh faced like a recent college graduate with the toned body of a head cheerleader, springy blonde ponytail to match. Is that jealousy swirling in my gut? Why yes, it is. I don't have a response, but that doesn't seem to matter because she keeps talking.

"I wonder who the real Aurelia is. He sounded pretty smitten when he talked about her."

He talked about me? I'm dying to ask what he said, but this woman assumes I was there and I feel weird correcting her now.

She sighs wistfully. "I'd gladly be his Aurelia."

An urge to growl at her hits me out of nowhere. Is this how I'm always going to feel when I hear other women talking about Winston? He's not even officially mine, and already I'm feeling super possessive.

"She's a pretty cool character," I say, trying to steer the conversation toward less touchy ground.

"Have you read it already? I thought the first copies were being handed out tonight."

How much do I say? I should play it off, but a more primitive part of me wants to stake my claim. "Winston sent me an early copy."

Her eyes round. "You *know* him?"

I shrug. "Yeah. We're friends."

"Do *you* know the woman he's hopelessly in love with?"

She thinks he's *hopelessly in love* with me? Warmth floods my chest, calming some of the insecurity inside. I press my lips together to contain the smile threatening to take over my entire face. I attempt a nonchalant shrug. She tilts her head, eyes narrowing as she assesses me.

"You don't really know him," she says decisively. "You're just messing with me. How rude." She spins around, pointedly giving me her back.

I don't feel a compulsion to correct her, instead looking

around for Penny. When she walks up, her eyes are as large as dinner plates.

"What?" I say.

"Oh, Anna."

"What?" I repeat, feeling my pulse kick up.

"I saw Winston on the way back from the bathroom."

My heart jackhammers against my ribs. I swallow thickly. "And?"

"And I think you need to meet him right now."

"I don't want to cut the line."

She glances around, her lips twisting, then grabs my hand, yanking me out of line. "Just come with me."

Blood pounds in my ears with each step we take. There's still a wall of people, but then we maneuver around a long coil of customers. The table comes into view, and Brody's sitting behind it. My feet slow and then stop as my brain struggles to process what I'm seeing.

Everything slots into place at once. The cologne. M.B. Winston. Matthew Brody. They both lost their parents at a young age. His extended absence from the library while Winston was out of town. It was him all along. I'm confused. I'm elated. I'm trying to figure out if I should be mad, when he looks up and his eyes lock onto mine. His surprise slides into pleasure, and he shoots up out of the chair. He breaks eye contact with me to say something to the people at the table, and it's at that moment I realize I have to get out of here.

I spin on my heels and practically run for the door. Thankfully, Rachel didn't re-lock it and it swings open, the bells above the door chiming merrily. I take two quick lefts, not sure where I'm going but knowing I need to get away from Page Turner Books. The Hill of Beans sign catches my eye and I duck inside, thankful it stays open late. One of the single bathrooms is open, so I lock myself inside and sit down on the closed toilet lid.

There are so many thoughts swirling around in my head. Brody is Winston. Winston is Brody. Brody's been writing me letters for over a year while also visiting my library. He struggled to talk to me in person for a long time, which is probably why he wrote me a letter. But why did he wait until now to reveal the truth? Obviously, it makes sense why M.B. Winston hasn't done any in-person publicity—he has anxiety. But he agreed to do an event for me.

My heart calms a little at that thought, awe at how much courage that must have taken overwhelming me. But then I remember how dejected I was when he didn't show up at the coffee shop. *He did, though. Just not quite how I expected.* Brody was there, and he was visibly troubled. I didn't say anything because I know how skittish he is. If he had told me the truth, what would I have done? I'd probably have been skeptical, but I'm sure he'd have been able to prove it. Would I have still gone on a date with Zach?

There's a knock on the door and I realize I've been in the bathroom too long. "Just a minute," I say, washing my hands before opening the door. I still need to do some thinking, but I'd feel bad taking up table space in here since I don't have my purse to buy anything. I head out front, wondering where I can go to think and also not loiter. I decide on Pritchard Park up the street. Thankfully, it's a weeknight so the drum circle won't have taken over the park.

I find an empty bench near the chess tables. Two men are in the middle of a match, quietly contemplating each move. I lean back, pondering what my own move should be.

There's no way Brody-slash-Winston hasn't lied to me at

some point. I definitely remember texting them both, and they have different numbers. That's a little sketchy for sure. But getting to know him in person and understanding his anxiety struggle, there's more than a small part of me willing to forgive him. I mean, Winston has seemed like the perfect guy for me for some time. He sent me thoughtful gifts and complimented me on so many things. Not to mention he *wrote me a book*. And now I know *Brody* is that guy?

My heart is definitely urging me one way, but part of me still needs an explanation. And I know just where to go to get it.

45

Brody

WELL, THAT WAS not how I saw things going. I mean, sure, I knew there was a chance I'd ruin everything by my deception, but in all of my imaginings of what would happen when I finally told Anna the truth, not one of them ended with her sprinting out the door. Especially not at a time when I couldn't chase after her. I felt so powerless seeing her confused face, quickly followed by her back as she jetted away from me.

Miraculously, I made it through the rest of the signing, but I am gutted. I should have known a happily ever after for me was too good to be true. Well, now I guess I do have to find a new writing spot. My career is on the rise again, thanks to my former relationship with Anna. I never would have written a fantasy romance without her inspiration. I definitely would have stayed in hiding as the reclusive M.B. Winston if I wasn't so desperate to show her how much she means to me. Alright, I did also hope the signing would help her forgive me a little, too. Wrong again.

The event ended an hour ago and there's been no word about what happened to Anna. Brett and the staff have cleaned up most of the event, including my signing table. I'm sitting in the lone chair they let me continue to occupy, staring into space, realizing this is definitely going into my Top Five Worst Days, when I sense someone standing over me. I look up into Levi's sympathetic face. "Dude, how are you doing?"

"Are you talking about the book signing or watching the woman I love run away from me as fast as she could?"

He grimaces. "Yikes. Yeah, that's rough, man. Have you tried calling her?"

"You heard her friend. She doesn't have her phone. My only recourse is to drive to her apartment and beg for her forgiveness, but she doesn't have her keys either, so…"

He claps me on the shoulder and squeezes. "Well, if it's any help, I'd give you a ten out of ten as far as grand gestures go. It definitely blew mine out of the water."

I give him a puzzled look. "When did you make a grand gesture?"

"I'm sure I told you about when I ruined Elizah's birthday party and she wouldn't talk to me for a month."

I scoff. "Uh, I think I'd remember that. Wait, is that the time her cake was knocked off the dock into the water?"

"Yep. See, I told you."

"You didn't tell me it was your fault."

"It was an accident, even if Elizah disagrees. *Anyway,* I knew I had to do something to make it up to her, so I called everyone on the guest list and organized a second birthday party, this one a surprise. I had the baker make two cakes, just in case, and then I got up in front of everyone and told her how much she meant to me and how I couldn't live without her."

My eyes widen. "I didn't know your extravagant proposal was also an apology."

He chuckles. "Two birds, one stone. It worked, though."

I slump down, tapping my fingers on my leg in a pattern. "It did. Too bad I'm not as lucky."

"Maybe you are."

"What do you mean?"

He grips my shoulder and points toward the door. I look up, stunned that Anna is standing in the store. Before my brain fully processes this information, my body's already out of the chair and halfway across the room. When she sees me coming, her eyes widen and I stop a few feet away, not wanting to crowd her.

She came back, which makes me immensely happy. But the serious look on her face tells me we're about to have a frank discussion and I have no idea what the outcome will be. My back is instantly sweaty, but I can't let my anxiety win. I take a deep breath through my nose and let it out slowly. I repeat the slow breathing again and again until the initial wave of panic is more of a low burble in my head.

"Anna." I pause, then open my mouth to launch into my apology when she holds up a hand. I close my mouth and wait to hear my fate.

Anna

Seeing him again has got my heart going haywire. I need answers and want to get them out before I'm tempted to ignore my concerns and just jump into his arms.

I open my mouth, but then pause, my eyebrows squinching together. "I'm not sure what to call you."

He swallows, his eyes not meeting my gaze. "Most people call me Brody, but it's up to you. I don't care what you call me."

"I'm very tempted to call you a liar."

He visibly flinches. "I definitely deserve that. Anna, I'm so sorr—"

Another raised hand cuts him off. "I'm not ready for an apology. I need answers first."

He nods. "You deserve them. Ask me anything. I'll tell you the truth."

"Why did you write me that first letter?"

"I couldn't talk to you. Every time I tried to, it came out awkwardly and in a stutter. I didn't know we'd become pen pals."

"Neither did I. When did you start wanting to be more than friends?"

He rubs the back of his neck. "From our first meeting. It's why my anxiety has been so bad around you."

"We're talking now and you seem fine."

He huffs out a laugh. "My brain still goes crazy around you. I've just been doing a lot of role-playing with my therapist. I have also been taking medication again and leaning heavily on my calming exercises."

I had no idea he was trying so hard and doing so much to spend time with me. The information rearranges pieces of our story around in my brain. "So the day we were supposed to meet, you were late because…"

"I saw you through the window talking to your friend, went into a spiral of imagining you rejecting me, and had a panic attack around the side of the building."

"Oh, Brody."

"I honestly was going to tell you who I was that day. I'd just worked up the courage to tell you and then you got that call."

I'd forgotten about that part. I guess in my worry and hurry, it had felt like two separate incidents. "But why didn't you tell me another time?"

He sighs. "I wanted to, but you started dating that one guy and you seemed to really like him. I didn't think I had a chance after that. Not until you told Winston you liked him. But by then, I felt so guilty I hadn't told you, I wasn't sure what to do. I thought only something big would do."

"Like agreeing to a public book signing?"

He gives me an embarrassed smile. "Yeah. Like that."

We're both silent for a bit.

"Can I apologize now?" he asks.

I chuckle at his contrite face. "Yes."

He gingerly reaches out and takes my hand, giving it a small squeeze. The contact zings up my arm and I squeeze his fingers back. "I'm so very sorry, Anna. You are an incredible woman who does not deserve to be deceived. I promise it's not who I normally am. I allowed my anxiety to get me deeper and deeper into this mess of deception, and then I didn't know how to get out. Honestly, I was afraid if I came clean, it'd ruin everything."

He pauses, his eyes flaring. Oh, to be a fly on the wall of his brain. Actually, scratch that. I'd probably be exhausted. "What?" I say.

"I just remembered it's still possible I did ruin everything. Did I? Don't tell me. No, do tell me. Wait, let me finish my apology before you break the news."

I can't help but smile at that. He's probably beaten himself up for all that's happened more than I'll ever know. His brow furrows.

"Where was I?"

"You were afraid of ruining things by coming clean."

He nods, his face a mix of pain and regret. My heart twists in sympathy.

"Right. I was afraid. And I let fear make poor decisions on my behalf. Because the truth is, I don't want to hurt you. I'm in agony knowing I have and, if given a second chance, I will spend every day from here to eternity telling you how amazing you are and loving you with everything I have. Because I do. I love you, Anna. So much. I'm so sorry. I hope you can forgive me."

How am I supposed to respond to that?

I release his hand and his head falls forward in resignation, but only for a moment because I reach my arms up around his neck, burying my head in his chest. His arms wrap lightly around me, but when I breathe in the cedar and citrus smell of his skin I've come to like so much, his arms tighten around my waist.

Something primal takes over and I move my hands to cup each side of his face, the barest hint of stubble rough against my palms. I angle my chin up while pulling him down to me. When our lips touch, sparks erupt behind my closed eyelids and I melt against his chest. His arms cinch tighter again around my waist, then one of his hands slides up along my spine until it's cupping the back of my neck. My hand, seeming to have a mind of its own, slides to the back of his head, threading through his hair. He tilts his head slightly, his lips pressing more firmly against mine.

I feel Brody's lips smile against mine before relaxing his hold on my neck and breaking the kiss. I drop my hands to his chest, pleased at the feel of his solid muscles underneath my hands. Reluctantly, I open my eyes. Brody's grinning at me with definite heart eyes vibes.

"So, does that mean you forgive me?"

I laugh. "Yes, that's what that means."

His eyes travel over my face as if he's memorizing every square inch. I look deep into his warm emerald eyes, amazed that I get both Winston and Brody.

A throat clears behind me and Penny's giving me a half-pleased, half-censured look. "I thought you didn't kiss on the first date."

"Technically, this isn't a date," I say. "And besides, we've already been on a couple of dates together."

"A couple?" Brody says, bringing my attention back to him. "I thought our waterfall trip was just a hike between friends."

I purse my lips and attempt a fierce glare, but fail miserably when my lips curve up into a smile. "It was *supposed* to be platonic, but then I saw you walking around without a shirt and jumping off cliffs. How could I not see you differently? I'm only a human woman, after all, not some warrior princess."

He grins. "Well, you're *my* warrior princess. If you'll have me, of course."

I roll my eyes, but the smile stays fixed on my face. "Let me think about it."

"Take all the time you need."

"Speaking of things I need, can someone give me a ride to the hospital so I can collect my purse?"

"I'll go get it," Penny says. "Do you have the other bag?"

"Is this it?" Levi asks, picking something up off a bookshelf.

I must have dropped it in shock when I saw Brody earlier. I nod and Penny takes it from him.

"I'll go make the switch," she says.

"That's so kind of you," I say, "but how will you get a hold of me? I don't have my phone."

She shoots me an exasperated look. "Easy." She holds out her phone to Brody. "Type your number in. I'll use you to get to Anna."

Penny wraps me in a hug before leaving.

"What do we do now?" Brody asks.

Brett grabs the chair Brody was sitting on and heads toward the back, calling over his shoulder, "I don't care, but you can't stay here. I'm locking up."

"Brody," Levi says, "why don't we go to your house? It'd definitely be more comfortable than finding an open business this late."

Brody looks at me. "Would it be too much of an inconvenience for Penny to drive to South Asheville tonight?"

I shake my head. "She lives near me."

"Great. Then, shall we?"

He holds out his hand, and I thread my fingers through his, pleased by the way our hands seem to fit perfectly. I squeeze his hand tightly. Now that I know who Winston truly is, I'm never letting him go.

Epilogue

Three Months Later

Anna

WHEN BRODY ARRIVES to pick me up, I'm already waiting out front. I pull him into a tight hug, then follow it with a long, lingering kiss. I finally let him go.

"Good morning to you too," he says with a grin. "What's gotten into you today?"

I shrug. "I just woke up happy. I have a feeling today is going to be a great day."

"I hope it is."

He picks up my bag from the curb, opening the passenger door for me, before continuing around back and nestling my bag in the trunk next to his. When he's seated next to me, he turns and grabs my hand.

"You ready for this?"

I grin. "Of course! I've been waiting for this conference since my boss approved the trip."

"Are you okay with us driving up to New York together?"

"Are you asking me if I regret choosing an adventure with you over a flight with Penny?"

He rubs the back of his neck and shrugs. "I just want you to be happy."

I lean across the center console and give him a peck on the cheek. "I'm always happy with you."

He smiles, his shoulders straightening. "Alright, then, let's get to it. You're in charge of the music."

I plug in my phone and scroll through my playlists until I find the one I made just for our road trip. The first song is a Frank Sinatra classic.

Brody laughs. "Did you make a playlist of every song that mentions New York?"

I suppress a smile. "Maybe."

"Of course you did. How am I even surprised?"

Brody and I have been officially together for three months. We spend most of our free time hanging out or hiking. Of course, I also see him most weekdays in the library working on his book. *Dragons of Moon Kingdom* turned into an international success. His publisher has been on him to send the manuscript for the next book whenever it's finished and they're releasing Ciara's sequel early to capitalize on the buzz around his fantasy romance. Petrocius Publishing is going to be at the conference we're headed to with ARCs of *Time and Time Again*. It looks like M.B. Winston is back on top.

There has been no mention of Brody's past online after his signing at Page Turner Books. I guess no one really cares about why he was so mysterious. Of course, everyone has gone gaga over the fact that M.B. Winston is so attractive. There are even more requests for him to hold in-person events. He hasn't done any since his debut in Asheville, but agreed to sign books at the conference. Hence the reason we're driving to New York together. I think him agreeing to take part was just an excuse for us to spend more time together, which I don't mind at all. I am completely and utterly in love with this man. He has made me feel so cared for and cherished every day we've been together. I have no doubt about his feelings for me and am so glad I didn't settle for something less. He was definitely worth the wait.

"I think I've finally figured out a nickname for you," I say.

Brody takes his eyes off the road long enough to give me an amused look. "Okay, lay it on me."

"B Dub."

His eyebrows crinkle together. "What now?"

"B Dub. I was thinking about B.W., but it has too many syllables, so I just dropped a couple."

"Okay…and what does that stand for?"

"Brody Winston. I know Winston isn't a real name, but since I kind of fell in love with you first through the letters, it has special meaning to me."

"That's sweet. It's certainly a different nickname, but I suppose it's not any stranger than Warrior Princess. Though maybe I should shorten it to WP or maybe just Dub P if I'm going with your logic."

I scrunch up my nose. "WP I'm okay with. Dub P sounds too much like 'dumpy' and I do *not* care for that."

"Fair enough. Maybe I'll just drop the W all together and refer to you simply as Princess." He winks at me.

I think about it for a few seconds. "I kind of like you thinking of me as a Warrior Princess."

"As you wish."

My eyes widen. "Are you quoting *The Princess Bride* to me now?"

He smirks. "Maybe."

"I'll allow it," I say, grabbing his hand and entwining our fingers.

Four hours into our drive, Brody signals and takes an exit off I-81 in Virginia.

"Bathroom stop?" I ask.

"Uh, yeah, it can be. While I was planning our route, I saw something I thought might be interesting. I hope you don't mind a detour."

I smile. Brody is fond of his detours and, most of the time, they turn out to be a lot of fun. "Sure, as long as it doesn't turn out to be another Ripley's Aquarium saga. I'd really like to get to NYC before the conference starts."

He scoffs, but his smile tells me he's not really upset. "How was I to know the sign was for an attraction four hours out of our way? Are you ever going to let me live that down?"

I rub his arm affectionately. "Probably not, because it's one of my favorite memories."

We pull into the parking lot for Natural Bridge State Park and I'm immediately intrigued. "What's a natural bridge? Can we walk across it?"

"It's essentially an arch carved out of rock by a river. We can walk under it, but not on top."

We stop at the visitor center and purchase tickets. A man punches them at the entry gate. I hold mine up to Brody. "Look! It's a little heart cutout."

He shrugs. "Well, Virginia *is* for lovers."

I laugh and grab his hand. "Guess we're in the right place, then."

We follow the walkway down to the natural bridge, though it would be impossible to miss as the arch is two-hundred feet in the air. I glance at a nearby information sign. "Did you know Thomas Jefferson bought this bridge, and it was privately owned until they turned this place into a state park in 2016?"

"I did not."

Brody's eyes are darting around the area. Is he bothered by the other people strolling around? Maybe we should get off the main thoroughfare. "Everything okay, B Dub?"

He scans the crowd again before meeting my gaze. "Y-yeah, fine. Should we take a picture of us with the arch in the background?"

"Great idea."

I pull out my phone, turn on selfie mode, then work on framing the arch in the photo before motioning for Brody to squeeze into the frame. The arch is just above our heads, like a limestone rainbow. I push the button, then look at the results. Brody's eyebrows are furrowed, and he looks like he's in pain.

"Uh, maybe smile for the next one?"

"Sorry."

I take a few more. Brody's now smiling, but it's not a genuine, carefree smile. I study him, noticing the tightness in his face and his fingers drumming against his thigh. The crowd must be getting to him. "Do you want to leave?"

His head whips around, a trace of panic on his face. "What? N-no. But maybe we could explore a little?"

I agree, and we take a trail with signs for a waterfall. It's an easy trail, and we reach the waterfall in about fifteen minutes. Lace Falls isn't as spectacular as Courthouse Falls or the other places we've visited around Asheville. It's more of a slide than a true cascade of water, but still pretty. The sound of rushing water is always soothing to me. I sit down on a rock bench and pat the space next to me. Brody joins me and I angle my camera to get the falls behind us. His natural smile is still missing. No one is around, so I'm not sure why he's so tense. I lace my fingers through his and angle my body toward him. "Are you nervous about the conference?"

He shakes his head, but then pauses. "A little, but knowing you'll be somewhere nearby is reassuring."

"I'll always be here for you. Well, unless there's a medical emergency, in which case I might be a little late."

He chuckles, a genuine smile finally appearing. "Hopefully, if that happens again, you'll have a working phone. Do you have my number memorized yet?"

I roll my eyes playfully. "Yes, it's hard to forget now that I know the last four digits spell 'book.'"

"I never noticed that."

I squeeze his hand before letting go. "I want to take a couple of photos of the waterfall, and then we can head back if you're ready."

Brody stands up and stretches. My gaze snags on the sliver of skin revealed between his pants and shirt. How did I get so lucky ending up with such an amazing man? He catches me looking and gives me a knowing grin. I press my lips together, trying not to smile back, but fail miserably. Finally, I shake my head and turn, raising my phone to take a few pictures. When I'm finished, I pocket my phone and turn, surprised when I see Brody behind me, down on one knee with a black velvet box in his palm.

He reaches out toward me with his free hand and I place mine in his, my heart beating a mile a minute. I know what this is and I'm ready for it. All of Brody's nervousness suddenly makes sense. He takes a deep breath, then looks into my eyes.

"Anna, you are an incredible woman. You're so loving and caring and kind and funny. You know just how to encourage me when I'm struggling with work. When I'm with you, I feel strong, capable, and grounded. You have made my life better in every way. Yours is the face I want to see first thing in the morning and last thing at night. I want to take you on a world's worth of adventures and share every part of my life with you. I love you so much and will spend the rest of my days showing you how treasured you are. Anna Jane Hollingsworth, will you make me the happiest man in the world by becoming my wife?"

The word "wife" has barely passed his lips before I shout, "Yes!" and pull him up into my arms. Pressing my lips against his, I channel all my love and joy into the kiss. Happiness swirls through every part of my body. Brody's arms tighten around my waist and we luxuriate in this special moment. When I finally release him, he opens the box, removes the ring, and slides it onto my finger. I bring my hand to my face to get a better look at the round cut diamond solitaire ring. The vintage-looking band has vine- and heart-shaped embellishments on the sides with little diamonds nestled inside the hearts, giving it a unique look.

"Wow, Brody. It's beautiful!"

"Not as beautiful as you."

I wrap my arms around his neck and pull him to me for another kiss. Voices increasing in volume ends our celebration. A family of four approaches and Brody holds his phone out toward them.

"Would you mind taking a picture of us? We just got engaged."

I can't help but beam at the family as the woman takes his phone and snaps a few photos. When she hands it back, we huddle together to look. My body is angled toward Brody with my hand on his chest, his arms circled around my waist, and we're both beaming. It's just perfect.

Find additional *Write for You* content including a bonus scene at MeganByrd.net/WFY

Want to stay in the know about future books? Sign up for my newsletter at MeganByrd.net/newsletter

ACKNOWLEDGMENTS

Anna Booraem, thank you for sharing all of your librarian wisdom with me, always championing my books. I love our monthly meet-ups and am so glad I found your Creative Writing Group when I moved to Asheville!

Susan Ward, thank you for your willingness to talk through therapy treatments for trauma and social anxiety and read some of my portrayals. (All misrepresentations and errors are mine alone.)

Cali Black, I cherish your friendship and the ability to bounce various aspects of author life off of you. You encourage, challenge, and inspire me!

Heather Gerwing, thanks for your wonderful insights and ideas that helped make this book better (and gave it a title!).

Special thanks to my early readers (Heather, Hilary, Lisa, Mandy, Suzie): your willingness to read and provide very helpful and constructive feedback in the early stages of editing was instrumental in making this book better.

A huge thank you to my Sweet Readers Facebook group who offered excellent opinions about titles, blurbs, and cover design (Ann, Brooke, Chantal, Heather, Hilary, Jenn, Jennifer, Judith, Karen, Stacey, Taylor).

Julia Hudgins and Jen Waite, thank you for answering a stranger's questions about your work at Pack Memorial Library.

Cathy, Carrie, Natalie and Tess—thank you for helping me with my blurb at 20Booksto50K in Las Vegas.

Hank and Susie, thank you for your support and help in getting my books into the NC Cardinal library system!

I greatly appreciate all the fabulous ARC readers and

Bookstagrammers who posted about the book on various platforms and provided support for me and the book. You are awesome!

Thank you to wigo_wiggles for helping my vision of Brody and Anna to come to life on the cover.

Mom, thanks again for your encouragement, support, and eagle eyes that catch typos and grammatical issues.

The most thanks goes to my husband and kids who have been great encouragers and support to me on this journey. I can't believe I wrote an entire series!

ABOUT THE AUTHOR

Megan Byrd lives in Asheville, North Carolina with her husband and two kids. She hates running, but loves hiking in the mountains toward a waterfall or scenic view and taking a variety of classes including kickboxing, HIIT, yoga, and Zumba. When she's not reading, writing, or chasing waterfalls, she enjoys visiting local bookstores, wandering through thrift shops in search of special finds, listening to live music, and catching up with friends.

Want to be first to know when the next book is available? Sign up on the website to receive a monthly e-newsletter and read about behind-the-scenes sneak peeks of her current work-in-progress, book recommendations, and other fun things. You can also visit MeganByrd.net/my_books to learn more about the inspiration behind her books.

Website: MeganByrd.net
Instagram: @megan.e.byrd
Facebook: Facebook.com/authormeganbyrd
Facebook Reader Group:
Facebook.com/groups/meganbyrdsweetreaders

www.ingramcontent.com/pod-product-compliance
Lightning Source LLC
Chambersburg PA
CBHW061337310726
48974CB00001B/91